CINDY M. AMOS

Oil Field Maven

America's Fabulous Fifties, Book 1

By Cindy M. Amos

Dedicated to
The brave Kansas men who toiled on Oil Hill
And to the women who cooked in their kitchens
Ad Astra per Aspera
"To the Stars through Difficulties"

ACKNOWLEDGMENTS

The author would like to acknowledge the following
for their support and encouragement of this book:
Kansas Oil Museum Staff, El Dorado, Kansas
Cameron H. Amos for color cover photograph
iStock for vintage black & white photograph
Pamela Bower for final proofreading
Cynthia Hickey of Winged Publications
& The Inspiration of the Holy Spirit

Keep me safe, O God, for I put my trust in you.
My soul proclaims, "You are my Lord."
My well-being hangs on your righteous balance.
Psalm 16:1-2

Chapter 1

El Dorado, Kansas 1951

Hell must have ascended and nailed him right to the middle of it. Duncan Reed passed his palm down the back of his neck to wipe away the sweat. A full crew of men stood at the ready as a monstrous fan belt gyrated around the powerhouse's interior. On assignment for less than a week, his first trip into the company's power generator pulsated with raw force. A nervous quiver shook the fan belt and a flapping resonance filled the air like chattering teeth.

Sol Edmunds, the larger-than-life floor supervisor, motioned with a gritty forearm. "Get back, boys." The men along the western wall responded by easing back a step.

Duncan leaned on the door jamb and slid a notepad from his shirt pocket. Second nature, his assessment began with a tally of the eight men out of harm's way. The giant belt cogitated through another cycle, straining against the spindles at each end of the building. As it shimmied up the eastern cylinder, an attentive worker guided it back into position with a greased wooden paddle. He scrawled a note and returned his gaze to the unstable east side.

A second man brought his paddle up to skim along the upper edge of the bucking belt as if to tame it. The belt retaliated with a bulging slap that seemed to set the entire rig loose. Secondary vibration contorted the rubber into a quivering snake, slithering around and around the spindles. The chattering teeth noise escalated to a full bone rattle, which solicited looks of dread on several dirt-smudged faces.

"No more, fellas. Back off." Edmunds crisscrossed his arms, his fists pounding his shoulders for emphasis.

A split second later, Duncan glimpsed the failure as it happened. The upper edge of the belt tore, making an ungracious slapping sound. Then it began to shear apart.

"She's going—everybody out!" Edmunds heaved the closest man to safety through the doorway right in front of him. Chaos followed as men careened for the exit, while the oversized serpent choked the life out of the powerhouse, its flap licking the stagnant air like a tongue.

Plastered to the plank wall, Duncan focused on every detail. Each piece would need to fit into his follow-up accident report, so he had to remain sharp. The west side workers had all gained freedom, and now the east side workers attempted to cross behind the front spindle. Right when the two men with wooden paddles ran past, the belt tore in half top to bottom.

"Heaven help us," Edmund exclaimed from the doorway. Free from the generator at last, the belt lashed out, striking two workers with unmerciful force. The slighter of the two men went airborne, landing against the far wall with a sickening thud. The stout man dropped where he stood, the air knocked from his lungs in a horrendous huff. The murderous belt thrust past him and coiled into a rubber mound in the corner. Spared by mere inches, the last four men dropped to their knees.

Duncan straightened from his post and pointed his pen at Edmunds. "Send for the ambulance." The supervisor scurried away, and a mousey-faced man peered into the room. Nothing stirred inside the threshold, an ominous portend. The man closest to the thrown victim checked his vital signs, while another laborer tended the heavy man.

Duncan pointed his pen again and pinned the mouse-man with a task. "Can you find Mr. Coates and advise him of the situation? The belt's gone out again, taking two men down with it. He will need to arrange a back-up, if we are to get this generator running."

"Yes sir. I'm on my way, Mr. Reed." Pained, he pulled a scruffy hat off, crumpled it over his heart, and then scurried away.

Fighting the urge to add a few notations, Duncan stepped past the motionless heavy victim to check the man by the wall. The laborer backed away, his eyes skittish. From the angle of the body, the man's neck had clearly been broken on impact. Light from a nearby window played a streak across him, highlighting something that glimmered on his hand. There, a narrow wedding band claimed the victim's left ring finger.

He squatted beside the man to be certain, unable to stop his throat from constricting. As he knelt on the floorboards, reality hit him with the weight of an anvil. How he loathed the follow-up portion of his job requirement—the notification of next of kin. He shifted toward the heavy-set man, while the victim's attendant shook his head and dropped his chin.

Death and industry made for strange bedfellows, a union he had never gotten used to during his ten years of service. *What a way to make a God-given living, chasing safety.* He took the notepad out and dated the preliminary accident report, May 4, 1951. It seemed hot for early May, even for central Kansas, but what did he know?

~

Neatness has no price tag. As the bungalow sat bathed in quiet, Lorna Rae had to hurry to get supper on the stove. When little Trudy awoke, she would demand her full attention. Tendrils of hair coiled damp against her face as she chopped the borrowed onion that would flavor their soup. Already too hot, a worry needled through her thoughts that she would have to serve more substantial meals with summer's pressing demands on the oil field laborers. If only Harley hadn't decreased her grocery money again this month without any explanation.

She raked the diced onion into the pot with the knife blade and fought back a tear, her reaction to the pungent vegetable. She looked for her next ingredient, a fat carrot. The chicken broth bubbled from a ring of heat below and lent her a soothing feeling, its aroma wafting to fill the tiny kitchen. She smiled when the embroidered tea towel caught her eye by the window over the sink. A wedding present from her mother, it hung from safety pins to form a makeshift curtain to block the afternoon sun. Otherwise, the swelter would be unbearable.

Standard housing for the oil field workers came with no embellishments, just a rectangle to contain family life. They were fortunate, as only the three of them had to fit. Poor Vivian next

3

door had four kids to shoe-horn into her cottage, but it never seemed to dampen the woman's spirits. No, she was lucky to have Viv for a neighbor. Plus, she tended Trudy now and then to free her up for an occasional outing.

She scraped the outer skin off the carrot and began to slice off wafer-thin pieces to make the soup seem fuller. If she got the carrots tender enough, she could feed them to Trudy. They'd blow the slice cool together, and all that attention somehow made it taste better.

Lorna Rae wiped the cutting board clean and cut the heat down on the gas stove. Ready to move onto the biscuits, she dried her hands and scouted the overhead shelf for her canister of flour. She frowned at seeing it emptier than she thought, lowering it with care. She had no more set it on the counter when a loud knock came at the front door.

"Golly gee, they will wake up Trudy yet. Lord, please do not let that unpleasantness come my way today." She stepped through the bedroom straight into the front parlor where a man stood on her front porch, waiting for her to answer the door. When he started to open his mouth, she shushed him with a finger to her lips to let him know she meant it. Not wanting to seem harsh, she allowed a smile to curl the edge of her lips. She shoved the screen door open to join him on the porch. "I have a toddler asleep in the back, which is just the way I prefer her right now, a wordless Kewpie doll. Now, sir, how may I help you?"

The man shifted his weight from one foot to the other, concentrating on her face. He stood dressed in a starched white shirt and dark slacks that looked like they had seen extra duty of some sort today. Maybe he had never seen a housewife before. Some men were all work and no play. This guy fit the bill. When he turned into the sun, she could see he was not as old as she'd first thought.

"First, allow me to introduce myself. I am Duncan Reed, and I work for Mr. Coates."

"Mr. Reed, here in El Dorado more than half the population works for Coates Oil Company. Oil Hill is his domain. I am Lorna Rae Holmes."

"So you would be the wife of Harley S. Holmes then? Is that correct?" He withdrew a notepad to double check the name and seemed satisfied with his pronouncement of it.

"Yes. I'm Mrs. Harley Holmes, but Harley does not typically come home for another hour, Mr. Reed. I'm afraid you are too early if you have business—"

"No, ma'am. I came here to speak with you." Again, he shifted his weight and gave his collar a tug while he swallowed in a gulp of air.

Unease crossed the porch as Lorna Rae sensed for the first time that something menacing might be hiding behind this nice man, something Harley could be trying to hide from her. After all, he had been siphoning off her grocery money for months. She folded her hands, found the apron tie with her fingers, and pressed the rickrack like she could somehow straighten things out.

"Mrs. Holmes, there was an accident today at the generator house." He paused, and his gaze softened.

A steam kettle seemed to go off inside her head as unbearable speculation tainted her reasoning. Harley had gotten himself hurt. How in the world would they afford that? "I…I see." Her thoughts got chopped up worse than the onion, and the almost-tear she had in the kitchen tried to come back.

"Mrs. Holmes, I'm afraid I have come here today with the news that Harley lost his life trying valiantly to correct a damaged belt at the generator house. He was struck and killed instantly, so I can assure you that no suffering was involved." He reached out to touch her but drew back almost as quick.

"Oh, I see." Her mind raced past the gulf of initial shock as the immediate truth of not having Harley to provide for the two of them poked a hole in her lungs. What would she and Trudy do? Try as she may to push past the question, no answer awaited. "Where will we live?"

"I am so sorry to bring you this kind of news, ma'am. Please accept Mr. Coates' condolences, as well as my own. The company will bury Harley and pay all those expenses, rest assured. You name the cemetery, and we will make the arrangements for the family."

"Rosalia. His people are from Rosalia. The family plot is there beside the church. Is he still here at the oil field?" She twisted the apron tie until it became limp in her fingers.

"No ma'am. The ambulance came and took both victims to the

hospital to officiate the death certificate. That is standard procedure. I came over as soon as I could. The other fellow didn't have any immediate family."

"Where will we go? Do I need to move right away? I certainly do not want anyone coming to clear out my things without me knowing." Somewhere a protective bristle stiffened her backbone, and she stood taller to defend her homestead, company housing though it was.

"No ma'am. Harley had this month's rent taken out of his paycheck like usual, so you have most of one month to make plans for where you will head. Unfortunately, there is a waiting list for housing here on the oil fields, one that I am on myself. But I hope something will open up for you and the little one, maybe something back home?"

"Not likely." Lorna Rae inched toward the door, unwilling to consider the possibility. "Daddy and I had it out over Harley, but I do not mean to make that any of your business, Mr. Reed. Do I need to sign anything for you, or do we leave it like this? You delivered your message and I received it, standing right here in front of God and everybody. Is there anything more?" Not intending to, she backed into the door and the frame slapped shut against the threshold, sending a loud crack echoing through the house.

A glance up at her visitor revealed his genuine concern. She had not anticipated compassion from a company man, and it proved to be her undoing. A cascade of unblocked emotion broke loose, and the tear she'd been working up all afternoon finally got emancipated.

A tiny hand pushed against her legs right through the screen. "I waked up, Mommy."

"Come here, baby girl. Mommy needs a hug right now." Though her knees trembled, her voice held steady as she brought the girl out and lifted her for the hug, rumpled clothes and all. "Trudy, this is Mr. Reed. He works with the oil company."

The toddler took a look at the visitor who had tried to soften his stance upon her appearance on the porch. "He's my new fwiend." Implausible, her declaration crossed the planks while she twisted several blond curls around her finger.

"I...I would like that." He eased off the porch and paused on the top step. "A day like this one is pretty tough…without having a new fwiend, I mean."

"She has trouble pronouncing her R's. Say goodbye to Mr. Reed, baby doll."

She flexed her hand to wave farewell. "Bye-bye, Mista Weed."

The man gave them a long look and finally lifted one finger to return the gesture. "I will see you at the funeral, then. Goodbye, Mrs. Holmes."

"Yes, we will see you at Harley's funeral. Rosalia Cemetery, please don't forget."

"No ma'am. I won't forget. You take care." He stepped away, headed for a car parked down the block.

Lorna Rae turned and came inside, her thoughts speeding by a mile a minute. Harley would not be coming home tonight. Not tonight, or any other night. It was over—the makeshift marriage her father had sworn her to had not lasted long enough to properly detest it. Yet she did, every blame minute of it. Her father would not be amused at this outcome, not in the least.

~

Duncan took a seat at his makeshift desk in the corner of the medical clinic as the company doctor flipped the Open sign to Closed. "No, Dr. Lucas, I don't suppose this particular incident had anything to do with the undercover maiming scheme. I saw the whole thing. It was an accident, pure and simple. Tragic, but an accident."

"Then we are nowhere closer to gaining the truth. Pity that, as your inauguration hasn't come off too easy, young man." Dr. Lucas patted his shoulder as he passed by.

"I would say it's been a rough spring so far. Guess I am still getting over General MacArthur being canned last month. What a perfect time to leave D.C. behind and relinquish the home fort to the Truman haters."

"You have to wonder what the Commander-in-chief might have been thinking in the heat of the moment. I suspect that General Ridgway may not have the same war-ravaged ilk that Doug MacArthur had. Change is difficult, especially with battles still raging."

"My kid brother is finishing a stint in the U.S. Navy. He wrote that morale has plummeted among the troops. Thank goodness his ship is headed back from Korea. I expect a visit next month." He brought out his notepad to begin transcribing details onto the company's standardized accident form.

"I would like to meet him and thank him for his service, if we can arrange it. Would that be during our company picnic? He could certainly attend as your guest."

"No, but thank you, sir. Sam is scheduled to arrive the week after, mid-June I think, depending on when the train can get him to Kansas from San Diego. I am hoping this place will be a true slice of American pie."

"Ah, R and R for the midshipman. Not to mention solid ground. Sounds like a healthy dose of Midwest normal." The doctor jiggled some glassware in the sink on the back counter. Soon water splashed to announce the end-of-day clean-up routine. "Say, if he's here for two weeks, maybe he could stay for the Independence Day celebration. Mr. Coates told me the citizens of El Dorado would be in for a treat this year."

"Fireworks are nothing but a distraction, sir, if you don't mind me saying so." Duncan rested his pen on the first blank and tried to recall the day's date. With pessimism as his newfound companion, the overtime work this evening would likely be quite protracted.

"Well, when the men striding terra firma cannot think of anything more lofty to pursue than maiming members of their own lot and wearing that disfigurement like some type of badge, maybe we need the distraction of looking heavenward, Mr. Reed. I wish you a focused report completion and a better day tomorrow. Mrs. Lucas promised to make my favorite meatloaf tonight, so I dare not be late. Remember to block out time for the funeral day after tomorrow. Mr. Coates requires his administration to attend in deference to the victim's family."

"Yes, sir, I will. You go enjoy that meatloaf. I have half a sandwich left that will hold me over. Here's to tomorrow and a better day." He lifted the soda bottle and tipped it to the doctor as he donned his hat to cross the threshold into a personal life, a realm Duncan didn't know. He inked in the words "Generator House Accident" across the top line and when the date came to him, he entered it next. With only two months until Independence Day, he had miles to travel to unveil the truth, a bloody path of sordid collusion. Why the image of a curly-haired little girl flashed to mind next he had no earthly idea, but he lacked any control whatsoever to stop it.

~

Rain blurred the vista beyond the hood of the hearse, which Lorna Rae accepted as God's protective provision. Still numb from the brief memorial service at the oil field chapel, she could not handle too many more details. Bless Vivian for playing the piano before the service. Otherwise, the whole affair would have been far too somber to bear. She had sat on the front row trying to keep Trudy from squirming as the men gave testimony to Harley's strong work ethic.

She had wanted to add an invective about his flawed family ethic, but her mother had taught her not to speak ill of the dead, so she sat quietly and held Trudy in her lap. Maybe red had been a poor choice for her daughter's dress, but all other options had grown too snug or too short. Time marched on, and now it had to leave their income provider behind.

Like trees in a forest, men that had busied themselves removing the simple casket now reappeared outside of the rain-streaked car window. In an instant, they would extract her for a graveside service interminable in length, given her present state. Trudy fidgeted against her on the seat, and she reached out to draw her closer.

"Listen to Mommy for a second. This is the funeral I told you about, where they put daddy's body in the ground. Remember, they are not hurting daddy. He is already in heaven."

"With Jesus?" The girl searched her face with innocent eyes.

"Yes, baby girl. He is with Jesus. Maybe they both wanted it to rain today, so God could water the flowers to tell us everything will be okay. You be good and stay close to Mommy, okay?" The car door opened in a flash, and a man's arm hooked inside. Mr. Coates bent down into the door frame like a humble patriarch and guided her hand onto the arm of his suit jacket. His expression bordered on kindness. The concern mixed in seemed genuine. He gave her hand a pat and stood to draw her out.

Lorna Rae slipped from the car shielded from the rain by a black umbrella. The steady drum of the downpour lent her entrance a mourner's cadence. Realizing she didn't have Trudy with her yet, she turned back to witness a second man dressed in black removing the brightly-clad girl from the back seat, carrying her on his hip to spare a muddy encounter. She sighed in relief and stepped toward the grave site.

The tent protecting the grave from the elements must have shrunk in all the dampness. Women from the oil field community sat beneath its shelter. A group of men huddled in the soaking rain along the tent's edge, some without hats or overcoats. Thank God above she had insisted on a brief graveside service.

Mr. Coates escorted her to the front row seat, while the preacher from First Methodist Church downtown took his position between two modest sprays of yellow daisies. She sat down and saw a red blur as Trudy slipped into the adjoining seat. When the attending gentleman straightened, Lorna recognized the man who had delivered the death news, Mr. Reed. His dark eyes fixed on hers for the briefest of moments, and then he stepped away into the crowd.

Across the belts hoisting the coffin above the rectangular grave, she spotted the Holmes clan, with Mama Reese wearing her navy blue Sunday dress. She nodded at the woman who immediately deflected her full attention to her oldest son. Lorna Rae reckoned this marked the last day of her being considered a Holmes, as the family members had only extended forbearance to placate Harley. No need existed to keep up that pretense any longer.

"We have come here today out of respect to this dearly-held man, Harley Holmes, a fallen co-worker, husband, and father." Clear-voiced, the preacher paused to acknowledge mourners on both sides of the grave with a nod. The rain intensified and a few more men crowded under the tent's edge for shelter.

"And beloved son." Mama Reese clutched her purse to her lap, while shooting the errant clergyman a caustic look for his inexcusable omission.

"Yes, ma'am, and such a beloved son." The preacher added the phrasing without breaking rhythm and proceeded to lay out the scripture-laden eulogy full of "thee" and "thou" swimming among other antiquated words that drew the finishing line on Harley's mortality. Hushed by the rain, the man of God soon closed his Bible and stepped toward her, whispering inaudible words of pity-padded relinquishment.

Lorna Rae fought the rain's comfort and sat rigid in the hard folding chair. With her gaze on the coffin, she recalled Harley on their marriage day, so attentive and eager to be wedded to her. How quickly things had degraded into something less than desirable when Trudy came onto the scene. As a wife, she had not been enough for him, and now the whole lousy situation fell beyond rectification. *What a mess.* Her attention trailed away and traced a rivulet of water running off the grave mound. An impulse shot through her to do the same.

Still beside her, the preacher mumbled the first words of a closing prayer, and she blinked before remembering to close her eyes. The funeral home attendants shifted into place as she lifted her chin upon the pronounced amen. When Trudy squirmed into her lap, she pressed the child against her chest, while the hoist squeaked and lowered the coffin into the grave. As it settled to the bottom, she yielded to an overpowering urge to stand, bringing Trudy with her.

She approached the vacuous hole that held her deceased husband and reached for the closest floral arrangement. Taking a fistful of daisies, she offered the child a flower and then tossed the rest onto the coffin. Trudy mimicked her actions without a word.

Thunder rumbled from a far horizon, and she gave in. Lorna Rae walked away from the gravesite, the mourners, and the truncated marriage to leave it all behind. With the hearse as her immediate target, she had almost made it on her own when a protective umbrella graced the sky over her bowed head.

The man pulled the rear door open and took Trudy, so she could manage the maneuver of sitting gracefully in a tailored skirt and high heels. The ground turned to mush under her feet, but she somehow got inside and reached up for her daughter.

"Trust God that tomorrow will be a better day." Humanity expressed itself in the eyes of the helper as he relinquished the child with a look that embraced the depths of compassion.

Well, well. Who'd have thought Mr. Reed would have such empathy in him? The door slammed closed to the pelting rain. Next the passing of attendees transpired, where humanity blurred once more into trees within a distant forest.

Chapter 2

Duncan stared at the blocks on the wall-mounted calendar and counted off nineteen days since the last maiming incident. If that trademark pattern held up, another event would occur by week's end. A series of red dots coded the predicted dates, another sickening aspect of the conspiracy against the employer and its insurance carrier. Happenstance never operated on a countdown, a fact he knew all too well. He gazed down the master work schedule to predict where the mishap might occur and saw nothing but routine well drilling.

Dr. Lucas peered at him beyond the clipboard in his hands. "I have a ten o'clock appointment coming in, a well-child visit. We will need some privacy, if it fits your morning schedule."

"Certainly. Thank you for telling me. Maybe I will mill about the new rig going in south of Stapleton field. This week may get a little uneven for us, Doc. I promise to keep my eyes open to help you, if you'll do the same for me."

"I am usually the last one to know, until the whole bloody mess ends up coming across that threshold for me to fix. These aren't bandage-and-go cases, you know."

"No sir. A lifelong debilitation is nothing to sneeze at. How's that young Jimmy Cantor doing on his light-duty job at the post office? Did that re-assignment work out?"

"Yes. He seems to be thriving over there, according to old Mr. Peterson. Call that a lucky pair-up, though Jimmy would work hard anywhere. That case makes no sense to me at all. Anyway, we cannot keep finding light-duty work for full-grown men on the spur of the moment. They need to conduct the labor out in the oil fields…or go work for someone else."

"Guess there is no need to do that, not when the benefits of their employment here accommodate such lighter duty." Duncan closed his planning book and pushed back from the desk. A movement outside the front window revealed someone walking up the sidewalk—the widow and her little girl. "Looks like your ten o'clock might be here early, Doc."

"I am not quite ready to open up. Could you go out and stall her for a minute or two?"

"I suppose, since I am slated to move into her bungalow in a few weeks. Let me work on making plans for her exodus and my invasion. Will three minutes do?" He stood to leave, eyeing his office mate.

"Perfect. I have to get the vaccines ready. Thank you, Mr. Reed. You are pretty handy to have around."

"I will remind you of that the next time our schedules get crossed." Duncan pulled the door open and closed it behind him, stepping out into a sunny morning. The little girl stopped her hopscotch progress up the sidewalk when she first saw him. They regarded one another with interest. He noticed the straps of her playsuit were being held to its bib by a couple of safety pins spanning the gap. "Hello there, Trudy. Do you remember me, your friend Mr. Reed?"

"I do wemembah you." She smiled and then bowed from the waist. A cascade of rowdy blond curls accentuated the childish gesture.

"I am so glad. Good morning, Mrs. Holmes."

She tucked Trudy's shirttail back into the playsuit and then folded her hands. "Yes, good morning, Mr. Reed. It's nice to see you again. I have not thanked you for helping shield us from the rain at the funeral last week. That meant a great deal to me at the time. You know, one of life's little unexpected kindnesses." Her gaze finally roamed upward and locked with his.

"You are most welcome. The doctor is not quite ready for your appointment yet, so I wondered if we might discuss your moving-out plan, so I could mesh it with my moving-in schedule. It seems I am being assigned your old bungalow for my temporary duration here. Such a small world, isn't it?"

"Oh, I see. Well, we wouldn't want to inconvenience you at all, Mr. Reed. My plans are to move to the Kansas City area and help my sister Della with her baby. She is due on the twenty-seventh, but prefers to be home from the hospital before we move up there. Knowing how uncooperative infants can be about being born on time, that may put us here right up until the thirty-first. I truly hope that is not the worst-case scenario for you, us moving out on the last possible day." She tilted her head and the morning light played across her light brown hair, lending a glimmer of life to her widowhood.

"No. Not worse case by a long shot. Are you planning to take most of your furniture with you? I must confess, I only own a bed to move in, little else." A trickle of sheepish exposure cooled his neck with the admission.

"Hmmm, might it work out for you that I leave the dinette table and chairs along with the living room furnishings? My sister won't have the space for those right away. I can arrange to come back for them at a later date, or when you move out since you're here temporarily."

"Yes, that's perfect. Let's strike a deal that I will keep your large furnishings except the bedding through the duration of my stay, until such time that you come back to claim them. I can be reached at the doctor's office, if you'd like to give me some notice that you're returning."

"Okay, I will call you, perhaps by summer's end. I should find employment by then and be ready for all my things."

He descended two stairs to help mask his surprise. "So you are intending to work outside of the home?" When the little girl came to him, he brushed a hand across her crown. Her eyes sparkled at the attention.

"I would like to pursue a dream of baking for a living. Of course, it did not fit well here, but I think I will try to find a place to start in Westport. That's the part of Kansas City where Della lives."

"I wish you the best of luck. Plus, I hope Trudy will get to make many new friends in Kansas City." When he touched the tip of the child's nose, she pretended to nip at his finger like a lion.

"Her first new friend will be her baby cousin."

Trudy shook her head and frowned. "I hope she doesn't cwy

too much."

"I bet you will help her remain as happy as possible. I had to keep my little brother entertained when I was a boy. Now, he's a sailor in the U.S. Navy and is coming to visit me in three weeks."

She shifted past him to ascend the stairs, a faint smile on her face. "Please thank him for his service. That war in Korea seems to drag on and on. Maybe Kansas will be good for him."

"I am hoping so, too. Okay Trudy, you be brave in there. Even if the doctor gives you a shot today, remember that he's a nice man and only does it for your own good."

"Okey-dokey, Mista Weed. You go be a nice man, too." She ducked under his arm resting on the newel post and marched up to smudge up the glass panel of the front door.

Mrs. Holmes moved past him, but her gaze darted his way. "Sorry about that. She can be fresh at times."

"Quite all right. In the absence of my mother, I don't usually get that reminder to be nice—and I probably need it. Trudy's a little darling, a bright spot in my day." He stepped down to the sidewalk and turned to give her his full attention.

"Thank you for saying so. I promise to be in touch about that move-out date. Goodbye Mr. Reed." She turned the door knob and let Trudy enter the office, then followed her inside with a swishing flow of her cotton skirt.

Duncan headed down the walk toward his car, thinking to drive out to the eastern oil fields and observe while the men drilled a new well. At the end of the sidewalk, the bell jingled at the company grocery store across the walkway and an idea came to mind. He veered left and headed straight for the penny candy aisle. He would leave it for the girl on the front porch of the doctor's clinic, with the hope that she could forget the temporary sting of the shot once she found the treat. The whole act lent him immeasurable pleasure, as if he had never enjoyed the opportunity to buy something sweet for a special little someone before. *Had he?*

~

Lorna Rae picked up the Tootsie Roll wrapper from the floor and crumpled the waxy paper into the kitchen trash can. Her worrisome thoughts parted long enough to acknowledge that it had been thoughtful of Mr. Reed to leave the candy for Trudy, knowing what the doctor had in store for her. Looking ahead at the likelihood of being uninsured indefinitely, she had asked the doctor to prepare the girl for starting school, which had equated to four shots. Her daughter's screams had punched a hole in her heart. Hard times would be coming, so they might as well get used to being uncomfortable.

She turned to the open shelves of the pantry to plan something for dinner. A child hooted out in the backyard, which came followed by several loud cries as the chase heated up. Her fingers landed on a can of green beans. Trudy would not eat those, so she shifted to the peas, thinking to forestall the green vegetable conflict for a day. They had already been through enough at the doctor's clinic.

"Ding-a-ling-a-ling," a woman called through the screen door.

Lorna Rae shifted to the back door and gave her neighbor a half-smile. "Hey, Vivian. Are you trying to tag me or is someone else 'it' right now?"

"Nope, my Bennie is 'it' and he's chasing all the girls. A twelve-year old shouldn't be chasing girls yet. Criminy!"

"Come on in. Can you stay a few minutes?"

"Not really. I have a pot of chicken and dumplings on, but Bert stopped by to tell me he'd be late. They have a union meeting tonight or something. I forget what he called it exactly."

"Please do not tell Trudy what's for dinner at your place, or she will invite herself over. I tell you, Viv, that kid is eating like a horse. Her clothes don't fit anymore. Goodness knows how we'll ever make it through this summer. I will have to guard Harley's last paycheck, for sure."

"Oh dear, Lorna Rae. I wish I could help you beyond praying every day that God will provide. Promise me you will write after you move to the big city."

"Of course, I will. Once I become a famous baker, I will name a cake for you, my oil field best friend." When she reached for her neighbor, the woman hugged her without hesitation.

"Now, I really came over to insist that you let me hold Trudy's birthday party along with my Mary Jane's, as the two of them are the same date exactly five years apart. It will be a family party, right here in the yard. Say you'll let me, Lorna Rae. By month's end you'll be gone, so let's give the children this last celebration.

What do you say?"

"My agreement comes with the condition that you'll let me bake the cake. I can at least do that." Lorna Rae tapped her thumb on her heart to express her sincerity.

"It's a deal then. Let's say at four o'clock on the twenty-seventh. I have a fold-out pin-the-tail-on-the-donkey game, and we can hold relays for the children. Let me plan everything. I'm the biggest kid out there, believe me."

"You mean angel, don't you?"

"Devil-angel is what Bert calls me sometimes, especially when I get to meddling in somebody else's business." Her mouth hooked into a smirk as she stepped toward the screen door. "I had better go stir my dumpling pot. I will send Trudy home in a few minutes."

"You are a godsend, if not an angel then. Let me get going on dinner, so Trudy won't beg to sit at your table. Have a peaceful evening, Viv. Thanks for the party idea. Trudy's going to love sharing a party with Mary Jane."

"Let's hope so. Hey, you kids get out of my iris bed. How many times do I have to tell you pip-squeaks?" She flung herself through the doorway in a melodramatic lunge and the screen door complained, then popped back into place.

Lorna Rae turned to fire up the gas stove and tamped the pan into place for another night of canned nothingness. "Lucky iris bed."

~

Danger lived at the base of every oil well, a euphemism that now came to life in front of him. Duncan walked to the far side of the drilling crew to get closer to the action. The rusted truck that bore the towering drill outdated his years, approaching thirty and wearing a ton of oxidation to fill its dented fenders. The rig groaned as the site foreman shouted something indiscernible to the crew. Several men backed away. The driver of the truck then thrust a lever toward the dashboard, and the drill rig vibrated with more power.

One smudge-faced man turned toward Duncan, so he nodded and folded his arms to indicate he intended to stay put. The worker beside him leaned in slightly and took a verbal cue from the tight-lipped man. With a hum, the drill pulled up and hovered, allowing the laborers to collapse on the well site to clear the mud and chipped rock collecting around the rim. Shovels clanged together on occasion as the crew made quick work of the excess material. Soon the foreman gave the signal, and the drill descended like a giant thumbscrew as the crew retreated.

Five men trailed over to a pickup truck across from Duncan where a corrugated water cooler sat on the tailgate. A hushed comment from the shortest man broke the group into tight laughter, distracting Duncan from the immediate job site. He strained to overhear the conversation that ensued, but could scarcely make out the first word.

Two shovels clanged together under the drill. As he diverted his gaze back to the well site, a commotion unfolded that gave chaos a bad name. A shovel blade slid along the revolving drill and subducted, taking its holder down with it. The foreman shouted to the driver while he lunged for the man. An egregious second too late, the drill stopped churning, but the man lay pinned by the downward force, only half of his trunk still visible.

Duncan broke into a run without thinking about maintaining his clinical distance. A groan tainted the air as he approached the well, trying to take in everything. What a sight.

"Up! Up the drill." The foreman screamed across the mayhem, veins standing out in his neck. The familiar hum sounded and right away the drill changed direction, backing out of the hole. Several men tugged at the trunk of the laborer, and his body fell back away from the massive drill, mangled and bloody.

The tight-lipped man came forward out of the water break group. "That's Glen Forshee."

A short man stepped up beside the first laborer. "Better get him to Doc right away, the way his shoulder looks."

The foreman wiped his brow, his face creased with concern. "He knew better than to risk going up under there. Anything can happen under that drill."

The victim moaned in response.

"Allow me to take him in. I share an office with the doctor and had planned to get back anyway." Duncan shifted closer to the downed man and put an arm under him to support his limp shoulders.

"Fine, somebody can ride with you and help tend him while you drive," the foreman replied.

The drive over might afford him the opportunity to ask a few questions that deserved answers. Duncan pointed at the tight-lipped fellow who seemed to have given the cue that set the whole accident off. "Let me have *him* then." The man clenched his jaw at having been singled out, which only made Duncan more suspicious of his role.

"Torguson, you're going. Everybody else help get Forshee loaded, and then we'll break for lunch. "Of all the cussed luck—"

"Luck or schemed, it's all the same bloody result," Duncan muttered under his breath while he assisted the foreman in getting the victim hoisted for transport. The affected arm dangled precariously, as though it lacked proper attachment to his trunk, while two other laborers shored up their efforts by grabbing the man's legs. In awkward unison, they shuffled toward his car where a grimy hand opened the rear passenger side door.

"Best get something under him," the foreman said.

"Right. Mr. Torguson, take my place here, and let me get something to protect the seat." Duncan shifted so the worker could take the load and caught the look of disdain crimping the man's face. He drew out a folded tarp from under the front seat. He tucked the seam into the seat back and held the upper portion up while they placed the man inside with care. Blood trailed out the door and streaked several of the men who had helped. He backed out of the far door and stood to exchange parting comments with the foreman over the top of the car. The sound of a man retching filled the stifling air.

The foreman gave a throaty growl and led the weak-stomached man away from the car fender. "Shorty Carlson, you go in place of Torguson. He is in no shape to help out."

"Okay, Mr. Delmar. Let me go." He brushed his pants leg free of dirt and gripped the door handle to get in the front seat.

Duncan pulled his door open and slid inside, aggravated at the apparent dodge and now stuck with the lesser accomplice, at best. He keyed the ignition, slammed the door shut, and stomped on the accelerator. A moan accompanied the lurch into motion, while the rescue picked up speed. When the wheels hit the pavement, his thought train shattered in a thousand directions, none of them productive.

The laborer pulled off his oil-smeared hat and laid it on his lap.

"You mind if I say a prayer?" Without waiting for an answer, he lowered his chin and squeezed his eyes shut. "Lord Almighty, Glen here's in a bad way right now. Please get him the help he needs and stop all this bleeding with your balm. I pray Doc Lucas will know what to do, amen."

"Amen." Duncan turned toward his passenger to get a better read on him. "Want to tell me what you saw, Mr. Carlson? I do not know how this could happen, if Mr. Forshee has been fully trained in matters of safety."

Carlson fingered the brim of his hat while his upper lip twitched. "All I know is the drill was engaged when Glen got caught. He knows that's a no-man zone. What in the world was he thinking? It sure beats me." He rocked back and forth in the seat as if to better cope with the tragedy, despite the forward momentum of the car.

"Okay. I wanted to be sure you saw it like I saw it—a man going directly against orders to stay back." Duncan clamped his mouth shut and navigated the stop at a busy intersection. A labored exhale echoed from the back seat.

His passenger fidgeted, replacing his hat. "Maybe we should just shortcut to the hospital." The man chanced a look in the town's direction and glanced back at him.

"It's company policy—Doc Lucas sees him first, whether it's quicker or not." He floored the gas pedal and headed into the last leg of the rescue, the oil company's main gate. He flashed a pass at the attendant and got waved through in an instant.

"They made me get a sticker for my truck windshield," Carlson said.

"I am not here for that long," he replied. Somehow, relief followed the disclaimer as if being shed of the oil field would exonerate him from further involvement. He tried to hold that thought, but the doctor's office soon loomed ahead, and the specter of a broken man filled his senses. "Let's hope we can catch the doctor before his lunch break."

"For Glen's sake, I sure hope so."

Duncan held his tongue, fearful of being too accusatory about the alleged accident. He pulled into his regular parking spot and killed the ignition. His passenger had the wounded man half pulled out of the backseat before he could make his way around the car.

He let the tarp drop to the ground as he hefted the man out, kicking the door closed behind him. They approached the front stoop to find Doctor Lucas on the front porch, descending to help.

The doctor angled up the first step when his eyes met Duncan's across the victim's hapless body. "Lots of blood loss this time."

"Too much blood loss." Duncan stubbed his toes on the next riser, corrected his gait, and lifted the victim onto the porch. "You first, doctor. Let me trail." By the time they had the man safely inside and laid out on the cot, his hands trembled uncontrollably.

"Get your accident report testimony started and let me go to work here," Dr. Lucas said.

"I will be right outside then. Mr. Carlson, please come with me." He grabbed the clipboard holding the blank form as the calendar mocked him from the wall. The red dot warnings fell two days short of accurate, setting a new trend of frequency. Duncan failed to be amused.

~

"See how Mommy does it? Fold it flat and even, so it takes up little room." Lorna Rae pressed the latest layer into her suitcase, a hard-sided rectangle that held her worldly assets. Her daughter stood vexed at the multi-staged process of folding a garment. "Pretend dolly's blanket gets a fold right down the middle. Use your hand to crease it like this." She allowed her hand to glide down an imaginary midline as the girl watched.

"I like long folds." Trudy performed a lengthwise fold on the stockings and crammed them onto the doming mound inside her satchel.

"But long folds act like no folds at all."

"That's why I like it." The girl dusted her hands and headed for the kitchen. "I have candy now."

"Okay. One piece, though. We want Mr. Reed's Tootsie Rolls to last." A thankful nudge accompanied the acknowledgment, as kindness could be a limited offering in oil field life. They would break away as soon as possible, leaving those smudged fields behind.

"I want one and one." Her daughter reappeared with candy held in one hand while the other fist delivered another sweet treat to her mouth.

"Most certainly not, young lady. That will ruin your dinner for sure." She stepped toward her and retrieved the wrapped candy from her sweaty little palm. "I think you have time for hop-scotch. Why don't you go see if Mary Jane is outside playing?"

"Okay." The girl's reply came garbled by the tacky candy. She turned and skipped for the back door.

"Stay in our yard or Miss Vivian's, is that clear?"

"Yes, ma'am." She pushed the screen door frame and slid out of the opening like mischief on the loose.

Lorna Rae paused long enough to capture the memory of her daughter at this house, her little bungalow of trim order. She would leave that as a gift for Mr. Reed, the beneficiary of her penchant for neatness. Something told her he would appreciate such tidiness, being an intellectual type with strict demeanor. At least he would be trustworthy, and her furnishings would be treated with respect. *A clean life is a good life, isn't it?*

She tugged at the top dresser drawer and found some personal items in the right corner beside her lingerie. Letters from her mother reminded her that Della had not written back with any details of transporting the two of them to Westport. These late days of May had blurred into a wait-and-see game, for which she found no enjoyment. With Harley gone, she had to steer into the future by herself. One thing could be certain—Lorna Rae Holmes would be ready.

She flopped the ribbon-tied letters into the shoe pocket of the suitcase and balled up a handful of unmentionables for packing. "Long folds are no folds," she muttered to herself, fitting her stockings into the crevice along the spine of the case. The contents leveled out and she smacked the lid closed about the time the screen door slammed.

"It's waining, Mommy." Trudy held up her drooping curls to prove it.

"Okay, baby girl. Come on with me and let's see if that soup is ready. We can dry your hair by the stove. I think we are all done packing anyway."

"All done," she replied, her palms turned upwards.

"Let's wash those hands." She led her to the sink and pushed the step stool with her foot.

The girl stepped up and offered her hands. "Is it going to wain on my biwthday?"

"Oh, rain does not last that long, Trudy. Let's hope it rains for a day and then goes away." Lorna Rae turned on the hot water, thinking she should use her share before the end of the month. Mr. Reed could inherit the luxury after that. Hot water represented another company benefit she would not be able to replace. Her life was waning like the shaved-off moon, and not in isolated droplets either, but a total downpour.

Chapter 3

Duncan stared out of the upstairs window as the rain turned the evening into a slick black unknown. For five days it had rained without cessation, making the route to and from work nearly impassible. The bridge at the end of the farm lane had overflowed from both sides, the water rising over the course of the day before his return. His car had not balked at the standing pool yet, but he would not press the issue if matters grew worse.

Dr. Lucas had mentioned overnight use of the cot in their office more than once, an offer he might have to accept if God had a re-enactment of Noah's flood in mind for Kansas. Goodness knows the depravity of his maiming case certainly warranted divine retribution. The liquid night drummed on as his thoughts ran deep to untangle the chronic maiming situation.

Seconds later, a knock at the door startled him. When a female cleared her throat immediately outside the room, he remembered his living situation.

"Mr. Reed?" Mrs. Hansen questioned through the planked door. "The call from Washington is on hold down in the main hallway. Are you able to take it tonight?"

"Yes, of course." He forced a step to the door and turned the worn knob. "I apologize. The rain has dampened my state of mind, I'm afraid. Thank you for notifying me of the call."

"You are welcome. I will be leaving to pick up Daphne from the Baptist Young Women's meeting here directly, so you can have your privacy." She swept at invisible dust along the door frame.

"Thank you, Mrs. Hansen. Your discretion is valued. I think you had better drive the old truck tonight. That creek is still flooding down the lane. The extra clearance will be handy."

"Oh, mercy. It is not a fit night to be out, but Daphne remains devoted to her meeting, nonetheless. Those young women pray for missionaries all around the world."

"May the Good Lord credit that to her account then, and to a mother who has to go out in this kind of weather." His feet descended the wooden staircase as he offered his last encouragement to the widow. At least he had been able to contribute to the household monetarily with his stay, though Daphne's fawning attention created needless complication. He picked up the receiver and muffled it against his cheek. "Reed here."

The homemaker passed behind him in a sweep of a full skirt and the medicinal scent of ointment. When the kitchen door closed moments later, the house fell quiet.

"Go ahead, sir. I am ready to report the week's progress."

"Have you attempted to get any information from the latest victim there, Reed?"

"No, Mr. McNaughton. That man, Glen Forshee, has developed an infection at the site of his wound and cannot receive visitors at the hospital yet. This case seems worse than a maiming, but I suppose a man takes that risk when he goes against direct orders."

"So you can verify that he operated against company policy and direct orders in the field by chancing injury under the drilling rig?"

"Yes sir, I witnessed the unthinkable act myself and have made official note of it. That report is in the mail to you right now." Unaware, his fingers entangled in the spiraled cord and he had to work against the coil to extract them.

"Reed, I want you to know the insurance company cannot continue to absorb these mounting expenses. We are sending notification to Mr. Coates that he will have to limit insurance claims for the next forty-five working days. We need you to help him draft a company memo spelling out the exceptions, which equates to obstetric deliveries and automobile accidents only. We chose to include vehicle wrecks because we do not think there will be any, given the nature of the business. Are these stipulations clear?"

"Yes sir, clear and fair, I believe. I will look up Mr. Coates tomorrow. Plus, let me ask Dr. Lucas for the number of expecting women seeing him for prenatal care right now, so we can get a handle on that exception."

"Good work, Reed. I knew you were the man for this job. Now stick with it. There's nothing done in secret that won't be made known. Keep watching and digging. You are close to breaking this case wide open."

"You give me more credit than what's due, sir, but I appreciate it." His throat grew dry at the acknowledgment. He felt far from the brink of discovery.

"Pay attention to everything. And remember, you are calling me next, after your move onto oil field housing."

"Right. I hope this rain lets up, so I can move my bed without having to tarp it."

"Do what you need to do, Mr. Reed. You can cover up or uncover. Goodbye."

The line clicked closed, but the ring of threat still clung to the air. Duncan turned for the staircase where his gaze fell onto an old photo of his host family during a happier time. Daphne's hair hung in braided pigtails, while her father allowed her to ride on the hood of his new farm truck. The accident-prone stagger-step of time had propelled them to this point, a fatherless household without laughter or ready income. *What robbery accidents can pull off, yet how unable to stop them humankind is.* He climbed the stairs downcast while thunder rolled across the valley.

~

Torguson eyed the core members around the table in a dimly lit back room.

Shorty squirmed. "Glen Forshee doesn't look like he is gonna make it."

"You're soft, Carlson. Don't go getting wishy-washy on us. Our plan is underway, and the big man is squirming. All it took was us little men uniting. See?" Torguson glanced left to check for support. Several members nodded. "We can take time off before the next draw, come mid-July. It will be hotter than fire by then for us drillers."

"Guess we don't have to make this any worse than it already is." Shorty's face twitched as he folded his fingers together. "The company picnic is coming up Saturday. Want to rig some minor diversion out at the lake?"

Torguson stroked at his beard stubble and reached for his mug. "No, nothing beyond a friendly game of horseshoes that is. We leave our work on the oil fields. I am past due to have some fun, anyway. Let's meet next on the second week of July. Any more questions?"

Shorty swung an imaginary bat through the air. "Is DiMaggio going to strike out this week?" The fellow beside him pretended to catch the strike and tag him out.

Torguson hid his smile inside the mug, but his eyes gleamed with success. "Maybe Joe's hitting streak will last as long as ours. Meeting adjourned then."

"I am going home to listen to the game." Shorty stood and scraped his chair against the floor planking before remembering to grab his slicker. "Infernal rain," he muttered. Several men chuckled as the group disbanded and emerged from the back room. Smoke leveled itself at hat height, seeming to double in the barroom mirror. "Lucky Strike Extra must mean smoke comes as a bonus." He waved a hand through the smoke cloud.

"There you go getting soft again, Shorty." Torguson picked up a matchbook pad at the end of the bar while he exchanged glances with the barmaid. "No time to be soft when there is so much to gain from being tough." He flipped on his cap and ducked into a curtain of rain.

~

Lorna Rae opened the oven door with care to maintain quiet. With the birthday girl asleep in the next room, she wanted to keep it that way. A tiny light came on in back of the oven to help her judge how done the cake was. She squinted and decided to keep it in a few minutes longer. A double recipe needed longer to set, after all. The door squeaked closed and she straightened, resting her hands on her hips. The storm rumbled, and a distant flash of lightning caught her attention out beyond the mechanic's shop.

A whole big world awaited her outside the main gate of Coates Oil Company. Should she be more excited to venture out and make something happen? Maybe the storm made it too cozy inside to dream about running away tonight. The stove warmed her arms while she glanced around the tiny kitchen. Nothing else needed to be packed away. In her efficiency, she had already taken care of all that. Three years would be drawing to a close with Trudy's birthday tomorrow. Within the week, they would move on to their next adventure, big city living.

She shifted to the back door, slid the curtain aside, and watched the rain in the weak light of a street lamp. Puddles outlined the walking paths the children had worn between the houses. No lights illuminated the neighbor's home. "Sleep well, Vivian. We will have the best party ever tomorrow. Hope you don't mind if I disinvite the rain." She folded her hands under her chin and bowed, though she kept her eyes open. "Hear this mother's prayer for her little girl, Lord. Watch over Trudy and keep her full of grace and love. I don't know what I'd do without her. Please let us hold this party tomorrow without the threat of overcast skies. I will accept good weather as a sign of your favor, dear God. In the holy name of Jesus, our blessed hope, amen."

The cake's aroma drew her back to the oven, so she lowered the door to glimpse its state of readiness. The cue she sought lurked in the corner, as the edge had pulled away ever so slightly from the pan. She folded the pot holder and grabbed the front edge of the rectangular pan, pulling it along the rack until she could lift it in one fell swoop. Up onto the stovetop it came with soft clatter, a perfect specimen.

"This baker is back in business." She turned the temperature dial off with a click and plopped the pot holder into a nearby drawer. "Time for bed, Lorna Rae, or you will pay for it in the morning." She passed the back door and slid the curtain back into place. A shadow shifted outside beyond the streaked windowpane—or had it been her imagination? She tiptoed through the bedroom in the dark, engulfed in weariness. She sat on the double bed where she would sleep alone again tonight. Trudy made a tiny gurgle in her sleep as she fell back on the chenille comforter. The rain tapped at the bungalow's roof, until she couldn't hear it any longer.

~

Mr. Coates sat down in the guest chair and leaned toward the desk. "I may be obstinate on many things, Mr. Reed, but I am downright flummoxed on this one." Dr. Lucas clucked in agreement from the back counter.

Duncan had worked all morning to draft the wording for the policy shift announcing a freeze on the medical benefits, due to the company's overrun on the coverage. Now, it appeared some assuagement might be in order. "This is a non-repeatable event your company is experiencing, Mr. Coates. Washington thinks we are getting close to breaking this open, so hang in there with us, sir." He slid the paperwork closer for his inspection.

Large-framed, the oil baron hunched his shoulders as he drew a pair of spectacles from his shirt pocket. "This blame rain is holding up drilling on three wells this week. If this keeps up, it will take us until mid-June to dry out. We can't afford to work, and we can't afford not to. I'm over a barrel…and I like my barrels full of oil." His last comment came with a growl attached.

Duncan tapped a pencil on a sheet he had torn from his notepad. "We will shut down any new medical expenses in the interim, sir. You might be relieved to know that Glen Forshee went home from the hospital today."

Mr. Coates borrowed the pencil and drew a line through the man's name. "What else do we have coming up in the way of medical expenses? William, what about this next exemption? How many babies are due in the next forty-five days?"

"You have caught your first break, Malcolm." Dr. Lucas stepped closer and put a hand on the man's shoulder. "I have no record of any due dates falling within that period. The first baby is scheduled on or around the end of August. As best I can tell from my records, that is."

Mr. Coates lined out the baby clause on the notepad sheet, and then hesitated. He touched the pencil tip to the paper and retracted it.

"Maybe you could buy yourself some goodwill by leaving the obstetric exclusion in the announcement, sir." Duncan leaned back on the window sill and crossed his ankles. "With that in place, the workers know you have their overall well-being in mind, as the moratorium won't put the *whole* family at risk."

"That is not the full truth, Mr. Reed, and you know it as well as I. Little Johnny had better not play with anything sharp, because we cannot afford to send him to the hospital these next forty-five days. What a conundrum we have fallen into."

"Sure, hospitalization will be out of the question, Malcolm, but I can treat little Johnny here without incurring any extra expense." Dr. Lucas swept his hand through the air. "Let me run a free clinic to absorb those minor injuries for the duration of the moratorium. Maybe we could ask Mr. Reed to add that to his memo to help quell any knee-jerk reaction to the temporary loss of medical benefits."

"Say, I like that tactic. They would still pay for any pharmaceuticals, but not the office visit. That would work. Good thinking, Will. Thanks for meeting me halfway on this. Usually when you try to lay low, fate has a way of really kidney-punching you. But I think we can maneuver through this lockdown of benefits without a flare-up."

"I will add the free clinic clause in here at the end, sir." Duncan noted the exact position by tapping his finger on the draft.

The big man scrawled something with the pencil and pushed back from the desk. "Very well then. I promise to stop back on my rounds after lunch and sign the final document for posting. It's time to go check on that new fan belt at the generator house and listen to the whirring sound of money being made."

"Oh, the little Holmes girl turns three years old today." Dr. Lucas looked up from his calendar. "She lost her daddy to your last fan belt."

Duncan must have exhaled louder than he had intended, as Mr. Coates turned his balding head in his direction. "I would be glad to go pay her a visit, sir, if you would like. After I get this final draft retyped, I mean."

"Yes, would you do that, Mr. Reed? And carry over a quart of ice cream with you. I can stop and speak to Mr. Anders over at the grocery to clear the expense."

"Uh, I would not recommend doing that, Malcolm, if I were you." Dr. Lucas followed the man out the clinic's door and stood in the morning sun.

"Why can't I go in my own store, dad-gum-it?" Mr. Coates tore the glasses off his face and shoved them in his pocket.

"Maggie Anders has a flare-up of gout, right smart and bad," the doctor replied.

"Oh, I see."

"I will be glad to bring the ice cream to the party out of my own pocket." Duncan stepped onto the porch and glanced across at the store. A mother led her three children down the walkway, her arms full of bagged groceries. The older boy strayed into a nearby puddle and landed a tacit reprimand.

"Fine. That solves that problem. Now, it's on to something more challenging like running an oil field." Mr. Coates tipped his imaginary hat and hastened down the sidewalk. He soon intercepted the family with groceries and patted the young girl on the head as he exchanged small talk with the mother.

"That Mary Jane Decker has a birthday today as well." The doctor nodded toward the young girl. "Since they live right beside the Holmes family, you can bet the girls will celebrate together."

"Guess that means I'll bring a half-gallon of ice cream then," Duncan replied with a grin.

"Or two. I had better find out when the party is, or you are liable to have a meltdown on your hands." The doctor ambled down the steps and caught the family as they passed.

Duncan let his gaze roam across the little village square past the land assayer's office over to the diminutive white clapboard chapel in the grove of trees to the south. A large puddle up the lane reflected the steeple in its entirety, fooling him into wondering which way was up. He tilted his head back to soak in the sunshine, a stranger of late to the oil field. He took a deep breath and tried not to let the rewording of the insurance suspension crowd his thoughts. *This is the day that the Lord hath made.* He would rejoice and be glad in it. Plus, now he had a party to attend.

~

Lorna Rae cupped her hands into a megaphone to get her message across to Trudy, but the other children shouted so loud she doubted her tips could be heard. "No, no, no. Try lower, dolly." Trudy's pinned tail landed on the donkey's right ear, which made the other players laugh. Ben Decker erupted in a condescending tease like a twelve-year old trying out his newfound devil horns. When Vivian removed the blindfold with a flourish, Trudy covered her mouth when she saw the location of her attempt, her eyes full of mirth.

A man stepped up behind her and the shutter of a camera clicked off a frame. "Might that be considered unfair advantage,

Mrs. Holmes, directing a blindfolded player in such an obvious manner?"

Lorna Rae whirled around, and her high spirits turned into cozy pleasure at seeing her visitor. "Mr. Reed? Whatever brings you out to the neighborhood today?" He looked well-groomed, like he'd had a haircut. The barber had managed to shave off a year or so from his all-business deportment.

He balanced the Instamatic camera between his hands with patience and captured the children grouped around the next participant, the older birthday girl. "Why, I am out rendering unfairness edicts and other regulatory digressions. Too bad this ice cream has to melt while I get all this circumstantial evidence recorded." When he looked up from the camera, he gave her a genuine smile and nodded toward the picnic table. There on the bench stood a paper sack from the local grocery.

"Really now, you shouldn't have, but I am as thrilled for it as I can be. Thank you so kindly, Mr. Reed."

"Not my idea. You can thank Mr. Coates. When he found out it was Trudy's birthday, he downright insisted. He had business to attend this afternoon, so I offered my delivery services and here I am."

"Well then, gracious. We had better get this ice cream into my Frigidaire for now. How wonderful to have to worry about the sun melting it. Why, I could just dance in the sunshine, I'm so fed up with all the rain." Heat came to her cheeks as she realized she'd been gushing all the while, to his apparent amusement.

"Can you take the ice cream while I say hello to the birthday girl?" He allowed the camera to dangle from a neck strap and motioned at the children under the cottonwood tree.

"Come help me first, will you? I can show you the bungalow, so you know what you are getting, if you're interested." Lorna stepped to the table and lifted the sack. Coolness crept up her arm right through the paper. "Uh-oh. I think we had better hurry and get this inside."

"Certainly, lead the way. I tried to come right over, but I'm afraid that brown paper isn't much of an insulator against late May. Guess I am inexperienced as a carrier of frozen products."

Lorna Rae snickered at his sheepish look as she walked up the rear sidewalk to enter the house. He stepped around her at the back stoop and pulled the door open for her. *How nice, a real gentleman.* "Give me a second or so to get this put away. Oh, mercy! There are two half-gallons in here. And one is strawberry—Trudy's favorite. How special. I will have to write Mr. Coates a note of thanks."

He pulled the freezer door open, and she popped the frozen carton inside. "I have to admit that the second half-gallon is my favorite. I can clean up any extra if nobody else likes it." He gave her a guilty look and tucked his lips to one side.

"Butter pecan? Are you kidding me? I ought to claim this whole carton for myself, though I know my next-door neighbor Vivian would arm wrestle me for it." She sniffed at the corner of the carton and made a pleasurable hum while she stuffed it on top of the other.

He pushed the freezer door closed and held her in his gaze.

Her knees trembled ever so slightly. She guided a wayward curl off her face. "On with the tour. I wanted you to see the bedroom and parlor to make sure they will do. Everything is connected, so you can walk from one room right into the next. For efficiency, I suppose."

"Yes, hallways are a waste of interior space. These bungalows are efficient, front-to-back aligned. I trust the plumbing is modern?" He stopped halfway through the bedroom to punctuate his comment.

"Of course. It is nineteen fifty-one, Mr. Reed."

He peered around the room until his gaze halted on her stack of suitcases. "Do you always have things so neat in here?"

"A clean home is a reflection of the housekeeper." She swept a hand down her skirt as if her appearance suddenly mattered.

"Point well taken." He stepped into the doorway of the front room, gave it his inspection, and turned to face her again. "Let me say, it does reflect well on you, especially for a woman whose world has been turned a bit upside down. I commend you for your orderliness and am most grateful to inherit the house in such fine condition. Thank you. I hope you didn't make any special effort on my account."

"Why no, Mr. Reed. I didn't know you were coming by today. But we should probably get back outside, before someone thinks something untoward of us being alone in here together."

"On my honor, I never gave the propriety a second thought. The ice cream and all—"

Lorna Rae watched his face redden and then led the way out the door, staying back to him so he couldn't see her outlandish grin. Though the perfect gentleman, he seemed to enjoy their time alone, which landed as quite the compliment. For a few seconds, freedom to be an attractive female filled her lungs. She smoothed back her hair. "I would like to introduce you to my neighbor Vivian, the biggest kid at the party."

He stepped up beside her with an earnest look on his face. "That would be fine, but please call me Duncan, if you will." The paved walk soon gave way to mud, and he guided her around the dry side of the picnic table with the slightest touch on her elbow.

"If you will call me Lorna Rae. You will only have a few days to use it, though. We seem to be crossing paths here at the oil field."

"My trail always seems to be temporary, ma'am, but I am honored to make a few friends along the way. Now, if you can excuse me, I have a birthday girl to dote upon." With that he stepped toward the cottonwood tree where the children gathered to attempt the next game.

Lorna Rae fought the feeling tightening her chest. Her daughter jumped up and down when their unexpected guest tapped her shoulder. A hug around the legs came next, and he wrapped the girl with his tanned arms. Her heart connected with her tear ducts at the adorable scene, and her eyes soon welled up in appreciation.

Vivian pressed her lips into a bright red circle as she ogle-eyed their visitor. "What in the world have you ordered from the Lillian Vernon catalog this time?"

"I am a widow living off my husband's last paycheck. I don't think I ordered anything." She put her hands on her hips and raised her brow to fend off any further banter on the subject.

"Well, maybe God ordered him then. You know I have been praying for you."

"Vivian. I am leaving within the week. Meet your new next-door neighbor, Duncan Reed. He brought over ice cream on Mr. Coates' behalf. I plan to fight you over the butter pecan."

"Better keep your spoon clean, lassie. I intend to take you up on that challenge. I can hardly wait to get a bite of that cake. It looks scrumptious."

"Everything is a matter of personal taste, Viv, my baking included." She pushed at the woman's apron-padded hip as she stepped toward the fun. The words barely off her lips, she locked gazes with Duncan who had lined up behind Trudy for the next game. When he nodded her over, she had no qualms about joining in. It was her party and she'd play if she wanted to.

~

God bless a well-placed spoon. Duncan turned with his boiled egg load and tipped his head to pass it onto the next player, Lorna Rae. She held her utensil in her mouth and reached up to hold his shoulders as he lowered the egg. From this range, the freckles across the bridge of her delicate nose were evident, and he took note like an explorer reading a landscape of uncharted territory. Focused on the transfer, she seemed all business until her gaze flickered directly into his. He now swam in a sea of opulent green to help confuse his mission.

She drew nearer as the children chided on both sides to hurry the pass-off. Her spoon angled and clinked against his, ready for the transfer. Her fingers tightened on his shoulders.

Duncan held his breath and dipped sideways. The egg rocked out of its cradle and rolled into her spoon. For a brief moment, it looked like a misfire that would end in a drop, but Lorna Rae steadied it and gave him a teeth-clenched smile before letting go to run for the head of the line. He would only have to endure one more such proximal transfer, as Trudy would end the game when she ran up front after his turn.

The girl turned around and crinkled her nose at him, her spoon clutched with both hands. Her knuckles blanched white with determination. "You gonna help me win this, 'cause fwiends like to win." She gave her head a Shirley Temple nod, and the curls all shook in unison.

"Yes, ma'am. You bet you are going to win. The birthday girl has to be the winner, after all." He tapped her head with his spoon to endow the winning touch, and it ricocheted back on him like a reverse blessing. How unexpected to enjoy the lighthearted moment.

"Now you get weady." The girl waggled her spoon at him and turned around to receive the next pass.

He knelt to be in position, and the egg soon came in a hasty hurry. The spoon handle nearly gagged him, but he recovered and stood with the load. As one hand protected the hard-boiled baton, he took a position in front of Lorna Rae and turned to make the final transfer of the relay. This time her attention seized on him from the start, and he bent to her height caught in the spell she produced up close. The egg teetered, and he lifted a hand that landed near the curve of her neck. Instead of solidifying his connection, a ripple of imbalance ran through him.

Her eyes gleamed as she maneuvered her spoon and literally took the egg from him in one fell swoop. When she turned to pass it on, the flutter smashed into his gut full force. Breathless, he watched her every move and before he knew it, Trudy passed by heading for the win. Vivian raised her arm to indicate the home team victory. Lorna Rae dashed around him to clutch the birthday girl so they could celebrate together.

A slender man pushed off the tree trunk and walked their way. "Is it time for cake yet?"

Duncan regarded the laborer and thought he had seen him before out on the job site. He nodded and tried to regain his decorum.

"Bert, you go wash up," Vivian replied. "We will settle in for cake and ice cream next. Make a line at the faucet, kids, and let's get those hands washed so we can eat."

The children left him standing alone as they responded to her command. Unsure what to do, he collapsed on the picnic bench while Lorna Rae lifted a box lid to check on the cake. Through the open slit he could make out a farm scene, complete with play horses. The corral fencing seemed familiar.

"Are those Tootsie Rolls for the fence post there?" He pointed to the partly hidden diorama.

"Shhh." A finger wandered to her lips. "Thank you for your contribution, Mr. Reed."

"Call me Duncan today, or you cannot have any of my ice cream." He froze a stern look on his face, until she capitulated.

"Okay, Duncan. Let's see if I can win back your good graces with my baking." She placed the top back on and retreated toward her bungalow. "Oh, do you want to wash your hands over here? I can show you where the outside faucet is."

"Sure, and then let me help you bring the ice cream out. I will carry the butter pecan, Lorna Rae, to protect you from your weakness."

"By golly, don't give it to Vivian instead. I hope you kept your spoon."

He walked behind her, ready to accept her challenge. As the faucet spurted the first handful of water, he brandished his utensil from his back pocket. "Maybe I need to give this a rinse-off. A hundred dirty hands probably touched that egg."

She snickered and grabbed a bar of soap hanging from a netted bag. "At least a hundred. Thank you for being here, Duncan. It sure adds to the fun. Trudy's fun…on her birthday."

"You are welcome." He tried to say more, but his hands brushed against hers under the water flow, and his ability to form words washed away. He accepted the soap and lathered with it before releasing the netted bag to its resting spot. It took a throat clearing before he could convey his next sentiment. "I am looking forward to sampling that cake. I heard you hope to be a commercial baker some day."

"Let's get that ice cream now." She left and went right for the back door, disappearing with a slam.

He reflected back on his words and the tone he had used to check if any offense might have been taken as he shook the water from his hands and turned off the faucet. A sliver of insight opened up to him that she might be anxious about his opinion on the cake, a test of sorts. Why that gave him a niggling satisfaction, he couldn't say. He stood knee-deep in a birthday party for a precious little girl, and he acted giddier than the three year-old. A carton of butter pecan ice cream soon poked out of the screen door and bobbed to catch his attention. "Good show, Lorna Rae. You are displaying great fortitude here."

"Somebody has to play the part of the grownup, right Duncan?" With that she shot out of the door, the strawberry ice cream riding the crook of her arm. A metal scoop rode in one hand and a large spoon in the other.

He tapped his back pocket with his free hand and gained assurance he had come ready for this next part, consuming a slab of mouth-watering cake. Hopefully, someone would take the horses off, but he was not opposed to choking down a fence post or two in the line of duty.

The laborer extended his hand for a proper introduction. "I am Bert Decker, Mary Jane's father."

"Pleased to meet you, Bert. I'm Duncan Reed. I think I've seen you around before." He took the hand and gave it a firm shake. Up closer, the man resembled Bing Crosby.

"Seen one driller, you've seen them all." A tease laced his comment as he broke away to pull up a chair near the table.

With Vivian's assistance, Lorna Rae revealed the cake and placed it in front of the two birthday girls. Trudy shook with delight. The older girl pointed to her favorite horse, so Trudy selected the other one.

"Whoa now, just a minute. You two aren't forgetting the candles, are you?" Lorna Rae shook a finger at them as Vivian filled her palm with a pad of matches. One by one, she lit the candles until the corral stood aglow.

"Oh, happy birthday to you," Bert began in a clear Irish tenor. The children took over from there, filling in both names of the guests of honor. Vivian brought the end notes down with her alto rendition, while Lorna Rae sang out with soprano clarity. Before anyone could say Jack Robinson, Trudy and Mary Jane commenced to spit-blowing to quench the candles.

"Hope you made a wish." Lorna Rae lowered the serving piece on the cake's far corner as the girls took the horses. "Let's allow our visitor to have this first piece, girls. I think he's dying to taste my cooking."

Duncan would scarcely argue that account, plus the far corner had managed to escape the spit-riddled blow-out of the candles, a most hygienic solution. He whipped out his spoon and saluted her with it as a gesture of thanks. When she tucked a smile away, her cheeks dimpled. Goodness, was that a blush working up the baker's neck? The cake made its way in front of him. It looked like chocolate perfection, moist, spongy, and set to disappear.

Vivian waved the scoop in mid-air. "Who wants ice cream with theirs?" The table's occupants erupted in overwhelming response.

The first spoonful surrendered to his mouth, where his taste buds took over the evaluation. By the second mouthful, he'd started humming. *Glory be.* The woman could outright bake. Duncan looked up without shielding his pleasure, and his gaze caught hers for an instant, transferring his satisfaction directly to the cook. She looked down again to cut the next slice, but stole a second glance at him through her lashes. About then, a rounded scoop of melted-edged butter pecan ice cream found its way onto his plate like a roaming iceberg. His spirits soared onto a higher plane. The two treats mixed to swirl the tastes, a pinnacle moment.

Trudy sucked the frosting from the horse's leg and poured some of her cherubic delight in his direction. "Hey, Mista Weed. How do you like my biwthday?"

"Like it? Why I think you should turn three years old every day—if it means I can eat this delicious cake."

"Amen, brother," Bert replied, working a big portion in his cheek.

"Never return a catalog order," Vivian added as she tapped Lorna Rae between the shoulder blades with her knuckles. The comment brought up a deeper hue of red on the baker's cheeks, though she tried to stay busy and hide it.

"Thank you, Rae. Really, I've never tasted anything so good before. You have got to market this. It will be a sensation." Duncan lifted a spoonful toward her and flew it right into his mouth, before he made matters even more complicated. As he swallowed the delectable load, he realized he had only used half of her name, like some term of endearment. He choked a bit until a glass of water showed up with an ice cream scoop balanced in the server's hand.

"I have told her that before, but she doesn't believe little ole me." Vivian's bug-eyed protest ended with a knowing smile across the corner of the table.

Lorna Rae shifted away from his spot to serve the impatient boy at the end of the table. When she turned back to the cake, her countenance had lightened. "It's Lorna Rae, both names together." She had corrected him in almost a whisper as she wiped excess frosting off the serving piece.

He took a long drink of water, hoping it would aid his recovery. He wrestled with proper wording for an apology when it dawned on him, a moniker for her business line. "Lo-Rae Cakes. It has a nice ring to it, don't you think?"

Bert raised his spoon as a vote of agreement, and Vivian smacked her hands together like he had landed upon a bulls-eye.

Lorna Rae passed by delivering a piece of cake to the last child seated on the far end. When she came back, she paused behind him. "I honestly do not know what I think, Mr. Reed, as I haven't had one clear thought since you put that egg in my spoon."

Her whispered message sent goose bumps up the side of his neck so high, he thought his ear might meet up with his part. Land sakes, what a party. He scooped up the last bite of cake and brought it home, savoring the sugar-slick frosting. Within seconds, another half-piece of chocolate-covered manna showed up on his plate. He dug right in like he couldn't get enough. Indulgence sure had its moments all right. Aware that he used to possess more self-control than this, he hummed again before downing the treat, his gaze ever on the cake's remarkable baker.

Chapter 4

This venture had all the makings for a total waste of time, but Dr. Lucas had suggested it, so here Duncan stood posting a letter off to his mother to gain an audience with the associate mail clerk. The second maiming victim on record, Jimmy Cantor, lost the four fingers of his left hand in a machining accident with a pipefitters group. As he waited at the front counter, a spirited young man appeared from behind a row of shelving.

The clerk approached the counter to render his services. "Good afternoon. May I help you?"

"Yes. I need a stamp for this letter. I am unsure what sufficient postage is due." Duncan yielded the letter.

The clerk accepted it with his right hand. The man's thick brown hair shone in the overhead light, still bearing comb marks from his morning's grooming. "One stamp will do it, if I am estimating right. Still, let's put it on the scale to be certain." He flipped it onto the scale and nodded when the reading confirmed his prediction. "That will be three cents, sir."

Duncan dug into his pants pocket and came up with three pennies. "Let me just get this one stamp for now."

"Sure thing." Once he saw the pennies, the clerk opened a drawer. He pulled the end stamp off a plump roll, using his hand stub to manage the tear-off. He placed the stamp on top of the letter and slipped the coins off the counter.

"Say, how are you getting along with your hand injury there?" Duncan tried to sound nonchalant, aware that a fine line separated concern from meddling. He needed to have this conversation, though, so he put more heart into it. "Hope it's not a hindrance to you, I mean."

The young man's affable expression dropped. He brought both hands up to the counter's edge as if to display the comparative damage. "Nobody would ever wish something like this on themselves, but I think I am finally getting on top of the situation."

"How so? I mean it must have been difficult—"

The clerk looked away as if someone might walk up from the back room and overhear the discussion. "Oh, yeah, painful, too. Dr. Lucas was a big help, but he could only do so much. Turns out, my fingers got pretty mangled."

Duncan pressed for more information. "Do you have any recollection of that day when the accident happened? You must have been shocked, right?"

An odd expression overcame the young man's face before he could shake it off. "No, I do not remember too much about that day, except that it hurt more than I ever could imagine."

"I bet so. They say that pain is a personal trial, and you have experienced that at a fairly young age. We can only hope to learn from such on-the-job mistakes to make this place safer for workers in the future."

"That's what the union says, but I am not so convinced that it's working. Say, I need to get back sorting today's mail shipment from Wichita."

"Take care, young man. Enjoy your work here at the post office."

"Thank you, sir. Good day." He walked out of sight while rubbing his stub.

Duncan licked the stamp and stepped toward the outgoing mail repository. The brass faceplate shined bright with wear around the mail slot from a thousand letters sent home. He slid the standard-sized envelop inside as his investigation took a quantum leap forward. Jimmy Cantor had referenced his union, but the oil field workers lacked such organized representation. He had gained a solid mention of collusion—a lead at last.

~

Lorna Rae pulled Trudy back against her legs as the doctor replaced the receiver. "Della sounds miserable, bless her heart. Thank you so much for allowing me to make the call. Here it is

May thirtieth, and we still do not have a baby."

"I am guessing this is Della's first?"

"Yes, that's right. She is two days overdue."

He stabbed the air with a tongue depressor, and the girl tried to snatch it. "You know how that goes, Mrs. Holmes. As I remember, little Trudy here did not show up on time."

"No, she came eight days late. Right now, I'll consider that the Holloway girls' family curse, one I did not necessarily want to share with Della. She's a bit more heavy-set than me, so I thought she might have a better go of it than I did."

"Many intricate matters have to come together through that placenta, so let's not wish her any complications—beyond a sour mood. Maybe you should be glad you aren't up there yet."

Trudy plopped down in the office chair nearby as Lorna Rae weighed the doctor's words of advice. "Yes, my hardship should not add to hers. It's just that Mr. Reed needs the bungalow by the first of June. That was our original agreement."

"I happen to know Mr. Reed has paid Widow Hansen rent for June, so his kid brother can stay there when he arrives midmonth. That means he can stay put, which might offer you some breathing room until the baby arrives, Mrs. Holmes. I'm sure Mr. Reed will be accommodating."

"What? I understand that stiff-neck is most difficult to deal with," a man replied through the screen door.

"My fwiend Mista Weed," Trudy exclaimed from the chair. She tried to stand, but the chair twirled under the weight shift. Lorna Rae caught her by an arm as she began to fall.

He walked into the office with a spring in his step. He pushed the chair back under the desk and gave the girl a slow wink. "How's my girlfriend doing?"

"Gweat." Trudy leaned away and in seconds, Duncan had her in his arms. The girl laid her cheek against his in an open show of affection.

Lorna Rae could barely stand to watch them being so close. "Hello, Mr. Reed. How are you today?" She smiled and looked his way with some reluctance.

"Better than I should be. And you? Is there a new baby in Westport yet?"

"I am fine, thank you. No, there's no baby yet. Dr. Lucas

reminded me that my little bundle of joy didn't get delivered on time either, so running late may be a family trait."

He shook his head to loosen Trudy's hand which had clamped to his forehead like a precocious nurse testing for fever. "Well, all things being what they are, I guess our moving plans will have to stay on hold."

The idea surged out of nowhere, but she liked the feel of it. "Not necessarily. What if we switched places? You would get the bungalow on time for your work convenience, while Trudy and I could enjoy a few days of living in the country with Mrs. Hansen. Would you please consider it, Mr. Reed?"

"I do have my room rent extended for a month—and you'd be long gone before Sam's train is scheduled to arrive, so that would not create a problem. Yes, I'm warming to this idea more and more. It sure would behoove my work to live onsite, if you sincerely mean the offer." He glanced past Trudy who worked hard to absorb all of his attention.

Relief flooded over Lorna Rae. She had found a way out of her predicament. "Of course I mean it. How wonderful then. That only leaves the small matter of getting Trudy and I moved out there. Our suitcases are packed and ready."

"If you'd let me, I'll borrow the old farm truck from Mrs. Hansen and load up your bed."

"And my bed." Trudy's little hand clamped around his chin.

"Yes, Miss Trudy, your bed, too. I have been looking for a way to help Mrs. Hansen and this is perfect. I plan to have the truck serviced while in town and filled up with gas." When he gave Trudy a celebratory squeeze, she grunted like a baby bear.

"You set the day and time, Mr. Reed. We can be flexible around your work schedule."

Dr. Lucas knocked the tongue depressor against the wall calendar. "Tomorrow is Thursday. I bet the auto shop would have a bay open for that oil change. The way days are getting longer, you should have plenty of daylight after work to make the move."

Lorna Rae almost shivered under the mounting excitement. "That would be just in the nick of time. It is perfect for us. How about you, Mr. Reed?"

"Fine by me. All I have to do is convince Mrs. Hansen to allow me the use of her truck. I will try not to give away our whole plan, though. That leaves me tonight to pack up, which should not pose a problem in the least."

Lorna Rae reached over and took Trudy from his arms to leave. "Don't forget those shirts she's been ironing for you."

A look of pure shock ran across his face at the mention of such a personal matter. "How did you know?"

She stepped toward the door, trying to quell the satisfied smirk tugging at her lips. "Oh, let's just say a woman notices little things like starched shirt collars. Bachelors typically need help with such finer details."

"She has you pegged." Dr. Lucas turned his back and wandered to the rear counter.

"I will be sure to get the shirts. If I do leave anything behind, she can give it to me when we arrive with your beds. That haul upstairs is nothing to look forward to, though."

She unlatched the screen door and stepped out onto the porch. "I am stronger than you think, Mr. Reed. We'll work together and get the job done."

He stood close, his face almost touching the screen mesh. "This is by far the best deal I have brokered in awhile."

"My deal, Mr. Reed, not yours," Lorna Rae whispered. With a coy smile, she turned and navigated the steps, while Trudy squirmed in her arms. The little girl managed to hoist over the top of her shoulder to blow him a soppy kiss with a fling of her wrist. Walking away as fast as possible, she heard his reply—an exaggerated lip-smack. *I did not just hear that.* The suitcases that had been mentally stacked only seconds ago took a tumble into the muted chaos of denial.

~

Duncan paced the clinic floor. He examined the nuances of his post office encounter in slow motion. "He expressed no shock at his predicament. That tipped me off at first."

Dr. Lucas shook his head. "I'd say Jimmy was the most downcast victim so far. He is such a young man with so much life left to live one-handed."

"It makes no sense at face value, which is why we have to search deeper for a motive. Another thing struck me as odd. He claimed the injury hurt more than he expected."

"Meaning he might have had some time to ponder it

beforehand?"

"Exactly. That does not line up with the incident being merely an accident either." He stepped to his desk and found little squiggles drawn on his desk plotter—a message from Trudy.

"Looks like you have something to work with after all. As time passes, folks tend to let their guard down."

"Have you ever heard mention of a union around any of the laborers?"

"A union? No, not that I can recollect. That kind of organization requires a larger pool of skilled labor, doesn't it?"

"I made mention of using his on-the-job accident so we can learn from our mistakes to make the workplace safer. That's when Jimmy said the union held a similar position, but he had doubts it was working."

"Sounds like a martyr who may be soured by his level of sacrifice for the greater good."

"Which might not be worth the cost. Now, he's relegated to living life one-handed."

"Such a pitiful shame. This maiming must come to a stop."

"Once I find the union, I can figure out how to stop it. Can you tell me? Is Glen Forshee in any shape for my interrogation yet?"

"Glen has not recovered the use of his left lung yet. I would hold off, though I understand why you want to be prompt with your investigation."

"Prompt, yes, but I do not want to be the last human he ever talks to. He took a horrible blow that day. How can a man willfully do that to himself?"

"Inescapable pressure? I don't know. A wild animal will gnaw off its paw when caught in a trap just to gain freedom. These cases could bear a similar desperation."

"Jimmy Cantor did not look free. No, he still carries the painful trap around, though his fingers are gone forever."

"Keep at it, as you may be on the verge of something significant here. By the way, thank you for taking some interest in getting the Holmes widow and her little girl on their way to a better life. I appreciate that investment of your personal time."

"Glad to aid the switch, sir. Besides, I need to be closer to the problem in this oil field community, close enough it stares me right in the face." He sat at the desk and pulled the case file front and center. He would record the Jimmy Cantor interrogation in detail and include a copy in his weekly report to Washington.

"You have the tenacity of a birddog, Mr. Reed. May it serve you well."

"Thank you, doctor. You wouldn't mind a few less patients coming through the door, would you?"

"Heavens no. The wife keeps dropping hints for a vacation out west this summer, so a lighter patient load would fit the bill nicely."

"A vacation sounds good." He placed the date at the top of the contact report as his thoughts wandered onto a more tender terrain. *What might it be like to vacation with someone who wants to spend time by your side?* He printed the postal clerk's name in all capital letters as the prospect of ever having a wife fazed in and out of focus. Beyond his control, the sound of Lorna Rae's voice whispered back through the screen to wrestle away his perfect deal. The kiss blown to the little girl had been an off-the-cuff response, a lapse of awareness. Nothing more.

~

Duncan drew a breath on the landing of the stairwell while Lorna Rae adjusted her hand grip on the full-sized mattress. Daphne Hansen occupied Trudy up in the bedroom, having escorted the pillows and linens up ahead of them. The matron of the house assumed a post at the front door down below, well within earshot. "You are stronger than I imagined."

Lorna Rae wiped her forehead and tucked the handkerchief into her waistband. "Mothers have to be strong. It falls in our line of duty. Plus, God stands ready to lend mercy where I lack."

Widow Hansen came to the bottom stair and looked up at their progress. "Amen, Mrs. Holmes. Steady now. You have only one more cumbersome piece, the box springs. After that, the child's bunk should be a breeze."

"Wish we had one of those, as it's quite hot today for not being summer yet." Duncan wiped his brow across his shirt sleeve. "All this heat is liable to reset the rain cycle again."

"The forecast calls for rain by Friday late," Mrs. Hansen replied. "Let me get the box fan plugged in down here. I can circulate some air."

Lorna Rae patted the mattress and squared her feet. "I am ready to take the summit when you are."

"One, two, three." He grunted with the effort and they slowly gained the next few risers. "Are you okay up there?"

"Steady as she goes, captain. Only don't push me along so much." She tugged at the top end and made it up the next riser. "Unless you are in a hurry."

He eased back his momentum from below. "Sorry, no hurry."

"Wight up heah, Mommy." Trudy appeared in the doorway, but her watchful sitter soon retracted her into the room.

"If I could only harness that energy—"

"You will, in time. I bet she will keep you going, even on the difficult days." Duncan grunted through the last words as he tried to assume more of the mattress's dead weight and still propel it upward.

She shuffled her feet once, and the mattress bottom glided over the top stair. "Are they all going to be difficult days? I have to start from scratch and build up a source of revenue to feed that energy machine in there." She puffed a breath through her bangs.

He pushed the mattress along the hardwood floor. "Hopefully, being at your sister's house will take some of the pressure off. Then you can start your baking line."

Lorna Rae stepped back into a nook and paused. "What if I fail to break into the market?"

Duncan brought his end of the mattress around and pulled toward the bedroom, walking backwards. Her talk of defeat had to be nipped in the bud. "You have an incredible product. The market is hungry for your baking. Do not underestimate yourself." He scrutinized her reaction, but she remained expressionless.

"I have the fan running now," Mrs. Hansen called. "The next trip should be cooler."

"See? The upturn of circumstance has already begun. Things are bound to get better." He disappeared into the bedroom and the remainder of the mattress followed, downy quiet. "You two stay back behind the frame in case this mattress teeters over."

"Yes, sir, Mr. Reed." Daphne took her charge by the shoulders and backed up to a chair in the corner. "Hey Diddle, Diddle. You sit in the middle." She patted the seat back, and Trudy filled it with a wiggle. A giggle soon bubbled up.

Lorna Rae peered into the room. "Thank you for being such a

good girl, doll baby. We have to go get the bottom part of the bed before we can put it all together."

"Then can I play?"

"Once we get the sheets on," Daphne said, "but you can help me, right?"

"Oh, yes. I can." Trudy kneaded her fingers together as if formulating a plan.

Duncan made a lunge in her direction with his arms raised like a goblin, and the girl laughed at the threat. "See, Mrs. Holmes, you have to be fearless like Trudy here." He headed for the door and held up a finger to let them know he would be right back in a second.

Lorna Rae backed out of the room ahead of him and took the steps with haste as if gravity had never been proven before. Mrs. Hansen patted her shoulder when she darted past. She offered an unconvincing smile in return and glided through the doorway.

As he passed, air movement across the foyer caught his attention, so he halted a moment to enjoy the fan's direct blast. "This is divine, Mrs. Hansen. Thank you for thinking of it."

She gave him a knowing look, her gaze trailing out the front door. "Sometimes all you need is the wind blowing in the right direction, Mr. Reed."

"I know she will be in good hands out here, if only for a few days."

"I will pray for her baking venture to succeed in Kansas City— with dependence on the Lord, of course." She held the screen door open to let him exit.

"His eye is surely on the sparrow, Mrs. Hansen." He stepped into the full heat that had to have topped ninety degrees in the last hour. "Oh, and you might find that your old truck runs better now. I had the boys at the shop give it a going over, so you can depend on it this summer."

She drew in a sharp breath and folded her hands across her chest, while a few wrinkles on her face seemed to ease. "Why Mr. Reed, how very thoughtful of you to remember my plight with all that you've got to handle on the oil field."

"I hope to leave a difference in my wake, even if for a short time."

"Then may God multiply the blessing back to you." She held

one palm skyward as if to call it down right there.

"Keep the prayers coming, Mrs. Hansen. You know I need them." He gave a wave and made strides toward the truck. Lorna Rae had already climbed up into the bed and waited by the cab. He tried not to focus on the trim ankles her pedal-pushers exposed. "Give me a few seconds here to get into position. This piece should be easier as it's less wobbly."

She shifted without looking up. "I am hooked back here."

"What's that? Do you need my help up there?"

"I believe so. I have somehow gotten hooked on a tack." Her fingers dug at the hitch-up while the box springs pressed tight against her trunk.

"Let me loosen this strap." He ran to the far side to untie the line. A tug at the looped knot rectified the situation, and he flipped the rope clear. "Hold on now, let me back the box springs off the cab." From the back of the truck, he grabbed the lower corner and pulled.

"Wait—I'm still attached. Glory be. What's next?" Her fingers fumbled to secure her freedom as the box springs tipped in the light breeze.

"Let me help." Duncan placed his foot on the rear bumper and hoisted up onto the wooden bed of the old truck. Only a rectangular wood frame covered in cotton ticking stood between them. In her growing exasperation, Lorna Rae took on a fragile countenance. She glanced up as if searching for something more than his assistance, a vulnerable look that struck him right between the pectorals.

"Cannot even the simplest of matters ever work out?" A little sob came up her throat.

Again their proximity worked against his well-planned steadiness. The box springs pushed against his shoulder, so he blamed his momentary imbalance on the giant. "See here? It's a staple, not a tack. That's why you can't get clear. Take a deep breath and hold still, so I can work you loose." Stooped, he glanced up to catch her nod and saw only staid defiance. "What? Do you want to do it yourself? It's an industrial strength staple, for pity's sake."

A rush of air came out of her lungs, as though she had relinquished her entire fortune into his hands. "See what I mean? I am not even strong enough for this task" She slurred the last syllable in full deflation.

Duncan spread his feet so the box springs would not toy with him. He needed to be a pillar of strength right now. With his chest tightened, he took several short breaths while staring right into her eyes. "You *are* strong enough. Reach deep, Rae. God has given you something that no one else has. It's up to you to bring it out and make it shine. If you want to bake, ask him for it and believe."

She trembled with a sob, making the next part of his plan almost impossible. He eased his fingertips along the wood frame, until he touched the errant staple that had detached on one side. He pulled it open and nodded his head for her to angle left. Once the fabric of her blouse shifted off the snag without further complication, he jammed the staple tip back into the wood.

"I do believe in God." Her words came heavy with intentionality. "But I have not had much opportunity to believe in myself."

He ducked his head as he pried into her business, pretending to put the finishing jab on the staple. "So now the horizon opens, and you have every opportunity. Plus, you have a fan club cheering for you. Think of Vivian and Bert, for instance."

"A fan club of two does not offer much support." The corner of her mouth twitched with the weak confession.

"Make that three and growing." He needed to look away, because some strange sensation had just unclamped in his chest. Too unfamiliar to control, he started to back off when a remembrance came to him. "As my mother is fond of saying, never ask what's next. She claims if we knew it would scare us to death."

Her eyes roamed his face and a snicker soon surfaced. "She is probably right."

"A baker has to take success one day at a time, right? You get up and bake because you believe." At that, he backed away and dusted his palms together.

"By the way, it's not Rae. It's Lo-Rae." A playful glint that birthed in her eyes accompanied the correction. Next, her little smirk flitted into a faint smile.

"Now, I hope you are good and rested, Miss Founder of Lo-Rae Cakes, because this box springs isn't going to throw itself up that stairwell into your new bedroom."

"Lead on, Mr. Reed. Don't worry about me. I have my half of the load."

He leapt off the back of the truck, tickled at her physical challenge. To test her readiness, he wobbled the frame while he feigned getting his grip. She caught it two-handed and righted it back to vertical.

"Good show back there. It is best to stay on the balls of your feet under the circumstances." He pulled the box springs until its full length cleared the truck bed.

Lorna Rae clambered down and resumed her hold on the far end. "Yes, it is by far the best approach to stay poised on ready and not worry about what comes next."

"Now you are talking like a real baker. Say, I wish I had asked for some compensation for today's moving favor, as I missed my last chance to eat your good cooking." He backed toward the house, and she followed on cue. Together they formed a fluid motion set against the box springs' rigidity. The front door soon creaked open, and they passed by Mrs. Hansen at her station.

The old woman's eyes were red at the rims, but her face beamed. "Only one more flight up to go." The door swung closed behind her.

"This will be the toughest run, so let's get it over with." He rested his end in a touch-and-go, and then hefted it higher to give his partner more clearance on the lower end.

"Mr. Reed is fishing for a reward—something for his sweet tooth." Lorna Rae's comment floated up as she maneuvered the first step.

"Well he's in luck," the hostess replied. The sounds of her heels echoed down the hall.

In steps, Duncan arrived at the landing and backed onto it, resting the bedding. "I meant *your* cooking," he whispered.

She rested her cheek against the cotton ticking. "Always leave the customer wanting more. Isn't that what they say in the business world, Duncan?" She spoke his name extra gently, like it was a bonbon.

"You are sounding more like a success every minute, Lo-Rae." He put a tease on the sound of her business name, because he was in no position to put a tease on anything else.

"Up heah, Mista Weed." Trudy ran back and forth along the

upper railing before disappearing back into the bedroom.

"Mista Weed," he replied, a mocking tone dusting the words with disgust. Hearing Lorna Rae snicker at him from down below, he wracked his brain for a fitting reply as he took the next step. "I suppose until you train that child to say her R's correctly, I must remain a weed and you will be Lo-Wae. Neither term seems complimentary in the least."

"To her, I am Mommy, which manages to steer clear of any mispronunciations. Unfortunately, you will have to remain a dandelion all by yourself."

He roared to shake off the deprecating moniker and better prove his nobility. The platform leveled under his feet, and he backed toward the nook.

Lorna Rae appeared with a pixie's mirth sprinkled across her features. With an inhalation, she swiveled the box springs for approach to the bedroom door.

Trudy poked her head out, her eyes as round as saucers.

Duncan roared again for effect. Laughter came from an indistinguishable source ahead.

"I hate to play the lion tamer," Mrs. Hansen called, "but I have a plate of gingersnaps on the kitchen table for anyone who might be ready."

"Me. Me," Trudy replied. She ran by, bouncing off the mattress that leaned against the wall. It teetered for a moment, but Lorna Rae stiff-armed it in quick response to make it stay put. Daphne filed out sideways as the box springs angled toward alignment with the bed frame.

With one last lift, Duncan fit the headboard end in place and stepped out of the frame. He walked to the foot of the bed and took Lorna Rae's place, relieving her of the load.

"See you at the cookie plate." She turned and left the room without glancing back.

"Not *your* cooking," he repeated loud enough for her to hear down the hallway. The box spring frame slipped into place without further protest. He stood to regard the room, thinking how it had been his just last night. The so-close-yet-so-far-away irony worked on him as he fit the mattress into place. When he stepped out of the door, he had to cut his stride short because Lorna Rae stood at the newel post waiting for him.

She knit her brow and gave her head a shake at his haste. "Guess I will have to owe you one home-baked reward." Her low volume meant it for his ears only.

"Now, that is one IOU I plan to keep in my pocket." His feet hit the stairs without a pause. He dared not look up or the feeling caged in his chest might take a crouching lion leap. Then where would he be?

Chapter 5

Lorna Rae packed the frosted sheet cake in tented foil and hoped that the cardboard base could hold the weight of a double recipe.

Mrs. Hansen scooped another spoonful of egg salad atop a triangle of toasted bread. "My neighbor Mamie Allison says the waterfall at Eureka Lake has not flowed in over twenty years. Why Daphne has not even lived that long. My, oh, my. I can hardly wait to lay eyes on it."

"I suppose that is a small price to pay for five days of rain this week." She tried to sound enthusiastic, but endless waiting for the phone to ring and announce the birth of her niece or nephew had siphoned all the levity out of her.

The hostess covered Lorna Rae's hand with hers and gave it a squeeze. "It was nice of Mr. Coates to send the invitation, so let's make every attempt to enjoy the picnic. You will hear soon enough from Kansas City…in the Lord's good timing."

"Thank you for allowing me to use the oven to stay in practice with my baking, Mrs. Hansen. I may have to hover around the dessert table after the meal to catch the reaction of some of the tasters. You would be honest with me if the recipe needed tweaking, wouldn't you?"

"Lying lips are an abhorrence to the Lord. Of course, I will give you an honest reply."

"Mr. Reed seems to be partial to my cakes, but I am unsure

whether I can trust his instincts or not."

"I believe Mr. Reed to be a trustworthy man, but his taste buds may not have much experience, with him being a bachelor and all." She shook the tin of paprika over the plate of finger sandwiches, but nothing came out. "Oh, dear. Here's yet another item for my grocery list."

"I can pitch in for the groceries, Mrs. Hansen. You should allow me, since we might be here for another week."

"We will see come market day. Maybe you could accompany me into town and help carry in the eggs."

"I would be more than happy to. I should warn you that Trudy has an uncanny attraction to eggs, one that does not always turn out to their benefit."

The widow snickered under her breath as she pulled a sheet of wax paper over the appetizer plate. "They would scarcely be the first ones broken by little hands."

"But as widows, we have to minimize our losses right now. All should be gain."

"Then pray as such, Mrs. Holmes, for the Good Lord to guide us. Some days it seems the world only wants to take away."

"Not if we won't let it. Are you ready to load the car?"

Daphne strolled through the kitchen holding hands with Trudy. "We are ready. I helped her get her shoes on."

"Weady, Mommy." Trudy stuck her nose above the table and sniffed at the cake.

"Scoot, you two. I will take the front seat and hold the food in my lap." Lorna Rae untied her apron and threw it across the chair back. "Ready, Mrs. Hansen?"

"We wouldn't want to keep the hungry men waiting, would we?"

"Men? What men? I am going to see the once-in-a-lifetime waterfall." Lorna Rae winked and picked up the cake, following her hostess out of the back door.

~

Not his intention to arrive late, Duncan feared he had missed the big spread for lunch. He ambled past a rousing game of horseshoes. Dr. Lucas tossed him a wave. Mr. Coates had his sleeves rolled up to meet the next team of challengers which included Sol Edmunds, the generator house foreman. He stopped long enough to watch the first series of throws, surprised to discover Mr. Coates held a sharp competitive edge.

"You can't catch me," a child shouted from the playground beside the lake. A gaggle of chasers followed him around the swings, daring to step along the water's edge in their sneakers.

Duncan traced the curve of the lake's bank around as far as possible from where he stood on the dam road. Carefree blue waters sparkled in the sunlight, but the drumming sound in the background truly captivated him. He followed the beckoning until he found the source, the upper falls. A curtain of water poured over the outfall with such a haste that made him feel like he was moving backwards. He dug his shoes into the sandy soil to stave off the unsettling effect.

Twenty feet below, the cascading water churned into froth as it plummeted from a ledge of stratified rocks. Carved out over time, a pocket of exposed rock layers formed a hard-surfaced beach of sorts down below. Many picnic goers explored the rock layers and walked along the chute of the falls back toward the entrance road. A teenager called to his friend as he ascended, leading Duncan to discover the trail to go down. Fascinated by the exploration, he wandered along the ledge and examined the fossil-rich layers. Water seeped from cracks between layers and added to the lake's discharge into the lowlands below.

"Mista Weed! Come down heah," a little girl called.

He found Trudy standing barefoot in a puddle looking as happy as a clam. "Hey there, fwiend. I didn't know you would be at the picnic today."

"Well, Mommy made a cake, so we had to." She giant-stepped out of the puddle and ran toward him.

He took a quick survey of the area and was surprised to find no one supervising the girl. Perhaps she had been put on autopilot. "Come this way, away from the waterfall, Trudy. We don't want to fall in there."

"No-siw-ee, because Mommy said not to. I play it safe."

He knelt to be at her level and noticed her outfit had squares of fabric that resembled a dress he had seen Daphne Hansen wear. "That's a good girl. Are you having fun today?"

"So much fun. The falls tickle my eahs."

"Mine, too. Say, did Mrs. Hansen sew that outfit for you?"

"Yes. Do you like it?" Her eyes turned into little crescent moons, she smiled so hard.

"I do like it. Are you here with Mrs. Hansen? I don't see your mother."

Her mouth drew into a pout, but it didn't last. "Mommy's sad because she dwopped the cake. She's hiding in the shade by that twee." A chubby-knuckled finger indicated a direction.

Duncan turned and scanned the rocky outcrop. Beyond the trail he had descended, several cottonwood trees had sprung from the creek's edge to take advantage of the surplus of water. A woman in a red shirt waved in their direction. She stood and began to walk over. All in the same instant, a mix of expectations ran through him. He decided to take it slow…from a distance.

Lorna Rae smiled, her eyes hidden behind heavy-framed sunglasses. "Hey there, Mr. Reed. We didn't know if you would be coming out today or not."

"I came but made a mess of it. How I could time my arrival to miss the lunch spread sure beats me. Maybe I should go back up and pick through the leftovers."

"Oh, not many of those I'm afraid. Too many men attending and not enough cooks." She pressed her lips together, accentuating the red tint she wore. A breeze blew and lifted her shoulder-length hair off the collar of her madras plaid shirt.

"Trudy tells me you had a mishap with your cake." When he held out one hand to beg an explanation, a small one quickly filled it.

"Did you have to go and tell my worst news first, little lady? Yes, true confession. The cake started to slide off the cardboard as I got out of the car, but I caught it. Unfortunately, it doubled over onto itself to make a real mess. I could scarcely serve it like that, could I?"

"Not to most people…but to me, yes." He hoped not to sound like a beggar, but the comment did come off in that general arena. Trudy dropped his hand and wandered to the edge of the rushing water.

Lorna Rae stepped across a crevasse and joined him on a slightly tipped slab of weathered rock. "You are not trying to appease my bruised pride at not being able to market my baked goods, are you?"

"Mommy?" Trudy called to her without turning around.

"No, not at all. This is a selfish request, at best. I am ravenous and the thought of monopolizing one of your cakes more than appeals to me."

She folded her arms with a nod of satisfaction. "Ah, true confession, is it?"

"Mommy, can you help me?" Trudy's tone sounded a bit more compelling.

Duncan turned around to face the girl and caught a light mist of spray from the waterfall in his face. What a relief.

Lorna Rae stepped up close enough her shadow got wet in the creek. "Do you really need help Trudy?"

"Not me, my tuwtle. See? His tail is wheah his head should be."

Duncan glanced at the raging current and saw the object of the girl's concern. A poor red-eared slider had been swept over the falls and now tempted fate through the harrowing run of the outfall, a run fraught with menacing rocks.

"Let me try to save him, Trudy. You stay dry on land. Is that a deal?" He stepped into the flow, submersing his sneaker in the refreshing water.

"Okay, Mista Weed. I will stay on the land wight heah."

Lorna Rae sidestepped down the shoreline, toeing the water's edge. "Duncan, really? It's a turtle. He will be okay in the water, won't he?"

He took two steps deeper into the drainage and tried to assess the turtle's progress. He would have to make a quick grab at this rate. "I think he'd prefer the lake to this, don't you?"

She wrung her hands as Trudy joined her on the bank. "I guess so. Mercy me, be careful as you go deeper."

With his last step, the bottom edge of his Bermuda shorts darkened with wetness. His feet slipped on the moss-covered rocks as he lunged for the turtle. It bobbed like a cork and spun out of his partial grasp, rotating head-first with the current. "Well, at least I managed to get him turned around."

"Save him, Mista Weed. Please." Trudy's voice squeaked through the last word, and she tore away from her mother as if to accomplish the rescue herself. Lorna Rae ran after her.

Duncan watched the two of them struggle on the rocks and

became sensitized to the vulnerability of the little girl. It may as well have been her floating down that watercourse, heading for harm. The parallel of their mutual helplessness lent his feet momentum as he came out of the creek in a power step and sloshed across the rocky bank to catch them. Up ahead, the revetment elevating the access road divided the creek and afforded him a better shot at the turtle. He raced past them and took a lead on the floating reptile. He selected an entry point and stood knee-deep in position to make the grab, as long as the turtle made the left fork of the creek.

Lorna Rae sauntered up, a smile tucked into one cheek. "It is nice to see such a high level of commitment, Duncan. Or, I could say you have gone crazy."

He leaned out over rocks collected at the base of the road supports to spy out his target. "Not at all. A friend of mine wants this turtle rescued, so I thought to oblige, that's all."

"Sticking with it is a worthy attribute, even if the object of your effort remains questionable." A small laugh stifled in her throat.

"No, no, no!" Trudy ran down to the fork in the creek. She pointed at the far branch. Sure enough, the turtle floated toward it—away from him.

Duncan waded out of the flow and eyed the terrain downstream. "Come on, girls. We are going through a tunnel." He reached out with both hands to connect and had instant success with the child. When Lorna Rae hesitated, he grabbed her hand and began to run beneath the road, pulling them along. Flies swarmed in the protective shade as they darted through to the back side of the park across a collection of loose rocks along the bank.

In a cusp up ahead, the creek took a sharp turn where the water slowed. He could launch a well-timed attack on the turtle there and put a halt to the rescue debacle. "This is the place, in the turn of the creek. Stay up here out of the water."

Lorna Rae slid her hand out of his and took Trudy by the shoulder. "Good luck. I think you might have him this time."

He splashed in without a glance back and waited for the hapless animal. In seconds, the red flash of color behind its ear appeared above the rushing water. He shifted deeper and prepared to make the grab off his left hip. The turtle spotted him at the last moment and clawed through the water trying to avoid the collision.

Duncan clamped the sides of its shell and lifted it from the creek. Though airborne, the turtle still clawed the air, doing the breaststroke.

"You got him!" Trudy jumped up and down at the water's edge to celebrate his triumph.

Lorna Rae took a step back and clapped her hands. Her red lipstick parted to reveal a pretty mesmerizing smile.

Duncan forced his legs to move against the current and managed a step or two back toward the shore before his balance began to falter. Having to hold the turtle tied up his hands, so he bent his knees to compensate for the water's movement. He guessed at the next step and the bottom slanted unexpectedly. Down into the water he went, turtle and all. Determined not to let go, he allowed the water to carry him downstream until he managed to get his legs under him once again. Smack dab in an eddy pool, he could no longer touch bottom.

"Help him, Mommy!" Trudy motioned, running toward him.

She ran behind the girl, her focus split between him and the water's edge. "Oh, dear me. Duncan, should I wade in?"

He gasped as lake water filled his mouth. "Come get the turtle, maybe. Let me try to get closer." He kicked and leaned shoreward, the turtle clawing at the water.

"Twudy do it." The girl started to step into the water, but her mother pulled her back.

Lorna Rae bent over her with a stern look. "You promised, remember? Mr. Reed made you promise to stay on land."

"Okay. You go, Mommy."

"Yes, Mommy has to go." Lorna Rae turned and came into the water with a few ginger steps. "Oh, wow, wow, Kalamazoo. The water is much colder than I thought." She shook her hands before making a reach for the turtle from a safe distance out.

"Hold it right there." Duncan kicked against the current again and shortened the distance between them.

Lorna Rae waded out further, her clam diggers wet up to her knees now. She extended out her full length and yanked the turtle from him in one sweeping gesture. "Oh, yuck. It's wearing moss for a fur coat." She shrank back toward shore where Trudy waited, her hands tucked under her chin.

Too wet to care, Duncan leaned back into the water and floated free for a few seconds. Unfortunately, he drifted out of the eddy pool and found himself at the mercy of the current once again. "Hey, follow me downstream." Water filled his mouth again, and he spat it out, surveying his next round of trouble around the bend. A willow tree dangled its branches in the current, but they appeared far too flimsy to offer any assistance. In seconds, he cleared the bend and floated out of the shade.

Lorna Rae ran just ahead on the bank, a remarkable sight. She waded into the water without the ginger steps this time, her gaze fixed on him. "Grab for me up here."

He spotted a large rock beneath the water's surface and managed to get a foot on it to angle his body against the current. He gained enough advantage that the link-up ahead looked possible. "Get ready."

She stepped out deeper and shoved her arm out. "Right here."

He reached for her and made the connection, though her hands slipped down the length of his arm. He pushed his legs under him where he struck the uneven bottom. Teetering, he grabbed for her with his other arm.

"Mercy me, Duncan." She strained under his weight and helped pull him closer to shore, one step at a time.

"Thanks for coming in for me. Hope it doesn't spoil your day." He tossed the water off his face in the chest-deep flow and searched her expression for an honest response. He thought to let go of her arm, but didn't want to quite yet.

She gave him a teasing look over her shoulder as she seemed intent on making it back to the bank where dry land awaited. "Spoil? Ha! You are worried about spoiling my roasting hot day with a dip in this refreshing water? I hardly think so."

Caught off guard by her playful demeanor, he searched for a reply. When she tugged at him to follow her into the shallows, he resisted, turning her back around toward him. His gaze trailed up her slender neck to her trim jaw line, where he enjoyed the attractive features of her face in the full sun. Dappled with water spots, he lifted her sunglasses off the bridge of her nose and tucked them into her loose hair. Her green eyes gleamed up at him.

"You are beautiful, Rae. You know that?" He slid his wet grip under her elbows, an open invitation to come to him at her choice. He held his breath, desiring a closer moment. The current became time, passing by them in fluid seconds of separation. Nothing else mattered.

She leaned toward him with a transfixing gaze and her lips parted. She made a throaty sound as if she might gravitate into his affections. "Oh, I don't think you would say something sweet like that, if you knew I had let your turtle go." A water splash struck instead of a kiss while her laugh announced her slip-away. She bounded up onto the bank.

He strode out of the creek with water sloshing out of his sneakers every step he took. "Why, you wouldn't have, would you?" She gave a squeal and headed back in full run, giving him reason to chase. Around a stand of willow saplings, he spied Trudy squatted on the rocks, petting her turtle like a kitten.

Lorna Rae stopped by the child and covered her mouth to mute her laughter. Trudy started to come to her, but opted for the turtle instead.

Duncan pulled up and drew a couple of deep breaths between Trudy and the water. He looked across the girl to her mother. Together they made quite a cameo image, both pressing an image onto his heart.

"I believe we should have that tossed-around cake now." Lorna Rae squeezed some water out of her shirttail and started walking back to the picnic.

He raked his fingers through his hair as he tried not to look at her. "Finally, somebody thinks of the rescuer."

"Hold my tuwtle, Mista Weed." Trudy handed him the reluctant animal that clawed the air for escape.

Duncan took the turtle and glanced in Lorna Rae's direction. She turned away, but not before he could see her merriment at his situation. "You are going back into the lake, so I can have my cake, buster."

"In a few minutes," Trudy said. "When I'm weady."

"As soon as the water at the lake is deep enough it can swim away." He put enough authoritative tone in the response to make sure he had the last word on it.

The girl ran by him and gave the turtle a love pat as she passed. "Soon enough."

"Sooner," he replied in a whisper, already thinking about that chocolate cake. He would eat it with a stick if he had to, but he intended to have more than his share, no matter what manner of calamity it looked like.

Chapter 6

Lorna Rae slammed the door to Mrs. Hansen's car to lock away what Duncan had left of her cake. She had not been too amused when he had fit the two broken halves together so the frosting merged into a filling instead. "You are not suggesting I package my baked goods upside down, are you?"

He stood from the picnic table and shook the crumbs out of his lap. His wet Bermuda shorts hung heavy on his muscular legs. "Think about it a minute. You have to cover individual pieces in some type of wrapper, right? If the cake is frosted, it leaves nothing but smear for the potential customer to see."

"Hmmm. But if it's filling on the inside, I have a neater package. Is that your point?"

"Yes, same great taste mind you, only frosted on the inside."

"You are impossibly fresh with your inane ideas. Truly you are. Still, I never stopped to think how I would accomplish the packaging, quite honestly."

"Lo-Rae Cakes—good from the inside out." He pitched the advertisement with vigor and made it even more believable by licking the corners of his mouth.

Lorna Rae glanced down at Trudy who was allowing the turtle to wander through the grass around the picnic area at will. The child rubbed her eye with the back of her hand, a gesture that meant only one thing, sleepy-time was imminent. "Somebody needs their afternoon nap. How about we escort Mr. Turtle up the lakeshore a ways and say goodbye to it now?"

"I agree, Trudy. He likes the water more than the land, so it's only fair we put him back."

"Okay, I guess. Can you hold him?"

Duncan shook his legs, looking uncomfortable. "Sure, I would be happy to. How about we climb the dam on those stone steps over there? We can lower him in on the other side which is plenty far from the waterfall."

Lorna Rae headed for the steps as the turtle changed possession. "Maybe we can dry out some over there, before we have to get back in the cars, I mean." Trudy soon ran ahead to make the climb, leaving the two of them to continue their private conversation. Pretty sure Duncan had run out of advice for her business venture, she reflected back to their earlier exchange in the creek. If he tried to get personal again, she would have to spoil the day with something off-putting. Despite being flattered at the masculine notice, she was days away from moving to Kansas City, for pity's sake.

He caught up in a few steps and held the target of his efforts like it had radiation contamination. "Please tell me what I was thinking for ever jumping in for the rescue."

"Maybe you wanted to save a little girl from having one more wound scarring her heart. She has been through enough, wouldn't you say?"

"Yes. Do you think she will even remember him? Your husband, I mean."

"I doubt it, since she was only two when he died. How many things do you recollect from when you were two years old?" When her foot struck the first stone step, she decided to run up the entire section and not wait for his answer. Escape turned to exhilaration when she arrived on top and nothing but crystalline blue lake appeared on the horizon. "Oh, my."

He came up behind her and shared the scenery in protracted silence. Finally, he cleared his throat. "Trudy won't remember me either."

"But I will...for your kindness through all this. Plus, we will see you again, when we return to pick up our furniture." She ambled down the slope of the dam, neither intending to outrun him nor trying to catch Trudy.

He quick-stepped in front of her and waggled the turtle to keep her amused. "But only if you come back while I am employed by Mr. Coates. Remember, I am here temporarily."

"That must be hard, moving from place to place so frequently."

"It has not been too difficult so far, plus I get to see a lot of America."

She let her gaze wander out over the lake, thinking how grand a new vista could be. "I would like to go see America's best, her national parks. That would take a lot of cake baking though. For the immediate future, I will have to settle for parks I can find around Kansas City."

"I don't recall seeing any national parks on the Kansas map as I prepared to move down from D.C."

"No, we don't have any. I meant smaller parks. And the Ozarks are nearby in Missouri."

"I find the tall grasses of the prairie quite mesmerizing. A meadow contains its own world. See how the grass grows right to the water line with no space between?"

"Yes, a prairie holds the subtle beauty of nature. But a mountain thrown up against the horizon would be a welcome sight now and then." Lorna Rae walked to the lake's edge which lapped up onto the mowed grass bank, swollen by the recent rains. Trudy came to her with tiny prairie violets clutched in her hands. "Are those for your turtle friend, doll baby?"

The child sniffed and leaned against her legs. "Uh-huh. I have to say goodbye, but I don't want to."

She placed a hand on her back to make her feel secure. "Be a big girl for me right now. Mr. Reed plans to put the turtle back in a safe place way up here, far away from the waterfall."

"Okay. I'm weady."

Duncan knelt and held the animal out. "Want to pat him goodbye?"

She sprinkled the tiny flowers on its shell while the turtle clawed at the air. "You be safe now, Ollie."

"See, he is strong like you are strong, Trudy. That's why God let you be friends today. Friends can say goodbye and still be friends." Duncan stood, his gaze directed at her.

Lorna Rae wanted to add her sentiments, but her throat had constricted watching how tender Duncan interacted with Trudy. When the child had tossed the flowers on the critter's back, unprompted tears began to well up in her eyes.

"Here you go, Ollie, right back where you belong." Duncan waded in a few steps and lowered the turtle. Its first contact with the water brought a frenzy of movement.

"Bye-bye my fwiend."

"Goodbye Ollie. I hope you appreciate your second chance at lake living." Lorna Rae stepped back from the water's edge as the turtle disappeared. She glimpsed a playground up the way off the dam road. A sneaky, self-serving plan began to take shape. "Look Trudy—I see a playground with swings. How fun would that be?"

"I want to swing. Please, Mommy, please."

"Duncan, would you mind if we went over there? Trudy loves to swing—and it makes her sleepy." Lorna Rae lowered her sunglasses enough for him to see her exaggerated wink.

He sloshed out of the water, his shoes squishing as he strode on land. "Oh? Does someone need her nap?"

"No nap. Swing!" Trudy ran ahead toward the cluster of shiny play equipment.

"Yes, someone needs her nap, but I refuse to say which one of us."

Duncan fell into step with her. "Meanwhile, I could use a little drying off."

She surveyed the playground which had been tucked into a sandy cove. "Rest assured this will not take long. She is two hours overdue, and turtles are only so interesting."

"Safety managers, too. Whatever it takes to purchase a nap. I will be glad to push."

"She has to sit in my lap, and I have to sing to her. There's a formula for success."

Duncan nodded, stifling a smile. "I like that scenario even better."

Lorna Rae stumbled in the sand, realizing she had painted herself into an awkward corner, innocent though it might be. Under no circumstance could she allow him to touch her—even for the noble cause of propelling the swing.

"This one, Mommy." Trudy hooked one leg onto a swing, but flipped right out the back. She stood and wiped the sand from her hands.

Heat crept up Lorna Rae's neck, an extra boost of warmth the month of June didn't particularly need. She needed to say something before things got out of hand—or in his hands. "Uh, Mr. Reed. I don't think I can—"

"Not to worry, Mrs. Holmes. I pushed my kid brother in a swing on many occasions. I know the ropes, or in this case, the chains." His left brow cocked like he had posed a challenge, subtle as it seemed.

Ready to get on with it, Lorna Rae slid onto the swing. Trudy climbed up her trunk and looped her arms around her neck. She closed her eyes and hummed a nursery rhyme about a muffin man. The first push came as a gentle shove forward. On the back swing, she felt a tug on the chains and his hand brushed hers. On it went in hushed to-fro rhythm until Jack and Jill fell down the hill. Trudy's head soon lay limp against her collarbone.

She turned back to signal him to stop. "Okay."

"You mean that's it?"

She nodded and pressed a kiss on her daughter's precious head.

"Fine. I get to pick next." Duncan strode from the swings and soon engaged with a family coming in from a bike ride. He jogged back animated, a catty grin across his face. "I need to dry out some, so we are borrowing bikes to ride around the lake rim."

"Oh my. Maybe I should take Trudy back and let her sleep in Mrs. Hansen's car." Her whisper strained to stay hushed as she pled her case for immobility.

"Your bike comes with a big basket on the handlebars. We should be fine. Let me see if I can borrow something to pad it with. Come on, pokey puppy. Let's get moving."

"You may have to help me stand up."

"Let me carry her. Will she wake up?"

"No chance of that. Please, take her." Lorna Rae tried to shift Trudy off her chest and into Duncan's arms, but the whole transfer turned out to be one big cozy hug that left her legs a bit wobbly. She blamed the swing. Maybe sitting on a bike would be a nice compromise after all.

~

The exhilaration of movement refreshed Duncan as they turned along a back portion of the lake. The fat-tired Schwinn bikes seemed well matched for the gravel road circling the water body. Plus, the rain had left them a hard-packed surface. They approached a low-water bridge that a recent deluge had scoured out. "Slow for the bump up ahead. Let's keep the princess asleep."

Lorna Rae angled her bike closer to his. "Thank you. I see it now."

Her voice trickled in his ears like a reward of sorts, not a whisper, but intimate nonetheless. He wanted to hear more. "Tell me about your life on the oil fields. Did you enjoy your time there?" He rode low across the washout.

She followed close behind and then pedaled to catch up. "Well, how honest do you want me to be? I lived in that bungalow all my married life, three years and eleven months. Harley took the oil field job as part of the deal he brokered with my father."

He decided to press the topic to keep her in conversation. "What kind of a deal?"

"A marriage deal. Daddy could not abide having me remain at home, once I turned twenty. Instead of letting me date to review my prospects, he decided to take a shortcut, at the farm co-op of all places. The Holmes family agreed to pay him with some outdated farm equipment plus a bull, and Harley, their second-eldest son, got me. The two fathers agreed that Harley could make better money at the oil fields and blessed his ambition in that direction. So that is how I came to be a wife at Coates Oil Company."

"Doesn't sound too romantic."

"No, love had nothing to do with it, but my dad got shed of me, and my mother could focus on Della, who had developed trouble in school. I prayed a lot but never questioned God, especially after I knew Trudy was coming along. Being a mother has meant the world to me."

"You are good at it, too. What about Harley? Was he a good family man?"

Lorna Rae snickered and shook her head. "He did not know the first thing about being a parent and barely wanted anything to do with her. My mother explained that few men knew what to do with babies, so I thought his behavior was normal at first. He got busier with work and lost interest in everything associated with home life, including me. That left me with more prayer and less husband."

He allowed her personal confession to ride the Kansas wind as they rounded a far corner of the lake. Houses dotted the next part of the shore, which broke the lake's calming effect. A few more questions came to mind about her husband, but one in particular pushed to the forefront in a business-before-pleasure kind of way. He needed to use care here. "In all that busyness, did Harley ever mention the union?"

Lorna Rae risked detaching her hand from the handlebar and smoothed some hair beneath a kerchief she had tied on at the playground. She blinked at him as if to celebrate her improved vision. "Oh, sure. They met the second Tuesday of the month, like clockwork."

"Really? I had no idea."

"Yes, and he talked Bert into joining up. Oh, Vivian could have spit fire over that. She confided that Bert regretted it later. Once you're in, you have to stay in though. I got the feeling they don't tolerate dropouts."

"What else do you know about the union? Who is the leader?"

"Harley and Bert went into town for the meeting, but that's all I know. I did suspect that the money Harley shaved off my grocery budget for the last five months had a connection to this union, though. He took money at the end of every first week, which is why I suspected it."

They pedaled past the first driveway that led to a modest block house half the distance to the water. The lake's calming influence had lost its magic on him by now, as he processed the new information, testing it to see how it fit against what he already knew. It seemed to link right in. To be fair, he needed to level with her. "I want to tell you something, but hear me out, okay?"

She tilted her head and angled her front tire even closer. "Of course. Why wouldn't I?"

"There is no union for the oil field laborers, at least not one recognized by the management. However, I have uncovered a reference to its existence during my investigation of this case. I am not at liberty to say much more."

A stunned look froze her expression. "This is part of your *job*? And now, you are discrediting Harley?"

"Yes and no. The company has a safety issue that I am here on assignment to resolve. That in no way tarnishes Harley's reputation. Remember, I saw the accident on the day he died, Lorna Rae. He made a heroic effort to tamp that vibration down before it shook the fan belt clear in half. Had he not attempted to regain control, he probably could have stayed back and played it safe. I cannot say for sure."

"Things happen for a reason." She stopped short with the rest of her reply and pedaled ahead of him.

A second driveway intersected with the lake road, and Duncan glimpsed a more attractive dwelling at the base of it. As they road past, he looked back over his shoulder to discover the wall facing the lake was constructed almost entirely of glass. The blue waters glimmered in the lowering sun and made him evaluate the tender ground he had arrived upon. Yes, discovering the truth mattered a great deal, but it was not the only thing that mattered.

A surge of energy to reconnect with the other bike rider flowed through his limbs, and he pushed harder to regain ground, a prayer ever on his lips. Backwards turtle notwithstanding, it had been a wonderful day in a lovely setting, and he would not let it shipwreck like this.

"Lorna Rae, listen. I am sorry for asking questions about your marriage. It was wrong of me. Please accept my earnest apology."

"No need," she whispered, the intimate tone gone. "I probably should get it off my chest as I get ready to move on. I have to be strong for Trudy's sake, after all."

"You are already strong, and getting ready to be a successful business woman. Watch out Westport, here she comes." He peered around trying to see her face as his bike finally caught up with hers. He could not have been more surprised to see tears streaking her cheeks.

She pulled the kerchief off her hair and wiped her face. She gave a nervous little laugh and stared over at the lake. "This is the first time I have cried since you brought me the news that day. All I could think of was how it was over, that farce of a marriage I had gotten myself into. But I'm done grieving Harley and what might have been. I have to look forward now. I have to."

"You get to," he replied, not meaning to correct her. Something more had to be said, as his peace-loving spirit had yet to be satisfied. "God is building up a modern-day Lydia in you, Lo-Rae. Rise up to your challenge and gain the life you truly want."

"I get to." She glanced over at him as she repeated his words back to him. Her radiance had returned. "Hey, look at you. Your clothes are almost dry."

"Good thing, as I see the playground looming there at the end of the road."

"Is this the dam road section coming up next?"

"Yes, ma'am. It is."

She smiled and glanced from Trudy over to him. "Then we will finish riding up high, won't we?"

"Yes, we are finishing high. Thank you for your company today and letting me eat your damaged cake."

"Are you ever able to say no to my cake?" Her tone teased, though she refused to grace him with any direct attention.

Nailed with her assessment, he mashed down on his pedals and rode past her in a surge. Holding on with only one hand, he looked back and locked her right in his focus. "Never," he replied. How cleansing it came to him, being honest with a woman he might not see again. His next breath tightened in his chest as Lorna Rae coasted up right off his handlebars.

"Guess that makes you my first corporate fan. Maybe I should keep that memory and frame it like my first dollar bill."

"By all means, you do that." His voice has turned husky in embarrassing revelation, but she didn't turn away. He glimpsed her against the backdrop of the lake, all loveliness and grace. He had made her cry, but Lorna Rae had come out of it even more beautiful. Not a bad outcome for a man who constantly managed his risks.

~

Lorna Rae balanced the cake remains in one hand as she tugged on her daughter to exit the car. "Don't begrudge having asked us to leave early, Mrs. Hansen. Trudy had plenty of fun today."

Daphne ran ahead to open up the house when the telephone rang. She soon reappeared on the back porch. "Call for you, Lorna Rae. I think there may be a newborn baby in Westport."

"A baby?" she repeated, almost knocking into her hostess.

The widow nabbed the cake from her and nodded toward the house. "Go ahead, young lady. This is what you have been waiting for, after all."

Lorna Rae ran up the back walkway, her thoughts all jumbled. Everything happened so quickly, she barely could make the adjustment. She came into the kitchen door and hastened up the hallway. Daphne held the receiver to her shoulder, her face lit with happiness.

"Hello? This is Lorna Rae. Oh, Steve. She did?" She paused to listen to the details and relief drained her last bit of strength. When Daphne tiptoed out, she perched on the edge of an antique settee. "This is wonderful, Steve. Yes, tell Della that I am thrilled. You will drive down Tuesday first thing? Okay, we will be ready. Congratulations, daddy. Be ready for that little blue bundle to steal your heart away. Goodbye now." She set the receiver on the base and found Mrs. Hansen standing at the end of the hall, her hands clasped across her chest.

"Is the baby a boy, Lorna Rae?"

"Yes ma'am, a healthy baby boy. Della's doing fine, too. Her husband is planning to come for us Tuesday morning, bright and early."

She stepped toward her and held out her hand. "You are an aunt. Isn't God good to us?"

Lorna Rae took it and captured the blessing that came with the touch of a concerned sister in the Lord. "He is—so good. I can hardly wait to tell Trudy that she has a ten-pound baby boy for a cousin."

"Goodness, such a big chunk of blessing." Mrs. Hansen chuckled and released her hand, turning for the kitchen. "Guess we will eat light tonight if you don't mind."

"Funny isn't it? When God fills you up with other blessings, you don't even need food."

"Like Jesus professed, the Spirit serves up a different kind of sustenance."

"Well, that might come in handy for us in the future, but at least Della needs to eat. A nursing mother can eat an entire buffet, as I recall."

"Yes, you are right there. She most surely needs your help. How perfect you can go."

"Right, perfect." Lorna Rae took the stairs one at a time, realizing her words did not exactly match her feelings. She had three days to get them to align while she packed their suitcases again.

~

Duncan took a knee to clench the right shot. The championship for the horseshoes tournament had come down to the wire, with Mr. Coates' competition drawing the privileged last toss. He braced for the heavy impact and when the wood chips settled, the tip of the horseshoe rested three inches short of victory. He clicked the image with his Instamatic and stood to catch the big boss in the throes of celebration. Handshakes abounded, so he captured several of those images as well. Someone made a comment about bragging rights, and the men shared a good-natured laugh.

He spotted some families still enjoying the playground and decided to get pictures with the lake in the background, though it meant having to shoot into the sun. He skipped the stone steps and approached the dam at its lower end, an easier climb. The bikes they had borrowed leaned idle on the monkey bar ladder, so he framed his next shot between the two front tires.

A hullabaloo ensued over by the overflow dam just above the waterfall. Several men started slapping backs as a tall man brought up the tip of his fishing pole. A hefty catfish writhed on the end of the line. The commotion drew the spectators up from the horseshoe pit, so Duncan gravitated toward the scene out of curiosity. An old pickup truck with its tailgate down served as the cleaning station. The men gathered around it. Aided by a strong net, the oversized catch plunked on the tailgate. A short man fingered the fish's whiskers, spreading them apart for show.

Duncan recognized the man as his passenger the day Glen Forshee took his injury. He stepped back from the hubbub and wandered around to look at the upper falls. He guessed the distance down to the water's surface to be over twenty feet. Hauling that lunker up had been an act of determination, which the crowd now celebrated. A hammered thud pierced the air followed by raucous cheering.

When the men aligned to be immortalized with their record-breaking catch, Duncan readied his camera and leaned in for a shot. There in the middle holding the cleaning board where the catfish had been impaled by a fillet knife was Liam Torguson. Obviously not sickened by the sight of blood now, the man simply gloated over the slain fish. Duncan took his picture and then counted the men who had been part of the original group, six in all including Shorty Carlson.

To remain behind the scenes, he retraced his steps down the

rock formation and soon landed on the spot where Trudy had discovered him earlier. Before his sidetrack thoughts derailed his intentions, he wanted another picture. The waterfall filled his viewfinder and he snapped the shot, playing the role of innocent tourist through and through. He may have stumbled onto something implicating here, all on account of a fat resident catfish.

"The turtle had better luck in the end. So what does that tell you, Reed? Slow and steady wins the race." He pocketed the camera as the tree line where he had first seen Lorna Rae came into sight. *Too bad I cannot afford slow anymore.* He climbed out of the rock-rimmed pool to make his way back to the car.

Chapter 7

Sunday's sermon on demonstrating the Christian life must have taken hold, as Duncan sat with a pink package on his desk that attested to it. He had gone to lunch early and dropped off his film at the drug store. Down the street, he found the right belated present for Trudy at Western Auto. The toy came with a six-reel package that included Cinderella, last year's big animated sensation. He had not hesitated one second to add the bonus reel that captured shots of America's most popular national parks in three-dimensional splendor. Lorna Rae would enjoy it, even if he had to slip it in on the sly.

He glanced out of the front window expecting to see Mrs. Hansen any time now. She always made her egg supply stop at the grocery a little before eleven o'clock. He would ask her to carry the gift to Trudy on his behalf. That would give him plenty of time to make his next appointment, the new well being drilled out west off Shumway Road. He checked for Bert Decker's name and found it on the labor assignment list. Since he made visiting each newly drilled discovery well a regular part of his safety inspection, he would act casual if the opportunity presented itself for a question or two.

A woman in a familiar blue dress stepped into his field of view, shifting his focus around with it. He stood, grabbed the pink box, and shoved the screen door open as he went out. He ran down the stairs and approached the egg deliverer.

He tipped an imaginary hat as the woman raised her gaze from the walkway. "Hello, Mrs. Hansen. May I say how nice you are looking this fine June day?"

"Oh, Mr. Reed. Good day to you as well. I have six dozen reasons not to like this heat, but it's what the good Lord has provided, so I will keep my objection in check. My neighbor's wheat is maturing and could use this heat, I suppose."

"It wouldn't be Kansas without all these fields of wheat and corn, now would it?"

"That's not all God is growing. I hope that gift you are holding is not for the new baby. Mrs. Holmes has a new nephew, you know. Pink would hardly be right—"

"Land sakes, I am behind. No, this is Trudy's belated birthday gift. I…well. The sermon yesterday from the Book of James assured me that my faith without any outward works might look post-mortem, so I wanted to send the girl a little remembrance."

Though she stiffened, her gaze fell on him with kindness. "That is mighty thoughtful of you, Mr. Reed. Would you walk along with me, so I can deliver these eggs as fresh and not hardboiled?"

"So there's a nephew, just like that?"

She bent towards him as if confiding a well-kept secret. "Yes, that is how babies arrive. We came home from the picnic right in time to receive the call from Kansas City. Mrs. Holmes is simply transported with happiness, whistling and humming while she packs. I believe she's relieved to get on with her life, don't you think?"

"She has so much potential for success ahead. I believe you are right." He held the front door of the grocery open as a wire spring protested his pull. "She finally grieved a bit over her loss at the picnic Saturday, which they say is a healthy step to moving beyond it."

"Yes, I believe she has started." She maneuvered her stacked cart through the threshold and headed down the main aisle of the store with her Monday installation in tow.

Duncan followed her to the fresh produce stand while he balanced the pink box in one hand. Conspicuous, he had thought to be shed of the gift by now, but the merchandizing widow had wanted to make her delivery first. When she started unloading the first dozen eggs, he aided her with the next carton.

"Thank you, Mr. Reed. It seems like we have been partners in more than today's egg delivery, does it not?" She turned and placed another dozen into the display.

Cool air circulated from a buzzing fan. Duncan wiped his brow, not catching her insinuation. His perplexed look must have given him away.

She continued her unloading task without hesitation. "Befriending Widow Holmes and her little girl, I mean. We have helped her through a difficult time of her life, in keeping with the Bible's directive to be mindful of widows and orphans."

A funny feeling started deep inside and wandered out to tighten his ribcage. Duncan had not taken on the Holmes family out of Christian concern. So what *was* his motivation? The investigation partly claimed some fault. He searched his heart and fell short of an adequate explanation.

"Now we can do the next kindly thing and let her go. Her brother-in-law arrives tomorrow morning for the pick-up, and off they will head to a most splendid life. I will be glad to deliver your memento to little Trudy." She straightened and reached for the box. "I'm quite certain you would not straddle them with a return of that wayward turtle. Would you, Mr. Reed?"

He surrendered the box, but refused her hidden accusation for being a hindrance. "There is no straddling pet to lug around in here, Mrs. Hansen. I also wish them every success. Let me know if Della's husband needs a hand tomorrow."

"Oh, I think between Lorna Rae and Daphne, they can manage. Plus, going down the stairs with bedding is quite a bit easier than going up, as you might recall. Let me deliver your farewell for you, and we'll leave it at that."

"I…well."

She reached and took the box from him. "Remember that you will be coming back out to the farm on Saturday to bring your brother to meet us, correct?"

"Yes, ma'am. We plan to check in before noon, if his train arrives on time. Or would you prefer to have us stop in town for lunch?"

"No, by all means, bring him right out. Daphne is so looking forward to meeting him."

A little wave of heat ran up his neck at the mention of her

cloying daughter, knowing he might be introducing his brother into a less than perfect scenario for R&R. "Let's leave it to Sam then, why don't we? He might like some of that good old Kansas beefsteak when he rolls in."

"Perfect. We can set up the grill in the backyard then. Bring him on out, and let us take care of him, for all he's done for our country." She gestured with the box in her hands and then set it in the cart. "Now, let me pick up a few things while I am here in the store. Thank you for providing a list of his favorite foods, so we can spoil him."

"You're welcome, Mrs. Hansen. I will be off to my next appointment then. Thank you again for the delivery. Please say goodbye to the Holmes family for me."

"In Christian love. Yes, I will. Good day."

He turned and sucked in a lung-full of air that smelled of strawberries and pickling alum, a fitful mix. That summed up his existence at Coates Oil Field, both sweet and bitter. A picture of the Sunbeam Bread girl on the door handle ahead brought Trudy to mind as the sweet, innocent part of his Kansas experience. Unable to stop it, Lorna Rae's face as she rode her bike by the lake slipped into the memory next. She seemed happy. So why did it land as a jab to his lower ribs? He grabbed for the door, rubbing his thumb across the bread girl's head. All he received was lukewarm metal in return.

~

Lorna Rae sat on the edge of her bed as the curtains fluttered in the night breeze. "What do you have there, Trudy?"

"A pwesent for me. Let's see, Mommy." Trudy tore at the pink paper to reveal the contraption pictured on the box which made her eyes grow big. "Let me have it!"

"Oh look, dolly. It's a View-Master. See here? It has one reel full of Cinderella."

She jumped up and down. "I love Cindewella."

Lorna Rae fought the packaging and finally got the right wheel in hand. "Here, take the viewer and let me get the reel put in." She fed it into the top of the machine and guided the viewer up to Trudy's face. "Look through the eye holes and tell Mommy everything you see."

Trudy gasped and stood stock still. "Theah she is—Cindewella with the mice."

Lorna Rae caught the excitement in the child's voice and let it warm her heart. Instead of sulking in the bedroom on their last night in El Dorado, they were off on a three-dimensional adventure. Gratitude flooded her senses as she pressed the lever to make the next scene appear.

Trudy's hands came up and took control of the View-Master. "She is going to the ball."

Lorna Rae flopped back on the bed, wonderment swirling through her emotions. "Yes, someone has been uncommonly nice to her, and she gets to go to the ball."

"Now she dances with the pwince." Trudy twirled about and almost got separated from the viewer. She hoisted it back in place and tripped the lever again. The guttural sound in her throat told of a threat. "Theah she is, the wicked step-mothah."

Lorna Rae blanked out on the fairy tale about the time her first tear rolled onto the pillow. Not to play what might have been, but it truly helped to know that decent people like Duncan Reed existed in the world, people not motivated by personal gain. Despite his bent toward serious endeavors, she had seen his more human side where compassion lived every time he looked at Trudy. She would hold that precious as they departed. Fond and precious.

Trudy tapped her legs with persistence. "This one has mountains, Mommy. See?"

She sat up and wiped her eyes. "I don't remember mountains in Cinderella, honey."

Trudy swung the viewer around. "I switched, Mommy. You look."

"Oh goodness. This is the Rocky Mountains. How beautiful." Lorna Rae pulled the viewer back and read the inscription on the center of the reel. The words "America's Parks" started in focus and then steadily blurred. She depressed the lever and returned the viewer to the bridge of her nose. Devils Tower appeared, looming in majesty against a striking cloud formation. She blinked and tears rolled down her cheeks. Duncan had sent her a personalized gift from a comment she had made in passing. It seemed such a small thing, a friendly gesture to which she was unaccustomed.

Trudy tugged at the viewer as she pressed her curls next to it.

"Show me."

Lorna Rae slid the viewer into place and kissed her forehead as the girl reveled at the photo. Duncan had been more than generous. What she could call it escaped her, but that did not make his gesture any less precious. Tears welled up again, and she pulled Trudy onto the bed to cradle her in her arms. If she angled her head, she might get a peek at the next scene. The curtains rippled in the breeze. She exhaled, allowing this last night to capture her imagination.

~

Ill at ease out in the bar, Torguson spit on the floor and glanced around the large room. He didn't recognize anyone from the oil fields, but he couldn't be too careful. This called meeting had none of the power of the typical union night. The exposure out front quelled his gumption. The bar maid had stymied his request for the back room, but he knew good and well no one was in there. She took their drink order a quarter of an hour ago and had disappeared.

Shorty Carlson spoke into a handkerchief smeared with grease. "Since they refuse to cover any medical bills, I'm not sure we can continue. Looks like the big man wins for now."

"Stop talking stupid, Shorty. That's why we called a meeting, to figure out a way around Mr. Coates' freeze on benefits." Torguson propped both elbows on the table and leaned in, drawing his leaders closer in collaboration. "It looks like we have two exclusions to work with."

"Well, I don't see how we can use the woman-about-to-deliver loophole, which required action back nine months ago." Shorty snickered at the insinuation and fingered his mustache.

Torguson stole a glance at the bar and saw no one tending it. "Not that I failed to try that approach. Seems like that leaves our activity cornered to vehicle accidents only."

Bud Gant, the thin man across the table, grunted in agreement. His lips parted and revealed a trademark gap between his front teeth.

"If we stage a collision offsite, they might not cover it, Liam. We have to keep the damage on the oil fields, which hits them right in the kidneys." Shorty punched a fist into his palm which gave off a loud whack.

Torguson shoved the man's hands off the tabletop and scanned the room to determine if he had drawn any unwanted attention. "Keep it down, Shorty, or else."

"Or else what? You going to rig drawing my number next? Bah. Not gonna happen."

Torguson popped his knuckles and glanced between the two men. "We need to concentrate on our next move, not bicker amongst ourselves. Think about this vehicle option. Where could we have an accident that involves a car?"

Gant switched his toothpick from one cheek to the other. "Not a car necessarily, just a vehicle."

"Go on." Torguson made his lips curl at the corners to encourage the man.

Gant returned the smile as the toothpick took up residence in his tooth gap. "A truck, the drilling truck. It's old as the hills with a predisposition to malfunction. I suppose if something was to go wrong, say the brakes gave out, no one would find that too hard to believe."

"Ooooh. I like that." Shorty leaned in and almost cooed. "I like it a lot."

"Give me a day or two to think on it. Swain is the drill operator. He is not a union member, so I have to be careful here." Torguson leaned back in time to catch a movement over at the bar. His previous acquaintance soon moved toward them with her tray full of their drink order. When she tried to retreat after serving the tankards, he caught her by the wrist. "If I was to go look inside that back room, would I see anybody?"

Her gaze steeled as she pried her arm free. "This isn't Tuesday night, and you're not Winston Churchill." She wedged the tray between them and walked away with the tip of her nose scraping the ceiling.

"Maybe not." Torguson shot a glance at his comrades as he lifted the drink. "But if this drill accident falls into place, feel free to call me Prime Minister, boys." He drank a long quaff and the sound of Shorty's snorting laugh blended with his liquid libation as it went down, a triumph waiting to happen.

~

Duncan checked the clock for the third time in five minutes. On edge from not having slept well, his unrest made it impossible to sit any longer at the desk, though he had only been at work for an hour. He pushed back and paced the floor from the front door to the back counter. With the doctor at the grocery store checking on Mrs. Anders' gout, he had the place to himself. At least he would not have to own up to his state of restlessness.

Never one for flying off-the-cuff in hapless spontaneity, but if he left for the Hansen farm now, he could help load the beds to get the Holmes family on their way. Hadn't he dreamt of doing just that a dozen times last night? Still, it came across as meddlesome and self-pleasing, as he knew Trudy would shower him with affection for the gift. *What about Lorna Rae?* What kind of reaction did he expect from her? That point made his stomach jitter. He could scarcely allow his mind to investigate it.

His pacing swallowed five more minutes off the clock. What if the brother-in-law came early? What if his scrawny arms could barely lift his share of the weight on the box springs? That would overtax the women, for sure. He really needed to go out there, as the scenarios stacked up against these weaker vessels. It could be a catastrophe if he didn't show. Plus, he would have the fortitude to face Lorna Rae—even accept a hug—if she gave him one. That would be a nice parting gesture. Yet, it would never have the chance to transpire if he stood here much longer.

Certain of his decision in the moment, he pushed his chair under the desk and picked up a hat to guard against the morning sun. About the time he had put his hand on the door latch, he saw a man standing out on the porch. The image iced him down to the soles of his shoes. "Mr. McNaughton? What are you doing here?"

"You missed your call last week, so I left D.C. to come make the overdue connection for you." The man smiled but scarcely meant it, his lips assuming the grace of a bent crow bar. "Are you heading out to the field, Mr. Reed?"

"No sir. Not at all. Come on in, and let's go over the case so far." He opened the screen door and swept his hat through the air as though to draw his boss inside.

"Thank you. I'm looking forward to it." In two stiff strides the man entered the office.

As the door closed, Duncan glimpsed the grocery store across the way and an egg saleswoman flitted into mind. *Let me deliver your farewell for you, and we'll leave it at that.* Her ingratiating words now would come true despite a fitful night and a clock-watched morning.

McNaughton pulled a guest chair over from the doctor's desk and made himself at home. "So you have new evidence since the moratorium went into place?"

"Yes, sir. From an unexpected source, the widow of the last true accident." To mention Lorna Rae he could manage, but to call her to mind proved too much. He sat down with a bruised sensation right under his ribs. McNaughton opened the file, and Duncan transformed into the best safety manager in the states, which took some concerted effort.

~

She blamed her downcast spirits on having to lug the furniture down the staircase once again, but Lorna Rae knew better. She shifted on the truck seat and checked on Trudy. The girl colored in the book Daphne had gifted her upon departure, a kind gesture. They headed east on the highway, which pushed the sun up the windshield as time and miles went by. Glad Steve had ended their pleasant chat minutes ago, she settled in for the ride to her future. So why was something indescribable tugging her back?

She withdrew a sketchpad from her purse and began to frame out a label design for her baked goods. Once she had block-printed the brand name Lo-Rae Cakes in the rectangle, she found it lacking and began again in a clean frame. This time the lettering came with more flow, like piping on a decorated cake. That treatment seemed a better fit. The motto Duncan had suggested came to mind, and she wrote it in beneath the larger lettering, "Good from the inside out." The lettering had run long and now sat off-centered, but the effect lent eye appeal.

Her thoughts tried to wander into a feel-good zone with Duncan at the hub, but she forced her attention back to the task at hand. She wanted to add something more, maybe a design that would help the buyer recognize her brand. The pencil tip doodled around the page edge, leaving butterflies and sunflowers in its wake. When she sketched out a stalk of wheat, it struck her as being appropriate for a baked product. She maneuvered it through several renderings. Finally, a twin stalk of grain-bearing wheat held favor above all other designs.

She looked up for a break in creativity, and the landscape

rolled in a continuum of grass on both sides of the vehicle. The prairie had a way of saying farewell that spoke directly to her heart. The big city didn't have any meadows, only concrete and high-rise buildings. She would be a part of America's prosperous surge to start the decade, which unfurled like a new frontier.

Steve shifted his gaze to her and then returned it to the road up ahead. "Say, have you heard? By the end of this month, they plan to run a signal for the first color television broadcast from the top of the Empire State Building."

"Oh my. That is truly amazing."

"This world is in for some rapid change, Lorna Rae. Just watch and see."

"Well, I hope all the prosperity means everyone will want to eat cake." She intended it as a tease, but recognized that deepest truths were often spoken in jest. Steve's snicker filled the cab and lifted the pressure off her chest momentarily. The truck passed a highway sign that indicated the turnoff for Eureka Lake up ahead.

By the time they crossed the bridge, the same daydream had taken over—the one where Duncan stood at the base of the waterfall, looking like he could slay all the injustice in the world. When he turned his gaze toward the shadowed tree line, she longed to step out from under her widowhood and come stand with him. Like the rainbow borne by the waterfall's mist, the scene flashed for a moment and vanished like a mere glint under the sun. Not meant to last, the warm emotion it generated soon trailed off to emptiness.

Duncan had not come out to say goodbye. That rainbow's glimmer had to be left behind. She needed to set her expectations on something more calculated, like building an empire of flour and sugar. Tony Bennett came on the radio crooning his way into "Because of You" and she punched in another station, a radio talk show.

Sentimentality only played on the heart strings. Hers had been played by someone else long enough. Trudy held up her coloring page. Every last crayon mark had landed well outside the lines. Lorna Rae sighed. They both had such a long way to go.

Chapter 8

The soda jerk popped a straw into McNaughton's chocolate malt as Duncan propped his chin on his palm in an attempt to cover his weariness from restless sleep. A hole in the wall, the lunch spot had been recommended by a clerk in the nearby drug store. Too narrow to be considered a full restaurant, the place did possess a vibrant atmosphere with its sparkly silver-and-red boomerang Formica, which helped compensate for his lackluster hosting.

McNaughton took a long pull on the straw while one eyebrow arched like a question mark. "Do you realize that today is the second Tuesday of the month?"

"Oh? I guess it had not fully registered with me yet. All I can think about is getting our hands on those company picnic photos. I have a strong suspicion that I will have some collusion captured with that catfish celebration by the upper falls." Duncan turned toward the street front to view the oversized clock by the front door. They still had a half-hour wait ahead for the film delivery.

"There is no question about your source on this information, is there?"

"No, sir. That witness is as honest as they come. It's the widow from the generator house accident. Her husband, Harley Holmes, was a union member. I think I went over that with you briefly, but may not have conveyed the connection to you in a clear way." Duncan dropped his elbow off the counter when the soda jerk came around to take his empty plate. Something like guilt tugged at his insides at the mention of Lorna Rae as part of his investigation.

McNaughton bid his time by taking another drink from the straw. Silence slung between them like corn syrup at a taffy pull. "Had you ever thought to rummage through Harley's things for a clue? You are living there in his old bungalow, right? She probably left his belongings in a closet somewhere, don't you reckon?"

"Though it seems like a breach of privacy, I guess I could look around. I don't think the union typed up their membership roster, so I don't know what to search for exactly."

"We never do in this business, but sometimes we get lucky. If they are holding some sort of selection lottery, there is bound to be a voting piece, even an initialed or numbered slip of paper. Otherwise, how could the victim get singled out?" He returned to his mission of evacuating the malt from its curved glass container.

"I believe talking to my neighbor Bert might be my next valid move."

"Or you could watch from the front porch tonight to see if he goes out. Say, we are downtown right now. Why don't you drive me around? We can take a look at the possibilities for a meeting place for this union. There cannot be all that many establishments open at night."

"That plan sure beats sitting here." Duncan slid off the stool, ready to get the investigation into motion. Maybe he could shake off the sleepy shroud on his day, once lunch refueled his energy level. The soda jerk tore the bill from his pad and slapped it onto the counter. Duncan reached for his wallet, seeing McNaughton content to suck the dregs from his malt and let him cover lunch. He laid a dollar and change on the counter, and then walked back to his car.

"Whew. The heat is firing up out here in the breadbasket. I may have to shuck my coat."

"Please do. It will make us less conspicuous anyway. We're lucky it isn't raining, quite honestly. The forecast threatens more by week's end. How long were you planning to stay?"

McNaughton smirked over the car roof as he removed his jacket. A pocket liner protected his crisp white shirt from the ink pens that rode inside. "Not that long, don't worry. Okay, let's tour around for twenty minutes and come back for the pictures."

"Got it, boss." Duncan fixed his frame behind the wheel and keyed the ignition. A few more comments came to mind, like he could manage the investigation on his own, thank you kindly. But maybe two heads were better than one, as he had not thought about digging through Harley's pockets for a clue. "First, I will drive the length of Main Street, and then come back up some of the side roads."

His passenger whipped out a small notepad and drew out a pen to start his cryptic notations. "Ready when you are, Mr. Reed. Let's not ignore the obvious."

"No sir. Now just what would that be, in your opinion?"

"After-hours meetings, likely in private. Sounds like a bar to me."

"Wherever you have roughneck well drillers, you are bound to have a bar or two."

He snickered and began to glance at the canvas awnings up ahead. "This is the Wild West after all, even if El Dorado is not Dodge City. It's close enough for us easterners."

Duncan allowed the car to motor slowly up the road, his mind less than devoted to the surveillance task. They passed a furniture store and came by an appliance retailer next.

"There's a Masonic Lodge, according to the lettering on the door." McNaughton made a notation on his pad.

"That group is pretty popular in these parts, and plenty cryptic. But something tells me they are bound by more honor than these union cads. Besides, I think that's just a stairway leading up to the second level."

"Good reminder to look beyond the storefront. Maybe the obvious won't give us what we are looking for."

"Maybe not. We could come back out tonight, if you want to step up the sweep."

"No. The last thing we want the union members to know is that we are looking for them. First, I want names and faces. Next, I want specifics on how they operate. With the moratorium clamped on, we might not witness their typical operation right now anyhow."

"Did I tell you that no babies are due during the forty-five day moratorium period? Doctor Lucas assured me of that."

"Fortunately, that's not something they can countermove on in the spur of the moment. I think we nailed them on that restriction. That narrows them down one alley, the other exclusion."

Duncan shifted in his seat, uncomfortable with the implications. Equipment would be at risk and the outcome might be a whole lot worse than maiming. A love song cooed from the radio, so he twisted the volume knob to off. "You expect them to switch their intentional accidents to vehicles?"

"Our purpose at headquarters was to force their hand, so to speak. If the pattern of fake claims is to continue at all, it has to be through the only avenue left on their coverage, automobile accidents. You are right there on site to stop it. We sit in good shape with less than fifteen days to go in the pattern."

"Don't remind me." Duncan could have groaned to a dead stop in objection, but the traffic light up ahead turned green, allowing the investigation to continue up Main Street. He felt exposed in the car, like he was taunting the enemy with the right kind of bait, a rolling Buick.

"Let's try a few side streets next. I am not getting a good feel for the town from Main Street. Turn at that bakery up ahead."

The subtle scent of yeast bread soon wafted over the sidewalk as Duncan slowed to take the left turn. He glanced at the storefront and saw loaves sitting in a row, waiting for midday customers. A woman emerged with a white paper bag in hand, her purse dangling on her arm.

"My wife's already needling me for a color TV console. She claims it's the next big thing. If we come back down here tomorrow, I might have to check out that appliance store."

An undeveloped block held a host of rampant-blooming weeds. Duncan mused that could be the picture of his wife or his life, both categories in need of some cultivation into something more productive. Funny how his job didn't seem like enough in the moment, a personal disclosure his boss would not care to hear.

"Aha. Here we go. Second-hand Sally's right beside a cesspool called The Tap Out. Did you get the name of this street, Reed?"

"Second Street I believe. Let me double check that at the corner." He encouraged the accelerator, and they completed the block in rapid fashion. "We only have five more minutes to kill. Which way from here?"

"Go left. I want to see how deep that bar goes toward the alley. They could have a back room for special clientele. Go slower. You cannot budge the clock with your lead foot."

"No sir, that's for sure." Duncan bit back the rest of what he was thinking, which involved stuffing his boss on an east-bound airplane. He blinked and tried to clear his mind. The alley soon opened up on the left. A beat-up Chevy pulled in behind The Tap Out building. A full-figured brunette got out and slammed the door.

His boss made a note on his pad and glimpsed up, a smile curling on his lips. "Barmaid. You may have to get to know her."

"Uh, I don't think so, sir. I believe these pictures will give us the real lead we are looking for." He pumped the gas pedal more than necessary, ready to get on with the film retrieval.

His passenger pocketed the notepad and swiped his hand across his lips. "Just remember my advice, Mr. Reed. Do not ignore the obvious."

Duncan clenched his teeth so as not to smart off at the lecture. Maybe the know-it-alls should stay in DC, where they made perfect bookends with the pompous elected officials at the capital. *Heaven help me, and show me the obvious, Lord, in case I miss it right in front of my eyes.* He pulled in at the drugstore and spied the neon sign that promised overnight film development, a claim on which he now hung his entire investigation.

~

Lorna Rae stepped into the butcher shop, determined not to let her display box slip into disarray. This counted as the seventh store she had entered that day. Morning had converted to afternoon without her consent. The savory aroma of frying sausage filled the storefront. The proprietor soon appeared from the back.

The man wiped his hands on a stained white apron and flexed his salt-and-pepper eyebrows, pressing furrows in his forehead. His eyes were dark, but honest. "How I can help you?" he asked with a mild accent.

Lorna hoisted the tray to show off her wares. "I am new in Westport. I have brought my business with me—cake baking. I package and supply the single-serve slices, and then I place them in stores to sell."

A bell tinkled behind her and the clerk turned away without a word, busying himself with a section of paper in which he wrapped a stack of pork chops. A portly woman in a starched maid's outfit pressed her hips against the counter. The meat order soon rested in her hands and she gave a tiny nod that jiggled her ample chin.

"You tell Missa Johnson that we got no liver 'til Friday. Yah?"

"More excuses, Ravi? What are we going to do with you?" She gave a look over her horn-rimmed glasses and turned to leave her question floating in the air with the sausage aroma.

"Now then. You give me deese cakes and I sell. Right?" He pointed at the tray only to find a smear on his hand, which he rectified by wiping it on the apron front.

Lorna Rae hesitated to add too much detail, hearing the man's broken English. "Yes, that's right. When I come back the first of the week, I will collect and pay you a share of what's been sold." The bell sounded again as the next interruption walked in, an older woman. She backed up with the cake tray and allowed the patron immediate access to the meat case.

"Four Kansas City strips, Ravi. And trim off the fat, as Harold will not stand for that. You good and well know it."

"Four strips, lean side only," he repeated. As he turned to the back counter, he gave Lorna Rae a little wink. A knife whacked the butcher block followed by the sound of tearing paper. Soon another filled order headed out the door. Once they were alone, he motioned her forward. "How I know deese cake is any goot? I plenty busy selling meat."

She rested the tray atop the display case and opened one edge of the wax paper on the first cake. "Why here, please taste one for yourself. It is the best cake in Westport, mind you. Yours will be the only shop in the area handling Lo-Rae Cakes. It's an exclusive to your shop, because you found me first."

The butcher kneaded his fingers inside the wrapper and pulled out a hunk of chocolate cake. He tossed it in his mouth and worked it around, his gaze frozen on the ceiling until his eyes closed shut. About the time he swallowed, his hand jutted out for more.

Lorna Rae stood like a statue, her middle an ice block while her feet turned to flames. She inched the first cake into his grip, wrapper and all. When he dug into it like a cave man, a snicker bubbled up from low in her throat.

The butcher made a production of stuffing his mouth with the sweet treat, crumpling the paper in his fist. His mustache twitched from side to side. Finally a smile erupted on his face. "Yum, yum. Ravi tasted and he likes. I take your cakes for sale."

She thought to start small, give the shopkeeper some room to maneuver, and maybe grow her success. "All right then. How many should we try to sell within a week's time? I can leave as many as you would like to sell."

"All, I take all you have. My shop busy, so I can sell all in a week. Not a worry to you. How much you make one cake? You get some coin and give Ravi some."

Lorna fidgeted and the tray dipped. "Yes, I think we can sell these for five cents apiece, that's three cents for me and two for you. Does that suit you?" She'd been fussing over this pricing issue for days, and didn't think she could cover her costs for any less.

"No. No suit me. I take a penny a cake, no more. You have new business. I want to help." One by one, he lifted the cakes and set them on top of the display case, all in a row.

"Fine then." Lorna Rae handed him the last cake, her fingertips gliding over the oval label that boasted the company name. She eyed the display and experienced the first sliver of satisfaction as her marketing plan took shape. "Now for next week, Monday is my baking day so I will deliver on Tuesdays. Let me bring a dozen more cakes, and we will see how sales go. We can adjust your inventory from there."

"So I pay you each week on delivery day. Good. Now, I get you meat order. What do you want to feed your family?" He gestured across the case.

Lorna glanced into the case, understanding that he wanted reciprocate business. She had some money—not much—but if he could invest in her, she could return the favor. "Well, I am cooking for my sister's family. She just had a baby. That sausage you have cooking in the back sure smells tempting, but it might be too spicy."

"Not too spicy—just enough. You see. I get some for you. How many links?"

"Four would be more than enough, Ravi." Before she could add her thanks, he disappeared into the back. When he returned, he offered her a bite-sized chunk of sausage.

"Today, we start business and eat lunch together. Life is good."

Lorna Rae accepted the sausage along with the sentiment that accompanied it. "Here's to being business partners, then." She bit the meat chunk, and a world of exquisite flavor spread across her palate. A hum of enjoyment came up her throat that launched the proprietor's eyebrows into his hairline.

Ravi busied himself gathering her order and took an extra link out, waving it at her. "Good partners. We get busy soon. You see." He turned and pulled the paper out a length, then wrapped her meat to go. His thumb smoothed a piece of tape across the opening and placed it on the case.

"Here you are for the meat." She slid a bill over the counter. "And for the cakes, I leave you twelve—make that eleven—and we will see how many you can sell."

"Next week, bring twenty. I sweet-talk customers and they buy. Trust me." He touched his mustache and seemed to blush.

Lorna Rae picked up the sausage bundle and nodded goodbye. Once outside the shop door, she remembered to breathe. She now had a business as a seller of cakes. *Imagine that.*

~

Duncan sat at his desk and thumbed through the stack of photographs as his boss took a quick smoke on the front porch. The good doctor had run across the way to check on Mrs. Anders' latest discomfiture over at the grocery store. With his offer to help identify some of the oil field laborers, Duncan sensed imminent traction. Now, they would be getting somewhere.

A matter of process, he dealt the photos out like a hand of cards, most of them landscape scenes at the lake. The imaging had come out sharp, which involuntarily triggered memories of the company picnic. He could almost smell the sawdust in the horseshoes pit.

Five or six exposures in, one snapshot made his hand freeze in place. The playground in the background, there laid Trudy in the bicycle basket with Lorna Rae leaning over her in an unguarded moment of motherly love. The honest emotion in her eyes unbuttoned him, one exhaled breath after another. Captivated, he realized that he had been missing them both. He caressed the picture with his gaze for a few luxurious moments, until he heard men's voices on the porch. He slid the picture into his desk drawer as the screen door squeaked open.

McNaughton tucked his pack of cigarettes back into his shirt pocket and approached him. "Got anything there, Reed?"

"So far, I have captured Mr. Coates on his way to winning the horseshoes tournament. I think the fishing champions are toward the end here." He flipped a few more exposures onto the desktop and halted at one shot directed into the old truck the men had used as a platform to cut bait. Quite by accident, part of the license plate could be made out. He flipped the next photograph beside it, and there stood the record-breaker, holding his prize catch.

Doctor Lucas rolled up his office chair and sat next to Duncan. He gave a harrumph and pulled his glasses out to get a better look. "Yep. That is Liam Torguson with the fish. To his right stands Shorty Carlson."

McNaughton hovered closer, his pen working overtime. "Slow up, Doc, as I'm trying to write down these names."

"This guy here with the split in his smile is Bud Gant. Funny, now that I think about it. These two share more than an interest in fishing." His finger alternated between Torguson and Gant. "It seems like I had to treat both men for the same socially transmitted disease within a year of each other."

The weighty evidence of a long-term collusion fell on Duncan as he examined the photograph. Torguson looked prideful as all get out, smug and untouchable standing in the midst of his men. They had likely been planning this whole insurance fraud thing for months before the first maiming episode happened, a thought that sickened him. "All right. How about this guy? Isn't that the foreman from the generator house?" He touched a pen to the man who stood on the outskirts of the group.

Doctor Lucas nodded. "Yep. That is Sol Edmunds, a big, quiet guy. Tell you the truth, I think he just likes to fish. If he was in cahoots with these others, I would be mighty surprised."

"We want to avoid making any unwarranted assumptions too soon, Doctor. I'll have Duncan check each man's employment record for any strikes against their behavior or marks against company loyalty. Let's leave no stone unturned, as the guilty must be held accountable. This offense may be punishable by imprisonment, given the scale of the insurance payout.

Duncan pulled up the truck photo and jotted down the visible letters on the plate. "We should find out who this truck is registered to, which may be included in the company's records, since we issue front gate passes."

McNaughton leaned in, looking like a salivating dog. "Whoa. Wait a second. Do these vehicles get some kind of decal or tag?"

"Why sure." Dr. Lucas shoved back in his chair and rolled toward his quadrant of the shared space. "Everybody has a windshield sticker, or the sentry at the front gate pulls them aside. Controlled access, I believe they call it."

"Then I am definitely going on the prowl tonight downtown. If any Coates Oil Field workers are gathered up, I can read it right on their windshields."

"Suit yourself," the doctor replied. He glanced at his office schedule and opened a file drawer.

Duncan sat motionless staring at his desk, where Torguson glared up at him with the impaled monster catfish in his grip. Now, they had more than a record-breaker on their hands. They had premeditated insurance fraud, and plenty of it.

"Let's split up, Reed. For heaven's sake, I can run these background checks, if you show me where the personnel office is located."

"Yes, sir. I will take you right down there. I sure appreciate the help. That will leave me enough time to make a site visit at a new drilling location this afternoon." He gathered up the photographs with the fishermen left on top. Before he could jam them back into the envelope, his boss had confiscated the incriminating shot.

"Let me keep this to match faces with the personnel files. I will make it part of my report. You can have another copy made with the negative, right?"

"If I need it, sir, I will. In my opinion, if you have seen one catfish, you've seen them all." He kicked the screen door open and plucked his sunglasses in place. He had more to guard against than solar radiation. June had clamped down on the oil fields with impressive force.

McNaughton stepped behind him, following him down the walkway. "You would have time later this afternoon to give that bungalow the once-over, right Reed? I would like to see any evidence you come up with firsthand while I'm here." He drew out the pack and tapped out a cigarette.

"Yes, sir. I will, depending on what time you want to launch that night patrol. By the way, ordinary men would eat dinner some time in between." Duncan glanced over his shoulder to see how his comment landed.

"Let's pick up some carryout and eat in the car. I have wanted a good burger with a side of onion rings for days now. Maybe tonight's the night." He flicked his lighter open and inhaled until the cigarette lit.

"It could be tonight." Duncan's thoughts diverged between the pending research and the waterfall pictures, both cascading ever before him seemingly out of control. He would double back to grab the picture of Lorna Rae and Trudy before heading home to the bungalow. That particular photo was his to keep, and he planned on it.

~

Lorna Rae wiped her hands dry from washing dishes and stepped into the front room because the light had been left on. There in a worn club chair sat Steve, sound asleep with the newborn cozy in the crook of his arm. She lifted the baby and murmured words of affection as she stooped to switch off the light. Della would be up in four hours for the one o'clock feeding and did not need to stumble about wondering where the baby had gone. She tiptoed down the hall and entered the back bedroom, where a bassinet hugged the wall by the closet. With a kiss to his forehead, she tucked her nephew into bed and prayed a word of thanks from her heart. Life was good.

Chapter 9

Boom Town could have been renamed Bust Berg for the lack of luck they experienced last night. Duncan cracked an egg into a scratched frying pan and checked to make sure he had the burner flame up high enough. As a bachelor, he knew his way around a kitchen, but cooking over a gas flame represented a new experience—and posed a challenge. He glanced around and noted the neat state of affairs bequeathed to him by the former occupant, a real gift. His eyes came to rest on the photo of Trudy and Lorna Rae, which now graced the Frigidaire's door.

Out of the friendship they had developed, he had taken an unauthorized step last night and boxed up Harley's things after checking them for clues. When Lorna Rae came back to claim her belongings, it would be one less effort she would have to make to be clear of the oil fields. He had left a note on Vivian's door at daybreak, asking her to come get the box of clothing, if she had an outlet for sharing with the less fortunate.

Part of last night's bust had been the rain, a blinding torrent. He had to keep the Buick's wipers on the entire patrol, which made it difficult to remain inconspicuous. Downtown had been a ghost town except for one hotspot. McNaughton had discovered a single scintillating piece of information linking his personnel research with the town's night life. Sol Edmunds bowled in the Tuesday night league, evidently come hell or high water. The guy was vanilla ice cream. Doc Lucas had been right with his hunch of noninvolvement.

Distracted while pouring his first cup of coffee, Duncan smelled the egg turning to burned protein. He slid in front of the range, but could not locate a tool to get the egg turned over to save his life. Frantic, he pulled the right drawer open and searched for a spatula. He found a useless pair of tongs.

He popped the left drawer open next, and there sat a long-handled turner that any safety manager could love. In his haste to extract it, half the drawer contents evacuated with the tool. He brushed a paper napkin away from the open flames as a pad of matches cut a few spins and came to rest near the back burner.

His attempt to save his breakfast ended with a split yolk and a burnt side that should have been rubbery white. Disgusted at the botched job, he threw the utensil down on the counter and began to gather the loose drawer contents for repatriation. When he grabbed the pad of matches, it flipped over in his palm to reveal a hand-printed message in black marker, the number nineteen. The two digits seared an image onto his awareness. He swallowed back a lump of disbelief. Just like that, he had discovered Harley's union talisman.

A knock came from the back door. "Yoo-hoo. Anybody home? Or is breakfast burning itself in there?"

Duncan shoved the matches into his pocket and stepped past the range to answer the door. "Oh. Good morning, Vivian. No, I get full credit for ruining breakfast. How are you this morning?"

"I am glad the rain quit, so the kids can play outside. I guess God had to water the flowers last night, but enough already. Know what I mean?" She laughed and stepped into the kitchen, her hair matted in pin curls that had not been brushed out yet.

Duncan forced a laugh as his analytical mind ran haywire with possibilities, now that he had the right drawing card. Vivian's husband was also a card-carrying member of the union, according to Lorna Rae. He needed to delve a bit. "Let me turn this catastrophe off before we get started." He reached to the range top and turned the gas control knob to off.

"Bert has eaten worse than that, believe you me. Say, what a great picture of Trudy." She stepped toward the refrigerator and fingered the edge of the photograph.

"I took that at the company picnic. She caught an afternoon nap in a bicycle basket that day, so I could dry off. You would think a grown man might know better than to leap into a flooded creek to rescue a turtle being flushed out of the lake." He gave her a wry smile and thought to rescue the egg from the pan next, turning to the range.

"Gosh, Lorna Rae looks remarkable. I mean, what with all she's been through. She has a resiliency that comes from her faith in God, that warrior-woman. I sure do miss her."

Her comment poked Duncan in a soft spot. A touch of melancholy filtered into the morning light coming through the curtains. "I can imagine you do." His reply took on a husky tone, and he took a quick drink of hot coffee to clear the unexpected emotion. For a second, he regretted having put the photo up, but when he turned around to regard it with her, it seemed like the right thing to do.

"Look at me taking up all your time. I am gonna make you late for work." She hurried into the bedroom directly adjoining the kitchen.

"I left the box at the foot of the bed." He followed Vivian a couple of steps, but decided to remain in the doorway to prevent any impropriety. When she grunted with the lift, he winced. "Better let me get that."

"I am no china doll, Mr. Reed." Her every word came strained through her teeth, expressing the exact opposite.

"Oh, I know what I wanted to ask." Duncan took the box and brought it into the kitchen, resting it on the corner of the table.

"Ask away neighbor. Need a cup of sugar?" Her facial features took on clown proportions, until she laughed at the unlikelihood.

"Not hardly. My boss from D.C. is in town—a surprise visit that kept me from seeing Trudy and Lorna Rae off, quite honestly. Anyway, this guy is a chain smoker. He is about to run me out of my own car. Doc Lucas even had to ask him to light up out on the porch to keep the clinic smoke-free. I could use some extra matches for him, and I remembered you had some at Trudy's birthday party. May I borrow them?"

"Follow me. You can have them in two shakes of a lamb's tail. I feel for you though. Bert smoked cigarettes when we first started dating, but I let him know right quick—it was either them or me." Vivian popped the door open with a flattened palm and shot through the doorway with a new mission.

Duncan hefted the box and followed her out to the stoop, checking his footing before launching across the yard. He noticed the worn path between the two bungalows had begun to grow closed with crabgrass along the edges. He needed to be a better neighbor, though he could hardly hope to take Lorna Rae's place.

"Just put that box of Harley's things right on the porch slab, the only dry place in the entire backyard." She clucked her tongue like a brooding mother hen and went inside the door. In seconds, she returned with the matches and plunked them in his hand.

"Thank you so much, Vivian. I don't know how much of this pad will remain after his visit, but I can return it if anything's left. As I see it, I have half a pack of cigarettes to endure yet, as his flight out is not until four o'clock this afternoon."

"Keep the matches, you poor man. I don't have another family birthday coming up until October, any-who. Oh, one more thing." A flash of interest lit her face, and she stepped back inside. She returned this time with a napkin wadded around something. "For your breakfast this morning, so you don't have to ingest that egg." She tried to stifle a laugh, but failed.

He pocketed the match pad and held something that felt light as a biscuit in both hands.

"Thank you, Vivian. You shame me with your thoughtfulness. Really you do. Have a nice day. I hope the children remember to wipe their muddy feet before coming in."

"They will—or else!" She jabbed a finger into the air, but her austerity soon melted into a loving smile. "God bless your day, Mr. Reed. Thanks for packing up Harley's things. I will write to Lorna Rae and let her know I took them away."

"Goodbye now. I cannot keep my boss waiting." He winked and fanned away some imaginary smoke, which gave her another laugh at his expense. With hastened strides, he returned to his bungalow and threw back the screen door. It had no more returned to the threshold with a slam, when he had the contents of his pocket emptied onto the tabletop. The match pad skidded across and flipped. Two black digits stared back up at him. *Lord help.* The morning had suddenly filled with double golden nuggets. Bert Decker held number twenty-four. Now, he had two indisputable playing pieces. McNaughton would have an absolute hay day.

Duncan eyed the wrapped breakfast treat, given out of

generosity by his friendly neighbor. He glanced at the burnt egg over on the range and noticed his coffee mug waiting for him, still almost full. Instead of dashing out with his breaking news, he opted to stay in his own cozy kitchen a few more minutes. Besides, a good breakfast would give him a better start on his day, his double-digit day. When he passed by Lorna Rae's snapshot, he blew it a kiss.

~

This had been Della's idea, though it made her stomach flip-flop. Lorna Rae rode silently in Steve's passenger seat on his morning commute into downtown Kansas City for work. The prestigious accounting firm that employed him sat proudly in the heart of The Plaza, home to Union Station and Hallmark Cards. Steeped in the city's history and bearing unmistakable panache, she had little expectation of her modest product finding any suitable home here.

Steve focused on the traffic, but gave her a nod of encouragement. "You will never know until you try, right? You have got the contact list, don't you?"

"Yes, here in my hand." She let go of the sample tray long enough to display the scribbled list, her best attempt to narrow the unknown market.

A crease of worry worked its way onto his youthful brow. "Okay. I will be praying God will open up the best possible door for you. Next on my checklist, do you have the bus route memorized? I am concerned you may get lost in town afterwards."

"Yes, I have the bus route memorized. And your address. And the telephone number." She tipped her head and glared at him to prove her point. "I can do this, Steve. It is a vital part of wanting the business. You have to go out and create sales. But I do appreciate the prayers."

"Sure, sis. One good thing about this area is there are lots of workers collecting down here. By high noon, they all start to get hungry."

"Is that the World War I memorial over there on the hill?"

"Yes, that's right. And over there is Union Station with the arches, just beyond the old Sweeney Automobile School. That building is the headquarters for Western Auto." His finger traced brick towers on the city's skyline.

Lorna Rae could hardly catch her breath. This was not little El Dorado, Kansas anymore. Kansas City was the industrious Midwest at its best. So much post-war progress evidenced itself here. Her business would be a part of it, a tiny part, but a sweet one. "I can do this. I plan to stay out there until this tray is empty, and the promise of next week's deliveries is full."

"You know I am willing to help deliver. I drive in daily, anyway."

"Thank you, Steve. I would be in a world of hurt without you and Della rescuing Trudy and me. I probably fail to say thank you enough."

"No, every night when dinner is on the table, you express your thanks. Plus, you are helping Della with the baby, too. She would be guessing at every turn without your advice."

"We Holloway girls have to stay close. It's the family way." The thought sent a warm trickle down her middle, as her birth heritage meant something to her.

"Okay, here we are. Let's start you here at this corner. Get ready and I will drop you at the curb when this light turns green." Steve signaled over to make good on his warning.

A nervous flutter tightened her throat. When she opened that door, she would be standing in the heart of The Plaza. "Lo-Rae Cakes, don't get the shakes." She shared a curt snicker with the driver.

"That's it. Keep your sense of humor, Lorna Rae. Use it if you have to. Now, go get your cakes out there and find your outlets." The light turned green and Steve pulled the car over.

"But I need folks with a sweet tooth, not a funny bone." She popped the car door and gave him an amused look, contorting her mouth as she got out.

"Call Della if anything goes wrong."

Lorna Rae stood up, her tray setting perpendicular to the impressive skyscrapers of downtown Kansas City. Twenty-four little cakes had ventured into the big city today, two dozen chances to be successful. Something told her she would need every last one of them.

~

The two matchbooks sat on his desk basking in the sun's indirect light. Duncan thought that represented an improvement on their typically nocturnal behavior. He took full responsibility for their conversion, as he would take full credit for their discovery. Somehow, the thrill fell short in the moment.

McNaughton gripped the edge of the desk and stared wide-eyed. He reached for his notepad and pen as a grin cracked his typically austere face. "I have got to hand it to you, Mr. Reed. This is a magnanimous turn of events. I had a hunch, of course, but this is the hard evidence we needed."

"Let the record show that Bert Decker was not a highly willing recruit. Harley Holmes brought him into the group. The men were next-door neighbors, so I think Bert assumed it would be a way to befriend Harley. Their wives are close friends."

"He didn't know what he was getting into then?"

Duncan opened the file and jotted down the number. "Most likely not. He could well be the last man recruited in, so that makes at least twenty-four members in the union."

"We know some of their identities from the photograph, based on assumption."

"Let's leave Sol Edmunds out. There is nothing else incriminating him at this point. Plus, he bowls on Tuesday nights, so he has a conflict with the union's regular meeting night."

"A fact the court would deem an alibi. I totally agree. Strike him off the list."

Duncan flipped back a page in his notes. "You can add on each of the maiming victims as confirmed members. Number one, Dennis Gregory. Number two, Jimmy Cantor. Number three, Glen Forshee."

"Plus the matchbook holders, Harley Holmes and Bert Decker."

"From the fisherman photo we add Bud Gant, Shorty Carlson, and Liam Torguson. That's eight men out of twenty-four, only a third of them. Still, we are building a pretty strong case." Duncan turned to regard his boss, looking for some direction.

"Don't forget, we have the moratorium in place. Pay-out wise, we have the bulk of our forty-five days left."

"But maiming schedule-wise, we're down to fifteen—make that fourteen days on the countdown calendar." Duncan tapped his desk calendar as if to have some of the pressure transfer onto the paper. "I would give anything to prevent this next episode. Really, it's starting to make me lose sleep at night."

"That's a sure sign of dedication. I would worry if you didn't care that much, Reed. Listen, you have your splitting wedge in place, and the log is poised to crack right in half, maybe with your next blow. Remember, this is a premeditated chess game, and it's their move. We have to think two moves ahead."

"What would you like me to focus on next, sir? I am happy to have your input at this juncture."

"Which one of these known members is the weakest link in your opinion?"

"Okay, I see where you're going with this. Take the next-door neighbor, Bert Decker. He's enrolled as an unwilling participant. I had a source tell me, once you're in, you're in. The union does not allow dropouts."

"So he is uncomfortable…and might be willing to talk. Good lead."

"Then there's the youngest victim, Jimmy Cantor. He seems to have…regrets. Maybe that translates into disloyalty, I cannot say for sure."

McNaughton slid his cigarette pack out of his pocket. "But it could be worth a slow pursuit. He might spill more details, since he put you onto the union in the first place."

"The last weak link, and I do mean weak, is the latest victim, Glen Forshee. He has grown stronger in his recovery, so maybe it is time for my perfunctory post-accident visit, since they know I'm sworn to promote safety." Duncan wrote the three potential leads in the margin of his notes. On impulse, he had the urge to add Torguson's name, as he'd love to interrogate the smirk right off that man's face. "What about the union leaders? Any advice?"

"Steer clear for the time being. Let's build our case beyond implications. All we have is a fish in a snapshot. We need to have something more red-handed than that."

"Before the next accident…if I could be so lucky in two weeks' time."

"I want a written copy of your interviews with all three of these targeted men. Put it in Friday's report and mail it on time, would you? Then I will call you, so we can go over our next move. Let me use this office number, as I suppose the bungalow does not have a phone."

"No sir, it's a residence for oil field workers. This is Boom Town, not Bean Town."

"And it lends great cover for you—just don't get lost in it. By the way, the matchbook pads need to come back to D.C. with me."

Duncan shifted in his chair and gave up the evidence. "Help yourself, sir."

"I need a cigarette. Be right back." McNaughton took the matches and stepped out to the porch to have his break.

Duncan closed the file and moved it to the edge of his desk. Maybe he could write a letter home and go see Jimmy Cantor at the post office, before his trip to the airport. Tonight he would be free of his boss and able to resume a normal life, one without onion rings and cigarette smoke.

He remembered Vivian saying something about writing Lorna Rae about taking Harley's clothes. She must have a Westport address for her then, something he never thought to ask. The waterfall picture came to mind. He considered mailing it to her in a casual note. The idea tantalized him until he knew he had to do it. Such a small investment too, a three-cent stamp.

~

Tired feet carried little promise of success. Lorna Rae looked at the half-dozen specimen remaining and wondered if Jesus could possibly replay the food multiplication miracle when he fed the five thousand up on the hillside. She could stand a modern-day version, offering up her tray with a sentence prayer like the young boy with the original loaves and fishes.

The door to a popular deli swung open, and a patron walked out, a toothpick in his lips. She slid the tray inside before the door could close. Heavenly aromas battled for top billing, but the draw of good old-fashioned melted cheese beat them all.

An aged woman with narrow shoulders and pear-shaped hips came strolling up behind the counter. "Well, what do we have here?" She blinked as if to unknot her caked-on mascara.

She raised the tray for the woman's inspection. "I am Lorna Rae Holmes, a new baker in the area. I am looking for establishments to sell my single-serving cake slices to their clientele. May I offer you a free sample?"

"Of all the crummy timing," she replied. "Leon, get your lanky frame front-and-center here, young man." She snapped her fingers until a scrawny guy with a crew cut appeared. "Lunch rush is over. I am going back to my office with this saleslady. You take care of any orders until I come back. Got it?"

"Yes, ma'am. Can do." The youth tightened his apron strings and immediately began watching the door.

"Right this way, Mrs. Holmes. It's been a long morning so far. I will be glad to get off my feet for a few minutes, to tell you the truth."

"Me, too. My toes are growing more corn than a Kansas farmer." Lorna Rae closed the distance between them and distinctly heard the woman guffaw at her joke.

She pointed left down a short hall and led the way. "Say, could someone talk to the shoemakers for us working women? I do not need spiky heels. I need foam insoles in a smart shoe that does not resemble something my grandmother would wear."

Lorna Rae glanced down at her scuff-toed penny loafers and felt a cringe of shame, but at least they were comfortable. "Hollywood is going to make us all lame, I'm afraid, with all those wicked high heels and peep-toe shoes."

"Isn't that the truth? Now come right on in." She walked around a cluttered desk, where the in-box cascaded like Niagara Falls. "Excuse the paper doll collection. I never have enough time back here to straighten things up." The chair squeaked when she plopped down.

Lorna Rae perched on the edge of the guest chair. A sense of camaraderie swept over her, so she decided to make less of a direct pitch. During her mental shift, she spotted a name placard on the desk. "Well, Miss Buckner, in our line of business, the food has to speak for itself. I would like you to try my cake, because if you don't like it, I won't stand a snowball's chance in June. Forget the rolling downhill part. Please humor me and sample one of these cakes."

The woman capitulated with a nod and selected a packaged cake from the left side of the tray. She pealed back the wrapper and let the moist chocolate gleam in the incandescent lighting.

Lorna Rae slipped back onto the seat. She had gotten inside the door, through the hall to the office, and now the ball headed down the lane towards the pins. She needed a strike.

The woman hummed once and kept eating until the entire

sample had been demolished. Bare-handed, she twisted a cap off a Pepsi Cola sitting on the desk. She threw her head back and drank the bottle half empty.

Lorna Rae could feel the momentum shift in the room, an odd sensation. Had they been on a ship, the desk top would have listed to port and dumped the paper doll mess on the floor. Transfixed in the divinely-appointed moment, she lost her ability to speak.

"Listen to me, Mrs. Holmes. This is a delicatessen. I serve sandwiches and an occasional pot of soup in season. Even though my customers want a little something sweet with their meal, I abhor baking. Cannot stand it and will not do it. Leon has been trying to concoct a proper cookie batter back there in the kitchen, but bread is his thing, fresh-baked and savory. We have a weak spot, all right. Isn't it funny that you walked right smack dab into the middle of it with your delicious cakes?"

"Oh, it's hilarious. I believe this is how great partnerships are formed, when two products can be offered hand-in-glove." Lorna fixed her gaze directly on the proprietor and allowed a small smile to curl her lips. "This would be a great nesting spot for these little cakes."

"No. Hear me out. I want big cakes, the full sheet, baked, filled and ready to serve. I really like your recipe, and I think my customers will crave it, too. I want to be able to reach in the display case and cut out the next square for the customer. It will keep moister that way and tantalize the eye, which is exactly how I plan to sell it, slice by slice. That will save you from having to wrap each piece. I will even provide you a stack of bakery boxes to bring it in."

A shiver ran through Lorna Rae, the thrill of success. Her business senses tingled as she examined the offer, which seemed almost too good to be true. "This is outstanding, Miss Buckner, truly it is. But I'll have to give my pricing some thought, as I have only sold by the slice up until today. Let me examine my costs and get back to you."

"One more thing. Not everybody is zippity-dee-do-dah over chocolate, which I frankly do not understand. Can you come up with a blonde version of this recipe? I mean something quite similar, only not chocolate. You could flavor up the filling if you wanted."

"I could change that version season to season, like pumpkin cream for autumn. Yes, that is doable, indeed. We need to decide if we would alternate weeks for each cake or double up each week. I certainly would not want to overdo it and leave you a bunch of uneaten cake."

"Like that's going to happen." She laughed and took another sip of the soda. "Okay, cautious baker-lady. Let's start with the chocolate cake first. If anyone complains, we will tell them we are working on an alternative. Give me the blonde cake on Week Two, so the customers feel some ownership for the switch. I am willing to bet on this—by month's end, we will be selling two full cakes a week, side by side."

Lorna Rae stood to shake hands. "You have a deal. Lo-Rae Cakes are now being sold on The Plaza at Buckner's Deli."

The owner shifted to her feet and offered her hand in a manly grip. "Get me your signage and we can put it up in the lobby. Why not? You have brought the icing on the cake, and taken the heat off of me. I would call that a red-letter day."

"Then I should get the sign done in red. Can you recommend a print shop?"

"Sure. Harry's is two blocks over closer to the post office. Be sure to tell him what we are up to with the cake addition. He comes in three times a week, that beanpole." She gave a husky laugh and took her soda bottle in hand. "When can I expect the first installment?"

"Let me aim for Monday morning, if I can get my baking done early enough. I catch a ride with my brother-in-law who commutes from Westport. Once we get the logistics smoothed out, he might be able to deliver the cakes without my help."

"Oh, you sound busy. I guess you have other drops to make, too."

"Just the butcher shop in Westport, and they get small cakes on Tuesdays."

"The butcher and the baker, which leaves me the candlestick maker. Hardee-har-har! Nobody's ever accused me of having waxy food before."

"Let's revise the rhyme to include a sandwich maker, shall we? Thank you for this opportunity. I am so looking forward to it. Big cakes, of all things." Lorna clapped her hands together, having thrown professional caution to the wind. If she seemed like a little girl giggling over her victory, that was fine with her.

"How about we go get those bakery boxes? I will have Leon shove 'em in a bag to keep the outsides clean."

"Great idea. I plan to take the bus back to Westport after I sell this tray empty."

"Consider those pitiful last five already gone then, as you are leaving them with me. I plan to cut them up as samples of what's debuting next week—give the customers something to look forward to at lunch."

"Miss Buckner, from my head to my aching toes, thank you most sincerely."

"So before you go, let's split a *corned* beef sandwich. Hardee-har-har! I couldn't resist."

"I hope your customers feel the same way about my cakes." Lorna Rae followed the owner back into the lobby, where she looked around while waiting for the boxes. A dated picture labeled "Harvey House Girls" revealed a younger version of the brusque deli owner as she stood in the two-story atrium of Union Station. The woman had been around food service for a considerable while—and she liked Lo-Rae Cakes. A yelp of joy unlatched from deep within her lungs. Lorna Rae only hoped she could hold off expressing it until she got outside. Big cakes meant big money, and it would roll in fast.

Chapter 10

Duncan called forth some patience as he stood on the portico of the small house.

From his wheelchair, Glen Forshee appeared but a shadow of a man. "Take me outside." A weak cough trailed his order. A haggard-looking woman pushed him toward the entrance.

Duncan held the door open to make the job easier as a lead weight dropped into his stomach. As safety manager, he had some heady topics to address. A matter of procedure, yet the man looked fragile. Even kid gloves would not abate the train wreck about to happen. In pursuit of company business, he felt obliged to make every effort.

He corralled his thoughts enough to speak a prayer over the situation while he followed the couple out onto the carport flanking the house. "Mr. Forshee, if you are not up to this interview, please say the word. I can always come back another day."

"I figured Mr. Coates would send somebody out. I'm short of breath, that's all." He straightened in the chair and nodded the woman back inside. She left and the door clicked closed.

Duncan sat on the edge of a metal yard chair that had rust spots everywhere. He slipped his notepad from his pocket and tapped his pen against it. "I need to go through the day of the accident with you to get your account on record. Anything you can tell us might make the workplace safer, so this never happens again. I assure you my department has the laborer's best interests in mind."

"They assigned me that well up the Shumway Road field along with Shorty Carlson. We have been working well drilling for nearly two years now, so we know the routine. The drilling takes time and is awful dirty, hot work." He smacked his lips together, sounding dehydrated sitting there in the shade.

"Did you have any tools in your possession, Mr. Forshee? Tell me about that."

"Only my shovel, like usual. 'Bout four of us were under the drill head working back the tailings brought up before the next round could start. We'd been going at it for almost an hour, and it got hot fast, so hot."

"Yes, I have made a note in the report. The Weather Bureau had El Dorado at ninety-two degrees that day. I guess your crew didn't expect that in May."

"You can say that again. Shorty cannot take the heat very well. He started looking like a sweaty pig, so the foreman let him sit out now and again to catch his breath."

Duncan wrote a note about Shorty alternating out and looked up to read the man's expression. "Was that kind of switch-out going on the day of your accident?"

"He had sat out a couple of rotations earlier, but was right there with us under the drill head at that point. We all knew lunch break was next. I set my mind on that to make it through the midday heat."

"Could you have been distracted then?"

The man looked up with a leer. "Distracted? No, I do not admit to being distracted."

"Mr. Delmar, the drill site foreman, testified that he gave the "all clear" call, and the rest of the workers heeded his directive to stand clear to let the drill operate—everyone except you, Mr. Forshee. Is that possible?"

"I haven't ever gone against orders. My record is clean. You can check it."

"That won't be necessary, Mr. Forshee. I am only trying to get your account to match up with what I already have on record. Could you be more specific about the moments leading up to your being pinned under the drill?"

"I heard the order, clear as day. He called my name out, so I got under there to get the rubble. Before I knew it, my shovel snatched my arm into the hole, and I was so shocked, I froze when I should have let go. The pain came next, the awful grinding pain of being pulled under with the drill rotating against me. After that, everything went blank." A wheezing breath followed, and he began to slump forward in the wheelchair.

Duncan glanced down at the notepad and jotted down the account to offer the man some extra time. "Is there anything else you remember? Anything at all?"

"Only that Doc Lucas tried to make me comfortable before the ambulance came. Guess I was too messed up for him to fix. He gave me something for the pain, but it didn't knock back right away. No sir, that took hours."

"Mr. Forshee, to get your account to match the site foreman's report, I need to go back over one point with you. Mr. Delmar gave the "all clear" signal to the whole crew, yet you say he called you out by name. Are you certain that Delmar called your name?"

"Of course he did. Who else would have a say? You can't blame me for doing my job. I wasn't distracted, Mr. Reed. I stood out in that godforsaken heat and did my job."

"I happened to be in attendance that day, Mr. Forshee. I observed the drill operation and the alternating pattern of digging and clearing. You were the only one who broke the rhythm of alternating, and the only one who disobeyed the "all clear" that Delmar gave. In the end, you were the only one who got hurt."

He spat on the concrete between where they sat. The spittle came swirled with blood. "Get off my property."

Duncan stood and closed the notepad. He realized the discrepancy was more than a crack in the story. It held the dark truth about the union. If he mentioned it while the man was on the defensive, it would give his advantage away. He had a hostile witness, a hurt, hostile witness. Everything inside of him hoped he would be the last.

He tucked the notepad in his pocket and looked the man in the eyes. "Good day then, Mr. Forshee. I will tell Dr. Lucas that you spoke kindly of him. I am sure he'd like to give you the clearance for your light duty assignment, when you feel like you are up to it."

Forshee shook his head. "I can't come back to the oil field in a wheelchair." He fumbled the cigarette pack out of his pocket and seemed in a rush to light up.

When the ailing man peeled back the cover on the match pad, a guillotine sliced the wind out of Duncan's lungs. A section of the matches had been cut off the pad partially up the stems, a purposeful act. Forshee's talisman may have been marked by the union, something he had not witnessed before. Straining to see the back cover as the man struck the match, all he could make out were two parallel black lines peeking out from under his grip, possibly the number eleven.

"I will get this report filed on record. You take care of yourself." He stepped to the car as the first puff of smoke circled the air above the wheelchair.

"You especially note the distracted part. I wasn't distracted from my job one bit." Forshee wheezed and gasped for air, coughing and inhaling the cigarette in alternating blows.

Duncan spared himself the tragic down-spiral of what had once been an honest laborer. Corruption took care of that, like smoke permeating one's airways. Part of that demise came self-inflicted in this case, but another part was the callous persuasion of one's fellow man. When the image of the impaled catfish came to mind, he fought the repulsion all the way back to his car.

~

Lorna Rae leaned over the batter bowl unsatisfied. Without the chocolate, the cake recipe tasted lifeless. She needed to add something to perk it up, but what? The steady beat of Della's back-patting to get baby Robert Thomas to burp added a stutter to the lapse going on in her baker's brain this morning. "Della, help me. This batter tastes as flat as they come. I need this to be every bit as good as the chocolate version, but it's not."

"You added vanilla flavoring?"

"Yes. That helps, but isn't enough."

Trudy picked up the coloring book and tipped the page toward her. "My monkeys have bananas."

Lorna's glance caromed off her artwork and landed on the facing page where an aardvark nibbled at an apple. The letter A stood tall and proud in the middle of the page. She checked and the banana page featured the letter B. "Oh, honey. I think your monkeys may be baboons instead. See how all the words start with the letter of the alphabet? Do you remember what that one with double bumps is?"

"B is for bananas." Trudy held her yellow crayon up as if to color the sky.

Della repositioned the baby to finish his feeding. "Good girl, Trudy."

"Del, what do you think of apples for the cake? I could grate it up small and it would lend the batter some flavor and fill out the cake a bit."

"I am unsure. That somehow sounds heavy to me. If the chocolate cake is light, then the vanilla cake cannot be heavy."

Trudy picked up the red crayon and began to make circles to fill up the apple shape on the page. "I only like applesauce, Mommy."

"Applesauce would lend the same flavor, yet not be as heavy. In fact, it might just make the cake moister. Where is your pressure cooker, Della? I am going to try making homemade applesauce and add it to the cake batter."

"Under the sink there, first cabinet to the right. Believe it or not, the recipe book says you can have creamy pink applesauce in just four minutes." Della words came in whispers as the baby showed some distraction at all the talking.

"What if you don't want it to turn out pink? My cake has to stay blonde."

"Then peel the apples, silly goose." Della snickered, and the baby's sleepy blue eyes popped wide open.

Lorna slid the heavy pot from its shelf with a finger pressed to her lips, demonstrating her willingness to be quieter while sharing the room with a nursing infant.

Trudy crinkled her nose up while echoing the tease. "Silly goose."

"We should call this the silly goose cake, shouldn't we?" Lorna Rae placed the pot on the burner and stepped toward a large bowl on the counter filled with fruit. She selected two apples and washed them under the faucet. "How much water should I put in the pot?"

"Only a quarter cup, unless you want it runny."

"No, runny will not do. Let's stick with a quarter cup then."

"I want yummy. Make me some, Mommy."

"Guess I could add another apple. You don't mind, do you Del?"

"Not at all, especially since I know who gets to sample this experiment tonight." Her whisper held childish intrigue, which soon bubbled into a full giggle.

"Okay, fellow conspirators. Now what about the filling? I need a hint of flavor for the filling, or the butter will overpower the sugar. Any ideas?"

"B is for bacon. I say bacon, Mommy."

Lorna Rae laughed at the girl's suggestion as she peeled the first apple. "I don't think anyone wants bacon for dessert, doll baby."

"I once had a dreamy cream puff with an almond filling that tasted divine. I have some almond extract up there in the spice cabinet that I use for Christmas cookies. You can help yourself, if it sounds good to you."

Lorna Rae glanced out the window as rain clouds shrouded the backyard. At least she had no deliveries to make today, but she did have to get her recipe down before Monday. She would use the apples for volume and put almond in the middle for an extra flavorful punch. "Almond Blondie Cake—how is that for using my ABC's?"

"I dunno. I plan to withhold my grade until dessert tonight. While I am thinking about it, can you remember to pick up some pork chops with your delivery next time?"

"Sure thing. They would be delicious with baked apples on top. Between the two of us, we'll make Steve a fat man yet." Lorna Rae picked up the third apple and saw a yellow butterfly flit by the window as she washed it.

"Trudy, maybe you should go play outside before the rain comes this afternoon."

The girl switched her mouth to and fro in protest. "Do I have to?"

"You get to, honey. I just saw a swallowtail butterfly go by. I bet he's on Aunt Della's lilac bush right now."

"I want to see. Let me, let me." Trudy slid off the chair and ran to the back door.

"Shoes, missy." Lorna pointed to their room, and she ran off to get them.

"Mister Big Cheeks is out like a light. I think I will put him in the bassinet and take a quick nap, too. Good luck with the cake and your secret applesauce ingredient. See you about the time it comes out of the oven."

"Fine. I will try to keep Trudy quiet. Maybe we can have a picnic on the back porch."

"Lorna Rae?"

"Yes, Della." She popped the second apple into the pressure cooker and picked up her third victim, glancing over her shoulder.

"I really love you being here. Having us all together is precious to me. I just wanted you to know. Plus, I'm proud of your baking business. When my hands aren't as full, I would really like to help out."

"Sure thing, little sis. Nothing would make me happier. Now, go get some rest and don't worry about us." She shooed her away and began peeling the apple, so it could become part of her latest creation, a silly goose ABC cake. Well, the name would need some work.

Trudy bounced into the room, her shoes on opposite feet. Out the screen door she sailed to go catch a backyard butterfly. The door fell closed with a soft swish.

Lorna Rae set the apple into the pot and checked the sealing gasket on the lid. Aligning the two-piece pot, she clamped the seal and turned on the burner. She studied the timer and attempted to set it to four minutes, give or take a few. After she cooled and strained the applesauce, she would dabble with the ingredients and test the new recipe. What an enjoyable day's work. Now, Della wanted to join her with the baking. Oh, joy. Pure apple-almond joy.

~

Duncan stepped up to the counter and watched the mail clerk sort a leather pouch of mail into private post office boxes. "Afternoon, Jimmy. How are you getting along today?"

He put down the pouch and approached the front counter. "Pretty top notch, thank you. Is it raining out there yet?"

"Hey, you seem more tan and full of steam than the last time I saw you. Two stamps today, please."

"Yes, sir. My father likes to say, 'You can't keep a good man down.' Guess I am proving him right." He dropped his chin and tugged the drawer open to retrieve the stamps.

Duncan reached into his pocket and withdrew some change. "Why, you truly are a testimonial for perseverance, all right."

"Well, don't go putting my picture on any posters just yet. I am making due just fine, though. Mr. Peterson says I am the quickest learner he's ever seen. So maybe this diversion is good for me. I may make a career out of being a postal clerk. Who knows?" He slid the two stamps onto the counter. "Six cents, please."

Duncan slid a nickel and a penny toward the young man. "Listen, I plan to have my kid brother visiting next week, on leave from the U.S. Navy. I bet he is about your age. Maybe we'll stop in, so I can introduce him to you."

"That would be swell, sir. Has he seen any action?"

"As much as Korea can dish out, I suppose. I will let him tell you all about it. Thanks for the stamps. Now, I have no excuse—I have to write my mother."

"Try to stay out of that doghouse, sir, or you may end up looking like something out of a Dennis the Menace cartoon strip."

"Ha! Right you are, Jimmy. Thanks again, and I'll stop in again next week." He waved with the stamps and headed for the door, his mind echoing with the man's "diversion" comment. He wondered what to do with it. He would write it up as part of his report to Mr. McNaughton, though it hardly seemed noteworthy. As victims went, Jimmy Cantor seemed to be the only one able to make peace with it, as Dennis Gregory had left the company, and Glen Forshee could hardly breathe, let alone get back to work.

Duncan came up the sidewalk rubbing the two stamps between his fingers, his mind locked a million miles away. Someone thumped him on the shoulder right in front of the grocery.

Vivian looked up at him with a knowing smile that played mischief in her eyes. "Hello, Mr. Reed. Did your smokestack boss get gone?" She shifted her paper sack and clamped the hand of her youngest son, who tried to wander off the walkway.

"Goodness yes. Now, I can hatch a thought without his prompting it—not all of which were positive, mind you. How is your week going?"

"Hot and hotter. I am welcoming the rain this afternoon, actually. I took the children over to the library, and they all have book to read. Let the rain cool things off. The Deckers are ready."

"Sounds like it. Hey, I wondered if I could borrow Lorna Rae's new address in Westport from you. I have been thinking about sending her a snapshot of the waterfall from Eureka Lake." A little trickle of embarrassment swept down the back of his neck at the personal request.

"Sure thing. I got my letter off yesterday. How about I put it inside your back door?"

"I would appreciate that. The door is not locked."

"Nobody locks anything around here, and for good reason."

"Because we are all honest people?"

"No, not at all. Because there's nothing to steal if they did break in. Ha! I could kill a burglar with my dirty clothes pile by the back door anyway. Keep that in mind if you ever sleepwalk and end up one bungalow short of a full trip."

"You are the best kind of crazy I ever did see, Vivian. Thanks in advance for the address. I have my stamps, so there's no excuse not to write."

"Well, I can think of one reason—if the right words don't come." She gave him a knowing look and turned up the sidewalk to head home.

"I am usually not at a loss for words. Not in this business."

"Let me venture a guess, your note to Westport has little to do with business." She looked at him with her clown expression and yanked the boy's hand to follow.

Duncan came up the clinic's sidewalk eyeing a dandy of a thunderhead cloud sitting on the western horizon. Maybe he could catch the top-of-the-hour weather bulletin on the radio as he finished transcribing his report to McNaughton. In an instant, he realized he needed three stamps, not two. He exhaled and tried to make a plan for the best use of the postage he purchased. In four steps, he knew the letter to his mother would wait. Besides, with Sam here at the end of the week, she could have news from them both. That sounded like a fine occasion for a phone call back home.

~

The rain pattered against the gutter as Lorna Rae stood at the back counter cutting the cake. Yellowed by three egg yolks, the cake looked impressive, but would it taste as good? She sliced a large rectangle and set it on the table in front of Steve. "Now, everyone please be honest. People will be spending an extra nickel for a taste of this cake, so I have to make it worth every penny."

"I want coffee with mine, Della." Steve pulled the dessert in front of him and gave it a once-over. "Step Number One—it looks delicious."

Della slid from her chair. "Want some coffee, Lorna Rae?"

"No thanks, I need to taste the cake without any interfering flavors." She cut a piece half the size of Steve's for Trudy and hoped the child wouldn't notice. Two more matching rectangles found their way to the table. The taste test officially began.

"Step Number Two—eat another bite." Steve half-laughed but stifled it with a huge fork-full of cake. He hummed his next comment.

"So moist, Lorna Rae. The almond cream turned out beyond expectation." Della shook her head and took another bite.

Trudy licked her lips and spread the filling in an arc beyond her tongue's retrieval. "This ABC cake is gweat."

"Oops. Looks like I may have to make napkins available for my patrons." Lorna Rae smiled before taking her first bite and sat patiently trying to assess her results. The creamy richness from the applesauce held the texture up, while the almond gave it a taunting taste that lingered on the palate. She had come up with a successful first effort, even if she tweaked the recipe a bit later on.

Steve hoisted his last bite in the air. "Hold down your costs. Forget the napkins. If they go around with crumbs on their mouth, count that as good advertising."

"Good from the inside out," Della replied. She winked across the table,

Lorna Rae soaked in the moment of support as thunder rumbled outside.

"It couldn't rain all weekend, could it?" A whine laced Steve's voice as he shoved back from the table and patted his middle. "I need to mow the grass Saturday. At this rate, it might be either too tall or too wet to cut."

Trudy finished the last of her cake and looked antsy to leave the table. "I like wain. It makes me feel cozy."

"You may be excused now, Trudy. I promise to read you a book after I finish the dishes." Lorna Rae took a sip of water and readied her taste buds for another analytical pass through her new recipe. Maybe the salt could be cut back a pinch.

Della stood and collected dishes off the table. "I need to fold some laundry while the baby is content. You really brought this recipe together, Lorna Rae. I would not change one thing for now. Maybe in the fall, you could do a pumpkin something-or-other."

"I was considering the same thing. Once again, great minds think alike." Lorna Rae rose and joined her sister at the sink. She rested her plate on the window sill and stared out at the pouring rain beyond the back porch. A streetlight on the next block lent a silvery sheen to the treetops below, and the whole world seemed magical.

Steve padded across the linoleum in his socked feet, which added a downbeat to the rain. "Guess I will catch the Jack Benny Show tonight."

Della rattled some plates into the dishpan. "You can hold your son while you're sitting."

"Nothing would please me more," Steve replied back up the hall.

"Except a second piece of cake." Della harrumphed after the comment, but soon giggled as she stepped into the laundry room to get her chore done.

Lorna Rae turned on the faucet and ran the water over the back of her hand until it felt hot enough. She found the dish soap and squirted a dollop of green liquid into the pan. Her thoughts began to drift elsewhere. For a moment she stood back in her own kitchen, a strange sensation because it felt so real.

"Here's a clean dish cloth to dry with," Della said as she passed by.

A tea towel landed across Lorna Rae's arm, a towel identical to the one she had pinned up as her kitchen curtain back at the bungalow. *Looks like mother gifted both of us with the same kitchen linens. How ironic.* A shudder rocked her shoulders as a humid breeze swept through the window. She reached to shut it but gave it a second thought, wanting to stay connected to the night. Worried that her cake might tumble off the sill, she brought it down and ate another bite. Yes, less salt would be better, but only a smidgen less.

~

The note card lay blank in front of him, its fold trying to

reacquaint the two sides of the paper. Duncan refused to let his know-it-all neighbor invoke writer's block on him at the mere mention of his choice of the right words. Right off the bat he had his first dilemma with the salutation. "Dear Lorna Rae" seemed much too personal. "Hey Lorna Rae" sounded like calling out a stranger.

He leaned back in the kitchen chair and locked his hands behind his head. The real source of his vexation hid. One second, it seemed like the friendly thing to do, share the waterfall photograph of a day mutually enjoyed. Call it a fond remembrance. The next second, he had to admit there was more to it. Restless, he stood up. He stole a glimpse of the photo up on the Frigidaire and saw the face of an angel, well-traced in curved cheeks and alluring eyes.

A silver-blue flash of lightning illuminated the night sky, so he closed the door to block out the thunder he knew would follow. He threw the lock and made the off-duty risk manager safe for the evening, but what about the rest of him? He paced the kitchen up and down its full length. "This is absurd. John Brown it, I will write what I want to write."

He settled back into the chair and the words came, line by line. He asked about Trudy and mentioned that Sam was due to arrive on the weekend, giving him an excuse to try out some tourist destinations around town. He added a teasing comment about her business pursuits and followed it with reassurance that she could go far if she aimed high.

When he pulled the pen from contact with the page, he realized the irony of what he had written. He might as well be sending her away with his blessing, far away on her voyage to success in the baking business. That would certainly make her happy, though he sensed the melancholy undertow of it himself. He added a line at the bottom about making friends with Vivian, since he knew it would lift her spirits. Before he could over-analyze it, he closed with a fond admission and signed his first name.

Cowardice tightened the skin on his back as he placed the waterfall photo into the heart of the note card and shoved the works into the envelope. In reckless abandon, he licked the seal and closed it, so he couldn't change his mind. Had it not been raining, he could have walked all the way to the postal drop, just to fend off the steam he had worked up over this attempt at communication. *What in the world am I doing?* Only thunder answered, and it failed to speak the tender language of the heart.

Chapter 11

Friday sat in his office like an unwelcomed visitor. Duncan looked at the wall calendar and could calculate that the maiming sequence had now bled down to single digits. A more discomforting week had never passed his way. Only his kid brother's arrival tomorrow would salvage his mental state, which could be weighed out as two parts angry and three parts exasperated.

He flipped through the personnel records that McNaughton had provided. Without exception, the laborers in the union had been employed at Coates Oil for less than five years. As he made a note of the similarity, he realized Harley Holmes fit that criterion also. Maybe he should ask Bert how long he had been employed to see if it would lead to any further discussion. He had a hunch that his neighbor did not fit this group, which might afford him an angle in.

McNaughton had been quick to point out that he had been lax with that particular trail of suspicion, adding to the friction he felt from the Washington office.

The telephone rang, and he pushed back to answer it. Dr. Lucas was out at Glen Forshee's place making a house call, according to his message board. Since McNaughton used the office line, he felt an obligation to man the phone. In two steps, he had the receiver in hand.

"Hello, Risk Management. How can I help you?" His words came clipped with impatience, but a long pause followed nonetheless. A commotion marred the background until the caller's breathing came loud and clear.

"Well, if this is Duncan Reed, you can help by coming to get me from this train station."

The words tumbled over in Duncan's mind until the image of the train station left no doubt. Sam had arrived early—a true harbinger of mercy. "You bet your spuds, I will. Gosh, it's good to hear from you—and a day early—but it could not be better timing for me. Which station is it? I can be on my way in two minutes."

"The passenger train station in Newton, Kansas. Go one block south of a gigantic grain elevator, if that helps." The commotion in the background increased another decibel.

"I will be there in an hour. Get your bags and stay put." Duncan heard the operator ask for another donation to the pay phone, so he hung up to forego the need for Sam to dig for pocket change. Energized with a break from routine, he strode to his desk, flipped the file closed, and tucked it away in a drawer. As he scrawled a brief note to the good doctor, the relief of being shed of the maiming case filled his lungs. Life away from work beckoned, and for the first time in a long time, he sorely wanted it.

~

Liam Torguson strolled up to the mechanic's shop, trying to look unassuming. "What do you say there, Swain?"

"Not much, Torgie. Got some repair work going today. That's all. A thorough shot of maintenance today will lend us better service for next week, right?" He leaned back under the hood of the drill rig truck and wiped the oil dip stick clean.

"Sometimes we can put off that upkeep. A few of us workers have met together to protect our interests against Mr. Coates' greed. We are planning to negotiate for better benefits and a safer workplace for the long run, I mean."

"Hmmm. Sounds like a labor union. That kind of thing always seems to benefit the average Joe, but I was not aware the likes of such might be happening around the oil fields. Besides, Mr. Coates has always been fair to me."

"Do you think he's gonna be fair to Glen Forshee? What about his medical bills, now that this moratorium on claims has been slammed down on us?"

Swain turned and reached for a can of Skelly Motor Oil, a

home-grown product. "Well, Forshee's entitled to benefits, as his accident happened prior to the clamp-down, or at least that's my understanding." He punctured a hole in the lid and soon had an amber-brown flow heading into the mouth of a funnel.

"But if the next victim isn't a pregnant woman walking into Doc's office to deliver her baby, they've got no coverage. You think about that, Swain. The oil field is dangerous work. We need better protection. That's what I came to say, so give it some thought." He kicked some dirt around on the shop floor to dust over a greasy spot as his words struck their target. Seconds ticked by, while the drill operator stuck to his task. "I can offer you membership in the union, if you sympathize with our cause and see the benefit of it."

Swain tipped the oil can up to slow the flow. "Yesterday, I came out here and did my job just fine, with no union representation. Come Monday, I hope to do the same, so I don't think I'm your man. Thanks for stopping by. I never get much company."

The refusal stinging his ears, Torguson stepped back into the light of day outside the shop entrance. He had to leverage the offer with one last twist of the tire iron, or he'd have no gain. "You know, for a man riding around on a risky hunk-of-junk like this drilling rig, you sure are leaving your fortune open to fate."

Swain shoved the dip stick in place and wiped his hands on a blue shop cloth. "Here's the difference between you and me, Torgie. You have fate, and I have faith in God. He's my fair representation. You ought to give it a try sometime."

Torguson spat his revulsion at the ground. Normally, he could see a sappy religious pitch coming from a mile away. He never figured Swain to be the preachy type, though. The whole faith thing left his offer dead in the water like an overloaded seaplane. "Well, try not to be surprised if you see our boys around. The rest of us believe in making this place better."

"Is Glen Forshee any better for getting under that rig? Ask yourself that, if you are heading up this union. They say a good leader sets the example, but I don't see you limping." Swain held up his hands to further provoke the open-ended question, while the blue cloth fluttered in the breeze.

Torguson had to leave a threat, his only way out. "A little

blood never hurt anything." He spat at the machine shed door and walked away, his temples throbbing and his fists clenched. With Swain flat out rejecting his bid for membership, he would have to find another way to stage the next accident. The cause had to move forward, despite the moratorium. The big man was on his knees. Swain represented a minor setback, that's all.

~

Lorna Rae caught the mail as it tumbled through the door slit, having seen the mailman coming up the front walk. Della had the baby down for his morning nap, and the house seemed quiet except for the squeak of the brass mail flap. With Trudy in the backyard playing horses in the sand, she had a few moments to sort through the mail stack.

Vivian's letter two days ago had been such a pleasant surprise. She had re-read its contents a dozen times. Vivian explained why Duncan had not come out to say goodbye. Not that he had any obligations to do so, but she had wondered a time or two what might have happened to him. A drop-in boss would be a real obstacle, a forgivable one.

She sifted through the mail. A postcard caught her attention, announcing a new store on the outskirts of Westport that offered an extended fresh fruit market right inside the grocery. She would have to discuss exploring that option with Della, since they could always stand to get a better bargain on apples for her cakes.

A smaller envelope eluded her grip and fell to the floor. When she bent to pick it up, she froze. It had her name printed in block lettering centered on the envelope like a business correspondence. The date stamp clearly showed it had originated in El Dorado. A wiggle of excitement that started up her backbone soon found itself thumb-pressed by a late-arriving worry. Had Harley left her some item of unfinished business, possibly an unpaid bill?

Lorna Rae stepped into the kitchen and deposited the rest of the mail at the built-in kneehole desk, where Steve conducted all the home business. Trudy made horsey noises that filtered through the screen door to tell her all remained well at the play corral. She slipped into her chair at the dinette table and placed the letter in front of her.

"Lord, please do not let this be some penalty for my having been Harley's wife. I hereby claim your freedom from any harm and healing from all that he tore off my well-being. On Monday, I am set to earn my first cake money, and you know I have supplies to buy with it. Please do not let the contents of this letter detract from that sum. I am begging for your protection, in Jesus' name, amen."

Her fingers trembled as she tore into the flap. The certainty of knowing would at least allow her to breathe without constriction. Then she could tackle the next hour, the rest of the day, and the open weekend ahead. Separating the contents from the envelope, she decided to save the paper to write out her next shopping list on, lending it a noble cause. She released such a deep breath, her shoulders dipped, until she straightened her spine and opened the card.

Her gaze locked onto the enclosed photograph tucked inside, the waterfall at Eureka Lake. Warmth from the memory flooded her senses, with so much water everywhere—and so much fun. She relaxed that day for the first time since Harley's death. The photo did the waterfall justice, and a ray of sunlight glimmered like magic in the pool below the falls. Part of a man's shadow had been trapped in the lower corner, his elbow extended while taking the shot.

Duncan. He had been the one with the camera that day. She folded the note card closed before her eyes betrayed her by peeking at the sender's signature to verify what she suspected. A rush of emotions took a fleeting run through her like a flash flood, washing away the dread she had prayed over only seconds before. "Thank you, God. Thank you so much. I think. Wait, I know. In your mercy, this penalty of being married to Harley remains behind me, in my past. I am so blessed by it, dear Lord, amen."

She opened the note card and placed her left hand strategically over the bottom to block the signature. She planned to tackle this message one line at a time and would not rush it. An old friend had taken the time to write, so she would honor that effort, even savor it. The block print helped her divide her attention to each word, like bricks building a message.

Dear Lorna Rae,

Sitting here in your kitchen during a drenching rain brings you and Trudy to mind. I hope you are well and the cake business has taken the Westport area by chocolate storm. Life seems to be drained from the oil fields lately, and I even noticed your path over to Vivian's has begun to grass over. Alas, I need to be a better neighbor. The waterfall picture came back so vivid, I thought you might like to have it, a cascading memory of a day well-spent. I'm looking forward to my kid brother coming by week's end, a real break from work.

Lorna Rae marveled at the flowing sentiment and wanted to read more, yet she hesitated to pull her hand away to reveal the close of the letter. How funny that nine-tenths of her go-ahead could be held in check by one-tenth of her whoa-up a minute. The horses whinnied outside and the impulse to pray again struck her. She closed her eyes and folded her hands together.

"Lord, you know what's best for me, but I clearly don't. Now that I know it's not a bill, I can hardly react. Forgive me for always suspecting the worst, when that's truly not your way. I release that negative mindset and claim your word when it says to think upon whatsoever things are true, honest, just, pure, lovely or of good report. I do receive this letter of good report from back home. Please bless its honorable intent and direct my heart according to your will, amen."

Emboldened, Lorna Rae dropped her gaze on the final line of the correspondence.

Reach me through Doc Lucas if you need to. Thinking of you fondly, Duncan

Her eyes played back and forth between the last two words. Not only had he been honest enough to admit he had been thinking of her, but he had qualified it. Something like a warm marshmallow expanded inside her as she sat in a borrowed kitchen where nothing belonged to her. Her entire world seemed to float in midair.

Della touched her shoulder as she walked by to check outside the back door. "Oh that Robert Thomas, he would steal my last second on earth, if I offered it to him."

"Well, you happily would, if it came right down to it." Lorna closed the note and slid it back into the envelope. This time touching the paper seemed more private, without any trace of pending threat.

"So who is your letter from? Another friend?"

"Yes. It's from the safety manager who moved into our old place. He is watching our furnishings for us. Duncan claims the path Vivian and I wore between the bungalows has begun grassing over, so things obviously don't stay the same for very long."

"Is he ready to move out or something?"

"No, he's just staying in touch. Oh, and he sent me a photo of the waterfall the day of the company picnic. Trudy had him jump into the creek to rescue a turtle that had been flushed out of the lake. The story had a happy ending. We released the turtle and went for a bike ride around the lake together, so he could dry off. Trudy slept the whole way in my bike basket."

"Wow. He sounds nice. Is he available?"

"Only to his work. He's on temporary assignment to improve the safety of the workers on the oil field. Duncan Reed is probably the smartest man I have ever met."

"Okay, that is quite a compliment. He must be ugly as a frog, or you would have said something more promising than the fact he's smart."

"Not at all, but I am not susceptible to nice-looking men that only have eyes for their careers. In fact, I am not looking at men with any interest at all, unless they want to buy or sell my cakes."

"So he *is* nice-looking—and he's written you a note. I'd say that holds some interest."

"You know going back to El Dorado is the furthest thing on my mind. But Duncan *is* crazy about my cake. He came up with my tagline 'good from the inside out' after he suggested I serve a dropped cake with the frosting pressed to the inside."

"I think perhaps his heart is also 'good from the inside out.' Are you going to write him back?"

"Maybe I will next week, after I see how my sales did at the butcher shop."

"Next week will be twice as busy as this week. Remember, you are starting the big cakes at the deli on Monday."

"You are insightful, little sister. Let me go put this in my room. Be right back."

"I will get the broom for you in the meantime."

"The broom? Why?"

"Let's just say somebody's horse corral leaked sand all the way across the back porch."

"Ooh, that little girl. She would steal my last second on earth, if I offered it to her." Lorna Rae stole a glance back over her shoulder and saw Della shaking her head. She gave her a wink as her fingers played over the envelope that had arrived bearing good tidings. *Thinking of me fondly. Will wonders never cease?* She stepped into her room and dropped the note onto her dresser. When the waterfall came back to mind, she paused long enough to retrieve the photograph and secured it into the frame of the bureau's mirror. In the corner stood a shadow-man, one she also remembered fondly. So what would she do with that?

Chapter 12

Duncan rested the duffle bag on the top step and turned to help Sam manage the ascent. He wished there had been some way to communicate Sam's injury to the Hansen women, but he had simply run out of time. "Mrs. Hansen, this is my brother Sam Reed. Sam, this is Ina Hansen and her daughter Daphne."

Sam bumped his helping hand away and drew up one step, then stopped to clutch his sailor's hat off in respect for the women. "My pleasure, Mrs. Hansen. Daphne, how are you?"

Duncan glanced up when he heard Daphne gasp in response and couldn't stop the embarrassment from filtering up his neck. Once he saw her expression, he knew that Sam's injury had nothing to do with her reaction. The two seemed down-right starstruck on each other.

"Daphne, remember your proper manners, please." Mrs. Hansen winged the young woman in the side with her elbow, which only managed to shut her gaping mouth.

"I can have Sam stay in the bungalow with me in town, if this isn't going to work out for you." Duncan spoke in a half-whisper, his attempt to target the proprietor with the room for rent.

Mrs. Hansen knit her brow and looked from one brother to the other. "Nonsense, we have been expecting him for nigh two weeks, and we want him to stay here and rest. Isn't that still your objective?"

"I sure want to stay," Sam replied. "I mean, there is no need to change plans now, since I am here and the room is ready. Right?"

"At least one of you Reeds is being practical. Come along, Sam. Daphne has baked some cookies we can enjoy." Mrs. Hansen dropped back out of the doorway to let him come in, which he did without any hesitation.

Duncan bent to retrieve the bag and found it amusing that Daphne seemed to be a permanent fixture in the doorway. He stepped inside and felt a nudge to show some tenderness to the girl. "Sam has been wounded, Daphne, and they lacked room in the clinic to treat him because he was better off than most, so they sent him to me."

She turned to face him while tears rolled over the rim of her cornflower blue eyes. "Dear Lord above. I have been praying for faceless men halfway around the world, and here God sends a ministry right to my own front door."

"He doesn't need your pity, though—"

"Mercy, no, Mr. Reed. He needs Christian compassion. Please, give me a chance." She wrung her hands as if trying to appear convincing.

"His skin graft needs treatment, at night and in the morning, with a special topical cream. Your mother can—"

"No, arthritis has her fingers tied in knots. I will do the treatments and count it my part in the war effort."

"So tell me why you got so frozen up back there when Sam arrived, if you don't mind." Duncan tried to ease off on his commandeering tone, but so used to interrogation to get the desired results, he may have overcommitted his resources.

The woman's face turned ten shades of red, accentuating her blue eyes as she shook her head. Strands of blonde hair that had escaped her braid fell across her face. She reached up and cleared the strays. "Because I am a silly nineteen-year-old woman who lives out in the boonies and never gets any decent company." Her bottom lip trembled and then she began to laugh.

Touched by her honesty, Duncan chuckled with her and gestured down the hallway.

"Besides, Sam is way better looking than you are. I wasn't expecting that."

"Oh, that is only the mystique of a man in uniform." Duncan

grinned and dropped the bag at the foot of the stairs before walking ahead to find Sam.

"Plus, he's not so old," Daphne added.

Duncan winced, but he hoped she hadn't seen it. The hallway opened into the kitchen where he found his brother, his much younger brother, leaning on the counter beside the sink.

"These are the absolute best cookies ever." Sam made another one disappear.

Daphne cleared some imaginary crumbs from the counter as an excuse to step closer to him. "Why thank you, Sam. I hope you are used to eating good food, because mother and I love to cook."

Sam smiled as he chewed and nodded at Duncan about the time Mrs. Hansen held out the cookie tray.

"Don't mind if I do. Might we have a few words in the front room, Mrs. Hansen?"

"By all means, Mr. Reed. Daphne, see to getting something to drink for Sam, will you?"

"Yes, mother. I would be delighted."

Duncan walked through the little-used formal dining room and noticed a thin layer of dust collecting on the walnut table. He had chosen the most direct route to get away from the cloying scene in the kitchen and hoped he had not trespassed into some forbidden zone.

"What is it, Mr. Reed? You seem out of kilter about something."

"Mrs. Hansen. I have paid for room and board, but now there's something more. I didn't know at the time I reserved it, but Sam is injured. A steam burn was so severe they had to do a skin graft. He requires medication with a topical cream on his back twice daily. I will have to impose on your good graces—"

"No imposition in the least, my friend. This young man is serving our country. Why, it's an honor to help him, not a duty. Not at all."

"Daphne mentioned your arthritis, ma'am. I would not want to cause a hardship for you. She claimed she would do the medicating for you but it seems, well, they seem kind of struck with one another. I don't know how else to put it."

"Leave it to me, Mr. Reed. I can chaperone the medicating, even if she's doing the direct application. About their being struck at first sight, you know Daphne well enough. Time will knock those stars right out of her eyes."

Duncan studied the woman's lined face, hunting for wisdom on human behavior where he had none. If nothing else, they could do a trial run. "Okay, for now, we will keep with our original plan. We should know soon enough if it won't work out. I expect you to be honest with me, Mrs. Hansen, if the chaperoning gets to be too much."

"I am honest with everyone, Mr. Reed. It's a tenet of my Christian faith, after all."

"Yes ma'am. I am just saying if problems develop, he can some stay with me at the bungalow.

"At least here, he has a soft bed—not a sofa—and two cooks." Her expression softened.

She had him beat. He fought back a smile, but couldn't quite manage it. "That trumps me by a bed and at least one cook."

Her bent fingers wrapped around his forearm in reassurance. "Sam will be in good hands here. Let's allow him to rest."

"What about when you come to town on your egg runs?" He asked mainly to test her, but they did need to have a plan in place.

"Then Daphne can come with me, or maybe if Sam's up to it, they can both accompany me. I could use the help."

"I agree, but we cannot leave them alone. We have to protect Daphne's reputation." Duncan had Sam's well-being more in mind, but wouldn't couch his concern in those terms.

"As usual, your honor accompanies your name, Mr. Reed. You have my agreement and my cooperation. Can you still join us for the cookout we had planned for tomorrow?"

"You give me a time, and I will be here."

"See you at high noon then. That gives us time to get the barbeque going after Daphne gets Sam's back doctored up."

"Let him sleep late if he's able. He is probably exhausted from the train trip."

"We can adjust the cookout accordingly. Please take his bag up to his bedroom before you leave. He certainly does not need to be lifting that heavy thing."

"Will do. Anything else?"

"Extend a bit of trust that we will be good for your brother. Watch and see. Farm life has a way of bringing out the best in people."

"I bet you're right." He winked at her and headed for the foyer to take the duffle bag up to his old room. As he ascended the stairs, he remembered helping Lorna Rae shove her box springs up that same rise. When he stepped into the bedroom, the dresser mirror revealed a smile on his face. Satisfaction made him look younger, much younger.

~

Saturday held a leisure aspect to it that offered Lorna Rae a welcome adjustment. With Steve home, the house seemed to bustle with activity. Once baby Robert had gone down for his morning nap, they had all teamed up to tackle the yard work. A narrow bed of neglected iris bloomed in profusion without any fawning attention. The purple bearded iris made her think of Vivian. She knelt and pulled out handfuls of nut-grass that had invited itself into the bed.

Della fixed a bandana over her ears and dropped to the base of the lilacs by the back porch to rid them of the unwanted volunteers. "Oh, tarnation. All this rain is making everything grow—especially the weeds."

"My neighbor Vivian has iris this same color. She claims Kansas can grow anything starting out as a bulb better than any other place under the sun."

"She's right about that. How I love perennials. They are so much less work. I used to plant annuals out front, but this spring I could scarcely bend over that far, so Steve planted some tulips and lily of the valley bulbs for me."

Lorna Rae pulled at a hardy dandelion until she heard the taproot snap. "I envy—no—I admire the way you and Steve work together, Della. That teamwork approach is so refreshing." She threw the plucked weed on top of an accumulating pile.

"Oh, we used to dream about what we could do if we had a place of our own, how hard we would work together to take care of it. Then we saw this place while riding through the neighborhood one weekend. It captivated our imaginations. We both felt it was the right place, and Steve got the financing all lined up to make it happen. That was a year and a half ago."

"I am ashamed that we never came to see you, Del. I couldn't talk Harley into anything for my side of the family. But come

Sunday, all roads led back to Rosalia and his mother's fried chicken dinner."

"I knew things were not good for you, Lorna Rae. I asked, but Mother would hardly say peep about you and Harley. She told me every married couple has to find their own way."

"That might have been true, if we had been a real couple. Guess what I had was more like bondage than marriage, but God looked down and must have pitied my plight. I am thankful for my freedom now and plan to make the most of it."

Della stood and dusted off the knees of her dungarees. She strolled over and cast a shadow over the iris bed. "Does that mean you decided not to write Mr. Reed back? Does freedom mean not interested?"

Something haunting hung on Della's earnest question, and Lorna Rae's first instinct to brush off the inquiry left her short of satisfied with the curt approach. "Time to be honest here. Duncan Reed is a friend, a genuine friend. Plus, he is good with Trudy. But he's wrapped up in his work and besides, I don't think he sees me as…Well, this is not the stuff romance is made of, I'm afraid."

Della came closer and picked up her weed pile. "Uh-huh. You say that, but what you mean is that *you* aren't the stuff romance is made of. Lorna Rae, you are becoming a successful business woman and have a bright future ahead of you. With your sparkling green eyes and hourglass figure, added to such a great personality, you are bound to attract some male attention. So here's some advice—choose the perennial over the fussy annuals. You will know what that means when the time comes but, believe me, there's a huge difference in upkeep." She smirked and walked over to the trash can.

Lorna Rae finished with the iris bed as the last of the nut-grass surrendered to her pinching fingers. She thought about how she felt the moment the waterfall picture fell out of the envelope. The first wave of emotion may have been relief, but the second wave hinted of intrigue. Duncan had a sharp eye for capturing the day through his lens, and he had proven to be a fairly good listener on the bike ride. His note had been cordial. Why wouldn't she write back and let him know how they were doing? She could update him on her business success as well.

Della passed by, dusting the dirt off her gardening gloves. "I am shifting around front to work on the hedge clippings, and then I can check on Robert."

"Hey, Del—I decided to write him back. Just a friend-to-friend kind of note, though."

"I bet he would appreciate that. Wish we had a picture to send back to Duncan. Remind me to get the camera out the next time my kitchen counter is full of cakes. We should document the start-up of your business, anyway."

"Great idea. You would make somebody a fantastic assistant, do you know that?"

"How about a baking lesson with your recipe instead?"

"Okay, baking school will be in session come Monday morning." Lorna Rae stood as Della gave a victory gesture and disappeared through the gate. She flexed her knees and glanced around the yard to identify the next trouble spot.

Steve walked past her heading toward the shed in the back corner. "Hey, you may want to switch to the front yard. I plan to start mowing back here and don't want anyone in harm's way. Besides, Trudy has a toad trapped under the front hedge and plans to capture him for a pet. Some parental intervention may be in order."

Lorna Rae sighed and walked through the gate. That active little girl sure kept things interesting for her. The backwards-floating turtle popped into mind, followed by a remembrance of the uninhibited turtle rescuer. At least Duncan had taken a turn at quelling Trudy's mischief at the lake. No, a brief note couldn't hurt, a friendly little conversation on paper that was all one-way and highly non-committal. She would write it this afternoon during Trudy's nap, if Della had a spare sheet of paper and an envelope. She crossed the front sidewalk and found Trudy, bottom up under the hedge.

"What are you doing down there, baby girl?"

"Making a new fwiend, Mommy."

"Try not to touch the toad, Trudy. He doesn't want to be touched."

"Oh, he likes it, I tell you."

Determined to put a stop to this particular capture, Lorna Rae reached for her daughter and lifted her backwards out of the hedge. To her amazement, the toad came along, locked in Trudy's hands.

She sat the girl on her feet. The critter managed to wiggle free at the same moment. With the most amazing leap, it disappeared back into the hedge.

"See you later, Ollie."

"Thank you, Lord Jesus." Lorna grabbed Trudy's arm and brought the girl up to the front spigot to wash her hands.

Trudy bent closer as the water started to flow. "What a gweat place foah toads."

"Not today it isn't," Lorna Rae replied. She rubbed her little hands clean awhile trying to stay out of the mud. "But it is good frog weather with all this rain."

"Wain makes lots of flowahs. And I like flowahs."

"You sure do, doll baby. Maybe you can color a flower next, and we will send it back to Mr. Reed for watching over our old house for us."

"Oh, goodie-goodie. Can we go in?"

"I need to check first. We do not want to wake up the baby."

"No chance of that," Della replied from the front door. In her arms the baby stretched, his mouth a circular bug trap.

Lorna Rae nodded to the side gate where Steve was busy making his outline run. "Don't blame the lawn mower." She stepped onto the porch and tweaked the baby's bare leg.

"Oh, I don't. I blame the man pushing the mower. He thinks we need to acclimate the baby to background noise, so he can learn to sleep more soundly."

"It sounds good in theory." Lorna scooted Trudy in between them and modeled wiping her feet. Trudy copied her every move.

"Theory, schmeory. His mommy needs him to take a full-length nap."

"Remember that teamwork approach, little sister." She snickered and came inside out of the overbearing June sun.

Della cradled the baby to and fro as if to make him drop back off again. "Teamwork, schmemwork."

"Hey, got any spare paper for my letter to Duncan? I might give it a go after lunch."

"Now you are talking. Just follow me, Miss Lo-Rae Cakes, Incorporated."

Lorna Rae poked at the baby, but couldn't miss Della's look of approval launched over her lowered brow. "Trudy is going to color him a flower, too, a nice friendly gesture." A little heat prickled up her neck. She couldn't remember friendship feeling like this before.

~

Duncan checked his watch. It read half past noon. "He slept this late?"

Mrs. Hansen gave him a sheepish look. "It would have been even later, but I accidently dropped a hymnbook on the landing. Sam is getting his morning shower now. You can help me set up the grill out back, while Daphne sees to his back medication."

"I am happy to help set up the grill, but since I'm here, shouldn't I do the application of the ointment? It only makes sense to me, being his brother and all."

"Well, are you good with that kind of care-giving, Mr. Reed?"

"I am not sure, but it's high time we find out. Show me your grill while I wait. We need to get those charcoals lit." He headed for the backdoor and walked out onto the patio. With the midday sun overhead, not a sliver of shade fell anywhere. "An awning would be handy back here. Keep that in mind, Mrs. Hansen, when you are ready to spruce up the place."

"This house has anchored a working farm for years, Mr. Reed. Mr. Hansen never took time for leisure. His brother gave us this grill, but Mil thought it a bother. I like the way it makes a good cut of beef taste, so I think it is well worth the bother, I guess."

"Thank you for including Sam and me in the extra effort, then. I could probably throw myself into that same all-work and no-play category. Then one day a man looks up and life has gotten away from him."

"Ah, you're much too young to talk like that."

"Not according to Daphne." With a grimace, he pulled the grill away from the house and ran the wire brush over the rim.

"Let me get the lighter fluid for you." She opened a storage room door and rummaged on a shelf that sat considerably askew.

He gestured with the brush. "Looks like a little carpentry work might be in order for that shelf." When he looked around for the bag of charcoal, he spotted it next to the storage room.

"Without a man around, some of that upkeep slips through the cracks."

Sam pulled the towel around his shoulders to better cover his bare torso. "Well, I am here now. I can tackle some of your projects, Mrs. Hansen. Be glad to."

"Hello, Rip Van Winkle. You might not be in any shape to take on farm work." Duncan slid the brush onto its hook and lifted the bag of charcoal. He poured a reasonable amount into the grill and sat the bag back on the patio.

"I only have heavy lifting restrictions and some range of motion issues. Believe me, my back will tell me when I try to do too much. Mrs. Hansen, I am ready for Daphne to apply that medicine now. Would you be available to come in with us?"

Duncan stepped forward. "Sam, let me take a crack at it, since I'm here and everything. After all, I have taken care of my kid brother before. Let me get this charcoal lit first."

Mrs. Hansen started to say something, but seemed to think better of it, handing him the metal container of igniter fluid. "Oh my, I forgot about the matches. Just a minute, Mr. Reed."

"I want you to call me Duncan, since this is a social visit." He splattered the fluid across the charcoal briquettes, until he felt satisfied it would light well. In seconds, Mrs. Hansen came back out and handed him the match pad. For a second, it triggered thoughts of his case, but he breathed a sigh of relief when no markings identified the matchbook. He tore a match out and struck it. With a flick of his wrist, it fell into the grill bottom and flames whirled full-circle.

"Let's get this ointment done. Where is Daphne, Mrs. Hansen?" Sam looked across the farm yard as if to search out an answer.

"She is still upstairs in her room. She must be fixing her hair."

Duncan leaned the grill grate against the charcoal bag. "I will take it from here. These coals need at least twenty minutes. Let me come back and check the heat before you put the meat on, okay?"

"Fine, Duncan. Give a shout if you need anything up there." She gave him a hesitant nod and returned to the kitchen behind Sam.

Duncan walked into the familiar house and headed for the sink to wash up. He heard Sam padding up the stairwell over his rhythmic splashing. He cranked the faucet off and dried his hands. The doctor was ready to operate.

Daphne stood in the doorway speaking to Sam in soft,

inaudible tones. When Duncan appeared at the top of the stairs, she skittered down the hall to her room, a long braid thumping against her back.

Duncan walked by the bed. The inflamed skin graft caught his attention. Adhered to Sam's right shoulder blade, it resembled the shape of the continent of Africa, puffy-edged and volcanic. He slowed his step and tried to imagine the pain Sam had lived through already. "Hey champ. Where is the tube of medicine?"

"On the table here." Sam's voice rumbled up through the pillow. He laid arms out, positioned flat for the application. "No wise cracks, either."

"No buddy. I am here to help. How much of this should I squeeze out each time?"

"Size of a BB. It goes a long way. I need to make that tube last. Put it right on the inflamed edge."

Duncan removed the cap and ran the tapered tip over his middle finger. He gave the tube a squeeze until a small bead of ointment dispensed. Stiff-bodied, the bead glistened in the indirect light. "Hold still now, I am coming with it." He bent and reached across Sam's left shoulder to deliver the requisite application. His judgment of the distance proved a bit off, and he contacted the skin graft with considerable more momentum than he had intended. The ointment slid across the seam of the target.

A volcano erupted. "May-day, I'm hit—" No longer muffled, Sam's voice escalated with his sharp pain. "Lord help. You are killing me, Duncan. Oh, heaven above, please help me."

The sound of footsteps came to the doorway as Duncan allowed the hurt of his brother's retort to infuse his frame. He had done the last thing on earth he'd intended—to cause Sam more pain. His stomach tightened so much, it soon became impossible to inhale.

Daphne stood in the doorway, her eyes fixed on the skin graft. When she lifted her gaze, it turned steely. "Get out. You cannot do this work, so get out."

"Please," Sam added. A sob punctuated the request, quickly followed by a quake across his shoulders.

Numb from the cataclysmic turn of events, Duncan stepped toward the door. He handed the ointment tube to Daphne without looking up from the oval braided rug at the bedside. "Your mother will be right up.”

Daphne sniffed and scooted by him into the room. She said something soothing to Sam and placed a fingertip on his left shoulder to comfort him. Her touch resembled a feather floating to rest atop a down comforter, a mirage of contact.

Duncan descended the stairway half-conscious. By the time he had gotten to the bottom, Mrs. Hansen stood there, her Bible in her hand. “They need you upstairs.”

She nodded and gave him a knowing look. “You watch the coals for me, will you?”

Nothing short of a dismissal, he worked to swallow his wounded pride. “I blew my chance in there.”

“God sees your intent, Duncan. You can be tenderhearted, yet come across heavy-handed.” She took a couple of steps and looked back. “Your brother won’t hold it against you. We will be down in a bit. The short ribs are on the top shelf of the Frigidaire if the grill is ready before we are.”

“Let him know how much I regret what happened—”

“Take it to your heavenly Father. That is where ultimate forgiveness lives.”

“That is the right place to start. Maybe afterward, I can forgive myself.” He wandered into the kitchen and spotted a bluebird perched on the electric line through the window. He turned the faucet on to wash the remnant of the ointment off his fingertip. The bird spooked with the running water noise and took wing. “Yeah, scary man on the loose.” His chide echoed around the empty kitchen. He felt hollow inside. The prayer came to his lips about the time his feet hit the threshold. Being outside soon eased the vise inside him. Now, nothing stood between God and him except a mile or so of June-blue sky.

~

Dear Duncan,

> *How sincerely kind of you to think of us with the waterfall picture. We had a most enjoyable day at Eureka Lake in your distinguished company. I am sending heartfelt thanks for your thoughtfulness. Trudy sends you her special flower in return.*
>
> *So much has happened here, and all truly wonderful. The cakes are selling! I have a distributor here in Westport,*

a butcher shop no less, but they have high volume sales and will serve Lo-Rae Cakes well. When I rode into downtown with Steve to garner business in the heart of Kansas City, I secured a verbal contract with Buckner's Deli located right on The Plaza. They want big cakes, uncut, and have asked for a selection to alternate with my infamous chocolate recipe. I have worked up a blonde applesauce cake with almond cream filling. Unfortunately, I find myself woefully short of any cake testers with experience fixing dropped cakes, so I must make due. Even today, Della has requested baking lessons. I am so flattered she wants to be a part of this endeavor.

Before closing, let me gush over my new nephew, Robert Thomas. He is such a good baby, sleeping and feeding on schedule. His cry is more like a kitten's mewling because he already knows he has his mother at his beck and call! In the evening I love nothing more than to rub my nose across his downy cheek and coo into his ear that his family loves him dearly. Trudy calls him Bobby to avoid her R trouble and is most tender whenever she takes notice of him. Mostly she tends her corral of toy horses in a sandbox by the back porch. I lose myself in the blooming iris out back, thinking of Vivian and all I left behind at the oil fields.

I pray that you are well and have kept everyone on the job safe this week. You are doing a most important work, but the irony that the safety manager seems to be the one at greatest risk does not escape me. May the little bungalow by the cottonwood tree shelter you from all harm, and may God shine his favor upon you both night and day. Should you come up to Kansas City someday, I would be honored to show you my cakes on sale to the public for five cents apiece. If thoughts are but a penny, I wonder what five cents worth would buy an entrepreneur like me to learn what might be on your mind.

Living life like a gift, because I get to, not because I have to—Rae

Lorna Rae fell back onto the bed, exhausted from the full day of domestic chores. A light emotion ran through her veins having written from so close to her heart. Duncan probably would not give the letter five seconds of attention, as busy as he stayed. Silently, she switched off the bedside lamp and untied her robe, ready for bed. The air lay heavy in the room as the threat of rain returned. Only the toad in the hedge would be happy about that. Come Monday, she had cakes to deliver. Cardboard boxes turned notoriously flimsy in the rain.

She thought back to her first dropped cake and how Duncan's admiration of it had remained undeterred. Perhaps there was more sturdiness to appreciate there than met the eye, which was more than what she could say for her cake boxes. The letter would serve as an apt messenger and, if he needed a friend, it would find its place like a bird nesting under the eaves of a house, out of the rain. Yes, definitely out of the rain.

Chapter 13

Duncan glanced out his office window and saw that Mrs. Hansen's Monday egg run had yielded his brother as a tag-along. He could not have been more pleased. He grabbed the letter to his mother and pushed the screen door aside to catch up with them. After helping deliver the eggs securely, he would invite Sam to the post office to meet Jimmy Cantor. He had sat on the bungalow's front porch late last night and prayed over it, among many other concerns.

"Good morning, Mrs. Hansen. Have your hens been generous this morning?" He smiled and gestured to take the wagon's handle, but Sam had no compulsion to relinquish it.

She fanned her face and kept walking to the store. "Yes. They gave above and beyond the regular. Those old girls must like the heat, but I cannot say as much for this old bird."

He remembered the eggs were heat-sensitive and picked up his stride to catch up with Sam. "How did your treatment go this morning? To suit you, I mean?"

"Soft and smooth without a moment's pain. I think the graft is healing faster now. Must be that fresh country air." Sam flashed him a tight smile, but his eyes hinted of something more enjoyable.

At a crossroads, Duncan could make mention of the angelic nurse now in charge of the treatments, or let it go unspoken so as not to call attention to the magnetic situation. Never a fan of romantic affinity, he opted for the silent treatment. "Mrs. Hansen, I have put a small sum on your account in the grocery store here, so if you want to add something beyond your basic provisions, say ingredients for a tasty dessert, you have the liberty to do so."

"Why, thank you, Duncan. I will be sure to pick up that cornmeal breading for our fish fry this evening."

He pulled the screen door open. "You are planning a fish fry?"

Sam wheeled the cart right in. "Daphne is in the garden digging worms for our adventure. I can hardly wait."

"Mil used to fish the stocked pond out east of the barn, but it hasn't seen much action lately. I thought fried fish sounded tasty for supper." Mrs. Hansen nodded to Mr. Anders, the grocer, and went down the aisle with her head held high.

Duncan let the fishing outing mosey around in his head, as he had wanted to keep Sam available for a possible get-together with Jimmy Cantor. His next idea shined down straight from heaven. Maybe Jimmy would want to go fishing. "Mrs. Hansen. Would you please plan to fix enough food for company tonight? I have a young friend over at the post office I have wanted Sam to meet. They are about the same age. We might invite him out to fish, if that's okay."

"Fine. We are already having company, but she's just family. My sister and her husband are going over to Hesston to purchase new haying equipment and plan to leave my teenage niece with us for the day."

"Then it would be a rescue of sorts, as I would not want Sam here to be overwhelmed with two fair lasses." Duncan raised a brow at his brother, who didn't register any appreciation for the interference. He lifted the first carton of eggs and handed them to her.

She placed the carton into the display and raised her hand for the next one. "Kathleen is the true belle of the family, but I have learned to find the beauty amid the brokenness. Except for my eggs, of course."

Sam handed over a carton and held one at bay. "I cannot remember the last time I went fishing. I am looking forward to it, that's for sure. Is there shade out there by any chance? I have to limit my sun exposure."

She accepted the next carton as a look of satisfaction softened her face. "Yes, by two o'clock, the elms on the western rim provide a bank of shade. Let's plan to eat lunch together, and then you can take the girls out midafternoon."

"I need to borrow Sam here while you do your shopping, Mrs. Hansen. Please take your time. After the post office, we will head back to my office, so meet us up there if you will."

"Yes, thank you both for your help. When you two work together, the Reed family resemblance is unmistakable. Maybe I *will* browse the produce section to see if any berries have shown up yet for a cobbler. One cannot rush the season, though."

"Heaven forbid we rush into anything." Duncan waggled his eyebrows with the tease, and she gave him a chuckle in response. He stepped toward the door and waved his letter at her to bid her farewell.

Sam lumbered up behind him at the screen door. "Is that a letter to Mother?"

"Yes, it is. I try to be regular while I am away, so she doesn't worry."

"I owe her one myself. Say, could I scrawl something about my recovery on the envelope there before you mail it?"

Duncan pulled the pen from his pocket and handed it to him. He walked out of the door, but remained on the covered porch to enjoy the shade it offered. The letter soon pressed against his back, so he leaned forward to play desktop for his kid brother. When the writing motion slowed, he set some framework for the next encounter. "Sam, I have a feeling about this young man at the post office. He could use a good Christian friend. Most of this is personal, but I wanted you to know he is involved in the case under investigation for work."

"I am not your infiltrator, am I?"

"By no means. I hoped you two might strike up a friendship while you're here, that's all. Let me introduce you, and we will see where it goes from there. If you feel good about it, invite him to go fishing with you guys this afternoon. No strings attached."

Sam swatted the letter into his midsection and looked at him uncertain. "And what? Four people are better than three around the old fishing hole?"

"Two's company and three's a crowd, so I guess four people really make two couples having a good time." He stepped out of the shade toward the post office, but didn't miss the grin that rode his brother's face as they departed. He had fallen right into that providential math lesson. He hoped it would add up to a table full of fish to eat for supper—and nothing more.

~

Lorna Rae walked into the downtown post office, her letter to Duncan riding the top of a cake box. The vaulting lobby almost took her breath away, easily the largest building she had ever been inside. Her footsteps echoed on the marble floor as she headed to the service counter. She needed postage and a whole lot more. Patrons were stacked three deep in two separate lines. She studied her options and selected the stouter clerk. The hope that her bait would find some receptivity there rose with each tick of the clock, adding needless stress.

The woman ahead of her requested a large quantity of stamps. The clerk had to step away and access his reserves. Upon his return, Lorna Rae managed to catch his apologetic gaze and nodded in return. She closed her eyes and said a short prayer for a crack in the proprietary door of the U.S. Postal Service, where delivery of mail came guaranteed despite the weather. For her, today held a high chance of opportunity. She needed that to translate into fair weather ahead for her budding business.

"Next customer, please," the clerk said.

Lorna opened her eyes and stepped toward the counter. She rested the edge of the cake box on the counter and took the letter in hand. "Four first class stamps, please."

"Four stamps then. And are you intending to mail your box today, ma'am?" He handed her the strip of stamps and held his question up with his eyebrows.

Lorna Rae slid her change onto the counter, but kept her fingers on it. "No sir. I intend this box to be a donation to the federal employees at this facility. I am a baker, new in the area, and my cakes are now for sale at Buckner's Deli down on The Plaza."

"Ma'am, we are not allowed to accept—"

She pushed the dime and two pennies toward him, her face animated with generosity.

"Then I am gifting the cake to you, sir. Do with it what you will. Carry it to the break room when you have lunch and share it with your friends. If they have the occasion to take lunch at

Buckner's, remember to order dessert to go with it."

The clerk looked over his shoulder as if to check how much operating room he had. "But I really shouldn't." He took the change and deposited it in his drawer.

She opened the box with flourish, fanning the baked aroma in his direction. "It's chocolate this week, but the blonde version—applesauce cake with almond filling—debuts next week. Please, take custody of this orphan. You would be assisting me greatly if you would."

His fellow clerk sidestepped over for a closer look and made a pleasant humming sound that twitched his mustache. "Come to my line next time, ma'am."

Lorna Rae's face flushed with heat as seconds ticked by. How was she going to sell any cake if she couldn't even give it away?

"Well, it *is* O'Malley's birthday today. He has been crowing about it all morning." The clerk closed the box and pulled it to his chest, accepting ownership.

"How very thoughtful of you. On behalf of Lo-Rae Cakes, please give Mr. O'Malley my best regards. We hope to see you at Buckner's Deli someday soon. Thank you for the stamps." She gave a fingertip wave as he stepped toward the back with his donation.

Lorna Rae wandered over to a heavy oak table and made quick work of affixing the stamp on Duncan's letter. She placed the other stamps in her coin purse where her first week's payment resided. When she had located the out-going mail slot, she advanced to it with the letter pressed against her lips. "Take the blessing with you, little letter, and be swift about it." Then she released it through the slot of the receptacle, part fearful of having released it and part restless to hear something back. *I feel as though I am learning something here today, Lord. Kind words are a lot like cake.* She turned for the exit realizing that she had tasted a mere tidbit, but it made her want more.

~

"This is my kid brother I told you about on leave from the Navy." Duncan ran his hand across the top of Sam's crew cut to accentuate the claim.

"Sam Reed. Nice to meet you."

The clerk offered his hand across the counter, and Sam took it for a hardy shake. "Jimmy Cantor. What can I do for you gentlemen today?"

"To start with, three first class stamps, please." Duncan slid the letter on the counter to dig out the pocket change.

Sam leaned over the counter as if to share a secret. "He gets the gold star this week. He wrote Mother like a good son—and I didn't. Guess I have fallen off the wagon on that one." He gave the clerk a mischievous, cock-eyed look.

Jimmy chuckled and pulled out the stamps. "That will be nine cents, please."

"Oh, look. I have a dime and two pennies. Throw another stamp in the kitty, will you?" Duncan produced the coins as Sam snickered beside him.

"Good thing I am planning to fish this afternoon and not spend it going out on the town with you, big brother. Looks like you have reached the bottom of your resources."

Jimmy's face lit up as he swapped the payment for the stamps. "Fishing, huh? It's been awhile since I have done any of that."

Duncan tore off a stamp and gave it a lick before pressing in onto the corner of the letter.

"How about coming out after work and give it a shot?" Sam launched the invitation just as natural as it could be. "It's a stocked pond that nobody has fished in years."

Jimmy reached over to pick up the letter. As he stepped toward the mail repository, he held up his stump to reveal the missing hand. "There's a slight handicap to deal with." He glanced at the back of the letter where Sam's message home had been scrawled and hesitated midstep.

Duncan could feel their attempt to reach him teeter on the brink. He had been so sure the two would hit it off. He couldn't have been that wrong, could he?

"So, we deal with it, right? You help me cast and I can help you bait. Between us, we can carry the cooler back full of delicious fish. That way the girls won't have to tote it and make me look pitiful." Sam snickered as he jabbed his thumb in his chest and leaned an arm on the counter.

Jimmy let the letter slide in and came back to the front, his face shining with new interest. "Girls—and fishing?"

Duncan backed away to take the pressure off the pitch. "Do

you know the Hansen farm out east of town? She's renting rooms where Sam is staying. The girls are Daphne Hansen and her cousin Kathleen, who's supposed to be a real looker. I can give you a ride out if that makes it easier."

"I have my own ride. Yeah, it sounds fun. Let me stop by the house and dig my own pole out of storage. I can leave here at four o'clock and be out there in twenty minutes."

"Perfect. I will have Mrs. Hansen watch for you down the lane then. Plan on staying for supper with us, too. She intends to fry the fish and even said something about a cobbler."

"Well, I hope we can deliver on the fish. The pressure's on, for sure." Jimmy pressed his lips together like he'd rather fight it than smile.

"We need to get back, Sam, or Mrs. Hansen's blueberries will bake before she can get them in the oven." Duncan headed for the door, a feeling of satisfaction making his step seem lighter.

Sam left the counter and fell in step behind him. "Good deal. See you at four-thirty or so. I am looking forward to it."

"Hey—don't pick out a favorite girl, until I get there," Jimmy teased. For a fleeting instant, he looked his age.

"Don't come late." Duncan volleyed the good-natured tease back over his shoulder, though he knew the truth. That choice had already been made, unless his brother's sense of sight trumped his sense of touch. With a fingertip's length head-start, he would bet on the soft touch that wore a blonde braid over a pretty face reflected in a pond. That would not be his business or his battle. No, he knew enough to steer clear of that territory. Besides eating the fish, he planned to keep his mouth shut about such pairing up. But he would keep his eyes open, because that's what older chaperones did.

His feet hit the sidewalk, and he saw no signs of Mrs. Hansen waiting up ahead. "It looks like we have time to show you my office. Maybe Doctor Lucas is in."

"Sure. Hey, I thought that went well back there. Didn't you?"

"Yes, but I will tell you what. I feel awkward being in the middle. I only wanted to introduce you guys because you're about the same age. I trust you to take it from here. I don't want your friendship based on my ulterior motives. You catch the fish, and I will come eat them. Simple as that."

"Perfect. After sharing a huge ship with hundreds of men, I think I can handle splitting a fishing hole with another angler."

"What about the girls?"

Sam gave him a fox-guarding-the-henhouse look and laughed. "Bonus. And I do love a good bonus."

"Hey, there's Dr. Lucas now. Let's catch him before he settles into his noontime nap routine."

"He sleeps on the job?"

"He calls it going over his files, but it never takes much 'review' to put him out for half an hour or so."

"Wow, things must be slow in the medical department."

"You are right, thank the Lord above, which is how we need to keep it while the insurance moratorium ticks away. Believe me, quiet is good."

"Gosh Duncan, you sound like a cautious old man. Maybe it's best for me to hang out with a younger crowd."

"Don't confuse responsibility with maturity, Sam. I came here to help these people stay safe."

"And I'm sure you will."

"Right up here. He knows you are visiting, so you might expect some questions."

"I'm happy to answer them to the best of my ability. I am no trained medic, though."

Duncan skipped up the steps and held the office door open. "Neither am I."

"Oh, no kidding." Sam faked a wince as he stepped through the doorway.

Duncan drew in a lungful of cooler air from the shaded porch and made a mental note not to set his brother up like that again. Of course he wasn't a medic, despite having an office inside the medical clinic. He promoted safety, and safety was more like wellness, before the doctor gets involved.

~

Just this once, Lorna Rae allowed the melodrama. She placed the last slice of cake in front of Della at the dinner table and detoured over to the kitchen desk. "Ladies and gentlemen, I have a very important announcement to make."

Della started to pick up her fork, but put it right back down. "I love important announcements. What is it, pray tell?"

"Today, Lo-Rae Cakes collected its first dollar in sales and here it is, fixed for perpetuity." She slid the dime store frame out of its paper bag and displayed the bill with the aplomb of a television game show hostess. "One large cake for Buckner Deli means one solid dollar bill for the business."

Steve clapped his hands. "Let's hope there are many more."

Della stood to give her a hug. "Way to go, sis. I know this means a lot."

"I like this chocolate cake, Mommy."

"Thank you, Trudy. Let's hope the mail clerks downtown like it enough to come to the deli and buy more. We do not want these dollars to trickle in, we want a downpour."

Steve looked up as if to check the ceiling for leaks. "Make that dollars, Lord, not more raindrops."

"Isn't that the truth? I need it dry tomorrow to deliver the twenty mini-cakes to Ravi at the butcher shop. He might have my second dollar waiting for me, or at least part of one. I may have only left a partial order there, come to think of it."

Steve gave her a stern look. "You should be keeping a ledger of your delivered quantities and your payments, complete with dates. I think I have an old ledger you can have to start with. Records are important, for tax purposes among other reasons."

Della sat down and picked up her fork. "Oh, Steve, you sure know how to throw cold water on our celebration." In seconds, she had cake in her mouth.

Lorna Rae set the frame down in front of her plate and took her seat. "No, he's right, Della. An entrepreneur has to be responsible in every aspect of the business. The pace only picks up from here, so I need to get the bookkeeping right from the start."

"That's the spirit, Lorna Rae. Early discipline equates to later success. Teach yourself to be a bean counter, cakes in and money out." Steve paused his lecture long enough to put some dessert in his mouth.

Trudy flashed her kid fork in circles at her uncle. "Bean cake? That sounds cwazy."

"Lo-Rae Cakes. Home of the cwazy." Lorna Rae clicked forks with her daughter and delved into the chocolate mound that started the whole craze. She traced the dollar bill's outline corner-to-corner as she chewed. Hope filled the part of the frame that the bill didn't cover, hope of something more than money that could also be kept for perpetuity. She glanced at the cake slices on the counter, waiting to be wrapped for delivery. Happiness lay somewhere between the two, money and cakes, a distance she planned to figure out.

~

Duncan pushed the small fillet around in the cornmeal, but the coating wouldn't stick. "Tell me if I am doing this right."

"No, switch the order. Egg batter first, and then you dredge the fillet in the dry crumbs." Mrs. Hansen took a step closer to supervise her directions. "This is a fine opportunity to practice being gentle with your touch."

He looked her in the eyes and saw only good intentions, so he eased his motion and slipped the fish into the beaten egg milk bath. After a full swim, he lifted it out the far side and allowed it to plop full-bellied right into the cornmeal mix.

"Now pat it like a baby's behind. That helps the coating stick."

"But I've never patted—"

"Imagine it then. Babies are delicate beings, totally in our care as adults. God intends it that way to make us refine our abilities. Gentleness is something only the individual can offer. The sentiment starts in your heart and is expressed through your hands."

"So I flip it now and get to be as tender to both sides, right?"

She poked the fork tines under a specimen in the frying pan and let it continue to cook. "Yes, use care not to lose the progress you have already made."

About the time he had started patting the baby's behind again, laughter erupted out on the patio.

"That one's still alive," Daphne called. A girl screamed right afterwards, a mix of terror and delight.

"Let me get him," Sam replied. He bent double and trapped the flopping fish. Jimmy brought the bucket closer while Sam plunked him back in. A splash celebrated the victory. "Good teamwork, partner."

"Sure thing. You want to trust me with that fillet knife now?"

"Jeepers no! The scales make 'em slippery as all get out."

Sam's resolve triggered unease inside of Duncan. He put the coated fish fillet on the platter beside the frying pan and then stepped closer to the door.

The next instant, Mrs. Hansen met him and placed a hand of restraint on his forearm. "Give it a minute. Let them work it out."

"I will hold it down by the tail, if you want to give it a try." Kathleen centered the fish-cleaning board in front of Jimmy. "I may have to close my eyes though, as fish guts make me squeamish."

Jimmy looked at her, and held his gaze. "If I get anywhere close to your fingers, you have to agree to let go. Do we have a deal?"

She reached into the bucket for a fish and placed it on the barn wood. "Yes, I trust you."

Jimmy swallowed and accepted the knife from Sam. "Oh, great. Now, I guess I have to trust myself."

"Let's get these washed off and take them to Mother for her next batch," Daphne said.

Duncan responded to the pull on his arm and stepped back to the counter to resume his cornmeal dredging. "Want to tell me about Kathleen's condition?"

"Handicapped from birth. No rhyme or reason to it. Her left hand is bent back at the wrist and lacks any useful function whatsoever. It has been remarkable to watch her compensate for it, and she's perfectly normal otherwise. Bright, pretty—"

"And possibly sympathetic to someone sharing a similar plight?"

"Oh, I am most certain of that. She can probably teach him a thing or two about the one-handed lifestyle."

"Given he wants to be taught, of course." He took the next baptism candidate into the milk bath with a glance out the screen door. Once or twice he heard exasperated noises coming from the cleaning station, but no big outbursts ensued. The couple stood shoulder to shoulder, combining their dexterity. Finally, Kathleen gave a hearty cheer as Jimmy held up the jagged fillet for admiration.

"Let me pick that up on round three." Sam opened the screen door to allow Daphne to bring in a bowl of fresh fillets. "Here is the next mess of fish, ready for frying."

"Not until I pat the baby's bottom." Duncan confiscated the bowl as the fry-cook began to snicker. Soon, her shoulders shook with merriment. Daphne caught the contagion and joined her mother in the hilarity. To egg it on, he slipped a fillet into the cornmeal crumbs and gave it a demonstrative patting, exaggerating his gestures while looking overly concerned.

"You gotta be kidding me," Sam said, disgust riding his tone.

Duncan relished flipping the specimen over and repeating his exacting care. "No really. You cannot be too tender with these fillets. Ask any seasoned chef, and they'll tell you it's true."

Daphne squeezed her mother's waist in a brief show of affection. "Mother, I haven't heard you laugh like that in years." That seemed to sweeten up Sam's disposition, and he held out his arms like he stood next in line, making Daphne blush. She gave his hand a squeeze instead.

"That's because you smell like fish. Plus, you are not in touch with your tender side." Duncan pointed to the door. "Better get back out there and finish the third batch, so we can sit down and eat these fish while they are still hot."

Sam moaned, but Daphne herded him along by bumping shoulders until they were back outside.

Mrs. Hansen broke her focus on the frying pan to give him a knowing glimpse. "They are getting along well, aren't they?"

"Yes, it would appear so. Perhaps even doubly so."

"I set the oven to warm to keep this first batch edible, so there is no need to hurry the young people. Let them have their fun. At least it's productive."

"And therapeutic. I don't mind really, except I am fairly hungry tonight." Duncan added another patted fillet to the platter and stopped to knock some crumbs off his fingertips over the sink. When he returned to his station, a lump of golden fried fish waited on a paper napkin.

She motioned with the spatula and returned to her frying. "Taste-test it, if you will. Make sure I am getting it done. There's nothing worse than serving fish that isn't light and flaky."

He picked up the fish, napkin and all, and lifted it under his nose to take a sniff. "Goodness me. How fine to be in the right place at the right time." He peeled the napkin back and bit into the fillet. The breading broke loose and laid the seasoning groundwork, but the fish carried it off with a flourish. He swallowed and gobbled the rest, making a strained effort to slow down and enjoy the morsel.

She lifted a large fillet onto a baking sheet. "Do you think they caught enough?"

Intuitive to her plan, he pulled the oven door open and watched the first batch slide into safekeeping. He shook his head, already hungry for another incredible sample.

Chapter 14

Lorna Rae took the last cake from the box and handed it to the proprietor.

Ravi added it to the cakes on top of the meat case in perfect alignment. "I tell you, Mrs. Holmes. This much rain is no good. My brother, his shop sits closer to the river. He had to sweep out the rainwater from this weekend. The ground can hold no more. You pray, right?"

"Yes, and I have been praying for the rain to stop. Believe me, it can get inconvenient after awhile. I hope your shop is safe though, Ravi. It seems to sit high enough."

"God must keep me safe. If I had to close even for one day, well, I hate to think on it." The bell tinkled behind her and his expression went from dire to fake-polite, ridding the wrinkles from his forehead. "What can I get for you today, ma'am?"

"I would like a four-pound beef roast with some decent marbling in it, please." The woman nodded toward her and fanned a well-exposed neckline. "Steamy today, isn't it?"

Lorna Rae knew this game, as the weather always provided safe territory for any Kansan to comment on. "Heat or rain, which one came first? It's a version of the old chicken or the egg question, and only my hairspray knows the answer."

"Isn't that the truth?" She strummed her fingers on the counter while Ravi pulled a sheet of butcher paper over her cut of meat.

"Have you tried these new cakes? They are all the rage here in Westport." Lorna Rae motioned at the cakes and held her breath.

The patron gave them a look, her nose hoisted in the air.

Ravi gave her a wink as he handed her the roast. "You not have time to cook dessert. You too busy getting your gravy oh so smooth."

"Ha, you are probably right about that. Have you tasted these, Ravi? I refuse to serve the best beef and then offer some pre-made dessert that isn't quite up to muster."

"Ah, yes. Ravi tried and ate more than one. I am big fan. Try for yourself. This is no regular cake. You see."

"How much?"

"Five cents for one cake. You can split two for four servings."

"Well, I do have some vanilla ice cream that would go with it. Okay, add two cakes to my order. I can let you know next week if your advice is any good."

Lorna interjected her presence into the conversation. "Thank you. I am the owner of Lo-Rae Cakes and I would appreciate the feedback, to be honest. Next week, I have a blonde cake debuting, applesauce with almond filling."

Ravi stood behind the counter, his fingertips pressed together forming a teepee of contentment. "That blonde cake good with pork, I bet."

The woman allowed her money to speak next as she laid two bills on the counter. She picked the cakes she wanted and placed them atop the butcher paper bundle. "Isn't this a bit of an odd pairing? I mean having a baked good for sale at a meat shop?"

"Apparently not." Lorna Rae lifted the lid of her empty box for emphasis.

The woman nodded and left the shop with her purchases.

"So you bring blonde cake next week?"

"Yes, if that is okay with you. We can alternate to keep you from being overstocked."

"No overstock. You bring both kinds." Ravi held up two fingers to make it clear.

Lorna Rae sensed the need to be sure. "You still want the chocolate, too?"

"Ravi likes chocolate." He smiled and looked like a little boy for a second.

Lorna Rae felt his sincere compliment trickle deep into her heart. She needed a town full of cake admirers like Ravi. Given time, she hoped to achieve that pinnacle. "Okay. Next week, I bring two kinds of cake, a dozen each, and no more rain."

"Ha-ha! Yes to cake and no to rain. You want your meat now? Or I pay you now?"

"Pay first. I have to keep my profit separate from my spending budget."

He laid the payment for the first week's sales on the counter. "Wise lady. You tell the owner of that downtown deli that Ravi's sausage is the best. I send her delivery right away if she places an order."

Lorna Rae counted the coins and slipped them into her change purse. "Yes, I will be glad to tell her about your sausage. Della wants pork chops this week. Can you offer any tips on how to serve them?"

"I have tips for the cake lady. Many, many tips. You be very successful if you listen to Ravi." He tore the butcher paper off with a flourish and laid it out flat to receive the meat.

"Let me have four chops. It's fine if one is smaller—for my daughter."

"But she's growing, right? I give you four nice chops. No small."

"Yes, she's growing all right. That makes her my good little eater."

He straightened from behind the counter and gave her an endearing look. "My daughter likes your chocolate cake." His mustache raised on one side.

"You are a good father, Ravi. Thank you for taking my cake to her."

"It is the best cake. Many more will sell. You see." He wrapped the bundle and handed it to her.

"I promise to talk to the deli lady tomorrow. Let me have her mention my name if she calls to place an order." She paid for the meat and got situated to leave.

"Just say Lo-Rae Cakes, then I know." He nodded his farewell and went to wash his hands at the sink.

Lorna Rae tucked the pork chops inside the empty box and made her way out to the street. She had just lost her personal identity to her business for the first time and was not the least bit put out about it. In fact, it felt quite promising, like an expansion.

~

Duncan caught a blur of motion in his peripheral vision and shifted in his chair to gain a better perspective. Jimmy Cantor came tearing down the sidewalk at a full gallop. He looked like an athlete running track, lithe and quick-footed. When he turned up the clinic's walk, Duncan stood and went to the door. "Hey Jimmy. Is everything all right?"

The postal clerk leapt up the stairs three at a time and planted both feet on the porch to come to a halt. "Mr. Peterson…agreed to let me deliver this straight to you…but only if I ran the whole way. The shipment from Wichita came in huge this morning, so I gotta get right back."

Duncan noticed the envelope in the young man's pocket for the first time. He popped the screen door open and held out his hand.

The smile he gave blazed a new trail that spoke of enjoyment of life as he handed the letter over. "Tell Sam I had a top-notch time fishing yesterday. Ask him if we can take the girls to the movie house Friday. I think that new Ava Gardner musical is showing."

"I will be sure to ask him and bring you an answer tomorrow. I think Kathleen went back home, but maybe Daphne can have her return for the weekend."

"That would be swell, sir. Just let me know." Jimmy gave a salute and literally flew off the porch.

For some inexplicable reason, Duncan stood and watched him all the way back to the post office. He had witnessed the young man's subdued monotony at the postal counter for days on end, but the combination of plentiful fish and pretty girls seemed to lend new zest. He turned to go back inside. Sam probably had something to add to the mix, too. "Good job, brother."

He sat down and placed the letter on his desk blotter. The postmark read Kansas City, not Washington D.C. The source of his correspondence had been deflected, another good sign. He thought to open it right there at work, even though he guessed it might be personal in nature. The door banged behind him and Dr. Lucas walked in.

"Glen Forshee died in his sleep last night. The coroner suspects a blood clot in his lungs. His wife said he had been coughing up blood for days. What a needless shame, the whole thing."

"We are on a better run now, doc. I think the moratorium is working to our favor."

He shuffled by and rearranged things on the back counter. "Are you going out to the new well drilling this afternoon? I have a string of appointments coming in."

"Yes, I plan to, if the rain holds off and lets the men work that is." He folded the letter and stood, tucking it into his back pocket. "Maybe I'll go have a bite to eat before driving out."

"Plan to attend Glen's funeral downtown at Maple Grove Cemetery on Thursday morning. Mr. Coates asked me to spread the word."

"You bet. I will pay more attention to who attends this time."

"We are all paying more attention—much more attention."

Duncan heard the vacuous defeat in the doctor's voice, having lost another regular patient. He understood such loss came as part of the job, just like his. But that didn't mean you had to like it. Gain was ten times better than loss, and it wore a dazzling smile.

~

Lorna Rae took the pickle spear that Leon had offered and sat Trudy down in the chair at the table closest to the deli counter. On a whim, she had caught the train into downtown and called Steve to order a ride home at five o'clock. The late afternoon clientele seemed thin, but she noticed the front case looked depleted. Even her chocolate cake had been decimated with only a quarter of it left for the remainder of the week. She looked at the box with half a blonde cake in it and wondered if she should have brought more.

Trudy began to nibble the dill spear, her nose wrinkling at the sour taste. Lorna Rae glanced past her to see Miss Buckner coming out of her office. Her knees trembled a bit because the woman packed an imposing figure. Instead of coming into the dining area, the owner disappeared into the bathroom. She sat down and pushed Trudy's curls out of her face.

Trudy held it up for her to taste. "So good, this pickle."

"No, honey. It's for you. Wasn't that nice of Mr. Leon?"

"Yes, Mommy. He is nice."

"I am so happy you remembered to thank him, Trudy. Those are good manners."

"What in the blazes did you do to me, cake lady?" Miss Buckner adjusted her slacks at the waist as her gaze bore down on the two of them. "We about didn't survive lunch rush today. Did Leon tell you?"

"No, ma'am. I…don't know what to say. What happened?" Lorna Rae stalled, her palms starting to sweat. The comfortable atmosphere a minute ago had heated up to unbearable.

"What happened? Let me tell you what happened. The postal clerks descended on us like a plague of locusts. The ordering line snaked clear out the door. Every last one of them ordered something different—until it came to your cake—which they all had to have. I about sold out, and it barely even sat in the front case a day yet. Criminy."

Lorna Rae squared her shoulders to the woman. "My goodness. I hardly know how you two handled it, Miss Buckner. What a scene that must have been."

"Oh, it was a scene all right, a scene right out of a dream. Do you know how long I have waited to have a gangbuster day like that? And it wasn't even Saint Patrick's Day."

"No. It's only June. What does that holiday have to do with it?"

"More than half of 'em are Irish, through and through. Plus, some loudmouth named O'Malley seemed to feel the call to provide some entertainment."

"Uh-oh. What did Mr. O'Malley do?"

"He sang 'Danny Boy' to the tops of his lungs. Everybody clapped afterwards. He did a fine job, actually. Land sakes, my meat inventory is now three-quarters gone, and my regular vender doesn't deliver midweek."

"I have a connection in Westport. I sell mini-cakes at the butcher shop there. He asked me to tell you about his sausage links, which are superb. I think those Irishmen might like a dish of sausage and potatoes."

"I'd have to put that on top of a bun to make it fit the menu. But I could do it, I guess."

Lorna Rae leaned back in her seat. "Have Leon work up an onion roll for that dish. Onion, sausage and potato—that is the ticket." Recipes came to her easily, and connecting people who served food seemed like a natural bridge to build.

"I gotta have deli-sliced cold cuts, including turkey and ham, by tomorrow."

"Call Ravi at Westport Meats. He promised me he would rush

any delivery you'd place, but it's getting late in the day."

"It's four forty-five. If he left early today, I am up the creek." She turned around and stormed into her office, appearing determine to make the call.

Lorna Rae stood and handed the cake box to Leon who had cleaned up the contents of the front case. "Find out if she wants to put this out when the chocolate's gone, maybe after lunch tomorrow. It's a half-cake, all I have with me. I really brought it so you could hand out free samples of the new flavor."

Leon smiled and nestled the box on the back counter. "Our sampling days are over, ma'am. This here's a gold rush we are experiencing, and your cake slices are the nuggets."

"Listen, I am suggesting a new butcher who's a friend of mine over in Westport. He makes a killer link sausage, the likes of which you've never tasted. Miss Buckner wants to serve it with potatoes on a bun. I posed onion rolls to blend the flavors. Could you come up with something?"

This time the smile came to him as if they had spoken of collusion. "Just watch and see, cake lady. I'll get the jump on this and still make the boss think it was her idea to start with."

"You're one smart man, Leon."

"Only in my bake shop really."

"Push the blonde cake for me, will you?"

"Like this." He plinked his little finger up and gave it the slightest motion. "That's all it needs. Come heavier next week, if she failed to mention it."

"No. She is too worried about her meat."

"Then you worry about the cake. I doubt you can bring too much. We may need you to come twice a week."

"Let me see what I can do. Thanks for all the support. I'd better get out to the curb, or I'll be walking home." Lorna Rae scooted Trudy out of her chair and walked outside, confident she had done all she could to make the sales rise as fast as possible. With the cake's disappearance, she had just cleared a dollar in a day, not a week. The ledger came to mind and she relaxed, remembering she had recorded the delivery before leaving the house.

Trudy pointed up the busy road. "Uncle Steve!"

Sure enough, Lorna Rae spotted his car at the traffic light. "Come on, dolly. We need to cross and get on his side of the road."

"Let's wun, Mommy."

"Yes, let's run." Lorna Rae clasped her hand and gave into the childish impulse, right there in the most dignified place in the city. She cared nothing about her image, not in the least.

~

The drill truck could not have moved more slowly, as if the humidity had given it gelatin to cross instead of air and land. Duncan opened his car door to observe from a closer post. He had seen some lightning along the southwestern horizon and knew the storm wouldn't hold off for long. A flash of white reflected off his car window, and he reached into his back pocket for the letter, forgotten in the moment. "Don't go anywhere. You are next." He tossed it onto the car seat and slammed the door, checking to make sure the window had been rolled all the way up.

A group of laborers moved toward the drill site where the foreman stood. Beyond him, a pile of metal fretwork for the oil derrick lay ready for use. He questioned whether raising such a lightning rod on the verge of a storm constituted a risk they should be taking. He would have to speak to Mr. Delmar, the site foreman, about that. He quickened his pace to allow more time to interact with the head man before the drill rig pulled in place.

The laborers separated into two unequal groups as several men lagged behind by the water truck. When the first group reached the drill site, the sun vanished behind the leading line of storm clouds. The foreman hailed the lagging crew members, and the men responded with something less than full enthusiasm.

"Afternoon, Mr. Delmar."

"Mr. Reed. You have come out to keep us safe today, I see."

"I hope so. Here's a quick question about that derrick rigging back there. I saw some lightning on the horizon and wondered if we should hold up erecting any of that in the face of a bad weather. Metal can be a strong conductor in an electrical storm."

"Not to worry about that today, sir. We won't get far enough before quitting time. Don't know if I can say that about the rain, though."

"I heard this is making for the wettest June on record. I am new in these parts, but it does seem like the rain comes every other day here lately."

"Hard to keep a schedule up at that rate, but what can a man do?" Delmar signaled for a laborer and the conversation halted.

Duncan stepped away from the immediate drilling site and turned to assess the proximity of the approaching rig. He found the truck progressing up the perimeter road at what was likely its top speed, half-past slow. It would have to dodge the water truck and angle in at the job site to clear the derrick workings. He noted that the visibility of backing the truck must be next to zero, given the towering crane riding its back bumper.

When the foreman began to shout directives at the crew, Duncan shifted his back to the storm and watched as all the elements came together. The men assumed a loose formation around the site, keeping one flank clear for the drill truck's approach. Several employed their shovels at the center-point where the drill would activate, leveling the surface for the start. Delmar shouted a halt command. The men straightened and backed away.

Almost at the last second, Duncan recognized Liam Torguson in the group that had been loitering by the water truck. Unease crept over his skin as he assessed the rest of the crew. A tall man standing at the edge of the loose group seemed familiar, but he couldn't recall if he'd been in the fishing picture or not. Too far away to render any identification, he made the reluctant decision to stay put. The storm rumbled behind him as the drilling truck arrived at the site. Delmar waved the driver in and shouted an order to redistribute the men.

Slow to gain position, the truck converged on the group. Duncan examined the angle and knew the driver would have to pull past and hook the truck's rear assemblage around to position the drill in place. He tensed when it looked like the truck had advanced clear past that mark. About that time, the tall man broke loose from the pack. Danger flared in Duncan's minds-eye. Forshee had made a similar move against orders and now lay dead at the mortuary.

His feet began running without his brain sending the command. His lungs caught on fire half the distance there. Delmar shouted something, but the tall man failed to heed it and stepped right into the path of the truck.

"No brakes," the driver shouted as he motioned in desperation out of the window.

"Clear the area," Delmar called in no uncertain terms. The

command echoed loud and clear. The men scattered in chaos.

Winded from his run, Duncan knew to pay utmost attention as the mayhem ran its course. He slowed and watched the tall man literally throw himself under the truck's front tires. In less than a blink, the most amazing thing transpired. The drill truck veered left to avoid him and went up on two wheels, leaving the tall man unhurt in the dirt. Like a drag strip trick, the truck circled left and collided with the derrick pile, where it teetered and fell back onto all fours with a deafening crash. Overhead, the sky tried to rip in half and dispelled a roaring quiver over the landscape.

"Shut down, Mr. Delmar," Duncan shouted as he passed the foreman on his way to the crash scene.

"We're down men. Go take cover at the water truck, as many as can fit. Use my truck, too." Delmar crossed behind him targeting the wayward worker.

"That individual should be placed on report," Duncan replied over his shoulder. He looked ahead and could see the driver slung back in the truck cab. "Lord, not another mortality." His beggared words were cut off by the need to inhale. He climbed up on the metal sections, trying to make the running board. Dangling on the back of the truck, the crane still swung like a pendulum from the forced landing. As he pulled up onto the running board, he discovered Delmar right behind him. His face bore a deep grimace.

"Easy now. Let's see if the door will open." Duncan depressed the latch and tugged at the heavy door panel. It gave way to reveal the driver, slumped with his eyes closed.

Delmar reached up and placed his hand on the man's shoulder, then gave it a shake. "Swain? Swain?" The driver moaned and began coming to.

Precarious on the running board, Duncan moved closer and leaned in between the driver and the steering wheel, a huge monstrosity that took up a quarter of the cab. "Mr. Swain, can you hear me?"

"Uh, what's that?" The driver's words came out airy, like he was exhaling without intending to communicate.

"Do you know where you are?" Duncan took a tight breath and looked back and forth between Swain and Delmar.

"I am up here with Mary, Joseph, and Jesus," the man replied. In seconds, his eyes opened to reveal blue irises that had been pushed back into mere rims by oversized black pupils.

Delmar eased back onto the running board. "Looks like a concussion. Can we use your car to run him back to Doc Lucas?"

"Sure. Let me drive closer. Try to keep him coherent, so he doesn't lose consciousness. You know, ask more questions." As he hopped down, Delmar shifted closer.

"So how's baby Jesus doing, Swain?"

"He is all grown up and protecting the world." Swain's slurred words came slow as he tried to pronounce each distinct word, but his meaning came loud and clear.

Duncan cleared the pile's rubble and stretched his stride into a run. Saving his breath for the exertion of doing his job triple time, he allowed unspoken words of gratitude to repeat over and over in a ticker-tape of consciousness. Swain was alive thanks to some tricky driving, and to a Savior who stood on never-ending duty.

He yanked the Buick's door open and there sat the letter, still unattended. He grabbed it and jumped in, slamming the door in his wake. "I promise to read you tonight, sweetheart. I'll get to you yet." He kissed the back of the envelope and leaned over to tuck it into his glove box, out of sight but definitely not out of mind.

~

Lorna Rae swished the beaters in the dishwater. Her attempt to ease into the topic ran on a thin wire. "Della, you are doing great with the baking. You know I appreciate all that you and Steve are doing for Trudy and me, but I think it might be time for me to start looking for a place of our own soon. Maybe by the end of July."

Della hovered over the batter she had just poured into the rectangular pan, a shocked look frozen on her face. "Why would you want to? I cannot imagine it really."

The hurt in her eyes knifed into Lorna Rae's heart. "Because we simply cannot stay forever, Del. I am so grateful to have been here when Robert Thomas came home brand spanking new from the hospital. It will always hold a fond place in my heart, all of us being under one roof together like a big family. But I need to settle in somewhere and get established, so Trudy can start school in a couple of years. You know, that kind of thing."

"What's the hurry, Lorna Rae? You are trying to kill me here, announcing a split-up right out of the blue like this." She shook the pan and tamped it on the counter, exactly like she'd been taught to rid the air bubbles.

"Well, you have gotten your feet under you, what with the night feedings tailing off. Little by little, you have come back into full swing."

"Huh? Not by a long shot. Please don't rush into anything. I want you to be happy and successful with the business. I want you here with us. Steve is willing to drive you downtown as many times a week as necessary. He is going anyway, so why wouldn't he? Think about the convenience of living here. You don't even have a car."

Lorna Rae searched under water and felt a slim knife that had escaped earlier detection.

"I do not want to be a nuisance. You know, the sister who moved in and never went away."

"Is this a privacy issue? Is it because you want to date? You can tell me if it is, because we can afford you all the privacy you need."

Lorna Rae snickered at her sister's ramblings. She didn't even have a private life and sure didn't need any space for one. She merely detested the thought of being in the way. "There is no privacy issue. In fact, I love you giving me advice. After I wrote that letter to Duncan, I felt a few pounds of needless stress lift off of me."

"Good. Now you are talking sensible. One more question, then we can be done talking about you needing to relocate. You don't want to move back to El Dorado, do you? I want you to like being in Kansas City."

"No to El Dorado, and yes to Westport. I am still letting Kansas City grow on me. It's so big and imposing. Okay, I guess I am paranoid about being in your way and rushing this moving out thing. I never even thought about the lack of a car."

Della puffed a breath through her straight-cut bangs and glanced at the oven. "Oh thank goodness. Now you are making sense."

"You will tell me when it feels like it's time, won't you, Del?" She started to pour the dishwater out when the oven timer buzzed and startled her. The dishwater slopped out and soaked her blouse. Unbalanced and now wet, she retreated to the bedroom, unsure of it all.

~

Duncan slouched in the padded chair he had dragged out onto the porch. The moonless night stood black against the horizon, but the storm had passed hours ago. The letter lay draped across his chest. The third time he read it, the redemptive work of its contents began to make a difference in his attitude. God's provision had placed Lorna Rae in a safe location where her start-up business could thrive, and she could raise Trudy without struggle. The traits that he admired about her were the very things that kept her away, which didn't make it any easier in the oil field neighborhood. On a tough day like today, a man might like to come home to a tender-speaking wife and loving children.

He had never given any thought to being lonely before. The job always paid the way to a new location that held the next challenge. Risk management did not exactly represent the type of stable nucleus a man could build a family around. Maybe it had been God's protection that he had never thought along these lines before. He would be thirty years old soon, quite a long record of being self-sufficient under the hand of God.

The letter had to be blamed. On that third time through, he read between the lines, thinking only of Lorna Rae. What had she really intended, speaking so honestly of her life? Hadn't he felt her heart beating through her expressions? And why did she offer a penny for his thoughts? Was it because she wanted to know if they might drift back to her? The sensation of having her close became so vivid, he began wishing he could be baby Robert Thomas, so that her nose might stroke his cheek. That way her words of whispered affection would belong to him.

He would have been left guessing at many of the answers if she had not signed off as Rae, his pet name for her. That one word gave him the answer, that she wanted his attention. A longing birthed right off that letter, a deep drawing. Miles apart, what would he do with it?

Bert stepped around the front of the porch. "Evening, neighbor. Vivian sent over this strawberry shortcake. She thinks you might be wasting away over here."

"Thanks Bert. Since my brother is in town, I have been taking a few meals out at the Hansen's farm where he's staying. That has probably been my salvation, as my cooking can turn caustic in a heartbeat." He laughed and sat up to take the dessert.

"She said to put the plate on the back stoop. How's Swain? I heard he saw Jesus today."

"I imagine he really did, after that stunt driving feat he pulled. What a way to go out, right? Delmar shook him back into consciousness as we talked him back off of heaven's doorstep. Don't know if that is the outcome he truly wanted, but his wife sure seemed grateful to lay hands on her man again."

"If I cut out like that on Vivian, she might chase me up to the pearly gates and make Saint Peter give me back. I am glad it turned out okay for Swain though. We have a bad lot mixed in with the labor force that makes the rest of us look callous and a little accident-prone."

Duncan wanted to state his case without spilling too many details, but it came as a relief to hear Bert side with the right. "Bud Gant has been placed on official report. Mr. Coates is having his lawyer examine the feasibility of taking legal action. Enough is enough."

"I see you got a letter there. Not from our old neighbor by any chance?"

"If I say yes, you cannot tell Vivian. She has been writing Lorna Rae, too."

"Okay, I will take that as a yes without your having to say so. I know Viv shifts right into matchmaking mode if the wind is just right."

"A man my age could use the excuse he is too set in his ways, but the night starts to feel lonely when there's nothing but words on a page and half a state between you."

"When the time is right, you will know it. I never gave a whit for silly girls until I met Vivian. Something opened up inside of me, and I couldn't seem to get enough time with her. One night instead of being content to take her home, God seemed to make it clear as a bell that I should take her home with me. The two week engagement period hardly endeared me to her father, but it was all I could spare. That's how love goes, all or none."

"Thank you for bringing the dessert over and for your words of wisdom. When this job ends, I will have some decisions to make, for sure."

"Listen for that still small voice. If you know the shepherd, then you will recognize the voice. What he blesses cannot be taken from any man. Have a good evening, neighbor."

"Goodnight, Bert. I will tell Swain you asked about him."

"Please do." His footsteps faded into the night.

Duncan rose from the chair, the letter in one hand and the strawberry shortcake in the other. In no mood for sweets, he walked through the dark house and pulled the refrigerator door open. He slid the dessert in beside the egg crate, a reminder of his inept ability to take care of himself. When he closed the door, the yard light gave him just enough illumination to make out the photo of Lorna Rae at the lake. He took it off the door and put it with the letter. Why his redemption always came on cold unfeeling paper, he would never quite understand.

Chapter 15

The Buick's tires rolled over the uneven stones that Duncan and Sam had used to line the farm road, when the low-water creek topped the passageway. Incessant rain had claimed the last three weeks, causing localized flooding all around Kansas. Sam put in for a medical extension for his leave and received it, prolonging his stay. They had tackled several projects at the Hansen place and rotated through surveillance duties in the chronic flooding basement.

The electric sump pump he had purchased in town would be his next installation project, which would save the residents from having to bail once the Reed men pulled out. He thought about Sam's departure and how it might prove difficult for all involved parties. He had spied Sam and Daphne embracing under the fireworks on Independence Day. The light display had been Mr. Coates' elaborate gift to the community, yet it seemed to solicit more emotions than patriotism. His kid brother was falling in love. He would not play the part of the hypocrite and try to talk him out of it.

In the dimming light of day, he spotted two people coming in from the barn. Sam had likely gotten his chores done and had a little company to sweeten the effort. He pulled the Buick into the barn drive to stay out of the puddles collecting in front of the house. Last week they had shoveled a few channels to drain standing water off the farm fields and into the creek. He needed to walk the front lawn soon to see if a similar solution would work. Tonight, however, he already had a date—his sump pump.

He exited the car and grabbed the box out of the back seat. Mrs. Hansen gave a wave from the back door where Sam had jacked off his rubber boots. An emerald green aluminum awning arched over their heads, last week's project. Sam had proven to be pretty handy with his tools, which made the job only half as difficult. In truth, Daphne would not be the only one sad to see Sam go. He approached the back porch and sat down the box.

Duncan knocked his cap askew and smiled at Daphne. "What's going on, brother?"

Sam straightened his cap and gave Daphne a coded look. "Do not get me riled. That basement started to flood at two-thirty this morning."

Daphne adjusted a wooden bowl on her hip that held ripe produce from the garden. "I went down and took a turn, so Sam wouldn't have to do all the scooping."

"Dinner's almost ready," Mrs. Hansen said. "Can you folks come in and get washed up?"

"Yes, ma'am," Duncan replied. "Do you need these tomatoes?"

"Hello, Duncan. Yes, have Daphne bring them in."

"I brought out a new contraption I think you will appreciate. It's an automatic pump that only runs when it needs to."

Daphne looked at him as if it were too good to be true. "You mean no more bailing?"

"No more bailing. We cannot leave that much work for you ladies, now can we?" Sam chucked the young woman's chin as he took the first stair step and got the reward he must have wanted, a coy smile.

Duncan followed Sam up and came into the kitchen. "I took a peek at the installation booklet. We may have some digging to do."

"Food first," Sam replied. He headed for the sink.

"You two have done way too much around here," Mrs. Hansen said. "Please know that I appreciate it. A little upkeep goes a long way."

Sam turned off the faucet and took the hand towel Daphne offered. "I plan to come back in December, when I complete my active duty."

"Well, I might be pulling out by then, depending on whether

this insurance case goes to trial. Still, we can work something out. One Reed is better than none." Duncan tried to laugh it off, but read the concern in Mrs. Hansen's eyes. A farm wife probably did not appreciate change. He'd had more than his share of it. "So, what's for dinner tonight?"

"I baked a whole chicken, since I didn't mind using the oven. I guess the morning rain cooled July off a bit for us today."

He stepped to the sink and wet his hands. "Yes, but it flooded the front yard again. I plan to take a look at that after I get the pump in the basement. The radio claims that the Kansas River is starting to reach flood level. That cannot be good news for the eastern part of the state."

"More to pray over." Mrs. Hansen spoke in a whisper as she bent to take the chicken out of the oven. "Daphne, wash your hands and put the mashed potatoes in that blue bowl, please."

"Yes, ma'am. I think Sam likes mashed potatoes. Isn't that right?" Daphne tossed him a meaningful look as she made her way to the sink.

Sam took his customary seat at the dinette table and glanced up. "As long as I am not peeling and mashing, I do."

"Spoken like a true KP king. You miss it, don't you brother? You miss living on a ship like a pack of wild dingoes stuffed in a sardine can." Duncan snickered and pulled his chair back. A sob soon echoed from the sink area.

"Now look what you started." Sam left the table and slipped his arm around the sentimental young woman. He spoke something into her ear and gave her shoulders a squeeze.

"Chin up, Daphne," Mrs. Hansen said. "Let's take it a day at a time. They are all golden and all given to us by God above."

"I agree," Duncan replied. "What might have seemed just an interim stay here may have been God's way of getting us all together to build something more. Look at all the good that's come of it."

"Like a sump pump?" Sam laughed while Daphne pushed his shoulder for the slight. He gave her a conciliatory kiss on her temple.

"Let's eat while the food is hot." Mrs. Hansen set the roasted chicken in the center of the table and took the hot pads back to the stove. "Tonight, let me say grace, as I have been more blessed than the rest of you put together."

Duncan allowed the aroma of home-cooked food to distract him for a moment, but remembered to pull out her chair before she joined them at the table. He might argue who the most blessing had fallen to though, as any time away from the oil fields came as therapy for him. Sam reached for his hand to link up around the table, and he clasped it with measured gratitude.

~

Lorna Rae stared out the front plate glass as the police lights flashed down the street. A megaphone repeated the message to evacuate immediately every few seconds. Her chest constricted. *How on earth could this be happening?*

Steve hastened to the desk and grabbed a handful of paperwork. "Get packed up. We need to leave in the next ten minutes. Lorna Rae, get your ledger and your labels."

"Right. Thank you, Steve. My head is not on straight. I never thought the flood would come up past Armourdale."

"I heard the stockyards went underwater this afternoon. The river is definitely rising, but I am not sure it has crested yet. With us coming into the evacuation zone, I would say we may have only a day before it does. I am not willing to risk staying."

Della came into the kitchen and surveyed the situation. "I have the baby's things all packed up with mine. Lorna Rae, do you want me to bring your baking pans?"

"How about two pans? If I need to, I can bake while we are gone. Where do you plan to take us, Steve?"

He halted his rummaging on the desktop and looked up, startled. "Oh, Lord help us. We cannot go east, can we? We would never get over the Missouri River. That makes my brother's house in Columbia out of the question."

"No, we need to head out over higher ground. We can go west on Highway 56 and stay up in the Flint Hills. Tallgrass prairie always marks higher ground."

Della nested some pans together, her brow knit with worry. "Where will we end up? We cannot take off without a plan."

"How about the Hansen farm where you picked me up, Steve? They would have room for all of us."

"Let's do it. We could be there in three hours. If we left right now, that puts us there by midnight. We could do a lot worse."

Steve crammed papers into a briefcase and snapped it shut.

"I will go get our things packed. Della, can you supervise Trudy? Have her put her horses in a bag for traveling, and please don't let her run off."

Della gave her a worried look as she bagged the pans. "Sure thing, Lorna Rae. Be quick, though. The traffic could be a nightmare getting out of town."

She hurried down the hall and dropped on all fours in the bedroom to retrieve their suitcases from under the bed. In seconds, she had them splayed open so she could stuff piles of clean clothes inside. All their worldly possessions would be riding west with them, running from the floodwaters. "Dear Lord, please let Mrs. Hansen have room in her house for us tonight." She closed the suitcases and tripped the latches, securing them closed.

"Time's up. We are out of here," Steve called. "Let's get moving."

Lorna Rae pulled the luggage off the bed and tried to balance the heavy load to stay in step. She grabbed her purse and left her little haven without even looking back. The waters were rising and her feet already felt wet. "Help us, Lord. Guide us to higher ground."

~

Duncan had agreed to stay fifteen more minutes to watch the sump pump cycle through to insure it worked properly. Sam had gone up for a shower and a late ointment application. He heard Mrs. Hansen rumbling around in the kitchen, probably up well past her usual bedtime. He pinched his eyes to clear the fog out of his vision. He needed some sleep.

The unmistakable sound of a car door slamming echoed through the back door. He stood from the table and flipped on the back porch light. Figures appeared in the distance. "We have company, Mrs. Hansen. Are you expecting anyone?"

She glanced at him from the stove, her fear evident. She shook her head and started toward the hall. "Daphne, can you come down?"

He could barely believe his weary eyes. "Good Lord above—"

"Who is it Duncan?"

"It's Lorna Rae Holmes and her family." As he shot out of the door, he heard her calling Sam down. He began running when he saw the adults struggling with suitcases and trying to tote the children. The evening rain had left everything a muddy mess. They had parked on high ground, though, out by the Buick.

Trudy began to squirm on Lorna Rae's hip as he approached. Not knowing what else to do, he made a beeline toward the child and took her right up into his arms. It felt like a miracle. He hugged her close and took the largest suitcase from Lorna Rae.

"Mista Weed!" Trudy held his cheeks and gave him a great big kiss.

"Girl, am I ever glad to see you." He nuzzled his nose into her curls.

"We should have called ahead. I am so sorry." Lorna Rae sounded weary. Her hands clutched the handle on the suitcase like her life depended on it.

"They evacuated Johnson County," Steve said. "We had ten minutes to get out."

"You are here now, and that's all that matters," Mrs. Hansen replied. "Please come on inside. Is the baby here?"

"Yes, ma'am. I am Lorna Rae's sister Della, and this is Robert Thomas. Would you like to hold him and let me help Steve unpack?"

Duncan tried to get a look at the bundle, but the porch's light didn't reach quite that far. "Lorna Rae?"

"Right here, Duncan. I need to get more things out of the trunk."

Sam stepped up wearing his pajamas with rubber boots for a classic first impression. "May I take the suitcase for you, ma'am?"

"Sam, this is my friend, Lorna Rae Holmes and her daughter Trudy." Duncan could not think of the next appropriate thing too include, not that he could tell his brother anyway.

"Oh, I believe I took your old room, didn't I?" Sam grabbed the suitcase without waiting for permission and turned for the house.

Duncan would have surrendered the suitcase he held so he could take Lorna Rae around the waist and give her a proper welcome. He could not take his eyes off of her. Sam didn't need the extra weight of two suitcases though.

"Let's get the children inside out of the night air," Mrs. Hansen said. She started ahead of him with the bundled baby, and Daphne opened the back door when she arrived.

It took every ounce of self-control he possessed to leave the others in the dark and come back to the house. Halfway out, he crossed paths with Sam who had come out to get a second load. "Should we give them your room? I can take you back to the bungalow with me, or we can settle in down in the parlor."

"Fine. The parlor then. I am not leaving. You had better think twice about that low-water crossing since it rained again tonight." Sam hooked one brow and left him to consider it.

Trudy pursed her lips and rubbed the corner of her eye. "I so sleepy, Mista Weed. Can we stay?"

Duncan put the suitcase down and brushed back her blonde curls. "Yes, honey. It's safe here from the flood. You can have your old room back. Won't that be nice?"

Daphne swept by him with clean pillow cases in her hands. ""Take her up to my room for tonight. We are putting the baby's parents in Sam's room. Lorna Rae can have my room, and I will double up with Mother."

Trudy fidgeted to get down. "Can Daphne wead me a book?"

"I promise to say your prayers, okay? Then tomorrow we can read some fairy tales. How does that sound?"

"Okay. Let me down for the steps, Mista Weed. I'm a big girl now."

"Straight up you go, and Daphne can help you get in bed. I will go help your mother." He eased the child to the floor and kissed the top of her head before giving her total freedom.

Mrs. Hansen leaned over the rail overhead. "Can you ask if they brought any kind of bedding for the baby? I hate to put him on the big bed, so I'll rock him until they come up."

"Let me find out. I will be glad to bring it in, but they are probably traveling lighter than that." He reversed his steps and exited the back door.

Sam came up under the awning, his arms full of paper bags. "They have the rest, I think. Steve's locking up the car."

"Guess we should teach him how to live like country folks, with a little more trust and a few less locks. Did you see any bedding for the baby?"

"No. We will have to make due."

"Daphne is upstairs helping put Trudy to bed. You should go

meet her. She is the sweetest little girl in the world."

"Well, I sure could read that on your face, the first second I saw you with her."

"That bad, huh?" Duncan walked away toward the vehicles when Della appeared. "Mrs. Hansen has the baby upstairs. She wants to put the baby to bed, but didn't know if you had brought something with you."

"Goodness, no. We will have to rig up a pallet. I'll go right up."

"First room on the left at the top of the stairs. She is rocking the baby, until you can advise her of your preference."

"Bless her heart. Lorna Rae knew this was the right place to come. I am so glad to be out of that car. Steve would not let us stop."

"That's because nothing is keeping the river from rising. Let's thank the Good Lord you made it out in time." Duncan walked further into the dark to find Lorna Rae. About the time he approached, Steve slammed the trunk closed. "Do you need me to take anything, Steve?"

He balanced three bags in his grip and headed toward the house. "No, I have this. Help Lorna Rae. She is cleaning up some of Trudy's things from the floorboard."

Duncan made his way around the car and found her, tucked into an open door. "Rae? Let me get you inside. You must be exhausted."

"Such a disaster back here. You would think we had camped in here for days."

"No, you're being a neat-nick. This can wait until morning. Come on inside."

"And my shoes are getting muddier by the moment."

He laced an arm around her waist and pulled her out. "Not anymore." As she turned to face him, he swept her up into his arms. She reached for the bag she had been packing, so he allowed her a moment to grab it before hauling her away. With one last clear thought, he kicked the car door closed behind them.

He walked with a deliberate, slow pace, since he had everything he wanted right in his arms. He smelled the fragrant shampoo in her hair and felt her arms around his neck. Every sensation made him acutely aware of the next. He had almost made the back patio when he felt a hot tear trickle down his shirt collar. It lingered like a caress. "You made it here, and that's all that matters." When she whimpered, he pulled her closer until their cheeks touched.

Mrs. Hansen held the door open to let them in. "Trudy is asking for her mother. I can put on a pot of coffee, if you'd like. I have decaffeinated."

"Yes, please." Lorna Rae stretched until her feet hit the kitchen floor. "I hope to be back down in a few minutes."

"Daphne put out fresh towels for you in the bathroom."

"Thank you so much, Mrs. Hansen. I knew this was our safe place."

The older woman folded her hands around the hand Lorna Rae offered her as if to transfer her peace. "Yes, dear. You will all be fine now. Praise God."

Duncan waited for Lorna Rae to disappear down the hallway before turning to his hostess. Before he could tell her what he had in mind, the hum of his latest improvement echoed up the basement stairwell. "Do you hear that, Mrs. Hansen? That's the sound of your new friend, Mr. Sump Pump."

"I am pleased to make his acquaintance." She looked up at him without a trace of fatigue, only appreciation. "What a miracle they made it here, of all the places they could have landed."

He glanced at the mess on the linoleum and decided to take his shoes off by the back door. "Yes, a real mud-clad miracle. Let me clean the floor up for you. I believe you promised our sojourner-friend a cup of hot coffee."

"Yes, I did. How happy for me to have a full house. Plus a baby, too. Goodness me." She went straight to the sink to begin her preparations.

"I will bring groceries tomorrow after work, if I can get over the creek, that is. For tonight, I will hole up in the parlor with Sam, if you don't mind. I would rather be able to see what I am driving into." True, he had blamed the rising creek, but wild horses couldn't drag him away. Not tonight.

~

"I have yet to even meet that Mr. O'Malley." Lorna Rae softened her chuckle by cupping her hand over her mouth. The two of them had laughed into the early morning hours until her sides hurt. When she lowered her hand to the couch cushion, Duncan's fingers brushed hers. The cozy feeling shot deeper as she made out his strong silhouette against the dim porch light.

"You have an entrepreneurial knack for this, for sure. I have been trying to read between the lines of your letter, but it is much more fun to hear it from the source, detail by detail." Duncan shifted his shoulders so he could look directly at her.

"Probably more details than you care to know. I guess that's fair warning not to get me started on the topic of cake baking, right?"

"No, not at all." His voice sounded whispery quiet as it traveled the gap between them.

Lorna Rae peeked out the screen door and noted that the murmur of conversation from the young couple had ended some time ago. Perhaps their evening had moved beyond words. "Tell me about you. I understand the case is confidential, so let's talk about Sam's visit."

"Everything that hinders my case could be put in a match box. Now, Sam's visit is another matter. On the first day, I almost sent him through the ceiling when I tried to apply his ointment too heavy-handed. Daphne kicked me out and now administers all Sam's medical treatments, which is just the way he wants it."

"Oh, I can imagine."

"Mrs. Hansen took pity on me and began my tenderness training with the proper dunking of fish fillets in batter. The day of that fish fry, my greatest success was matching up Jimmy Cantor from the post office with Daphne's handicapped cousin Kathleen. Sam tells me her parents are allowing them to court."

Somehow the shift from tenderness to courtship pulled Lorna Rae into a realm she had given up on long ago as girlish foolishness. From out of nowhere, she wondered what it would be like to kiss Duncan. Would the compassion he expressed in his luminous brown eyes ever transfer to his touch? To break the spell, she tucked her legs under her and angled toward him. "Show me what you have learned so far…with the tenderness training, I mean." She placed her hand on his to lend permission.

Seconds passed. Duncan's hand remained on the sofa. Giggles floated in from the front porch and ended with a muffled throaty sound that marked unmistakable pleasure. At long last his hand moved from under hers, his fingertips trailing up her arm. He broke the touch and then it re-alighted below her earlobe as he began to trace the line of her jaw.

Lorna Rae sat breathless, her heart pounding to a deafening rapid-fire beat. She might have her answer to the kissing question sooner than she thought. She wet her lips and soaked in the warm effect of his satiny touch. When he leaned closer, she managed to inhale.

His thumb touched her lower lip and halted. "My, how I have missed you, Rae," he whispered. "Maybe I am not so good at reading between the lines, but your letters sure saved my sanity a time or two when things got tough."

Lorna Rae could feel his lips brush her temple. Goosebumps dropped into her ear and tightened the skin down her left side. Anticipation started to tug at her chest. "Guess I liked being thought of fondly. Not too many letters came to Westport signed like that." She lowered her face until her forehead rested on the cleft of his chin. His beard stubble evoked a sensation even deeper inside.

His tenderness demonstration dropped to her throat where he clasped her, much like the wind holds a milkweed seed. "Sometimes I can be too honest."

His confession ringing in her ears, Lorna lifted her face to look him in the eyes. She discovered that look of compassion she remembered, unmistakable even in the dim light. When his hand roamed up her throat, she dared not speak.

"Rae, I—" His lips dusted enchantment onto her cheek as he drew even closer.

Hypnotic, she lingered under the spell of his proximity as she waited for his next touch, the one she had wanted since he had swept her into his arms at the car. They belonged together as more than friends. This would seal the sentiment. Her heart rumbled in affirmation.

"Would you...allow me?"

The rumble returned, drowning out his whispered question. Lorna Rae reached up and touched his lips to give him a tactile answer when the rumbling grew more insistent. The interruption turned out to be a persistent knock at the screen door.

Sam walked in pulling Daphne behind him. "Time for some

shut-eye, big brother." He flipped off the front porch light, and they stumbled through the parlor to the hallway.

The intimate moment shattered like crystal from a plunging chandelier. Lorna Rae felt Duncan pull her to her feet to evacuate the men's sleeping quarters. "Allow me to walk you to the bottom of the stairwell."

Without waiting for her answer, he tugged her into Sam's wake, so she could follow giggling Daphne upstairs. Only she had nothing to giggle about. Duncan gave her hand a reassuring squeeze that came across as a middle school substitute for the kind of goodnight gesture she had in mind.

"Thanks for agreeing to help Mrs. Hansen with her egg run tomorrow. Come see me at the office afterwards. I have a surprise planned for you."

"But now it is not a surprise, silly." She tried to keep the disappointment out of her tone. Standing side by side, the lip match-up would not happen without some concerted effort, given their differences in height. Anyway, the spell had been broken.

Duncan touched her nose and nodded up the stairs, dismissing her. "Don't count on it."

Lorna Rae padded up the stairs barefoot like a reprimanded child. Disappointment would be her teddy bear tonight, and she would hold it in her arms thinking what might have been. She pushed the door open and discovered Trudy lying across the middle of Daphne's bed, leaving her few options but to do the same. *I am definitely crosswise, so why not sleep like I feel?* She found her gown and made quick work of getting into bed. Trudy flopped over and crowded her toward the foot of the mattress, where she wrestled with the unfinished night for quite some time.

Chapter 16

Duncan stood under the cottonwood tree and watched his surprise run its well-intentioned course. Lorna Rae rushed into her neighbor's arms with a yelp. He had almost kissed her last night, an act he had regretted all morning. What she really needed were her old friends, and he had planned a heaping dose of re-acquaintance under feigned pretense.

Lorna Rae turned from Vivian and gave him a mixed look. "Oh me, oh my. Guess the joke is on me. Duncan said he had trouble operating the gas range, so I told him I'd look at it."

"He has trouble all right," Vivian replied with a roll of her eyes. "I think they call it operator error. Yes, that's it. The hand that stirs the pot scrapes out the burnt residue."

"Okay, okay. Guilty as charged, but how else could I get Lorna Rae over here to reunite with her friends?" Duncan toed the dirt while accepting the blame. Every time he looked at Vivian's animated expressions, he felt like he had stumbled onto the TV set of "I Love Lucy."

Vivian clapped her hands with excitement. "The whole summer reading program is coming over from the public library this morning. We planned to do the reading here under the cottonwood tree. The librarian promised to bring some outdoor-themed books to read aloud."

Duncan stepped past her to gather up the girl in his arms. Glee washed across the child's face as her arms clasped his neck.

"When Vivian mentioned it to me, I thought you and Trudy might want to join their ranks."

Trudy wiggled in delight. "All of my fwiends came to see me."

"So much fun, right? Now make sure you say hello to everyone, even the boys." Duncan kissed the crown of her head and sat her down on the ground. When he straightened, he caught Lorna Rae's wounded gaze and immediately wondered what he had done wrong. He tossed her a farewell wave and made a beeline to his backdoor, where he sought refuge inside his borrowed kitchen. An unspoken complication had surfaced between them. She had been quiet all morning, letting the girl babble on. Maybe he had really botched it last night. They seemed so close, until Sam charged inside.

He avoided notice of the dirty dishes hiding in the sink and pulled last week's newspaper off the table to clear some space. Keeping house proved harder than it looked, as did most tasks in the kitchen. He ambled into the bedroom and took a few moments to make the bed look presentable. Not that he expected company, but he could do better than this.

After a cleanup task or two in the parlor, he glanced at his watch. He had less than half an hour before the preliminary hearing for Bud Gant's charges. McNaughton had made his intentions clear—he had to attend and represent the insurance company's interests. Duncan redirected his attention and flew out of the back door with a bang. He glanced over his shoulder and caught Lorna Rae staring at him. He regretted looking over there.

He had a job to do, and making connections in the oil field neighborhood only clouded his purpose. Today, he would take down the number two man in the illicit labor union. Tomorrow, he would be one step closer to its leader. If he knew what was good for him, he might stop holding hands late at night and get on with it. *Come on, old man. Find yourself.* The challenge rang hollow as the Buick came into sight, his chariot to the arena of justice.

~

Lorna Rae sat on the back rim of the group, stewing in the midday heat despite lots of shade. Not that the library would have been much more pleasant, but Kansas did not typically produce this kind of steamy humidity. The librarian read the last page of "Miss Hickory" where the twig figure had magically merged back into her spot on the tree after leading a fulfilling life. The parallelism didn't escape her, sitting right smack dab in her old neighborhood. Well, she would not surrender as gracefully as that. She had miles to go and other people to meet. Maybe there would be better people, ones that acted on their intentions and didn't leave you hanging.

Vivian leaned over, mischief in her eyes. "Duncan must have been mighty glad to see you last night," she whispered. "Did he…you know…did you two?"

"No." Lorna Rae spoke it like a hush, but knew Viv could be tough to squelch, once she had a train of thought going.

"Then it's only a matter of time. I've seen him sitting on the front porch at night leaned back in his chair, your letter resting across his heart. He has been lonesome, even Bert sees it."

Lorna Rae tried not to see the eager taunt in her friend's eyes. Hadn't she felt equally as sure late last night? Yet something gnawed at her about the whole thing. She had wanted that kiss and not gotten it. If it had been a business proposition for a cake deal, she would have clinched it herself. Instead, it blew away into nothingness.

Her gaze wandered to the children. Trudy sat beside Mary Jane, their arms laced together in friendship as they listened to a story about a bunny. Duncan had not hesitated to kiss her daughter, not for a second. Her motivations came pure as the driven snow, to love and be loved.

Lorna Rae stewed over the reflective thought that her intentions may not have been as sterling. Since Duncan held a temporary job at the oil fields, he would be on his way when the case closed, maybe by the turn of seasons. An uncomfortable churning started in her stomach that leaked its unease into her limbs. He would leave as sure as summertime rain, and they had more than their fill of that. That made her the mud puddle left behind. She straightened in her seat, trying to break from the sensation.

"What's wrong?" Vivian's face animated with her inquiry.

"Too hot, I guess." Lorna Rae fanned her neck to better look the part.

"I have ice cream."

"I'll take some."

Vivian started first, hatching the inescapable giggle that came out more like a snort. She slapped a hand over her mouth, but her eyes carried the message forward. Her shoulders shook.

Lorna Rae determined not to give way to the levity. She crossed her ankles and tried to focus on the bunny story. When Viv leaned over far enough she could feel her shaking, the contagion inexplicably spread. She snickered and caught it in her fist, pressing her other arm into her midsection to stabilize.

"Officer, I would like to report a five-alarm fire," Vivian whispered. A snort followed, the kind that cannot be hushed, though another parent down the line attempted.

Lorna Rae let the giggles carry her worries away. She and Viv shook shoulder-to-shoulder for the remainder of the bunny story. In a stroke of luck, it ended with a funny last line, so the children soon joined suit. The librarian rose from her chair as the program concluded.

Lorna Rae patted Vivian's hand, her bad mood erased. "I will take that minimum daily requirement of coolant now."

"Have a double," she replied in a rush. "It may have to last a while." She pinched her nose to stifle the next giggle, which only made it sound like an elephant trumpeting.

Lorna Rae stood and took in the scene. Beyond the hubbub of mingling children, the bungalow sat like a familiar friend. "I think I'll go over and check on my furniture."

"Lunch will be ready in half an hour. You are my guest, so wander back like a boomerang. Don't be too shocked by the state of things over there."

"That's a fair warning. Can you keep Trudy busy?"

"Let's leave that to Mary Jane. She drew a new hopscotch board on the back sidewalk after breakfast this morning."

Lorna Rae threw up her hand and walked the familiar path to her old home, purposefully treading the edge where the crabgrass threatened to encroach. She pulled the screen door open and walked into the kitchen. A mess in the sink became her first order of business. She scrubbed the stovetop next. An errant shirt claimed the chair back at the table, so she brought it into the bedroom. She exhaled when she found the bed had been made. Thank goodness Duncan wasn't a total slob.

When she stepped over to clear another shirt from the closet doorknob, something on the nightstand caught her attention. She picked up a photograph and recognized the setting as the company picnic. Trudy had awakened in the basket right at the moment Duncan had taken the candid snapshot. Her matronly image stared back at her with open candor. She looked happy.

Winded by a sucker-punch of a guilty conscience, she perched on the edge of the bed to regain her stability. From the curled edge of the photo, Duncan had been handling it quite a bit. Not that the revelation translated into anything of promise, but it did speak of a private moment where a man might admit he had been thinking of you fondly. She found her letter on the nightstand. So moved, she couldn't bear to touch it. She stood and placed the photo down right where she had found it. Smoothing a hand over the chenille bedspread to eliminate any trace of her presence, she sensed an untangling of sorts.

"Heavenly Father, please bless the admirable man who sleeps here. Should you intend something more between the two of us, then I ask you to bless that as well. Let my heart surrender to you first, Lord. Please prepare my heart, because I do not know my way around this territory. Shine your light on my path, amen."

Tidying the parlor proved inconsequential compared to the rear of the house. She noticed Duncan had moved an upholstered chair near the front door, likely his front porch perch. She ran her fingers over the chair back, trying to imagine him out there reading and re-reading her letter. A lovely coolness ran through her, a cozy assurance that everything would be okay. Maybe she would pass on that ice cream offer after all, though Vivian would be shocked to high heaven.

~

Duncan drove in relative silence the familiar road out to the Hansen farm. Lorna Rae turned to check on Trudy in the back seat, and the delayed nap held its sway. He caught her gaze when she faced back around.

He tightened his grip on the wheel. "You didn't have to clean up the bungalow, but thank you for doing it. I will count that as my surprise for the day."

A smile flitted across her face as she stared out the windshield at the countryside. "You are welcome. It had an element of déjà vu to it, but different all the same. I tried to respect your things."

He slowed the car for the low-water bridge and thought it had receded some since that morning. The sound of splashing water crept through the open windows and seemed to refresh the mood. "We have gone over twelve hours without rain. I think that is a good sign."

"Yes, a good sign. Steve thinks we might be here the better part of a week. I heard Della say he is thinking about returning by himself first, to clean up the flood mess. She does not want the baby exposed to mold or anything harmful."

Duncan assessed her last comments, working out a timetable in his head. He might only have two weeks to enjoy her company. It would have to do. His thoughts jumbled as he let the car drift out of the water and come to a slow stop at the rise.

Lorna Rae leaned forward and examined the hood of the car. "Is something wrong with the Buick?"

"No, nothing's wrong. I am buying a few extra minutes, that's all."

"Oh, don't worry about Trudy. If you park over by the barn, I can leave her in here to sleep off her active morning. Those Decker kids wore her out."

"I meant a few minutes for you and me." As soon as he started his explanation, a huge frog must have leapt into his throat. He tried to clear away the complication as she turned in the seat to face him. A jazzy rendition of "I Only Have Eyes for You" played over the radio to fill the lapse. "We are all crowded in here at the Hansen's, like one big happy family."

"I like it though, and Mrs. Hansen seems pleased as punch."

"What I am saying is, I want some time with you alone—you and me. Even if it's only two weeks until you go back to Westport, Rae. I would like to take you out on dates. We can include time with the family, but have our own time, too. If you could give me an answer in the next day or so, I'd appreciate it. Seems the calendar works against me at every turn lately."

Lorna Rae dropped her gaze from the windshield and gathered her hands over her heart. When she turned back to him, her eyes sparkled. "Yes, I would like that immensely. Let me speak to Della about babysitting Trudy. I am quite certain she will."

Duncan held his elation at bay, keeping his eyes fixed on a beautiful woman who had just consented to be the object of his affection. Part of him wanted to evaporate the distance between them and launch the intimacy right then and there. The other part of him sat paralyzed, weighing the risk against the unknown gain. Proper words failed him.

As the singer sang the last ooh-ooh-ooh in ascending notes, Lorna Rae slipped across the bench seat and came to rest right beside him. When she situated her frame, their shoulders touched. A shy smile birthed on her face as she regarded the countryside once again.

His foot found the accelerator, and they proceeded up the road to the farm drive. He wheeled the Buick in and headed toward the barn to shield Trudy from the late afternoon sunlight. Truth be told, he could stand a little nap himself. "Come out my side, and we will try to keep her asleep." He cut the engine and opened his door with care.

Lorna Rae grabbed the hand he offered and followed him out. He bent to close the door at close range to maintain quiet as she held her other hand on her chest. The girl stirred, but went right back to sleep.

He tugged on her, expecting some feisty resistance to walking hand-in-hand. "Need this?" He would hardly put it past her.

She bit her bottom lip to quell a smile. "Not until we get to the house."

He stood taller and gave her hand a little swing of enjoyment. This courtship was heady stuff, all right. He might just grow fond of it, from the feel of things. Mrs. Hansen appeared at the back stoop and waved. He returned the gesture with his free hand. When Lorna Rae did not attempt to pull loose, he gained some confidence that he had made the right move. Two weeks would show them a direction from here, one way or the other.

~

Torguson propped his elbows on the hood of Shorty Carlson's truck and let the scorch from the sun burn a few seconds longer than comfortable. "We're gonna have to call a meeting."

Shorty looked pretty uncertain as he checked the wiper blades under the pretense of maintenance. "But boss, what with Gant being in trouble with the law, I'm not sure you can get a turnout this month. Besides, the second Tuesday has come and gone."

"Each member pledged their commitment. I am calling them

on it. Let everybody know the meeting is mandatory. Make it this coming Tuesday night. Same place as usual. We will be rolling the lottery and making the next pick, so be ready."

Shorty gave him a sheepish look and eye-balled the far wiper blade. "I don't know if a man can really be ready for that, boss."

"Let's try to add some extra cash this round. We are a few members short of a quorum, so that pinches our bank account." Torguson eased his elbows off the hood, but leaned his hips onto the front quarter panel. He savored the sensation as long as he could bear it. "Man, I hate July."

"From what I can tell, it hates you right back." Shorty gave a little laugh, until a torn-off match stick found its way onto the hood. "Looks like the rain could be an issue. First the Kansas River, now the Neosho. A flood makes for a bad distraction."

He pushed back off the truck, sick of the whole mess but unwilling to give up without total victory. "At the oil field, I am the lead distraction. Try not to forget it." They needed to strike again before Gant's trial, to show the big man who the real boss was. One more fellow would have to lose a few fingers, but it wasn't going to be him.

Shorty plucked the match off his truck and seemed a bit unsettled. "DiMaggio made it forty-five games in a row last night. That's quite a hitting spree he is on."

"I like mine better." Torguson spit on the curb and threw his hands up in the air, releasing his sergeant-at-arms to convene the next meeting. If all signs were dead on the money, it was going to be a hot one.

~

The morning sun rose out of the kitchen window, and Lorna Rae regarded it with a sigh. She had agreed to a baking lesson that morning, both for Della and for Daphne. Now, she would have to go through it with halfhearted vigor. She separated the pans and fashioned two work stations on the counter.

Last night had been their first night officially courting. Duncan had fallen asleep with his head on her shoulder, right there on the sofa. No romantic exchanges had transpired, no innuendo or suggestive hints of attraction, and certainly no kisses. Exasperating though it had been at first assessment, she remembered the unmistakable happiness deep in her spirit. The time they shared meant something special, even if he had been half-wakeful through part of it.

The flooding slapped a vise-grip hold on the men. Yesterday, Steve learned the Kansas City stockyards had gone underwater, including an area called West Bottoms. In Manhattan, the downtown district had flooded eight feet deep. With the crest yet to come, Lorna Rae wondered how bad it could get from here. The sump pump hummed on automatically and echoed up the basement stairs. At least they were safe here in their little haven.

Mrs. Hansen took the tea kettle off the stove and began to fill it with water. "Good morning, Lorna Rae. Are you ready for your baking school this morning? Oh, mercy. Our water pressure seems to be down. I better have Sam check the pump house. We might be 'water, water everywhere and not a drop to drink' right here in the middle of the flood."

"Let's not even tease about that, Mrs. H. If I cannot have a shower at least every other day, things might get unfriendly around here." She chuckled, but she meant it.

"What a blessing from God that both Della and Daphne want to bake with you. Who knows, you could open up a branch line while you are here. Think about it. I can say a word on your behalf to Mr. Anders at the grocery store, if you get so inclined. We could deliver the cakes with my eggs, so it would not double my gasoline bill."

She pulled the flour off the pantry shelf and studied her hostess. She seemed most sincere. "Do you mean let Daphne bake without me living close by to oversee it?"

She turned the burner on and settled the full kettle in place. "As long as she adheres to your recipes and maintains your packaging style, it would work. Aren't you open to expanding your market?"

"I had not given it any thought beyond my immediate reach, to be honest. But there isn't any reason for that, I suppose, as long as quality standards were in place."

"God has a reason for you being here, maybe to lend you further success with your cake business. I suggest you remain open to it and see where he leads you."

Mindful that they had now progressed beyond a conversation about cake sales, Lorna Rae stopped at the kitchen window to conduct a heart check. The sun rose in strength, climbing the morning sky with full purpose. Yes, she could allow God to direct her life, if she could ever figure out where the next turn in the road would fall.

Trudy ran into the room clutching her coloring book and crayons. "Daphne wants a chicken." She slung the book onto the table and pushed the chair into place.

"Let me get your booster seat in place, young lady." Mrs. Hansen reached for the phone book and, upon closer inspection, opted for two. "You won't need these long at the rate you are growing, big girl."

"I'm so big." Trudy dumped the crayons out and selected the red one.

"A big mess," Lorna replied under her breath. Mrs. Hansen walked by and patted her shoulder. She heard a shuffling upstairs and realized they would have company soon, forcing her next confession. "Mrs. Hansen, I wanted you to know that Mr. Reed has asked permission to date me while we are back here."

She turned toward her with a motherly look. "And did you say yes?"

"I did, only it hasn't been what I assumed."

"Love takes its own way. Try not to be quick to push it where you want it to go."

"Thank you for that good advice. I find myself off-balance, to say the very least."

"Imagine what he must be going through then. He's had nothing but work all his life." She made a clucking sound and checked the kettle. "I married a man like that—a good man."

"A good man. Yes, that is my impression, too. I admire him for his safety work. He is the smartest man I have ever met, a maven out on the oil fields."

"Admiration is a fine starting point. I promise to keep you both in my prayers."

"I somehow knew I had to get here when the flood struck. I needed to get to your house, Mrs. Hansen. Bless you for taking us all in."

"The blessing is already mine, dear. How about some hot tea before the day grows too hot to even consider it?"

Lorna Rae nodded as Della and Daphne made their appearance in the kitchen.

Della pulled her hair into a ponytail while Daphne took two aprons from a drawer. "Robert Thomas seemed a bit fussy this morning, like he didn't want his nap after his feeding. Maybe it's the change of scenery."

"It could be our well water making your milk taste different. I wouldn't be too alarmed." Mrs. Hansen poured the hot water into matching china cups with delicate handles. "Anyone else want a cup?" She returned to the counter for the tea bags.

"Yes, please," Della replied. "Okay sis. We are here and ready. Let the lesson begin."

"Ladies, let's keep this in mind. Either of you could carry off the Lo-Rae Cakes distribution in your area, with or without me." Lorna Rae looked from one astonished face to the other. "After all, the creek is rising, and we have no idea which side I might end up on, so my baking instructions today will be thorough."

Della pulled the apron over her head, and Daphne tied it behind her. "Fair enough then, but we fully expect you to come back with us and conquer Kansas City with your business prowess."

Careful to be detailed and ever-watchful, Lorna Rae took the younger women through the complete baking cycle, posting ingredients on the cabinet door and allowing them to do the mixing independently. The cakes had gone into the oven at the same precise moment, and she had taught them what to watch for when the cakes were done. When the combination of visual, olfactory, and timing cues aligned, they would know when to take the cakes from the oven. Della had removed the chocolate cake and Daphne the applesauce one. Both gave the appearance of having turned out to perfection.

Mrs. Hansen lowered the oven door to dissipate some of the heat. "I believe you have two A-plus students."

"Remember, wait to pull the filling from the refrigerator until the cake has cooled to room temperature. Be sure to whip it one last time before putting it between the layers. We will work on the standard cutting size after you get these removed from the pans. Let's allow them to cool for ten minutes first."

Trudy hopped off the booster seat, causing the phone books to topple onto the floor. "I melt my cwayons." She chased the red crayon and finally corralled it at her mother's foot.

"Trudy, do not make a mess now. Mommy is very busy

teaching Aunt Della and Daphne how to bake."

She gave her head a rebellious shake. "I bake too."

Lorna Rae rubbed a tiny ache out of her brow, closing her eyes to aid the process. "Della, do you have that diagram of the cutting pattern?"

"Sure. I tucked it into the bag with the pans. It's right here."

Mrs. Hansen dropped her china cup and it shattered. "Oh, Lord. Please no—"

Loran Rae opened her eyes. It took a few seconds to decipher what she saw. Trudy stood at the open oven door, her hands clasping the racks where a red crayon melted from what remained of the three-hundred fifty degree oven. The high-pitched scream came next as Trudy reacted to the hot metal in her hands. Lorna Rae lunged for the oven, knocked her hands off the rack, and kicked the door closed.

Daphne ran some water over the tea towel and handed it to her. Trudy let loose another ear-pricking scream and tears began to flood her cheeks.

"Let me get some lard," Mrs. Hansen said, her eyes filled with worry. "We may have to take her to Doctor Lucas if it turns out too severe."

"Hush baby, hush." Lorna Rae pled as her mind tried to catch up with her actions. She knelt and attempted to open Trudy's fists so she could apply the cool compress. When she managed to get a peek of her right palm, she saw nothing but blisters rising out of the damage.

Daphne's face blanched white. She stepped back so Della could get a glimpse. "Third degree burns, the worst kind,"

Della gulped. "Let me get Steve in from digging up the front yard. He can drive you to town, Lorna Rae, while you hold Trudy."

"Yes, please go get him. I…don't know what else to do." Her mind swimming, Lorna Rae pulled the girl against her wishing she could take all the hurt away. Maybe if she'd been paying closer attention, it might not have happened.

"Doc Lucas will see you without charging. He knows what to do. God, help him." Mrs. Hansen wrung her hands as Daphne left the room. She soon returned with Trudy's shoes and slipped them on the child without a word.

Lorna Rae scooped up the girl who proceeded to wail right into her ear. She deserved it for her negligence. Something turned to stone inside of her as she fixed the car in her gaze and walked on shaky legs for it, the cooling cloth dangling from Trudy's grip like no help at all.

~

Kicked in the stomach each time the girl cried out, Duncan sat on the clinic's porch waiting for the doctor's verdict. A statue that looked like Lorna Rae sat in his office chair, watching the doctor's ministrations to assure the wound was hygienic. His treatment must have burned like the threshold of the sun, as the little girl found the full capacity of her lungs and used it profusely. He held his head in his hands, helpless to make any difference.

When Steve left for the chapel to pray over the dire situation, Duncan wondered if he should have joined him. Still, he had felt the nudge to stay close by, not understanding it but willing to obey.

"This first week is critical. We have to keep her hands free of any germs. I could cover them with plastic gloves, but the skin also needs to breathe. We can use gauze instead." Dr. Lucas pushed back on his chair to address Lorna Rae directly. "The next part is difficult treatment. You are not going to want any part of this, but you have to."

Duncan snapped to his feet and stepped toward the screen door, not wanting to miss a word of what the doctor had to say. His chest heaving, he took breaths in short bursts as if he were mad at the world. How hard to regain ground after safety had lapsed. He dreaded the acrid aftermath.

"The burnt skin has to come off—daily. This is an indelicate task, and Trudy is not going to cooperate. I suggest you remain the comforting parent, Mrs. Holmes, and get someone else to inflict the painful remedy."

"But I am a single parent, doctor. Can I do both?" Lorna Rae spoke in a quiet tone, her face pale.

"No, it cannot be done by one person. You will have to restrain her, and the helper will have to scrape her palms after they have been soaked in a nightly bath. I can give you a scouring mat to use for the treatment."

"Perhaps Daphne would help me. She is showing some promising skill with first aid."

Duncan stood beside Lorna Rae, not realizing he had stepped

inside. "I will do it." Though part of him seemed paralyzed, one point he was certain about. He would not be able to stand seeing anyone else inflict pain on that precious child. Not while he was around.

Lorna Rae stood to face him, her expression beyond fragile. "Duncan, I don't think—"

"We are close, Doctor Lucas. The child considers me her friend. I think it helps going in to have that type of foundation established."

"True, but you could forfeit everything you have built, going through something traumatic like this. You are going to hurt her—on purpose."

"Is this truly the best treatment?" Lorna Rae's tone held a beggar's plea.

The doctor reached out to Trudy who had balled up on the examination table and rubbed her back. "Yes, it has to be done."

Duncan held out his open palm to Lorna Rae, and she slipped her hand in his. "I will scrape her hands then."

Lorna Rae turned to face the doctor and seemed a bit less fragile. "I will hold her and pray to high heaven she can forgive us. Now, show us exactly what to do."

Duncan tried to send a message of stability to her through their hand connection, but sensed quite the opposite, as if he had gained from her. United, they faced a mighty foe, the unbridled pain of a child.

Chapter 17

The rain fell in torrents for much of the day. Lorna Rae never questioned that Duncan would come help her with Trudy's treatment. The sound of his footsteps in the hallway below lent reassurance that recovery fell within their collective grasp.

As he greeted their hostess, Duncan's forecast for gloom echoed up the stairs. "On tonight's news broadcast, they reported the barracks at Fort Riley had been destroyed by rushing water. Topeka is being evacuated tonight, almost twenty-five thousand people. They are afraid the Missouri River is changing its course. God help us, as Kansas may never be the same."

Impervious to troubles beyond her own pending flood, Lorna Rae allowed the threat of high water to roll into a distant catch basin, as she could not absorb that statewide magnitude of worry right now. Her little girl would soon be under assault. It knifed her in the stomach to think it would be at her own hands, or more specifically, at Duncan's hands. "Yes, God help us."

He proceeded to the top stair, his expression reserved. "Is she ready?"

"Yes, she is bathed and dressed for bed. Daphne and Sam are acting out a story, one of her favorite stories, 'The Three Little Pigs.'" She turned down the hallway to hear Sam's huff-and-puff, unaware she had stopped until Duncan's hand covered the cap of her shoulder.

"Father, I pray that you find our hearts innocent of anything but love tonight as we start this harsh treatment. In your kindness, shield Trudy from the pain we must inflict for her recovery from the burns. We ask in the name of Jesus, amen."

Lorna Rae stepped out of his grasp and walked with determined steps to the bedroom door. Daphne closed the book and tapped the big bad wolf on the head. Sam stood and flashed a toothy smile at Trudy who pulled the covers up to eye level as if to hide. "Bedtime, baby doll. Your friend Mr. Reed is here to help me with your treatment. Remember, we talked about this in the bathroom. Off with the bad skin to bring out the good." Daphne led Sam from the bedroom.

"No, I don't want to. Go away, Mista Weed."

Duncan's presence filled the room. "Hold her, Lorna Rae. Trudy, I want you to help me by not pulling away. I expect you to be brave." He pulled back the seal on the scouring mat. It snapped like a brittle nerve.

"Let's get ready, Trudy. Mr. Reed came over a flooded creek to be here tonight. We have do what he says." Lorna Rae pulled her out from the bedding and sat her down in her lap.

Duncan approached and knelt on one knee. "Secure her arms. Let's start with the right hand first." With steady resolve, he pressed down on the encrusted skin and began the scouring treatment with side to side pressure.

Trudy matched a howling scream with a voracious kicking spell, while Lorna Rae tried to subdue both. The first five seconds chewed her motherly instincts to pieces and spit them out onto the carpeted floor. Trudy slipped from her grasp, so she struggled to get a better hold.

Duncan paused to await a more stabilized treatment surface and switched hands with his next swipe, attacking the sloughing skin on her left palm. He worked with steady, even strokes.

Trudy ratcheted up her volume, and within seconds, the unmistakable cry of a newborn answered back. As she kicked and thrashed to rid the hurt, Lorna Rae pinned her limbs back and began to sob. What an atrocity of motherhood.

Duncan finished the palm scouring in a final pass. With patience, he removed the gauze drop cloth that had caught all the damaged skin. He wadded it up, stood, and left the room without a word.

Lorna Rae rocked back and forth in an attempt to get Trudy to shush. She hummed into the child's ear, and in a few sob-shaken moments, managed to calm her down. In another minute, the girl had fallen asleep. With a gentle roll, Lorna Rae got her into bed and pulled up the sheet.

Wiping a tear on the sleeve of her shirt, Lorna Rae wrapped fresh gauze around the child's hands, grateful for the lack of resistance. The treatment left her aching front to back. When she tied the final knot to hold the second bandage, Duncan crept into her thoughts. He had been stalwart earlier, unflinching in his task. She would have to sincerely thank him for that gift of steady assurance, as she had been a basket case.

~

Duncan failed to realize he was standing in the kitchen until his hostess spoke.

"I mean the pump house, Duncan. Can you check it before we are totally out of water in here? I am so sorry to have to ask, but at least the rain is tailing off to a drizzle now."

He gathered his wits, not easy after what he had just been through. He wiped a hand through his hair and studied the thinning stream of water coming out of the faucet. "Maybe it has clogged up with debris. Sure, I can take a look. Have you seen Sam?"

"I sent Sam and Daphne out to collect eggs when the screaming let loose."

"Good idea. Wish somebody would have sent me out, too."

"Listen. You have to lift the pump housing from the ground and tilt it back. Mil once showed me a little red lever inside that resets the pump. I know nothing about the filter, if you think that could be clogged. There were half a million things I should have asked that man."

"I should be fine. Maybe you could get me a flashlight, though. The sun has already set. I will try to bring those two egg collectors in when I come, so they don't get trapped in the barn all night with the next round of rain."

"Someday there won't be a next round—"

"I hope you are talking about during the summer of 1951, Mrs. Hansen, because I cannot wait until the promised Day of the Lord to get dried out." He stepped toward the door to get the next chore addressed.

She chuckled as she rummaged through a junk-filled drawer, where she eventually located a silver flashlight. "Please do not give up on God, even when he seems slow in arriving." She brought him the flashlight and delivered it with an understanding look.

He took possession, bobbing the heavy tool. "If anyone needs me, I will be out back."

"Lorna Rae needs you, all right. Like I said, give God some time."

Duncan stepped onto the concrete patio and noticed the barn door ajar. His kid brother was inside, probably receiving a kiss an egg from Daphne as the old hens clucked and fluttered harmlessly around his ankles. Such tasks were not doled out to him, though. He always got the ugly work, the on-the-edge-of-safety work. For some reason, that allotment raked his ire tonight. Impatient, he held the flashlight to shield his brow and scanned the backyard for the pump house.

A square-topped structure stood in the center of the yard. Sitting on high ground, flooding did not appear to be the source of the problem. He strode out to the small shack and pushed against the front planking. When it resisted, he pocketed the flashlight and sank to his knees. Using both palms, he shoved the housing back. The hinges squeaked but held fast. From the moment the housing thumped on the ground, the pump began to hiss.

Duncan drew out the flashlight in slow motion, his irk flattening to something akin to dread. In the pale light of dusk, he could make out the convoluted structure of the pump tapping the well, but the lever escaped detection. His thumb slid across the flashlight's switch, and yellow light illuminated the mechanism. The pump hissed again, but the red he saw came from the tongue of a hideous brown-blotched snake coiled around the whole works, not the lever.

"Saints above and Satan below," he whispered. His eyes widened when the snake moved toward him with a girth thicker than his forearm. The hissing became constant. He tried to arrest the creature by shining the light right into its eyes. Within seconds, he could tell that approach held no merit. He stood to keep from being struck in the face, while the snake slid out of the hideout toward the swollen creek. He might have saved a few frogs from their fate by not allowing the expatriated reptile to escape. Having inflicted enough pain for one night, he stood motionless and let the animal slip away unharmed.

The patter of light rain tapped against the tin roof of the pump housing and mixed with the rapid thud of his beating heart. He closed his eyes, lifting his face into the steady drizzle. He remained like that for some time, allowing the day's hurt to rinse off. He recalled the traumatized version of Trudy, staring back at him with tear-swollen eyes. That look of betrayal left a hurt-filled taint—one that ripped him up on the inside.

His knees quaked, so he dropped back onto the soggy turf. With the flashlight illuminated, he searched for the red lever and soon found it on the lower right side. Lighthearted laughter trickled across the yard from the direction of the barn. He refused to look. Ready for resolution, he reached beyond the cobwebs and toggled the red lever a couple of times. The pump responded and ran through a motor-driven sequence before turning off. He planned to give it a minute before trying again, somewhat heartened that the water pump appeared to be working fine now. He turned the flashlight off and tossed it to the ground.

Still on his knees, he spoke a quick prayer of forgiveness for the gut-stabbing hurt he had caused Trudy. He prayed against the mounting flood and for their collective well-being through the night. A recurring flaw came to mind, birthed from his incessant need for analysis, so he asked for forgiveness for that. When he opened his eyes, he found Lorna Rae by his side.

"Trudy fell asleep a short minute after you left. I wanted to let you know, so you wouldn't worry anymore tonight. Mrs. Hansen told me I could find you out here."

Her words came to him in a slow, deliberate way. Duncan managed to nod in response, too damaged by a cumulative build-up of pursing safety at all cost. A joy robber, it held him at smoking gunpoint right here in front of this pump house, down on his knees. Seconds ticked by and the guilt began to dissipate, leaving room for something else that felt more life-lending.

Duncan stared at Lorna Rae. Rain dripped through her hair as she looked up at him, her gaze full of admiration. He needed the pump to disappear and all the flooding hardship with it, aggravating complications that burdened his life. "I'm waiting to reset the pump one more time."

"So we wait." She reached out and touched his shoulder.

The heat transfer short-circuited his brain. He slid his arm around her back and pulled her closer until their faces were mere inches apart. When she looked at him through wet lashes, the dam holding back his self-control gave way. His cheek slid across Lorna Rae's until his lips found what they needed. For her part, she seemed ready—possibly even hungry-ready. Her reciprocal touch transfixed his unrest. After he broke off the extended embrace to catch his breath, she soon returned for a second round, a thrill he met with unbridled enthusiasm. During the kiss, the pump cut on and off by itself, a real healer.

Lorna Rae leaned away and gave the pump house a brief inspection. "It sounds like the pump is working fine now. Should we go back inside?" Her gaze searched his face.

He touched her bare neck and played the wetness up and down her skin with his thumb as if to gauge his answer. With her delicate features flooding his brain, he could not imagine standing to move away, even if he had to. "Remember? I am on reset—"

She managed a tiny gasp when his next kiss landed and then shifted up against him.

Duncan held her tighter and decided right then he would take his sweet time about going back inside the house. Catastrophe could take a long time-out for the rest of the evening, since he had finally found something better to do than chase safety. His kid brother probably had a dozen or so eggs to carry back to the farmhouse. He would collect his own harvest, one plucked fruit at a time, if his sweet cake baker would let him possess enough focus to keep a count going. After she inched up and whispered something breathless in his ear, he realized counting would not be a feasible option.

~

Torguson leaned across the table to put the squeeze on his sergeant-at-arms. "Tell me, Carlson. Who's not here? Do not make me repeat myself a third time."

"Bert Decker, Harley's next-door neighbor. Maybe he isn't interested anymore." Shorty looked up and several men nodded.

Torguson rotated his steely glance around the table to connect with each member. They needed to stick to their game plan. "That is not how we build the union, is it?" Their next strike would likely split things wide open, given the moratorium. The day it lifted would be a sorry day, indeed. To have things lined up well ahead of time would be his best strategy. "You told Bert to be here, I suppose."

Shorty gave his sweaty face a wipe. "Yeah, I stopped by his house yesterday evening on my way out. He got the message, but showed little interest, to tell you the truth."

"I think he might show a bit more interest now." Torguson reached for a blank matchbook pad behind him on the bar. "Just to remind everybody—when you fail to show for the meeting, your number automatically comes up. That's union rules."

A low murmur followed his comment as Shorty reached out to neaten up the pile of match pads already in the center of the table. His hand shook while it reclaimed his own pad. Several others rapidly followed suit.

"If you could be so kind as to provide me that number, Shorty, I will write it in." Torguson flipped out his box cutter and slid the blade open.

"Bert is number twenty-four." Shorty rolled a black marker toward the leader and took his hands off the table.

Torguson ripped the cap off the marker with his teeth, keeping the blade in his left hand. He wrote the two numbers square on the back cover and flipped the matches over. With a slash, he cut a swath of match sticks out and then threw the pad at Shorty. "Deliver this with the message that I will let him know when." He gave the members a steely smile as he collected the detached matches and stuffed them into his shirt pocket. "Meeting adjourned."

"That's it, fellas," Shorty replied. He grabbed the chosen match pad and scurried away.

Torguson leaned back in his seat as the members rapidly disbanded. *What's the hurry when the night holds nothing but rain?* The barmaid soon stepped over to clean up the empty tankards. "Bring me another one. I feel like looking at you a while longer."

"Suit yourself, Liam. No harm in looking."

"Action, honey. You know I am a man of action." He chuckled as she walked away from his charming invitation to spend some time at his table. She'd be back. They always came back.

~

Lorna Rae had returned inside with only half a brain in her head. Her thoughts skittered around like a drop of water on bacon grease. Only when she heard footsteps coming up out of the basement could she get her bearings. She wiped the stovetop clean for a second time and flashed Sam a smile when he emerged from the narrow stairwell. She ran some water over the dishcloth and wrung it out to dry.

Duncan soon hovered over her shoulder at the sink. "Good water pressure you have there, Miss Lo-Rae Cakes. You served some mighty fine cake earlier tonight. It seems too long since I've had such a treat."

"How's the sump pump? Will we be safe tonight?"

"Like its cousin outside, it is working full-strength. I'm heading home now. Want to walk me out?" Duncan nodded toward the back door.

She felt him untie her apron strings and batted his hand away with a coy smile. "Not that I want you to go, but I will be happy to show you out if it's time." She stepped around him and lifted the apron over her head to hang it on the pantry knob.

"I am taking the farm truck tonight. The creek has swollen too high for the Buick."

"That doesn't lend me any comfort. Mrs. Hansen said the radio reported that Fairfax Airport is underwater in Kansas City. TWA lost their overhaul base."

"Well, that is what happens when you build your airport on bottomlands. The Missouri River is reclaiming its floodway. Too bad it had to pick this summer to do it."

She opened the back door and stepped out under the awning. His arm soon threaded around her waist, spinning her around into his full grasp. "At least the incessant rain brought me back to El Dorado."

"At most it brought you back." He closed the gap between them, his eyes scanning her face. "I needed a miracle like that, Rae. I needed you back. Everything fell flat when you left."

"Shh. Try not to tell all your secrets, Mr. Risk Management. A woman could take advantage of that." She batted her lashes a couple of times to let him think she might.

"Not all my secrets," he whispered.

She tiptoed up to meet his goodnight kiss and developed a cramp in her calf before he released her. It was pleasurable pain, the kind she would return to in a heartbeat. Duncan may have been thinking along the same lines, as she soon found him leaning over her, hunting for more attention. "I must say, this dating business seems to be giving you an outlet for your compassion."

He hugged her, his nose nuzzled against her ear. "I will be dreaming about you, Rae. Stay safe for me. I will come back for dinner tomorrow." With a peck on her cheek, he stepped away.

Lorna Rae backpedaled toward the door as darkness wrapped around Duncan's figure. She should have drawn out their farewell, because the night rapidly dropped off the deep edge of hollow. Their attraction came with unexpected magnetism, a force she had never known before. She opened the back door to the sound of the sump pump running as the truck's headlights raked the house and disappeared down the lane.

~

Duncan made every attempt to pull in the diesel truck without a sound, coasting to a halt by the bungalow's front porch. One glance at the neighbor's house revealed no need for such concern. A light shone from every room. He popped the truck door open and checked his watch in the cab's light. It read ten thirty-five. A hacking sound came from the side yard, and he stepped under the cottonwood tree to figure it out. A stooped figure worked the flower bed over with a heavy hand. "Vivian? Is that you?"

"Yeah. Can't tell you what is going on, because Bert swore me to secrecy."

"Okay." Though her answer confused him, the hour was ridiculous for gardening. "Does this have anything to do with the rain?"

The front door swung open and Bert stepped out, his motions jerky as he looked around. "Viv, get back in here and help the kids. Duncan? You have a truck?"

"Yes, I had to swap the Buick out. The creek has overrun the low-water bridge coming out of the Hansen's farm."

He dropped off the side of the porch and drew up next to him. "Thank the Lord. Listen, I need to borrow that truck tonight. We have to move out. There's trouble. Union trouble." His voice lowered, Bert shot him a desperate look. "I searched, but can't find any other way out."

"Where are you heading? I suppose Mrs. Hansen might want her truck back."

"Wichita. I have an uncle in the aircraft industry where jobs are plentiful right now. The oil fields have become too dangerous for a family man. My first responsibility is to these kids."

Duncan glimpsed a rare opportunity opening in front of him and gained new courage to face it. "Okay, Bert. The truck is yours to use under one condition." He steeled his features before laying down his terms. With a direct shot at the union boss, he did not hesitate to take it. The night grew young under the cottonwood tree, a true reckoning of determined pursuit.

~

The morning broke clear through the east-facing window where Lorna Rae stood basking in the healing light. Trudy stumbled in, her gauze bandages hanging loose. "Here, sweetie. Let Mommy retie your bandages for you."

She scrunched up her face and her eyes formed half-moon squints. "Mista Weed was mean to me last night."

"No, Trudy. Mr. Reed was firm with you, because the doctor wants us to make your hands get better. We talked about this yesterday. Mr. Reed did not like doing it though. It stung his heart to hurt you like that." Lorna pulled the knot apart and began to unwrap one hand.

"He likes safe things."

"Yes, you are right, he does. Safety is his job at the oil fields."

"Like a policeman?"

"In a way. Oh, look at this, doll baby. Your hand is so much better already. It's working. That scrub treatment is working to make your skin heal."

She offered up her other hand, her eyes full of fear. "Will he come back tonight?"

"He plans to come for dinner. Then, I promise you a big bubble bath before he treats your burns again. I don't want you to dread it all day, though. See how much better you are? That makes it totally worth it."

"Mista Weed is mean to me, so he cannot be my fwiend."

Lorna Rae unwrapped the second hand, which had not been as

severe. A blister had popped, so she tried to pick off the dead skin.

Trudy flinched and pulled away. "Mommy, do not be mean."

"No, sweetie. Mommy loves you too much to hurt you." She gathered the child in her arms for a reassuring hug. "Should we see if Daphne will braid your hair this morning?"

"Oh, yes. She is nice to me." The girl skipped out and pattered down the hall.

Lorna Rae rose and took the gauze bandage box from the medicine cabinet. The braiding had been prearranged as a distraction for the daily re-wrapping of her damaged hands. But Goldilocks did not need to know anything beyond Mother Bear's determination to take care of her every need. Her thoughts drifted to Papa Bear, who had fallen into the doghouse as far as Goldie was concerned. She clucked her tongue, hoping Duncan could maneuver his way out.

~

Mack Swain sat on the examination table across the room from Duncan's desk, his pupils catching the brunt of a flashlight test being administered by Dr. Lucas.

The doctor whipped the light beam out of one eye and into the other. "Any continued discomfort? Dizzy spells? Particles floating in and out of your vision?"

Swain shook his head and his comical glance fell on Duncan. "No, no, and no. I am ready to go back to work, doc. My wife called me a heaving dam of pent-up water."

Duncan laughed at his state of productive energy raring to go. "That's powerful talk given the flooded conditions we find ourselves in, Mr. Swain. Maybe I could have you read through my accident report to make sure you saw it transpire the same way I did."

"Be glad to, Mr. Reed. I had a hunch something ill might have been lurking for me that day, so I might have been a little on edge when I pulled Old Gypsy up on two wheels like a nimble hot rod."

Duncan scooted his desk chair a bit closer. "Were you working off of a mere hunch? Or did you have some inkling of the workers' unrest?"

Swain squared to face him. "Half a truth is a lie. I was approached late last week by a worker trying to foment sympathy for a labor union balking against the moratorium."

Duncan took out his notepad and began scribbling the details of Swain's voluntary confession. "They needed your vehicle?"

"Yes, that's right. As operator, they needed my cooperation to stage the accident."

"Interesting choice of words you are using, Mr. Swain. Are you saying that the workers had a premeditated plan to have someone injured on the job? I am sure you know that this case is being prosecuted, so please consider your answer."

"I am anything but at fault here, so truth is my ally. He offered me membership in this union and wanted my cooperation to pull off the stunt. I declined that day under threat, as he said I was tempting the hand of fate. I told him, I don't live by fate. I live by faith in God. Therefore, I saw no need for the union's protection."

"How did your response go over?"

"Not too great. He asked me to think about it, hesitated by the door, and walked away."

"How long have you worked for Coates Oil Company, Mr. Swain?" Duncan posed the question with the union demographic in mind.

"Seventeen years this fall. This company has been good to me." Swain looked back and forth between Duncan and the doctor. "Can I go back to work now?"

"Yes, I plan to sign off on your medical suspension and let Mr. Coates know you are fit as a fiddle." Dr. Lucas went to his desk to make good on his word.

Swain stood and tucked his shirttail in. "Tell me—does he really care about an old drill rig driver like me?"

"Oh, yes. He inquires about your welfare almost daily. That's how Malcolm built this company after all, by attention to detail. Here is your signed work release." Dr. Lucas handed him the slip of paper that bore his permission to continue living a working man's life.

"Much obliged, Doc. Mr. Reed, do you suppose we could put off my reading of your report? I could bet there's a discovery well I need to be drilling somewhere between here and Shumway Road." Swain gave him a sheepish smile and rocked onto his tiptoes.

"Sure thing. Let me follow you out then, Mr. Swain." Duncan jumped from his chair and had the screen door open in seconds.

The drill driver stepped out of the clinic and started down the steps. Duncan cleared his throat. "One last detail—since half the truth is indeed a lie. I need the name of that union visitor you mentioned. I can keep it anonymous, if necessary."

Swain looked up and down the sidewalk across Boom Town. Energetic children played over in the park, and women walked out of the grocery, their arms full of daily provisions. A painting could not have portrayed a more innocent setting. "That man was Liam Torguson."

"Do you think he's the union leader?"

"The way he talked about their cause, he seemed to be. He claimed they were interested in worker safety, but right after that he said something else that spoke otherwise."

"What was that, Mr. Swain?"

"He said 'a little blood never hurt anything.' I didn't think that sounded in anyone's best interest, at the job site or otherwise."

Duncan fought back his loathe for Torguson and his methodology, paving the way to reform on a tide of other men's blood. "He likely meant it as a threat."

"Failed to work on me." Swain pointed skyward, indicating the source of his assurance.

"Keep the faith then, Mr. Swain. I will send for you if we need anything further. In the interim, please drive carefully—on all four wheels."

He turned back and gave him a catty smile. "Figured I might get a lecture on safety after that particular stunt. Thanks for not totally disappointing me."

"You're welcome." Duncan gave him a salute and re-entered the office to record the testimony word-for-word. Far from the circumstantial evidence the insurance company needed, at least a finger pointed at the number one man. He vowed to unravel the rest.

Chapter 18

Lorna Rae stared from the doorway as Duncan lay across the bed, reading the new book he had given Trudy. The girl squealed when the bad wolf threatened the grandmother in classic storybook tension. Duncan gave her a protracted growl to play the part. Trudy shrank back and giggled. A glance at her watch made her react. "Hey, you two. I think we need to save the second half of the book for tomorrow night. It is getting late, and a little girl must go to bed."

"Aw, Mommy. Wed Widing Hood is in twouble. She needs me."

Duncan popped the book closed and swung off the bed. "I will be back in a minute to start the treatment."

Lorna Rae smiled as he passed, knowing he had made a purposeful effort to win Trudy's trust back. That scored points with her, as a lesser man would not have bothered.

"Please remind me," he added from the doorway, "I have got to work on her R's."

"Good luck with that, Mista Weed." Lorna Rae gave her best impression of Trudy and laughed when he swiped his wolf paw at her. "Remember to give Della the warning that we are about to start. She wanted to take the baby outside and spare him the commotion."

"Will do," Duncan replied.

Lorna Rae waited until she heard his footsteps on the stairs before starting Trudy's bedtime routine. She put clean clothes away in a drawer and tidied up the dresser top. "Okay, baby girl. Time to get ready for bed. Let's hit the bathroom and then say your prayers."

Trudy slipped from the bed and walked to the doorway. "Does God heah me, Mommy?"

"Yes, he does. He hears each and every one of his children. You can be sure of that." Lorna Rae followed her to the bathroom and helped as needed. Finally, the cotton gauze she had set so carefully into place that morning had to come off for the treatment. She checked for improvement and found considerable, but the crusty skin surface still looked plenty tender.

Trudy looked up at her with a poked-out bottom lip. "I pway Mista Weed goes away."

"Oh no, baby girl. That would hurt Mommy's heart something terrible. We want Mr. Reed to stay and keep us safe." Lorna Rae leaned over to toss the bandages into the trash. When she straightened and cleared the hair from her eyes, Duncan stood in the doorway. He had likely heard the whole exchange.

He looked at her with a hint of flirtation and nodded down the hall. "I think I'm ready if you two are."

A blistering flush worked up Lorna Rae's neck as she contemplated his presumptive readiness after she'd exposed her true feelings. Maybe as adults they should focus on the task at hand and not be making moon eyes at each other like a couple of teenagers, if that was possible.

She followed Trudy into the bedroom and felt a sudden allergic reaction to the bed. "Oh, here. Let's try sitting in this chair. It could help me hold her still a bit better, I think. Come here, sweetie." Lorna Rae slipped into the cushioned club chair and patted her lap.

"You may be right. I like this setup better." Duncan knelt in front of the chair and lifted Trudy to her. He brought the scouring mat up, half hidden in his hand. "Hold your hand out, Trudy. That shows you trust me."

Lorna Rae held her breath, knowing how obstinate her daughter could be. Relief soon took the pressure from her chest as Trudy obeyed. She placed a protective arm around her body and one across her legs. Duncan had no way to escape her kicks from this angle, so Lorna Rae had to keep the girl restrained.

He placed the gauze along the padded chair arm and shifted her hand, palm up, onto it. Without further ado, the scraping started. Trudy screamed and thrashed to get away. Between the second and third stroke, she landed a solid kick on Duncan's chest which must have hurt, as he sucked in air. Lorna Rae needed to be an octopus-mom at the moment, as two hands were not nearly enough. The lull between hands soon came as he left to wash out the scouring mat.

Lorna Rae scooted back in the chair and took a deep breath. "You are being a big girl, Trudy. Soon you should be able to play with your horses again."

Trudy sniffed and leaned on her. "I want to play again. Bad oven."

"Trudy, you know not to touch the oven. Hot things can burn. Mommy needs the oven for her cakes, but you have to be careful near it from now on, okay?"

"Okay, I will twy."

Duncan came back and knelt in front of the chair. "Part of being safe is knowing where the danger is. For you, it was the hot oven. Safe hands do not get burned. Do you understand?"

"I can be safe and not touch. I pwomise."

Lorna Rae pressed her cheek onto the child's head and felt her tense when the hand treatment continued. She whimpered a couple of times, but nothing like the wailing last evening that had sent them over the edge of forbearance. Not that good things hadn't precipitated from that edge, because they most certainly had. She whispered a prayer into the child's hair and before she knew it, Duncan tapped her hand to signal the end.

Lorna Rae pushed out of the chair and guided her by the shoulders. "Now hop into bed, little bunny. It is time to say goodnight."

Trudy wiped her tears with the back of her hand and climbed onto the bed. "Mommy, does Sam weally have to leave us?"

Duncan froze midstep. He turned to regard the girl and backtracked to close the gap between them. "Sam serves in the Navy. He promised he would keep America safe and he has."

"Sam got a boo-boo, too. He should stay away fwom the oven, like me."

"I will be sure to tell him that. He can come home before Christmas. How about that?" Duncan leaned over and tried to put a finger on her nose which solicited her typical biting reaction. He smiled and brushed down the curls on the back of her head. "I will be waiting for you downstairs, Rae." His gaze raked across the room while his warm smile lingered.

Lorna Rae got into position to lead Trudy's prayers as the light went out overhead. "Now I lay me down to sleep, I pray the Lord my soul to keep—"

"God, please bless Mommy, Missus Hansen and Daphne. And bless Sam in the Navy."

"And God bless Mr. Reed who helps make Trudy's hands heal, so they can be perfect all the rest of her life, amen." Lorna Rae patted the sheet covering her daughter and stood up to go downstairs. She would not envy the porch couple their shared sentiments tonight though, as goodnight was much more workable than goodbye. God meant life to be lived together one day at a time, of that she was most certain.

She tiptoed down the stairs only to find Della climbing up, the baby asleep on her shoulder. Steve touched the small of his wife's back to follow her up. Lorna passed with a smile and headed straight for the parlor. Yes, distance posed a problem. Too much distance trumped the element of time and could snuff out the best of goodnights. She would use care not to let that happen. When she entered the parlor, Duncan stood to welcome her to their date time.

~

Duncan studied the overhead signs as he guided the Buick into the curbside drop-off lane at the Wichita Municipal Airport. Glad that he had talked Sam into the change in transportation venues, he had purchased two extra days to get the Hansen farm in shape.

Sam shifted in his seat and stared out the window. "Keep left for now."

"Did you leave Daphne a checklist?"

"Yeah. Not that she needed one, but I couldn't help it."

"You know, five months is not that long, and then you will be out. You can go back to D.C. or anywhere."

"I plan to come back to Kansas. I'm pretty sure of that." Sam turned and gave him a look that solidified the plan.

"If I solve my case, I may be gone before the end of the year. You know my job makes me a rolling stone like that." Duncan eased ahead and thought he saw the right color combination coming up on the next marquee.

"So, get a new job. Right? That would be one solution." Sam cocked his eyebrow as if to lay down a challenge. "I am looking forward to the change-up. Farm life suits me."

"Will your ship head back to South Korea next? I don't want to have to worry about you in direct fire again."

"Naw. We are stuck at the San Diego shipyard for the duration. I don't believe our troops will be over there much longer anyway. We've held the thirty-eighth parallel all summer, so a truce might be right around the corner."

"That hope will certainly keep me listening to the nightly news. It would be outstanding if we both ended up in the same place, wouldn't it?" Duncan pulled over to the curb and stopped the car.

Sam hopped out and opened the back door, dragging his duffle bag out by the handles. "I would like that, brother. Thanks for the ride in and everything."

"Be sure to write me, Spunky. I still need a dose of that big brother admiration you carry around." He reached through the cab and shook Sam's hand. "Remember, Trudy says to stay away from the oven."

"Got it. Watch over the Hansen women for me until I can get back." Sam's voice cracked a bit as he slammed the car door and hit the sidewalk toward the entrance.

Duncan navigated out of the airport loop and headed for Kellogg, the primary east-west corridor south of town. Before he could correct it, he had exited on Southwest Boulevard which wound around the airport's eastern flank. A conglomerate of huge buildings sat on the next corner, marked by a sign that read "Cessnair Flight." Quite by accident, he had stumbled into the heart of the aircraft industry. Turning in out of curiosity, he pulled in front of a massive display window and saw an airplane inside, spit-polished and ready to serve its new owner.

Piqued by the whole setup, he took a guest parking spot, killed the ignition, and strolled up to the marketing facility to see what he could find out. Maybe they needed someone committed to safety in the aircraft industry. As the underbelly of a small commercial airplane passed overhead, he thought his kid brother would be proud he had taken his career advice.

~

Lorna Rae came right over the moment Mrs. Hansen raised her voice.

The woman stood at the checkout counter, looking at the proprietor of the grocery store like he had gone crazy. "What do you mean Maggie is not here? Mr. Anders, you simply cannot run this place without her help."

"That is what I told Doc Lucas, but he stuck to his guns. Maggie can hardly stand up because of her gout lately. He seems to think if she's home, she might stay off her feet."

Lorna Rae fiddled with a rack of canned snuff, popular with the working men. Once she had that aligned, she started on a shelf holding BC Powders and miniature tins of aspirin.

Mrs. Hansen seemed fired up about this inexcusable situation. "What can I do? Beyond bringing eggs in twice a week, I mean. Surely Maggie would let me help her."

"I could come in and work her morning hours," Lorna Rae offered. "My little girl needs to nap in the afternoon, so I need to be home by one o'clock."

Mr. Anders rubbed his palm down the edge of the counter. "Well, that does sound tempting, Mrs. Holmes. You came back home right when we need help the most, so perhaps we can assist one another. I understand you are baking cakes, too. Maybe we could take on some of your product and see how it sells."

"Oh, yes. I can have a cake baked for tomorrow, if you would like me to start right away. Would that be of any help?" Lorna Rae continued straightening the penny candy boxes.

"You know what? I cannot stand sorting out the penny candy the kids keep mixed up. It snaps my last straw, so I try to avoid it at all cost."

Mrs. Hansen pulled her cart out of the way of paying customers and held her ground. "Both you and Maggie need a break, Fred. Let us help, for pity's sake."

"Okay, okay. Mrs. Holmes, you start mornings as of tomorrow. Ina, you can have the laundry to take home. Maggie washes clothes for some of the single men on the oil fields, twenty cents a load, washed, dried and folded. There is a backlog already heaped up in the rear storage room."

Mrs. Hansen clapped her hands together. "Fine. I accept. Daphne and I will do the laundry . I can bring it in with the egg delivery. You can pay for both at the same time to keep it simple."

"I will see you in the morning, Mr. Anders. Please tell your wife her friends are rallying to her support, until she can get back on her feet again." Lorna Rae stepped around the egg cart and could hardly wait to get back to bake up a storm. She had a job and a new place to sell her cakes—most splendiferous.

~

McNaughton's voice drew thin across their spotty connection. "I am calling to tell you what a solid effort this is with the Swain confession. I think things are beginning to clamp into place on this case."

Duncan covered the receiver and cleared his throat. The pause must have unsettled McNaughton as he lost a bit of his poise under fire. "I am not sure this could have turned out any better for us really. Don't you think so?"

"Yes, sir. Swain's testimony is strong, albeit hearsay to the courts. We still need more witnesses to testify against the leader in order for it to stick."

"Or find some incriminating evidence in his possession. Want to search his house?"

"We likely won't find the kind of evidence we need there. Maybe we should try to bust up the union's next meeting, ambush them in the act." Duncan fiddled with his desk blotter, knowing the regular pattern of meetings and subsequent accidents had been more of a scatter-shot this month. That made the union unpredictable.

"Nice piece of work on that Decker confession. He fingered the same guy, Liam Torguson. I really think you should pay that man a visit. Think about it. How much better is it to go in on your own terms than wait for his? You know I have a valid point."

"Yes, but you may be rushing things a bit. Remember that Decker is this month's selection—but he left town. That has to rankle the head man, right? The loss of support equates to loss of control of his members. He should be squirming right about now, as his kingdom starts to cave in on itself. I want him to get desperate, because desperate people get careless. That's the break we need, not leverage. We need him to get careless…and then we have him."

"Suit yourself, then. Do you want me to come down for the

trial on this Gant character?"

"No sir. I've got this. You know my pace, slow and steady, but I always get my man."

"Well right now, you have your number two man—which isn't all bad."

"Trust me, Mr. McNaughton. I plan to get Torguson. He will leave himself exposed, and I will be right there to get him when he does."

"Call me if things get hot then. Otherwise, I will sit tight and expect your weekly report. Nice work, Reed. Keep it up, you hear?"

"Got it, sir. I will be in touch." He lowered the receiver and realized he was ready for that new job, if any offers surfaced. His old job came with a certain pinch to it, like dress shoes that failed to fit anymore. He wanted to walk barefoot through the lush summer grass.

His mental digression brought Lorna Rae to mind next. What a pleasurable walk through the summer grass she represented. A tiny celebration went off inside his chest and dulled his concentration. The daydream lasted until Dr. Lucas kicked the screen door as he entered the office.

"Some kind of good. That is exactly what these new cakes are. You ought to try one."

"Cake? Where did you get that?"

"At the grocery there. Lorna Rae Holmes works behind the counter now."

Duncan jumped to his feet and gave the doctor an untrusting look before heading out to verify the situation. The aging man had chocolate cake smashed into the corner of his mouth.

"I will have some cake all right." He banged out the screen door and ran across the width of the village square to see what the commotion was all about. When he entered the store, everything appeared in peaceable order.

Lorna Rae stood up from behind the counter, a scoop of dried black-eyed peas in her grip. She poured them into a paper sack and busied her hands tying it with a string. "May I help you, sir? Did you come in looking for something in particular, or are you just browsing?"

Duncan stood stupefied, seeing her at work so exposed like

this. How in the world could he keep her safe in here with so many patrons coming and going? Trying to work past the new predicament, he gazed around the store and spotted her trademark cakes, good from the inside out and all lined up in front of the counter. "I will take two of these cakes and one explanation of what you are doing here."

Lorna Rae's smile turned into a day-old baked good right before his eyes. She took two cakes off the shelf and put them by the counter. As she punched the register keys, she glanced at him like she did not remember who he was. "That will be eleven cents for the cakes, please. As for the rest, Mrs. Anders had the gout so bad that Dr. Lucas ordered her to stay home. Mr. Anders needed help, so I took on the store work and Mrs. Hansen took on the laundry service for the interim. I get to work the morning shift and sell my cakes. Isn't that marvelous?"

He fished a dime and a penny out of his pocket, then plunked them on the counter. "What about Trudy?"

"Daphne watches Trudy for me. I get back in time to feed her lunch and put her down for her nap. Then I can help Mrs. Hansen with the laundry, if she needs me. And bake, of course."

He looked at her across the counter and sensed nothing he could say would make an ounce of difference. She had found gainful employment right across from his office. He could visit on a whim, so what left him so irritated with the whole set-up? Safety, his old nemesis, reared its ugly head. He took a breath and tried to calm down. "Good luck selling the cakes then." He picked up his purchase and took a step toward the door.

"Nice to see you also, Mr. Reed." She batted her eyelashes at him and gave him an ingratiating business-like smile.

Duncan stormed out of the grocery and turned away from the office. The next thing he knew, he had arrived at the chapel. He sat on a wrought iron bench out front and pinched the wrapper off the first cake. He took a bear-sized bite and let the sweetness overtake his foul mood. He finished it with the next bite and soon had to unwrap the second cake. He traced the outline of the peaceable structure in front of him, from its easy-open doors to the tip of its steeple. That is when he realized what had put the prick in his predicament.

Lorna Rae was like his faith. He wanted the personal

relationship, but didn't want to share her with anyone else. Instead of being selfless, he had been jealous. Call keeping her safe false piety at best, as his motivations were full-blown self-centered. He had gotten too involved, and now his personal connection had led to a short-circuiting of his control. Detesting his own jealous reaction, he stood and walked into the empty chapel.

A long corridor led to the front pulpit where a wooden cross hung center stage. Hard wooden chairs comprised a choir loft. He knelt by the platform and closed his eyes, knowing he needed saving from his preoccupation of risk avoidance. The need to always control a safe environment sat like ballast rock on his chest, and he needed to give it to God. He prayed, unsure what the outcome would be, but inner peace might be nice.

He stayed for some time, turning the authority back over to his Lord and Savior, Jesus Christ. When he stood, he felt lighter, like the burden had been removed. As he came out into the daylight, he sensed the compelling need to tell Lorna Rae he was truly happy for her new work. Buoyed with purpose, he strode into the grocery and approached the front counter, only to find old Mr. Anders on duty like usual.

"Is Lorna Rae here?"

"Mrs. Holmes went home at one o'clock, but I am sure you can catch her tomorrow." He nodded and stepped toward the rear of the store.

Duncan dropped his head. She likely thought he had gone crazy, being so irate about her job. He should have been proud of her instead, which he would be sure to tell her at the next available opportunity. He headed back to his office, a thousand thoughts running through the maze of his mind, but none coming to any logical conclusions.

~

Lorna Rae took a cup from the rack and ran the faucet to fill it. "She finally fell asleep. I think I can forego those bandages tonight. That could be what makes her so uncomfortable." Mrs. Hansen wrung out a man's shirt from her pre-soak pail. The water clouded with dirt. "Mercy, this oil field work is dirty business. I do not know how you ever stood it. I thought farming used to soil Mils' clothing. Grease and oil make up a whole separate category of grime."

"Let me help you, Mrs. Hansen. I can put the next load through the ringer-washer. Is this one ready?"

"Yes, please go ahead and take it. I will go fetch the first load off the clothesline. This winter when I am eating beans out of a can, remind me that I needed this money, because right now it isn't endearing to me." She wiped her hands dry over by the sink and made her way to the back door. "It seems so different around here without Sam, doesn't it? I guess that means Duncan won't be around every night, either."

"Well, I thought he would come help me with Trudy for a couple more treatments, but we had a spat at the store today, so I don't know if he will be out or not." She grabbed the wet shirt and started for the washer in the utility room.

"Was he unhappy with you taking the job?"

"Seems like it. He came into the store like an explosion, bought two cakes, and stormed back out. I gave him my polite customer service smile, but I am afraid it missed the mark of being genuine." Lorna Rae glanced inside the tub where the rest of the load waited. She no more wanted to wash these clothes than bathe the man in the moon. "Do you know what I would really like, Mrs. Hansen? I would really like to say 'no thank you' when the world offers me the unfit work, the hard, hot, dirty work that no one else wants to do."

"Please tell me how, because I have not been able to say 'no thank you' since Mil died. It's a widow's plight, I suppose." She stepped outside to perform her duty at the clothesline.

Lorna Rae sulked, running water into the wash tub. Sam had gone back, Della and Steve might be gone within days, and she had a lovely new job measuring out dried beans and inconsequential whatnot. At least she could look her customers in the eye at the point of sale and tell them she baked those wonderful Lo-Rae Cakes.

Time on her feet came as a tradeoff for building her business. She had moved up to three points of distribution, if the ones underwater in Kansas City still counted. The more she thought about it, the less they seemed to matter. With her tub full, she proceeded to scrub the dirt loose from the fibers and send them through the wringer one reeking piece at a time. *Nasty business, this oil field laundry.*

Chapter 19

If it was the last thing he ever did, Duncan would make up with Lorna Rae first thing this morning. He never wanted another sleepless night like last night. How agonizing it had been. Not to mention lonesome. He had missed Trudy's treatment, which he realized at twelve o'clock, much too late to do anything productive about it. His entire world seemed out of kilter, and he wanted it back plumb-line straight. That had been his prayer over his paltry breakfast and should motivate him to get things corrected. It had taken him being out of sorts to realize he was in love with Lorna Rae. This separation between them had to end.

Duncan walked to the office from the rear of the parking lot, a vigorous trip. Good to his word, Doctor Lucas had brought him cut flowers from his wife's garden. That evidence now sat on his desk in a canning jar. He checked his attitude, thinking himself most humble and apologetic, given the heaviness of conscience he had nursed through the night. Yes, he felt ready to win back Lorna Rae's good graces. The hour remained early, a fact he would use to his advantage. Perhaps she could even agree to stay in town and enjoy lunch in his affectionate company.

With dripping-wet flowers in hand, he exited the office and hit the boardwalk at a healthy stride. A family passed and he gave the mother a cordial greeting as the children ran ahead. He thought to buy some candy for Trudy and brighten her day on the farm. The sun shone from behind a cloud bank, proper imagery for his emergence from such a foul mood yesterday. He quick-stepped it onto the grocery's porch and opened the screen door, tucking the flowers behind his back.

Lorna Rae stood at the front register, which he counted as his good fortune. He only had to wait for the current customer to finish his business, and she would be all his. He strolled down the aisle, feigning interest in the produce displays. Someone had a multitude of luck growing their eggplant crop, though he disdained the vegetable's chalky taste.

Lorna Rae laughed as she accepted a package from the customer. The man, in turn, seemed to be enjoying a few extra moments of her company. When he happened to turn away from the register, his identity became clear. There stood Liam Torguson.

Duncan dropped his pretense and inched closer to overhear their conversation. This encounter raked across his good humor, making it difficult to wait his turn. His elevated blood pressure created a throbbing in his ears.

"Yes, Harley used to feel that way, too." Lorna Rae turned with the package and spotted Duncan for the first time. She quickly looked away. "Thank you, Mr. Torguson. Stop by on Tuesday then. The laundry will be ready."

He shifted toward the door a step, but then hung back for some invisible reason. "Call me Liam, please. I never got to tell you how sorry I was to hear about Harley's accident."

"Thank you for your sentiments, Liam. I know the two of you went way back. Trudy and I manage to get along day-to-day. The Lord is providing."

Torguson gave a half-grin and stared at her a moment or two beyond respectable widow admiration.

Duncan stepped up in line, holding the flowers below counter height to keep them out of sight. He fixed his eyes on Lorna Rae and tried to block out everything else, especially the flirtatious Liam Torguson.

"Hello, may I help you, sir?" Lorna Rae held a certain lilt in her voice as if to toy with him, albeit from a public place.

"I'd like two of those Lo-Rae Cakes please." He held onto the customer pretense until Torguson pushed the door open and exited. The rubber band tightening his chest relaxed a bit. "May I say you look lovely at your job today? I am grateful for both, just so you know." He popped the surprise bouquet into range and allowed her to examine them as evidence of his earnestness. They held a certain whimsy, though several stems had begun to show signs of wilt.

"Thank you for your complimentary notice of me this morning. I hope you slept well last night. That will be eleven cents, please." The clank of the cash register followed.

"Not too good a night of sleep, if I can be honest." He placed the coins on her side of the counter, so he could lean a bit closer. "Why did you have to accept the package from Torguson?" he whispered. His annoyance crept back despite his best intentions.

"That is his dirty laundry I accepted, for your information. It is part of my job. I take it home to Ina and help her wash, dry, and fold it for twenty cents a load. That's what widows are forced to do, eke out a living to stay alive." Her whisper amplified with the last word, as if she was making a point. A vein popped out on her neck.

"Oh, I see. Well, these flowers are for you. They are helping me make amends."

"Let me think about it, though it seems like such a nice gesture. I must take everything into account you see, like your horrible attitude." Again, her whisper amplified on the last word, and several other customers within earshot turned and looked at them.

Duncan stood dumbfounded, as she was surely judging his motives without knowing a thing about Torguson or the danger he posed. A red flag of unease waved across his line of sight, but without sharing confidential information, he could not breach the impasse. He would have to think of something else. His gaze dropped to the penny candy, and a little curly-haired girl came to mind. "How is Trudy? Does she need me to come back out?"

"What? To make her cry again? No, I don't think so."

Standing in a landslide, he knew he was losing ground fast. A woman appeared in line behind him and plunked two small eggplants on the counter. He grabbed the two cakes and clutched them to his chest.

Lorna Rae held up the dime and penny in similar possessive fashion. With a keystroke, she placed the coins in the register and offered him a plastic smile. "Thank you, sir. I hope you enjoy your cakes."

"I certainly plan on it." He growled his disappointment at the outcome and stepped toward the door, feeling something more needed to be said. He glanced back and all he could see were the eggplants, now in Lorna Rae's hands. His knee-jerk reaction got the better of him. "Those things are inedible—they taste like chalk." Both women looked equally shocked as he turned and left the store deflated. He had botched the romance repair work, a first-class failure.

~

Lorna Rae opened her suitcase and placed her things in the guest room bureau. Della and Steve had taken baby Robert Thomas back to Westport to tackle the storm damage as a team. Once Trudy awoke, she would move them lock, stock, and barrel out of Daphne's room so their host family could return to some semblance of normal. She suppressed the feeling of being left behind, because she knew she had some unfinished business here and needed to address it.

The waterfall picture fell from the stack she picked up next, and it fluttered onto the bedspread. Lorna Rae sighed. She should make a decision about Duncan soon, as he had been uncharacteristically distraught at the grocery today. Doubtful that love should look like that, she still had a difficult time fully dismissing him from her affections. He seemed to wrestle between the bounds of protection and control, only one of which struck her as admirable.

She tucked the remainder of her things away and noticed much of Trudy's clothing had been gobbled by the dirty clothes hamper. She could do a load this afternoon and get it on the clothesline while the sun remained high in the mid-July sky. Thank the Good Lord the rains had ended. Kansas could dry out at long last.

Lorna Rae descended the stairs and heard Daphne and her mother talking in the kitchen. She walked in to find the young woman at the table with her Bible. Ina stood at the sink scrubbing something in a wash tub. "Oh, goodness. I forgot to come back and help you with the laundry order. I got preoccupied with moving into the guest room, so Daphne could have her room back. I am truly sorry. Can I help in any way?"

"Well. You could do the last shirt there and let me start supper for tonight. I left the rest in the washer trying to get this pre-soak done first. This fellow does dirty work."

Lorna Rae pulled an apron from the drawer and tied it in place. "I am glad to step in. Daphne, were you reading aloud? I would cherish hearing some comfort from God's Word. I have been perplexed as of late and hardly know which way to turn."

Daphne opened the book and its tissue paper pages slipped into place. "Mother and I had been discussing how Solomon had been gifted more wisdom than anyone else on earth, yet he strayed from his faith under the influence of his pagan wives."

"Love can turn the world topsy-turvy, that's for sure." Lorna Rae thought of another man of faith, a genius she greatly admired. Yet a simple thing like courtship had become his stumbling block. Now, he looked all too human. However, to Duncan's credit, he had not waivered on his faith in God. She dumped the dirty soak water and began to refill the tub.

"Better to enter a home where there is mourning than one where a party is being thrown, because the living should be soberly reminded that death awaits us all." Daphne looked up and the color drained from her face.

Ina clattered a large skillet onto the stovetop. "No. That's all right, Daphne. I had to claim that verse many a night after your father passed away. We are called to live soberly. King Solomon's wisdom shows itself here."

Lorna Rae added a pinch of soap powder to the soak water. She turned and plucked the last shirt from the paper wrapper. She dunked it under and pressed out the air pockets with her fingertips.

"Sorrow is superior to laughter. It may sadden your face, but it sharpens your understanding." Daphne gave an exasperated exhalation, but continued on with the reading. "The end of something is better than its beginning. Patience is superior to pride."

A tiny lump formed in Lorna Rae's throat at the thought she might be looking at the end of her friendship with Duncan. Had there not been so much to admire? He seemed so attentive to her in thoughtful ways. Plus, he held a genuine fondness for Trudy, too.

A mat of something papery floated up in the soak water. Lorna Rae dabbed at it with her finger and it separated into several pieces.

"Never ask, "Why were things so much better in the good, old days. It's not an intelligent question to pose." Daphne slammed the book closed. "That does it. I cannot stand any more."

Lorna Rae glanced over at the reader as a sensation overcame her that made her skin crawl. She turned back to the basin and lifted one of the sticks out. It was a match, now flimsy from the soak. She put it on the window sill and dipped the next one out. It had a bit more length, but the same angular cut on the bottom. She placed it up to dry and dug out the next stick while the tingling sensation crept down her entire right side.

"Daphne, please bring your Bible over here. Something is wrong, truly wrong." Without turning around, Lorna Rae heard the woman's chair scrape and knew she had taken her seriously.

"Whatever is the matter, Lorna Rae?" Ina came beside her at the sink. Soon, they all stood gawking at the waterlogged matches aligned on the sink, seven of them—all sliced from the pad.

Lorna Rae shook her head. "Duncan once told me everything he needed to solve his case could be put in a matchbox. Could this be it—cut matches? I have a horrible feeling about this, as I remember Harley would grab the kitchen matches every time he went to those union meetings. I have a sneaking suspicion Duncan might want to know about these."

Daphne went on tiptoe to get a better look at the matches lined up on the sill. "Do you mean this L. Torguson on the laundry label could be mixed up in his case?"

"Yes. Duncan must have been trying to protect me earlier at the store, only he couldn't tell me. Lord forgive me, I judged him for that treatment and not favorably, mind you." Lorna Rae wrung her hands on the apron to dry them, a shallow absolution for her wrong-doing.

"We should pray for protection from such evil. Then you need to call Duncan and get him to come out here—the sooner the better." Ina pulled her close and Daphne stuffed her Bible between the three of them. "Lord, by your almighty hand we pray you allow this evil maiming to end at the oil fields. If the end of something is truly better than the beginning, we claim that now in the power of Jesus Christ. Keep this household safe and protect these working men from further calamity. Give us the courage of Joshua, and protect Duncan as you guide him to resolution. Do not hinder his good work, Lord. In Jesus' name we pray, amen."

"I have to call him and make him come over. But I have been so foolish, why would he even want to?" Lorna Rae walked toward the hall where the phone waited.

Ina gave her a knowing look and opened the Frigidaire. "Tell him I am inviting him for dinner. You know that man is a terrible cook."

Lorna Rae allowed the involuntary snicker to break her defeated mood. Somehow with divine help, she would look past the obvious and find the underlying wealth right in front of her. A noble, admirable man had affections for her, and she should be most grateful. All she needed was the chance to show it—and she would. She dialed the clinic's number, each subsequent digit heavier than the last. The amends rested in her court now, and God was filling her with the gift of reconciliation, a most penitent state if ever she knew one.

~

Torguson sat at his makeshift desk, a useless ironing board in his bedroom. Restless, he had been fighting the urge to slide over to The Tap Out and have a cold one. The day's heat had peaked hours ago, but ninety-five degrees didn't go away just like that.

He studied his master plan, a mixture of calendar, black lettering, and cut-off matches. It was all coming together nicely, except the vehicle slip-up. He blamed that on Bud Gant for his sophomoric melodrama that day under Swain's drilling rig. So what if Gant got sentenced to time inside from the court case? That would go down as his screw-up, not the union's fault.

He evaluated the upcoming weeks, trying to pinpoint the perfect date for their next happenstance. Mondays seemed upsetting, so early in the week to face the loss an accident represented. That would certainly clip the big man behind the knees. He picked up the marker to write in the member's number that had come up in the lottery, but had trouble recalling the exact one. He pushed back in his chair, glancing around the room to find the dungarees he had been wearing Tuesday night. He found them slung over a box fan in front of the window, but the pockets didn't contain the match pad. Oh right, he'd given it to Carlson to return to the loser.

As he pulled back under the desk, it all came back to him. A member had been absent, Harley's old neighbor, so he forced the number up automatically. Carlson had given him the man's number, so he wrote twenty-four into place on Monday, July thirtieth. He now had a plan.

His gaze skimmed over the masthead of the calendar where he had stapled a series of cut-off matches. There they stood in line like pickets in a fence. A smug sensation deepened in his chest. He was leading a reform against an industry giant, a real David-and-Goliath story. Men wrote their way into history books with movements such as this.

He thought to add the latest brigade of matchstick warriors to his infantry and pushed back to retrieve the shirt he had worn at the meeting Tuesday night. A cursory search yielded plenty of other worn shirts, but not that particular one. He had seen it somewhere—but when it dawned on him where—the realization kicked him in the gut. He had accidentally given it to Lorna Rae Holmes at the grocery for laundering. Without a doubt, he needed to get it back.

Low-level panic set in as he raced around the house getting shoes on and finding his keys. He didn't know where Lorna Rae had taken up residence since she had left the oil fields, but he knew a union member who looked at lots of addresses, especially those for forwarded mail. He tore out of the house slamming the back door as he went.

Nothing but a temporary setback, he should have things leveled out by nightfall and maybe even steal a kiss from Lorna Rae, the lonely widow who had been looking pretty good earlier at the store. A country boy with rugged good looks, he could pick up right where Harley left off. Why hadn't he thought of that before? An image of the fawning safety manager came to mind, trying to get Lorna Rae's attention across the store counter. What a laughable situation.

~

Lorna Rae dropped the receiver. "Duncan is not answering. I guess he has left for the day." She tried not to let her failure to connect ruin the evening. Trudy clamped on her leg begging to be swung around. She picked the girl up under her arms and twirled her several times. After the world settled back in place, she put her on the floor again. "Why don't you color a picture before dinner?

We can send it to Aunt Della and tell her we will be coming back soon."

"Okay, Mommy."

"I need to help Mrs. Hansen with supper. Go get your coloring book and bring it to the kitchen table, okay honey?"

"I will, but I don't have a wed cwayon now."

"You will have to use the other colors. Now scoot." She pretended to swat at her bottom, but the girl had already started up the stairs out of reach.

"I need to set the table," Daphne called from the dining room. "Is Duncan coming?"

"No, I cannot get him to pick up. Maybe I should drive into town after dinner."

Ina stirred the ground beef as it browned in the skillet. "Try again later. I would feel better if we all stayed together, until this unholy business gets settled."

Lorna Rae stepped to the sink to wash her hands and eyed the drying evidence on the sill. She should probably put those away somewhere safe, until Duncan came for them. Perhaps she could go to work early and deliver them right to his office. Trudy came into the room, flapping her coloring book against her legs.

Ina poured a can of diced tomatoes into the skillet. "We have all day tomorrow, right? It's Saturday and Duncan should be off."

"Oh, I totally forgot we won't be going to town tomorrow. That's all the more reason for him to come out here." Lorna Rae wiped her hands and lifted Trudy into place on the booster seat. "Do you still want that onion chopped?"

"Yes, please. They can simmer in with the tomatoes."

Daphne returned to the cupboard and retrieved another plate. "Mother, I am going to set an extra place setting, just in case."

"That is ever being the optimist, isn't it Daphne?" Lorna Rae picked up a medium-sized onion, and it crinkled in her grasp.

"I believe in the power of love, if that's what you mean. Plus, Duncan has dropped by many times in the past without an invitation."

"That's mighty thoughtful of you, Daphne." Ina turned and gave Lorna Rae a corrective look. "You might want to say a prayer or two while your hands are busy chopping."

"What's the matter with me, anyway? I want him here more

than anyone." Lorna Rae faced the sink and tried not to look up at the matches, but didn't succeed. Duncan needed them, but did he need her? The onion chopping commenced and soon her eyes filled with tears. The pungent reaction a perfect prompt, she gave in and had a good cry, right there at the kitchen sink.

Chapter 20

He knocked at the door, impatient as all get out. Still, he could not let his hurry interfere with the business at hand. When he lifted his fist to knock again, the wooden door swung open.

"Hey, Mr. Torguson. What brings you by?"

"Hey there, Jimmy. I just need some information. I am hoping to have a hot Friday night on the town with a little help."

"I got plans myself. What do you need?"

He flashed a crooked grin and scraped his shoe on the concrete stoop. "I am trying to look up Harley's widow, Lorna Rae Holmes. You know, pay my respects and maybe see if she is ready to move on."

Jimmy tossed his hair back, a clouded look overtaking his features. "She lives off the oil field these days. I think her mail reroutes to Westport."

"No, she works in the oil field grocery nowadays. I thought you might know where I could look her up closer by."

"Not really, unless she moved back to the Hansen farm out east of town. I really can't say. Hey, I need to get on down the road for my date."

"No sweat. Glad to see you're doing okay, Jimmy. Come on back to the union meetings anytime. We are about to break even on this thing, thanks to brave men like yourself."

"I am not feeling all that brave, Mr. Torguson, but I have me a girl that doesn't seem to mind, so life is looking up."

"Glad to hear that. Thanks for the directions. See you around." He snapped a fake salute and headed back for his truck. He got in, turned the key, and let the engine rumble. The front door had closed within an inch, but he got the strange sensation Jimmy was standing there eyeballing him through the remaining crack. "Stay out of trouble, kid—because I sure won't." He floored it in reverse and swung the back end around like a man on the verge of control.

~

Duncan sat on the front porch trying to estimate when the sun would set. Darkness would be an improvement at this point and match fairly well with his mood. Today he had proven he knew little about the female persuasion, or this touchy thing called love. How could he have held Lorna Rae so close, and then lose her like that? He just could not reason it out.

A car came up the lane idling slowly. He leaned forward so the chair would rest on all four legs. Someone probably had gotten lost, since few cars came this far into the neighborhood. It slowed to a stop and the window rolled down.

"Hey, Mr. Reed. How's it going?"

Duncan tried not to let his surprise show. "Well hey, Jimmy. What are you doing around these parts?"

"I came looking for you…if you have a second."

Something in the young man's weighty tone made Duncan snap out of his self-pity stupor. He stood and walked to the edge of the yard. The wind rattled the cottonwood leaves overhead, sharpening his hearing. "Go ahead. What's on your mind?"

"I had a visitor this evening, someone looking for directions. Guess he figured since I worked at the post office, I kept track of where everybody lives."

"Go on, Jimmy. I fail to see what this has to do with me."

"Well, I knew you had been writing to her, since you come in and get stamps from me and all. Plus, I brought you a letter back from her—Lorna Rae Holmes, I mean."

The bottom fell out of Duncan's stomach at the mention of her name. His thoughts scrambled in every direction, but he squelched the progression trying to battle his tendency to control matters. He opened his mouth, but nothing came out.

"Torguson is no good, sir. You are the better man. That's why I drove over here on my way to Whitewater to see Kathleen. Guess I had better get going now." The car pulled from the curb, and left nothing but another rut in the muddy road.

Duncan knew he had either a split second to make his decision or all night to stew about it. He ran into the bungalow and grabbed the car keys. He was, in fact, the better man. And he intended to prove it to Lorna Rae tonight beyond a shadow of a doubt.

~

Lorna Rae looked at the clock again and knew she would never make it through the night without trying to contact with Duncan. Time seemed to stretch out their impasse in exaggerated proportions like avant-garde artwork. She found no beauty in that type of expression, as she found no rest for her current concern. She whispered the same prayer under her breath she had uttered fifty times before.

Mrs. Hansen pulled the yeast rolls from the oven, browned to perfection inside a square pan. "We should try to serve the meal now, and hope for the best."

"Of course, we need to eat. No use moping." Lorna Rae took her apron off, hazarding a glance at the window sill. Her tiny slashed-up stowaways had dried.

Daphne walked by with the tea pitcher headed for the refrigerator. "Do you want Trudy to have a glass of milk?"

"Yes, please. Daphne, I am grateful for you. Really I am. You are so good with Trudy, a real godsend for me." Lorna Rae touched her sleeve,

Daphne smiled back at her. "A child livens things up around here. That makes it fun for me, so you're welcome." She swapped the tea for the milk jug and poured a jelly glass full.

Lorna Rae took the glass and walked by Trudy, tickling her neck with a kiss as she passed. "Come on in to the big dining room, doll baby. It's time to eat."

She held up the picture of a green turtle. "I am all done with Ollie."

"So I see. Is that for Aunt Della?"

"No, Mista Weed, Mommy. He's coming ovah heah."

"Well, we will get it to him, I promise. Now come with Mommy, and let's eat this nice meal that Mrs. Hansen has been so busy making all evening."

"I need my boostah seat."

"Let me bring it." Daphne hooked the roll basket onto her hip and picked up the phone books.

Ina nodded to the seat by front hallway. "Leave an empty place beside you, Lorna Rae. It shows you have faith in those little prayers you have been whispering."

She blushed, not realizing her words had been audible. Without disgracing herself by arguing with her hostess, she sat one chair down from the end. Daphne sat across from her and put Trudy by her seat, accentuating the lopsided affair. Ina took a seat at the head of the table.

"I would like each of us to stop for a moment and express our thanks for the smaller blessings this day has brought. These are genuine gifts that God bestows, and we shall not miss this opportunity to give thanks. Daphne, you go first."

"I heard on the radio today that a truce along the thirty-eighth parallel indicates the war may soon be over. That means mothers all around the nations will get their sons back, and the United States will have preserved the interests of NATO." Daphne took her napkin and placed it in her lap, her elation lending radiance to her countenance.

Lorna Rae felt a shameful rebuke riding her conscience. Here she had fumed over her insignificant personal trauma all afternoon, while Daphne had the greater good of the entire nation in mind. The young woman had cast a wide prayer net, while she only managed narrow.

"Lorna Rae, you go next, dear."

She looked up at Ina Hansen, a woman who could so easily have been defeated by her widowhood, but had summoned the strength to re-engage a full life. That took fortitude built on faith, the type of resilience she desired for her life. "I want to give thanks for this family who took us in, for the Christian kindness and generosity they have extended, and for treating us like family members even though we aren't. May God bless this house and all who reside therein."

"I will add your unspoken request to mine." Ina nodded and closed her eyes. "Heavenly Father, bless this meal to nourish our bodies and commend us to thy service, amen."

Before Lorna Rae could open her eyes, the sound of a car door slamming shut echoed from the front lawn. She gasped and gave her hostess a surprised look.

"I should get the door then." Ina slipped out of her seat and touched Lorna Rae's shoulder as she passed.

Trudy held up a roll that had a giant bite already taken out of it. "I like these."

"Go ahead and serve her the beef ragout, Daphne. Otherwise, she will only eat the bread and fill up on it." Lorna Rae listened as a man's voice rumbled in low tones from the hallway. A shadow fell across the door, and she turned with high expectations to regard their guest. To her immediate shock, there stood Liam Torguson. An icy constriction raced down her back.

"Mr. Torguson has graciously conceded to stay for dinner. Isn't that nice, ladies?" Ina exaggerated her glance at Lorna Rae to prompt an answer.

"Yes, how very nice of you to drop by, Mr. Torguson. Please do take a seat. Mrs. Hansen had hoped for company tonight, and here you are." Lorna Rae motioned to the seat beside hers, already set and awaiting occupancy.

Torguson pulled off a ratty baseball cap and twirled it onto the marble-topped sideboard. He nodded at Daphne and pulled out the chair. When he sat, he scooted it closer to Lorna Rae.

An unnatural repelling pushed against Lorna Rae, so forceful she adjusted her chair in its wake. She somehow could not get far enough away from this man. With any small excuse at all, she would be flat-out running away.

"So what's for dinner?"

Ina passed him the casserole dish containing the main dish. "My hearty beef ragout with spring peas and yeast rolls. I think Daphne has some chocolate cake for our dessert."

Torguson sent a lewd smile across the table. "Well now. Thank you, Daphne. I owe it to your friend Jimmy Cantor for letting me know Lorna Rae has been staying out at your place."

Daphne's neck turned ten shades of crimson. She quickly pretended Trudy needed her assistance and feigned disinterest in furthering the conversation.

Ina passed the peas and gave him a servile smile. "So, how do you know Mrs. Holmes?"

"Her husband Harley and I went way back. We were both

raised in the Rosalia area, so we went to high school together, played football, chased girls, and raced cars." He shoveled a loaded forkful of ragout into his mouth and immediately reached for another.

Ina motioned down the table. "You can pass the peas along to Mrs. Holmes, once you take your serving."

Liam took two spoonfuls of peas and let them roll all over his plate. When he passed the bowl to Lorna Rae, he held it firm until she extracted it from his grasp.

"Thank you, Mr. Torguson. I don't believe Harley ever enlightened me much on his rowdy high school days." Lorna Rae busied her hands with the peas, at a loss as to what to say next. She knew the men had affiliated over the labor union, the last topic she would ever choose to bring up, given the circumstances. She passed the bowl over the table to Daphne and squinted.

Daphne braved up to take the bowl and the conversation. "Mrs. Holmes is teaching me how to bake her special cakes. She started a business in Kansas City and has made quite the success of it."

He turned to grace Lorna Rae with his full attention. "I saw those cakes for sale at the grocery store. I might have to try me one."

Trudy held up a yeast roll with a bite out of the corner. "I like these."

"Trudy, is that your second roll?" Lorna Rae let her discomfort come across as agitation in her tone, a slip she needed to correct. "Try to show us what a good meat eater you are."

Trudy growled like a tiger and began to devour the ragout in wild animal style.

"Oh, you sure can tell she's Harley's kid, all right." Torguson took a roll and stabbed it with his fork to open it. "Got butter, by any chance?"

"Allow me," Lorna Rae replied. In a split second she slid out of her chair and flew into the kitchen to retreat. The impulse to wretch rose so strong that she clasped the sink and squeezed her eyes closed. The same prayer bubbled up, only this time she meant it double. When she opened her eyes, her little evidence sticks stared back at her. She needed to hide them, and she needed to do it quickly.

In a bustle of slapdash motor coordination, she managed the

secretive task and soon reappeared in the dining room with the butter dish in her hand. To her utter amazement, Duncan Reed now stood in the far doorway, his back pole-straight and his jaw flexed at the odd scene before him. "Thank you, Lord," she whispered, taking the butter dish to their guest.

Ina gave her a twinkling-eyed smile and gestured to her side of the table. "Lorna Rae, please bring in another plate for Mr. Reed while you are up, will you, dear? He has graciously agreed to dine with us tonight."

"Yes, ma'am. Please have a seat, Mr. Reed. I will be right back." Lorna Rae came into the kitchen wishing she had been clever enough to invite him to wash his hands, so she could deliver her surprise. Now, she would have to wait. Maybe serving dessert would afford her the break she needed from Torguson's watchful eyes. She slid the plate out of the cupboard, grabbed some flatware, and returned to the fiasco dinner. "Here you are now. Let's enjoy our dinner."

Duncan held her chair out, ever the gentleman. "After you, Mrs. Holmes."

Lorna Rae took a long moment to look him right in the eyes, her first genuine expression all evening. He stood fairly close, so he could not have missed her earnestness.

He flexed his brow and nodded for her to be seated. "So, what brings you around these parts, Mr. Torguson? It's a little far out of town for your usual carousing."

Lorna Rae started to gasp, but swallowed it back. Why had she thought this could be a respectable gathering with the two of them sitting at the same table?

Torguson took a long drink of tea and sat the glass down. "I am actually hunting for my laundry. Lorna Rae, I know you said it would be ready on Tuesday, but I had an important note in my shirt pocket that I hoped to retrieve before it got lost in the washer."

Ina placed her fork down and wiped her mouth with her napkin. "I'm doing the laundry for the store, Mr. Torguson. Surely it can wait until after dinner, can't it?"

Trudy held up a yeast role with a nibble taken out. "I like these."

Duncan stole a roll from the basket and held it up just like the girl. "Anything Trudy likes, I like—because we are friends." He pointed a finger at her across the table, and she gave him the requisite response, the growl-and-bite of a lion.

Torguson nodded and took a heaping helping of peas into his mouth.

Lorna Rae leaned back, unable to control any of the circus-like cloaked motivation running inside three rings across the dinner table. Daphne blinked her eyes twice in rapid succession, so she tried to figure out the code. Anything beyond "trust God" was missed on her. She finally took a bite of her roll and could agree with Trudy. "Eat your food, baby doll." Her meal largely untouched, she felt like the reigning hypocrite.

When both men looked at her at the same time, Lorna Rae's head began to throb. Whether any redemption could be found in this setting escaped her for the moment. She could throw the laundry at Torguson and send him on his merry way, but that seemed too simplistic. She had no experience at this cat-and-mouse stuff. It ruffled her feathers to be this deeply involved. All she could do was pray. She bowed her head right there and closed her eyes. That is when she felt it, a feather-light touch on her knee beneath the tablecloth. *Praise God.* Duncan knew she was suffering, and now he was here to take control.

"Would you care for some peas, Mr. Reed?" She lifted the bowl with longing in her eyes.

"By all means," he replied.

When his hand overlapped hers, Lorna Rae welcomed its unmistakable warmth. A bonding moment, she took it as a sign they were on the same team, an alliance of the heart.

Chapter 21

Duncan assessed what he had learned at dinner. Ina Hansen knew her way around the kitchen. Daphne knew how to handle a preschooler. Trudy knew a good yeast roll when she tasted one. And Lorna Rae knew when she was in over her head, because she had shaken like a cottonwood leaf the entire meal. Fortunately, he had sent her a soft signal under the table.

Torguson had no business being there. The laundry excuse he gave seemed implausible. Duncan would remain suspicious regarding that ploy, yet not turn his back. The women were safe as long as he remained in their midst. And he would, until Torguson walked out the door with his laundry in his hand. That way they could both get what they came for. *Call it a draw.*

Irked that he lacked the upper hand, he glanced around the table. Ina asked a few conversational questions and listened intently as her guest gave his answers. Her mouth seemed a bit more puckered than usual, like she had to keep tight-lipped about something. Maybe she had not known Torguson was coming to dinner—and she failed to appreciate the drop-in.

Daphne entered the room balancing three dessert plates decorated with squares of chocolate cake featuring white cream filling in the middle. Lorna Rae soon followed with three more plates. She stopped at his left shoulder and set one plate in front of him.

Duncan winked the instant she looked at him. Time-constrained, it represented the best he could do. He heard her respond with a tiny hum as she passed, a pleasurable hum, he hoped.

Torguson took his plate without a word of thanks and started to devour his cake. Repeatedly stabbing with his fork, he finished in five bites. He ate like a man in a hurry.

Ina pushed back from the table, having only taken a taste. "I see you are through with your cake, Mr. Torguson. If you will excuse me, I'll collect your laundry order for you."

"Yes ma'am. I do need to head back to town soon."

Duncan watched for Ina to make eye contact with him and immediately found it odd that she avoided doing so. The night grew stranger by the moment. A caution flag went up mentally, as things were not what they seemed.

Trudy stuck her fork into the square and left it standing straight up. "I need some milk."

Duncan saw a means of escape and took it. "Me too, Tootsie Roll Trudy. Come on and let's go get that milk." He planned to have a word with Ina to make some sense out of the awkward conduct around the table tonight. The child beat him to the kitchen door, but not by much.

He tugged the refrigerator door open, while Trudy sat her glass on the table. In seconds, he retrieved the milk and joined her. He poured half a glass and resealed the jug.

She held up her coloring book and showed him a turtle colored in looping green lines. "I made this foah you, Mista Weed."

"Why, this is our old friend Ollie, isn't it? You have done such a nice job, Trudy. Remember that Ollie is a red-eared slider, so you need to add a dash of red right through here." He traced his finger behind the turtle's eye. Something on the next page felt lumpy to the touch.

Trudy poked her bottom lip out. "But my wed cwayon is all gone."

"Oh that's right, from the big meltdown when you burned your hands. Tell me—are they all better now?" He reached for her, but she shied back.

"You no touch me." She scooted out of the chair as Ina came by with the laundry package.

She picked up Trudy's milk and escorted the child toward the dining room. "Coming, Mr. Reed?"

"In a minute. Guess you will have to trust me not to drink out of the milk jug."

"I trust *you*." She accentuated the last word for his personal benefit and walked away.

Duncan picked up the coloring book and turned the page to satisfy his curiosity about the lumps. He found feminine handwriting scrolling around a drawn heart. In the middle of it, a line of cut-off matches had been taped in place. Shock filtered down his shirt collar. Hungry for more information, he read the handwritten message:

You have my heart in a matchbook. Love always, Rae

He closed the coloring book as all the oddities began to make sense. Torguson hadn't been after a note at all—but he sure needed to retrieve these matches. They were the only circumstantial evidence tying him to the maiming case. Somehow Lorna Rae had figured it out and saved the matches out of the laundry for his investigation. God bless her. In doing so, she'd handed him Liam Torguson's head on a guilty verdict platter. And he would sure take it.

He tucked the coloring book on top of the refrigerator for later retrieval and slid the milk back inside. One glance out of the kitchen window revealed dusk had settled its purple twilight onto the horizon. He had almost run out of daylight. Now, he would have to work fast.

Lorna Rae stood in the doorway squeezing her hands. "His order is missing one shirt."

Duncan truly wanted to give her some appreciation about lip-level, but fought the urge and remained focused. "Think hard about where that shirt could be."

"It needed a presoak." She pointed to the sink and then to the window sill. "Oh, I think it must be out on the clothesline yet."

Duncan reached up for the coloring book, flipped the front cover open and tore a corner off the first page.

Lorna Rae stared at him and slowly cocked one eyebrow.

"Come on. I am walking you out to the clothesline." He placed his hand on the small of her back and guided her to the door.

She nodded toward the dining room. "Really, you should be protecting them."

"I am." He popped the torn paper into his mouth and began to chew it.

Lorna Rae raised both eyebrows. "What in the world?" She pushed the screen door open and stepped outside.

"I am simply giving Torguson the wet note he's so desperately looking for."

She gasped and headed for the clothesline straight-away. "With God as my witness, this day could not get any crazier."

"Don't count on it." He removed the wad and separated it into pieces, then twirled them between his fingertips. "Here, let me put these in his pocket."

She unclipped the clothespin on one shoulder and paused to let him tuck the wet paper pieces into the pocket.

"Okay, now fold it so the pocket side is up to better aid his inspection."

"But that is not how I fold a man's shirt."

"Work with me, Rae. That's all I am asking."

"Fine. Pocket-side up. Anything else?"

"I want you to escort him out front to his truck."

"Me? What about you?"

"I will be busy with a side project, but I plan to meet you out front. Here's our code—if he is making a clean break, no strings attached, you look me right in the eye when you come out. If something is up, do not look at me, even for a second. Clear?"

"Don't look at you if I need help. Got it."

"Good girl. I knew I could count on you." He stepped toward the pump house and dropped to one knee.

"You want to tell me anything about this side project?"

He lifted the housing and eased it back. The pump let out a slight hiss. "Believe me, you don't want to know. Go back inside and give the man his shirt. I need you to buy me two minutes while you say your goodbyes. Then bring him out front. I promise to be there waiting for you."

She creased the shirt in half and then folded it in quarters, leaving it pocket-side up. "My knees are shaking over this, Duncan."

"Remember who the good guys are."

"I know, silly me for worrying." She walked in silent steps back to the house.

Duncan waited until he heard the screen door shut before he

turned and focused on his target, the pump house occupant. He inched closer and the hissing amplified. "Hey, it's Friday night. How about we go for a ride?" His first grab being his best chance, he forcibly cuffed the snake by the neck and loosened its thrashing body from the pump mechanism. "On such a hot day, I figured you might be around."

Livid, the snake entwined his arm with all five feet of its length. *I believe this ought to make for a first-rate distraction on Torguson's ride home.* For a leader not opposed to spilling other men's blood, a few well-placed snake bites might lay the groundwork for reconsideration. Just for insurance, he planned to follow Torguson all the way back to town.

He rounded the house and ducked under the height of the untrimmed lilac hedge to access the man's truck. One glance at the narrow gap behind the bench seat told him the snake would never fit. He lowered it into the passenger side floorboard, where it landed with a hissing thump. "Goodbye, Ollie. Now, don't get too comfortable under there." He paused to read the license tag and committed the number to memory.

Duncan reviewed his options as he strode over to the Buick. Number One, Lorna Rae might come out and look him dead in the eye. No harm done. Number Two, Lorna Rae might come out in Torguson's grip and not look at him. That could cause some momentary trouble. Number None, Lorna Rae comes out and gets in the truck. No, he would never let that happen.

In the seconds that elapsed, he tried to remain calm and focused. Being level-headed had always been critical to his success. Maybe he could give himself a break on the need-to-control guilt trip. In reality, he possessed a keen sense to protect, which was not the same thing at all.

Locusts began to call from a nearby oak tree, building to a deafening crescendo. The words in Lorna Rae's message flashed to mind. He leaned back on the car's front quarter panel, and the metal soon radiated as much heat as her sentiment had—torch hot.

A low click sounded by the front stoop, so he stirred to full attention. Lorna Rae appeared on the top step. Her gait seemed hindered as if being restrained. He shifted off the Buick, his midsection tightened for the worst case scenario.

Torguson followed Lorna Rae down the front steps and caught

her playfully around the waist with his free arm. They angled toward the driver's side door.

Duncan stepped in front of the pair to confront them. "Liam, you are not taking Lorna Rae with you."

He tossed the laundry into the cab through the open window, keeping his grip on her tight. "Says who? She wants to go out with me, right?"

Duncan braced, shifting his weight on his back leg for extra momentum. She had three seconds to look his way.

She cleared a curl from her face, but her gaze remained locked on the ground. "I guess a short drive might not hurt—"

Duncan lowered his shoulder and rammed right between them, a deft move that separated the captive. Momentum from the blow sent Lorna Rae tumbling against his chest. Wrapping his arm around her, he gladly took possession. "Go back inside, Rae." He let her go, but not before they made eye contact. She had played it his way, a beautiful thing.

Torguson spit and pulled himself into the truck. "Hey. Maybe some other time, Lorna Rae." He slid his hands up the steering wheel. "You can't be around every night, Reed."

"Don't bet on it." He iced the statement with a leer.

The truck started and backed out of the yard in haste. When it hit forward gear, gravel scattered from the driveway. Torguson gave him one last look before heading up the lane.

Duncan watched the taillights half the distance to the low-water bridge. Once satisfied, he darted up the stairs and flung himself through the front door. Inside, the women all started talking at the same time.

He held up a hand to halt them. "Hold on. First things first— great job on being so level-headed. Lorna Rae, get an envelope and put the match heads in it, tape and all. If I don't come back, put it in the mail to my boss, Mr. McNaughton." He reached into his billfold to produce the business card.

Lorna Rae pressed her hands to her heart. "What do you mean, if you don't come back?"

Daphne looked at him with an incredulous stare. "You are not going back out there?"

"Yes, I need to follow him back to town. Ina, I need you to make a phone call to the police. Tell them the safety manager at

Coates Oil Company suspects criminal mischief and give them this tag number." He scribbled the number on the back of the card. "Be sure to tell them what direction we are driving in from."

Ina folded her hands, waiting with the patience of Job. "Is there anything more? Beyond continuous prayer, I mean."

Trudy pushed in front with a pout. "What's going on heah?"

Duncan knelt and gave the girl's nose a tweak. "Tonight, we are catching a bad guy, Squirt."

"Oh, good." She gave him a cheesy smile.

"Most incredibly good." Lorna Rae's voice turned velvet with the tribute.

Sensing victory, Duncan stood and touched her chin. "I need to get going."

~

Lorna Rae had not been born yesterday. She knew this could run off the edge of dangerous. She followed Duncan out to the Buick, her hand riding on his shoulder.

"You cannot simply let him go, can you?

"What justice would be served by that, Rae? This is what I do—risk management. The pendulum swings on both sides of safe." He opened the door and slid inside.

The slamming door provoked her heartfelt admission. "But I desperately want you on my side of safe." Her statement lacked the impact she had intended, so she leaned inside the car to deliver more persuasion by direct contact.

Duncan did not let her get off easy. After a heat-scorched kiss, he keyed the ignition and the Buick roared to life. "Believe me. I *want* to be on your side of safe." He winked and eased her back out of the window before he floored it. Seconds ticked by while the car diminished to a pair of rounded red taillights dipping across the low-water bridge.

Lorna Rae stood in the front yard, her hands on her hips. The night had begun to cool, and the three-quarter moon had just cleared the barn. "Dear God, please go with him—so I can have him back." She remembered that she had an envelope to address, so she hastened back inside.

~

His trip out had been well worth his time. That young Daphne had not been too bad to look at across the table either. Lorna Rae had been squirrely tonight. She might be a tad too high-strung for him. Liam glanced at the town lights and caught a glimpse of the smokestack flame ever-burning at the oil refinery. "Making money off our aching backs, but that is all set to change. One more strike of the red-hot iron ought to bring the big man down."

He reached over and connected with his prize, the clean laundry. He peeled the paper back and ran his fingers across the top piece, the shirt that had gone missing. He dug into the pocket and felt wet paper pulp. Now, he could be satisfied that he had recovered everything he needed. He pulled off unpaved Sharpville Road and headed west on 12th Avenue into town. The skyline glowed up ahead, separating the city from the country. Maybe he would head over to The Tap Out and raise a little hellfire. The night was still young.

He turned up the radio in raucous celebration. Something knocked against his leg, so he shifted his foot on the accelerator and mashed down. It banged against his leg at the back of his right knee, but his dungarees padded the blow. He dropped a hand from the wheel and tried to feel around for the culprit. He soon struck something cool, smooth, and slithering.

"Son of a beast." He hauled it up from the floorboard, a nasty-tempered snake. It hissed and twisted to protest his grip. Before he could stop it, the strike came right at him. He turned his head, and it landed a fang-piercing bite on his cheekbone. The truck veered sharp left, so he made a focused effort to correct it. As he adjusted his grip higher on the snake's neck, he tugged it toward the open window to be shed of it. One failed yank revealed the snake had entwined its lower body around his leg.

In a panic, he released the steering wheel to better work the snake free. The city lights cast a pallid glow onto the blotched-back monster. The sight of it made his stomach lurch. The truck drifted left, so he returned one hand to the wheel and retook the right lane. With the intersection of Highway 77 looming ahead, he made a split-second decision to throw the animal into the floorboard. At least he'd be able to protect his face. His dungarees would have to protect the rest.

Lights rimming the highway's corridor gave him a target up ahead. He eased up on the accelerator to slow for the right-angle turn, but the truck failed to respond. Coiled around his right leg now, the snake had jammed the gas pedal. He shifted back and gave his right leg a kick toward the passenger side of the cab to dislodge the animal. Instead, its body served like a tether to his post. He caught a glimpse of his face in the rearview mirror, and two puncture wounds had leaked twin blood tracks down his cheek. A pair of headlights approached behind him.

He clenched his teeth and reached into the floorboard with both hands. The snake came up in full strike mode and his hand position failed to prevent it. The piercing pinch landed just under his chin left of center and ripped open a major artery of pain, before he could pry a thumb into the creature's mouth and dislodge it. He mashed the brake pedal and the wheels locked up. With snake in hand, he passed under the lights of the highway and fully missed the turn at the intersection. Blue police lights blocked the highway corridor in both directions.

The banks of the Walnut River fell into its swollen flow immediately west of the highway. He yanked the wheel left as the grill pummeled through the wooden guard rail with a crack. Panicked, he over-corrected his steering. The truck began to roll sideways down the riverbank. His head hit the roof as he choked the snake, sirens blaring in the background. A torrent of cold water rushed into the cab as the windshield met his forehead, and everything merged to black.

~

Duncan pulled the Buick over on the emergency lane of the highway as the police worked the accident scene. He pulled the notepad out of his pocket and began to record the failed escape in chronological sequence. An ambulance nosed into the split guardrail, and soon two drenched policemen emerged from the riverbank. The attendants manned a gurney, and the four of them disappeared back down the bank.

He would not deny the truth. It had been sickening to watch Torguson's truck sway and lose control on the dark side of safety. He sat in the lamplight and thought of Lorna Rae, recalling the look of fear in her eyes when she let him go. Maybe she had been right about her side of the pendulum. A family needed safety—not risk.

He made note of the time and location as another police car arrived. The driver accessed the trunk and came up with folded towels. They walked over to the crash scene as the gurney crested the bank. A body rode on its surface, covered head to toe in a white sheet. The wet officers donned the towels as the medics loaded the gurney into the ambulance.

Duncan made his final notation "dead on impact" and shut the notepad. He now faced a choice, head into the office to file a report that closed the case or return to the Hansen farm and alleviate some well-founded fears. He started the Buick and wheeled around, retracing his route to the farm. Tonight he would trade professional obligation for something of considerably greater value—a loving family.

Epilogue

Duncan followed the realtor as he showed off the features of the three-bedroom home.

"This Westlink area is perfect for a young family. Plus, there is a school within walking distance." The agent stopped for dramatic pause and pulled open the curtain facing the backyard. "Of course, the greenway is a huge selling point, as well."

Duncan gestured parallel to the canal's length. "I assume that's a flood control structure."

"Yes. When it's not conveying water, it can be a playground for the children."

Lorna Rae looked up at Duncan, her eyes shining with hope. "I saw a real playground on the corner where we turned in. That would be fun to have nearby. This house also has double ovens for my cake baking—and it falls within our budget."

Duncan soaked up her attention, but knew he had one more card to play. He made eye contact with the selling agent. "Can you give me some time to think about it? I promise to call with my answer before closing time tonight."

"Certainly, Mr. Reed. Feel free to look around more, maybe explore the backyard."

Trudy perked up and broke her record-length silence. "I want to!" She grabbed Lorna Rae's hand and started tugging.

"Go ahead, you two. I need to retrieve something in the trunk first." Duncan stepped out of the room and walked down the hallway with purposeful strides. He heard footsteps run up behind him.

"What are you bringing in, Duncan, your safety meter?" Lorna Rae's tone teased as she rubbed his shoulder blade.

"No, I keep that up here." He pointed to his temple and walked out the front door. Majestic twin oak trees stood on each side of the front walk, lending plenty of shade.

Trudy ran for the side gate past the garage. "Ovah heah, Mommy."

"Okay, come find us out back, Mr. Serious." As Lorna Rae threw him a kiss, the diamond ring on her finger glinted in the late summer sun.

Duncan opened the trunk and pulled out the sagging trash bag. It had seemed such a small gesture, when he pulled away from the bungalow that last time. Now, he grew hopeful for the impact. He swung the bag over his shoulder and went to hunt up his future family.

Crossing the backyard, he found a rear gate and stepped onto the lush greenway. Lorna Rae stood down the slope, trying to convince Trudy not to get wet in the ribbon of water there.

"Come on you two. Wait until you see what I found over here." Duncan animated his nod and walked down a series of chain link fences. When he arrived at one with an open gate, he stepped inside.

Lorna Rae caught up with him, breathless from the run. She tilted her head sideways, unsure about the situation. "Duncan, I think you are trespassing, sweetheart. Come out before the residents see you."

"Let's pretend they don't mind, Rae. How else can we get to know our neighbors?" He restrained his smile until he had turned away from her, but glanced back over his shoulder to make sure she followed. He soon spotted a gardener, working a promising patch of ground off the back of the house. "Excuse me, ma'am. Are you expecting company?"

Lorna Rae ran up and tugged him back to curb his enthusiasm. When the gardener stood up, she let out a squeal. "Vivian?" The two women embraced, while Bert poked his head out of the backdoor to see what the ruckus was all about.

"Come on out, neighbor." Duncan waited until Bert had joined them in the yard. With delayed pleasure, he extended his sack to

Vivian.

Several children ran outside next. Mary Jane picked up Trudy and swung her around. Vivian bugged her eyes comically as she peeked into the bag. "My iris bulbs! Oh, Duncan, bless your thoughtful soul. I get to have my iris back. Lord, have mercy."

Lorna Rae turned around, her green eyes misting with tears. She pressed her fingertips over her lips and came to him. "You really didn't have to—"

"But I wanted to." He drew her close, knowing that something much more precious than flower bulbs had been redeemed from the oil fields. Rae would make a great wife living in prosperous Wichita, Kansas, the Air Capital of the World.

Bert stepped over and slapped him on the back. "Welcome to the airplane business."

"Where it has to be safe...or it won't fly." Duncan kissed Lorna Rae's forehead. Confident a bright future lay ahead, he embraced it with his whole heart.

"A piece of cake," Lorna Rae replied, her smile a mile wide.

"Chocolate cake—it's good from the inside out." Duncan bent and kissed the baker, standing right there in wide open August sun, in front of God and everybody.

AUTHOR BIO

Cindy M. Amos writes romantic inspirational fiction in both contemporary and historical genres. From her background of field biology and nature study, her themes center on man living close to the land. She writes from Wichita, Kansas, where she lives with her aviation engineer husband and two come-and-go college-aged sons. During growing season, she ranches weekends on the Amos family's fifth generation operation in the Flint Hills of Morris County surrounding historic Council Grove, making the tallgrass prairie her second home. Her inspiration for *Oil Field Maven* arose from a chance visit to the Kansas Oil Museum in El Dorado, Kansas, which allowed her to retell the story of a close-knit community whose hard work and dedication drove America's postwar economic success. The author witnessed the once-in-a-decade waterfall at Eureka Lake in the summer of 2015, and captured the plight of a hapless red-eared slider riding the cascade in this book for all to enjoy. Find her complete book list and sign up for her Nature Ink newsletter on her website at: http://cindymamos.wixsite.com/natureink

OTHER BOOKS BY CINDY M. AMOS
Landscapes of Mercy Series
Redeeming River Rancher
Saving Bicycle Man
Justifying Sound Strider
Sanctifying Ace Aerialist

Lifting Lock Runner
Salvaging Doctor Junk

National Parks 100th Anniversary Romance Collection
Everglades Entanglement
Mesa Verde Meltdown

Christmas 3-in-1 Collection
Running Out of Christmastime

Taming the Cowboy's Heart Collection
Warming Stone Cold Lodge

50 States Collection
Secondhand Flower Stand (Kansas)
Red Cloud Retreat (Nebraska)
Tidewater Lowlands (North Carolina)
Canyon Country Courtship (Utah)

John Denver 20th Anniversary Collection
Calypso Reimagined

Loving the Town Hero Collection
Cascading Waterworks